DO

Spur was ready b en Rogers rode up. H ed carefully with the Winchester. The girl sat astride behind Rogers, her arms locked around his chest, her skirt riding up to her waist.

At this angle McCoy could hit Rogers without endangering the girl. Spur refined his aim. Rogers stopped for a moment.

Spur fired.

The round hit Rogers in the left shoulder, away from the girl. He nearly fell off the horse but held on. He grabbed the girl wih his good right hand, and crashed through the brush with his mount and pounded down the road.

"I'll kill her if you try to shoot at me again!"

LARAMIE LOVERS

Spur dropped off the branch and crouched behind the tree. The Circle S. At least he knew who they were. Someone crashed brush behind and to his left. Spur froze against the tree knowing that a moving figure is easy to distinguish in brush.

The sound came again and he saw movement. Automatically, Spur lifted the Spencer and sent three rounds into the brush where he saw the motion.

A scream, then cursing followed quickly. All was quiet for a few moments. Then a piercing bellow of pain.

"Come help me, you bastards! He done shot me bad. Gut shot me. Come get me out of here."

Other Spur Double Editions:

GOLD TOWN GAL/RED ROCK REDHEAD
SAVAGE SISTERS/HANG SPUR McCOY!
INDIAN MAID/MONTANA MINX
RAWHIDER'S WOMAN/SALOON GIRL
MISSOURI MADAM/HELENA HELLION
ROCKY MOUNTAIN VAMP/CATHOUSE KITTEN
COLORADO CUTIE/TEXAS TEASE
DAKOTA DOXY/SAN DIEGO SIRENS

SPUR DOUBLE:

DODGE CITY DOLL

LARAMIE LOVERS

DIRK FLETCHER

LEISURE BOOKS  NEW YORK CITY

A LEISURE BOOK®

June 2007

Published by

Dorchester Publishing Co., Inc.
200 Madison Avenue
New York, NY 10016

ISBN 10: 0-8439-3372-0
ISBN 13: 978-0-8439-3372-7

Printed in the United States of America.

DODGE CITY DOLL

1

The polished derringer lifted again aiming at the sheriff's chest. His hand came up weakly, his voice only a whisper now as the pain eroded his strength.

"Why? For God's sakes. Why are you trying to kill me? I don't even know you! I've never done anything to you or yours. Do you get some wild kind of thrill from this?"

Sheriff Clyde Wilson touched his belly where only a small spot of blood showed through his pants. The first shot, which caught him totally by surprise, sliced into his lower abdomen, ripped through the intestines and lodged somewhere near his spine.

Damn, it hurt! He'd never experienced anything like it. Gut shot was not the way to cash out of a game.

"Give me just one reason, damnit!" he roared, the pain flooding over him again, dulling his vision. "Just one reason why. I deserve to know why you're killing me. Maybe I'm not the man you want. I know damn well I've never hurt you!" His voice faded to nothing as a surge of blinding pain started in his bowels and grew and grew as it billowed and splashed and bored its way through his body until it hit his brain and he cried out in agony, sure that he was dying.

A moment later, to his shock, he discovered he was still alive and he hurt as much as before. He shook his head and opened his eyes.

The twin muzzles of the little gun came closer. He didn't have the strength to lift his hand, let alone knock the small weapon away. But the derringer had already wounded him grievously, fatally, if he didn't get help soon.

The two figures sat in a closed black buggy at the edge of town. Both were dressed conservatively, a silver star shining on the sheriff's chest.

"Damnit, tell me why!" Sheriff Wilson gasped and shuddered. He lunged across the buggy but met only the muzzle of the derringer as it discharged. The .45 caliber slug rammed through his dark coat, shattered a rib and plunged in three pieces into his heart, killing him instantly.

The buggy swayed as someone got out. A slap on the horse's hind quarters sent it skittering away down the lane out of town.

Spur McCoy sat in the town marshal's office in Kimberly, Kansas, about six miles west of Wichita. He had picked up his orders in the larger town at the telegraph office, scanned his directions from Washington, D.C., the headquarters of the Secret Service and just made it on the stage heading west.

"Just heard about Clyde Wilson this morning," Marshal Paul Sanderson said. "Damn, known Clyde now for twenty years. He was a good lawman. You say it's happened before?"

"He's the fourth lawman to be murdered around here in the last four weeks. Three of them have been on the stage line heading for Dodge City. You're the new marshal here, I'd reckon."

"Right, the new marshal. I'm not quite used to that title yet."

"This is the first place a lawman was killed in this string. I'm investigating all the murders. Some people think that the same person or persons may be doing all of them."

"Somebody with a big hatred for lawmen?"

"Happens."

"Sure as hell does, McCoy. How can I help?"

An hour later McCoy had checked over a report by the undertaker who was also the county coroner. Death came as a result of a shot to the heart by a large caliber slug, probably a .45. There was a second gunshot wound in the lower abdomen with considerable bleeding. One curious fact recorded. Both wounds showed "severe powder burns indicating the weapon had been extremely close to the victim when shot."

Marshal Sanderson scratched his jaw. "Wasn't like Marshal Jones to be careless. He'd been town lawman here for ten years. Never a lot of trouble. We ain't a big cattle town like some of them. But Larabee Jones was a careful man."

"Where was he found?" Spur asked.

"Out along East River Road. He was in a buggy, not his own, and the horse was walking free, like nobody had tied the reins. The old black was just munching away on spring grass when we finally found Larabee."

"So he could have been shot anywhere and the horse driven or chased out there or maybe it wandered."

"Peers as how."

"Not much help."

"Happened near a month ago, and we ain't got a thing, not a clue and no suspects. Nobody heard nothing. Widow Jones said her husband didn't have no enemies she knew of. He didn't gamble or carouse with the fancy ladies. Marshal Jones was a short, kind of fat little man. Never raised his voice. Not one to pick a fight or hold a grudge. Funny kind of man to be a lawman, but he was a good one. Whole thing is a blamed mystery to us, Mr. McCoy."

"Well, keep it open, Marshal. I'm moving on down the line, see if I can get a line on the killer and stop him. Bad for the way people think about lawmen if somebody keeps killing us off all the time."

The remark brought a wry smile from Marshal Sanderson. "Hope that same polecat don't come back this way looking for another lawman to do in."

Spur waved and caught the afternoon stage for the next small town, River Run, fourteen miles down the road.

Another lawman had been murdered here, six days after the first one. Spur went through the same routine. The case of death was listed as two .45 rounds, one belly, one heart. It wasn't hard to figure which one had been fired first. There were intense powder burns around both wounds.

Again, there were no known enemies. The sheriff

was respected, ran a good office, was fair, did his job and kept the town as clean as possible. Yet somebody met him in a black carriage, shot him so close that powder burns were deep. One wound in the belly looked as if the muzzle of the weapon had been pressed against the man's pants as the weapon was fired.

Boys going to school found the buggy the next morning, the horse cropping grass in the small public park. No one had remembered seeing the rig the previous night. It belonged to the doctor and had been left in front of his place after a house call. He forgot to move it.

Back in his hotel room, Spur looked at his reports. He had missed the stage; he'd get he next one in the morning. The first two victims were found in buggies. Both had powder burns. Which meant it had been an up close job.

After seeing the results of the first two kills, Spur decided it was the work of the same man. No two people with a killing rage would kill two lawmen exactly the same way. It was one guy, but who and why and where was he now?

The next day he took the morning stage and covered the other two towns where lawmen had been murdered. He found the identical pattern. Death came from two .45 slugs, one to the belly and a second in the heart. One lawmen had scratches on his face. He was found a half mile out of town at the side of the road. The fourth lawman to die was in a buggy as well, parked in front of his own jail.

No suspects, no witnesses, no clues. The new lawmen in each town were at a loss to explain the killings, nor could they offer any idea who could be responsible. They agreed it probably wasn't a local man.

By now every lawman in the state of Kansas had been sent a flyer warning him about the danger from person or persons unknown. There had been no robberies or other killings in the towns so affected. The only motive seemed to be hatred for lawmen of all kinds. The sheriffs and marshals were warned to be on the lookout for any suspicious characters.

Spur looked at the map in the sheriff's office. There was only one direction the killer could go, on west, on down the stage road. Four killings so far, the last one here just two days ago. If he was lucky he could prevent the next one, but what town would it be in?

He picked the next biggest town down the line. That was Greensburg. County seat, with a sheriff and nearly twenty miles from this spot on the map. The killer might stop before there, or go past the town, it was a chance he'd have to take.

Perhaps he could stop a killing this time and nail a killer.

The stage came in on time and they got away quickly. As they neared the next stop several hours later, Spur's pulse picked up and he looked forward to the confrontation. He had a feeling that this was the right town, that something would happen here.

In was his job to stop the killing and to nail the killer.

He slid out of the coach, caught his carpetbag off the top of the rig and walked toward the hotels. He saw two of them, and from habit picked the best one, a three story affair called Pride of the Plains Hotel. It was to be hoped.

Spur McCoy stood taller than the average man at six feet two inches. His best fighting weight was two hundred pounds even, which made him slightly on the thick side, but it was all toned muscle, no fat. His reddish brown hair touched his shirt collar but was usually covered with a low crowned, gray Stetson. The sandy hair extended down almost to his jawline in mutton chop sideburns fronted with a full moustache of the same shade.

He stared out at the world through curious green eyes and was an excellent shot with pistol and rifle, was murder with a shotgun, and could ride as well as most cowboys but not as well as the Comanches or Sioux.

During the big war he had served in the infantry, rose to the rank of captain, took one small wound, and retired to Washington, D.C., where he was an aide to the senior senator from New York, an old family friend.

When the Secret Service was created by congress in 1858, he had been one of the first members of the force. It was originally started to defend and protect the currency against counterfeiting, but soon its scope broadened into general law work, especially where there were no other federal law officers to handle disputes across state lines.

Spur served in Washington for six months, then won the job as agent in charge of the western region, from St. Louis to the Pacific Coast.

His direct boss was General Wilton D. Halleck, the number two man in Washington who gave him his assignments through the wonders of the telegraph.

Boss of the operation was William Wood, the director of the Agency who had been appointed by Abraham Lincoln and by each President since.

Deep in his traveling kit, Spur carried an identification card that had been signed by President Lincoln, and a pair of carefully worded letters from General Halleck that made him a full colonel in the army and the orders to take over any military equipment or personnel he needed. Those letters were hidden between the covers of a book, carefully taped together.

He usually worked undercover, using a variety of names, since his real name was quickly becoming known in the west, especially by outlaws and ne'er-do-wells.

He walked across the street, his eyes always moving, watching everything, everyone, as if he were walking through Apache country. Spur moved like a cougar, smoothly, alert, ever ready to dart one way or the other to avoid or confront.

Low on his right hip rode a tied down, well worn holster that carried a long barreled Colt .45. He had been known to drive six penny nails with .45 slugs from that weapon from thirty yards.

Spur stepped up to the desk of the hotel, registered under the name of Colt Smith. He paid for his lodging with a ten dollar gold piece, asking tor two nights. The fee was fifty cents a night.

"What floor ye want?" a wild eyed young man asked as he scratched a pimple on his neck.

"Second floor," Spur said.

"Fine, put ye in 204, that's center and looks down on the street. Ye a bounty hunter, mister?"

"Not so you could notice. Why, are you a wanted desperado?"

The kid laughed, gave Spur his key then sobered. "Truth of the matter, I am. Wanted in New York by my wife, but I ain't about to go back. She was as ugly as a box of rocks. Now her ugly wasn't just skin deep. No, sir. Her ugly went right down to the bone!"

Spur laughed, picked up his bag and walked up the stairs to 204. The room was like a thousand others he had stayed in. A square box with one window, thin curtains blowing in the afternoon breeze, a bed, a small dresser with a mirror that had wavy lines in it and with the silver peeling off the back. A washstand with a large crockery bowl and a pitcher filled with water. He was lucky. This room had a straight backed, wooden chair. It would come in handy for locking his door at night.

Spur looked down on the Greensburg street: dusty from two months without rain. Littered with horse droppings. A few merchants picked up the droppings every morning from in front of their stores after they swept the boardwalk. But not enough of them picked up the manure to do much good.

The main street was a block long each way, with only a few businesses on the side streets. On the far side he saw that houses crowded right up to the back of some of the stores with only an alley between them. Not exactly St. Louis or Chicago. Maybe a thousand people.

He pulled the wooden chair up to the window and sat down looking out. Somewhere out there could be a killer, one with a particular twist. He hated lawmen, any kind of lawmen, anywhere, at any time. How could he find a man like that?

He would see the sheriff and stay glued to him like a second skin until something happened—or until word came in of a lawman murdered by the same method in another town. Then the chase would begin again.

Spur nodded, affirming his moves. He had to stay ahead of the killer, be out front, ready to stop the crime and catch the murderer. Sure, easy to say. Now he had to get out on the street and do it.

2

Spur made sure his six-gun was loaded and ready. He eased it in and out of the holster twice to be sure it didn't hang up, then left his carpetbag on the bed and went out and locked his door.

He found the Sheriff's Office & Jail a block down along Main Street. Greensburg was a normal Western town. This one's main reason for being was cattle, a few coming through on trails, but most of them raised on the unending flat great plains that stretched interminably in every direction around Greensburg.

Spur pushed open the sheriff's door and saw that it was made of two-inch sturdy oak. A wise precaution. Eight feet ahead of the door, a counter went across the room with a narrow pass through. Behind the counter sat two men, one in his forties, one barely out of his teens.

"Sheriff in?" Spur asked. He saw the older man flinch, his hand went to a holstered gun on his left side. Then he stood and came to the counter.

"I'm Sheriff Bjelland. What can I do for you?"

"Colt Smith is my name, Sheriff. Wondered if we could talk privately?"

He held out his hand. "Possible, but I hold your six-gun while we talk."

"Good move, Sheriff Bjelland. More than glad to oblige." Spur gave him his hogleg and they went into the back where the four jail cells had been built solidly into the structure.

"You must have received the notice about lawmen getting killed between here and Wichita."

"I did and I've taken special precautions. Haven't been going around much alone anymore."

"Good idea. I'm here to try to catch the killer. You heard about Sheriff Wilson, I imagine."

"Known Clyde for twenty years." He looked up, curious. "You one of them Federal marshals or something?"

"Close enough. I'm going to be watching your backtrail for the next few days. Hope you don't mind."

Sheriff Bjelland squinted as he eyed Spur. "How do I know you're not the gent who's trying to kill me? You got a paper says who you be?"

"Do you carry a paper like that around, Sheriff? Something like that can get a man killed."

"Don't need to carry no paper. These folks hereabouts know me. I don't know you."

Spur reached in his shirt pocket and took out the telegram with his orders on it. He unfolded it and handed it to the lawman. The sheriff read the long telegram through.

"Never heard of this Capital Investigations. Who are they?"

"The Secret Service of the United States Government. We can't advertise who we are. You never can tell who is watching the telegraph office."

The sheriff folded the yellow paper and gave it back to Spur.

"Makes sense." He stuck out his hand. "Glad to meet you, whatever your real name is. And I'll be damn glad when this foolishness is all over."

"The four lawmen back the stage line don't think it's foolishness, they think of it as dead. Just be careful. I'll try to stay with you like a blanket. Do you check doors after dark?"

"Used to, guess I just decided not to. My deputy will do it tonight."

"You'll stay here the rest of the day, and tonight? Sleep here?"

"I'm a widower, nothing to go home for. Yes, I'll sleep in. You go look around, get acquainted with our town, try and spot your killer. I've only got two deputies. One is here now, I'll tell the other one about you when he comes on, so he don't drygulch you. He's a bit fast with a gun."

"Obliged." Spur took back his six-gun, pushed the long barreled weapon in his holster and went out the door. He walked the street from one end to the other on both sides. A few more stores than most places this size. That must mean there were a few ranchers and farmers out there who came to town now and then for supplies.

He went back to the hotel for supper. Just as he stepped into the lobby a woman came down the stairs. She wasn't a flashy "stopper" type that he had seen in Denver and St. Louis. Rather she had an understated kind of beauty and elegance that caught his eye. She was dressed in a pretty and he guessed expensive outfit that had a little jacket, and he saw earrings and a string of pearls around her neck.

She looked his way and their eyes met for a moment. She turned away and smiled softly as she walked into the hotel's small dining room.

He followed her in, saw her sitting at a table for two alone, and without a moment's hesitation walked to her table. "The place is terribly crowded tonight and I wondered if I might share your table?"

She looked up without surprise or fear as if she had guessed he might be coming over. She checked the dozen empty tables in the dining room and smiled.

"It is crowded. Won't you please sit down?"

He liked the soft voice, the easy way she had handled it. He was not sure what she would do.

He sat down and put his hat on the floor beside him.

"You must not be a cowboy, you don't eat supper with your hat on," she said. There was a touch of an accent but he couldn't tie it down.

"No, Miss. I don't. I grew up in New York. Oh, my name is Colt Smith." He used his cover name automatically.

"Colt, that does sound like a cowboy, or at least a weapons manufacturer. You're not that Colt?"

"No, afraid not."

"Just as well. My name is Lila Pemberthy. Are you new in town, too?"

"Yes, how did you know?"

"I saw you register earlier this afternoon."

They ordered their meals. The menu was easy to understand and limited. There was a choice of country stew or a steak dinner. She had a small portion of the stew and coffee. Spur ordered the biggest steak and all the side dishes. She watched him eat with amusement.

"You here on business?" she asked.

"Yes, Miss Pemberthy. Land. I represent a firm in Chicago and St. Louis that is interested in land speculation. My job is to find good land, cheap and buy it."

"That sounds interesting."

"Are you just traveling?"

"In a way. Actually I have a week's engagement to sing at the Bar None Saloon. Usually I sing in the opera house or some kind of hall. But there isn't any such thing here."

"A real entertainer! I'm honored to share your table. What time do you perform?"

"Three times, seven, nine and eleven. I've done the eastern cities and decided to come west for a change. My goodness, things certainly are different out here."

Spur smiled and cut up his steak. "Different isn't always pleasant. I hope you have some protection at that time of night when you leave the saloon."

She laughed softly. "Oh, yes, the barkeep arranges for an escort back to the hotel. It's only a block. It's quite safe really. I always carry a six-inch long hat pin. It can be a remarkably effective weapon."

They chatted about the weather and politics and the problems of travel, then she stood. He rose quickly.

"May I see you back to your room?" he asked.

"No, finish your supper. But my room number is 305, if you need to know."

Spur chuckled. "Was I that obvious?"

"Not quite. Will you come to hear me sing tonight?"

"If I can squeeze in the door. I bet the saloon will be jammed."

She nodded and left. Spur watched her walk away. She was interesting. He needed something to help him charge through this current assignment. How to find a killer when you don't even know for sure that he's in town, or that he's going to stop here?

He thought about it as he finished the steak, mashed potatoes and gravy, carrots, peas, pickled beets and three kinds of bread, butter and jam. The coffee was hot, plentiful and better than he usually found in hotels out here.

When the food was gone, he had decided if there was a better way to do the job, he couldn't think of it. He basically had to watch the town, watch the sheriff, look for strangers and anything unusual.

Then with a whole lot of luck, he just might stumble onto the killer before he could strike again.

That was the plan.

It wasn't a great plan but it was all he had.

Maybe Lila Pemberthy would help make the time go quicker as he waited. Maybe. On the other hand, she might be a totally proper lady who would not even let him past her hotel room door, and surely never see her trim ankle.

After supper, Spur toured the town again. Most of the retail stores were closed. He bought a box of .45 rounds at the hardware just as it was closing, then began to investigate the saloons.

There were seven in the small town. Four of them offered games of chance, everything from faro to poker, roulette, monte, Boston, seven up and euchre. Two had dance hall girls with dresses cut so low they left little to the imagination. The girls almost never danced. They spent most of their time flat on their backs, fucking up a storm in the two cribs upstairs.

The stairway up to the cribs were the most popular spots in town. Clients sat on the steps, waiting their turn. The only rule was that they had to have a beer or a whiskey in hand as they waited, or they forefeited their place in line.

Spur stayed in the last watering hole, the saloon that had a picture of Lila displayed on the door and again inside. It was the Bar None Saloon, and Lila was billed to sing at seven, nine and eleven, just as she had said.

He fell into his routine of playing some low stakes poker and listening to the saloon talk. In a strange town that was often the quickest way to get a feel for a place, learn what was going on and why it was happening.

A few of the men there had heard about the sheriff in the next town getting killed. None of them thought it could happen in Greensburg.

He won four dollars, then lost it again and quit fifty cents behind when Lila's first show came on.

The saloon was packed. All the poker table chairs were filled and thirty or forty men stood shoulder to shoulder behind them waiting for the songs.

There was no stage. A piano with two keys missing hunkered against the far wall. They had cleared back the poker tables for eight feet to give Lila some room near the piano. A piano player hit a few cords and the crowd cheered.

Lila walked out from the room behind the bar.

She was a looker.

Lila had a flare for theatrical makeup, yet she used only a little to highlight her natural beauty. The dress she wore cost more than the average cowboy's wages for three months, and it fit perfectly to show off her small but slender and well proportioned body, clinging delightfully.

Lila played it like a duchess, at least. She was a lady, and there was no need to announce it, or caution the men not to swear or use profanity. Lila was here!

She walked across the saloon to a hush, turned and nodded to the piano player and her voice wrapped around the sad song of "The Girl I Left Behind." It caught a lot of the men by surprise and there was a tear or two before she was done.

Lila moved out of that into "Jimmy Cracker," then "Old Dan Tucker," and plunged ahead into "My Love is Buried On The Wabash," a Civil War tear jerker.

When she paused at the end of the four songs the applause thundered amid whistles and stomping feet on the wooden floor.

Lila smiled at them as if they were children. She

was with them yet not really there, detached, unreachable, a memory/dream figment of the perfect woman of wonder that caught at them all. She was performing for them, yet alone, as if she were singing only for herself, or better, individually, for each man who heard her. Through it all her loneliness and her aloofness remained.

She sang again, roaring into "Garry Owen," the famous Seventh Cavalry battle song the troop used. This time she paused because the men knew where the ending was and they clapped and cheered and stomped.

She sang a dozen more songs. Many of the men remembered them from the East and the South. After every song the cheering raced through the crowd. More men crowded in from behind and gradually they pushed forward until she had only a small area to move around. She sang "The Bloody Monogahela" about the war and then "Rosie, You are My Posie." She closed with the haunting "Somewhere A Girl Waits For Me."

When the last song ended, the crowd waited in silence a moment, then burst into applause. The barkeep shouldered his way through the crowd, made a path for Lila and led her out of the saloon and into the back and small office where she had a tiny dressing room.

The men in the saloon cheered for five minutes, then the barkeep and owner shouted that Miss Lila would be singing again at nine and eleven, and the place settled down.

Spur went out and wandered the town, checking the other saloons, and soon spotted the sheriff making his rounds. He was checking doors and looking in at each of the saloons.

Spur waited for him to come away from the bakery door.

"Huh? Oh, you, Colt Smith. Yeah, I caved in. Figured I better earn my money. If that means some asshole shoots at me, I'll just shoot back. Got to be that way. Kind of the way I'm made, know what I mean, Smith?"

"I know. Figured it might happen. I'll be half a block behind you. Look sharp."

Nothing happened on the rest of the rounds.

They walked together from the next to last saloon to the Bar None.

"Usually stop in here last before I close up," Sheriff Bjelland said. "Mike's behind the bar. Known Mike since we both were kids in Missouri. You know there are over three hundred thousand souls living in St. Louis now? Christ, what a mob! Glad my folks got out of there when they did. Back in 1850 there weren't more than maybe seventy-five thousand."

They went into the Bar None. It was jammed. Lila was in the middle of her routine. It seemed to be the same songs in the same order for every show. Nobody minded. Most of them had never seen a lady sing this way before. They were mesmerized.

Spur found a spot against the wall near the piano and stood up. She noticed him at once and he thought there was a flicker of a smile between numbers. He was just wishing again. She was the picture of a lady, regal, proud, detached, desirable and totally unattainable.

Sheriff Bjelland slid behind the bar to talk to Mike. There was no place else to stand.

Lila closed with the same song she did the last time, "Somewhere a Girl Waits For Me." Again it had a shock effect on the men—a lot of them did have a girl somewhere waiting. Then, after a pause, the applause shook the place and they cheered for more.

Mike and Sheriff Bjelland made a path for Lila back to the office, and the customers drifted away, it being well past bedtime for the working men among them. A few cowboys had another beer before the long ride back to their spreads.

Mike came over to Spur and gave him a note. He opened it wondering what it said.

"Colt. Can you wait for me? I'd like you to see me back to our hotel . . . if you're not too busy buying land." It was a delicate feminine hand and could only be from Lila.

"Tell her, of course," Spur said, and Mike hurried through the rapidly emptying saloon.

When she came out, she had removed some of the makeup, but she still looked stunning. Her brown hair was piled on top of her head to make her look a little taller, he decided. She wore a soft brown sweater that matched her hair. He stood at the table he had taken when she walked up.

"Do you mind if we sit a minute? I always need to simmer down a little after I sing. It might not look like it, but I really work hard singing."

"I could see it. You don't just say the words, you seem to be feeling them. It could be emotionally draining."

She nodded. "That's the right words. I've never

figured it out quite that way before. I'd like a glass of white wine, but I don't want to drink it here. Would it . . ." She looked up at him for a moment then away. "No, I guess not. Forget the wine. I'm exhausted. Let's just walk back to the hotel. Performing never seems to get any easier."

She held his arm as they walked into the darkness. He could feel some nervous tension ebb from her.

"Oh, I hope you don't mind my grabbing your arm. I just feel safer this way. It isn't the darkness that is scary, it's all those men who looked at me while I was singing. Some of them thought I was their sweetheart. Some of them looked at me and remembered a mother, or a wife, or maybe a lover back east somewhere. It always happens. I . . . I just don't want to have to deal with them."

"I understand. I really don't mind your holding my arm. In fact I rather like it."

They went across the dusty street to the other side and down the boardwalk. The walks were always built by each store owner, covering the area in front of his store. Usually these walks were on the same level, but here and there, there were a few inches to step up or down.

At the hotel, they went up the broad steps to the first floor lobby and up to the second floor. They paused a moment, then went on to the third. He led her down to her room, 305, as he remembered.

"You have your key?" he asked.

She smiled. "Mr. Smith, I've been living in hotel rooms for the past three years. I've never lost a hotel key yet. And if I ever do, I have the three basic skeleton keys that open most door locks made today."

She smiled up at him and nodded. "Thank you for your escort service, Mr. Smith. Perhaps we'll see each other in the dining room again."

"Good night, Miss Pemberthy. I was delighted by your singing." Spur turned and walked toward the stairs. He paused there, saw her go in her room and close the door. He heard the faint click as she turned her lock.

McCoy checked off one good deed and went back to the street. He wanted to be sure that the sheriff was tucked safely in his office. That meant looking at the Bar None to see if he'd left and if he was checking doors again.

This was the third day since the death of the last lawman. The next attempt could come any time during the next four or five days. Spur shrugged. He didn't need all that much sleep anyway.

3

Spur spotted Sheriff Bjelland inside the Bar None Saloon and waited for him to come out. For the next hour, Spur tailed the lawman, never letting him know he was there, as Sheriff Bjelland checked store doors and hurried a few late drunks on their way home.

At last, a little after one in the morning, the sheriff went back to the jail, locked the door, leaving one deputy in charge of the night shift.

Spur walked a few doors down Main Street and sat in one of the chairs outside the bank. He tipped the chair back on its rear legs and watched the town. It slept. Most of the lights were out.

He tried to put himself in the killer's shoes. How would he do it? What kind of a ruse would he use to get the sheriff alone? Did he have a hatred for all lawmen, or just those in Kansas? What would motivate a man to do this random killing?

At the end of the half hour he gave up and went back to his hotel and crawled into bed. For a moment, he wondered if the beautiful lady in room

305 was asleep. He decided she was, blew out the lamp and settled down on the lumpy mattress.

McCoy did not see the songbird at breakfast. He had opened up the dining room at six-thirty. He ate three sunnyside up eggs over a stack of hotcakes and drank two cups of black coffee. His first check of the day was with the night deputy, still on duty at the jail.

Nothing had happened during the night; the sheriff was safe and sound, snoring in cell number one.

The next potential trouble spot Spur could figure: the stage was due in slightly after ten that morning.

Spur followed the sheriff to breakfast at the Johnson Cafe, saw him deliver two official documents, and hold a long discussion with the owner of the Mercantile, who was also the town's mayor.

The stagecoach was late when it pulled up in front of the freight depot with its four prancing horses. The flat landscape allowed only four instead of a team of six they had to use in the mountains.

The big Concord stage rolled in ten minutes late, but there had been no real problems, just a tired horse that wasn't exactly pulling her share.

Spur leaned against the Saddlery Shop as he watched the weary passengers get down from the Concord. Two men and a woman, and each seemed to be traveling alone. He checked the men critically.

One was a drummer of some kind, whose sample case never left his hand as he supervised the unloading of two heavy boxes from the boot.

The second man was a cowboy, with saddle, rifle

and small carpetbag. Neither of them looked like a loco killer hunting his fifth victim.

The trouble was, if you didn't know who the killer was, he could be almost anyone.

A young man hurried up to a woman who had arrived and hugged her tightly, then grabbed her valise. They chattered away as they walked down the boardwalk toward a buckboard. All accounted for.

Four passengers got on the stage. The horses had been changed in quick time. The two new teams were hitched and the driver made sure the passenger doors were closed. Then he cracked his big whip and the four horses strained ahead, got the heavy wagon moving again, then went faster and faster and raced out of town.

Spur grinned. It was company policy on most stage lines to charge quickly in and out of each town, giving the local population a show. Outside of town a ways the rig settled down to a steady pace once the show was over.

A pistol cracked through the sudden quietness after the departure of the stage. The shot came from down toward the sheriff's office. Spur leaped off the boardwalk and sprinted toward the sound.

Another shot boomed, a deeper sound, more like a .44 or a .45 caliber. A wagon passed out of the way and then Spur could see the sheriff's office. A man lay in the dust as the lawman kicked away a revolver. The man on the ground held his right arm which was already bathed in rich, red blood.

"Get me a doctor! I'm bleeding to death," the shot up man screamed.

"Too bad," Sheriff Bjelland said.

Spur rushed up and grabbed the weapon out of the dirt. It was too small for a .45. Looked like it could be one of the Remington New Line Revolver #3's, a .38 caliber.

Spur walked over to Sheriff Bjelland. "What kind of a coyote is this one?"

"Damned foolish one, Colt. I served some papers on him and he thought it was all my fault. His argument is with the bank, not me."

"So he can't be the one we're looking for. Especially not with that little .38 caliber pop gun."

Spur helped get the man to jail, where the local doctor came and bandaged up the arm.

Spur faded out of the jail. All the killings had taken place at night. No reason why the bushwhacker should change his tactics now. Which meant McCoy had himself some spare time. He walked down to the livery stable and rented a horse and saddle and rode out of town a mile or two.

He stopped near a bank near the creek and unlimbered his .45. Spur set up some small rocks on a boulder and did some target practice with his long barreled .45.

The ten-inch barrel made the weapon a little slower to draw, but it gave Spur what he tested to be seventy-five percent greater accuracy. He was willing to give up a few hundredths of a second for a killing shot. He set more small rocks on top of the boulder and got back forty yards and tried to hit them. His hit rate was too low.

Spur came up to thirty yards and nailed the rocks almost every time. With a shorter barrel he would need to be nearer twenty yards to get that kind of accuracy.

He rode back into town, turned in the rented nag and walked the town again.

Nothing.

Back at the hotel he lay down on his bed and concentrated on going to sleep. He would get a few hours now and be up most of the night. Darkness was the time the killer liked best, it seemed. Spur could do darkness.

All evening he trailed the sheriff, from one doorway to the next, to the saloons. Nowhere was there any contact, any secret messages, any tries by anyone to talk to the sheriff covertly.

This evening the sheriff went into the jail just before the late night show by Lila and when Spur came in he waved.

"You can relax, Colt. I'm staying inside the rest of the night. You can listen to Lila sing and then have a good night's sleep."

Spur did listen to Lila. He waited after the show and she came out and sat at his table.

"Thank God he isn't here," Lila said when she sat down. Her face showed a strain, her eyes not confident now at all, but frightened. She checked around the saloon again, then visibly tried to relax.

"I really need that glass of white wine tonight," she said. "If I can persuade you to walk me to the hotel, I might even let you have a glass yourself."

"My working day is over," Spur said and they headed out the door. She caught his arm again and held tightly. This time she looked around all during the walk. Spur kept watchful at the alley and at deep recessed doorways. His right hand hung close to his .45, but there was no problem. No one approached them and soon they were inside the hotel.

"Oh, I'm so glad to be here!" Her eyes sparkled and the fear had vanished. "If I remember right, I promised you a glass of white wine, and the only wine I know about is an almost full bottle in my room. Would you like to climb an extra flight?"

A short time later in her room she automatically locked the door and glanced at him. "I always lock the door as soon as I come in, long time habit. Don't think it means anything other than just locking the door."

She took the bottle of white wine off the dresser. It had been opened. She picked two wine glasses from the top drawer and held them up.

"Courtesy of the Bar None Saloon," she said and laughed. "I've more than earned them. I must be tripling business for him this week. I wonder how much he's taking in. I might just come right out and ask him tomorrow."

She poured the two glasses of wine and smiled.

"Now it's time for you to tell me about yourself. Start by telling me where you grew up."

McCoy sipped the wine, it was good. "I was born in New York city and grew up there. My father runs some businesses and I worked for him for awhile after school."

"I bet you went to college, didn't you?"

"Yes, Harvard."

"And you graduated?"

"Yes, a few years ago. Business courses mostly."

"But you didn't like Daddy's kind of life, so you moved west and went into land speculation?"

"Close enough."

"Then what happened? Were you in the war?"

Spur told her about the war, his two years of fighting and then how he was called to Washington.

"Tell me about the parties. Do they have wonderful parties in Washington? Were the ladies all beautifully dressed and the men in their black ties and so handsome?"

"Yes, there were parties. I never went to many, I was busy working for the senator. He went to the parties. But I did get to a few. Yes, the women wore expensive gowns and it was all very exciting."

"I sang at a party once in Washington," she said. "It was kind of fancy. But then I had to leave to catch a train. I just love to ride on the trains, don't you, Mr. Smith?"

Spur said he enjoyed travel by train. Lila tipped her wine glass up and emptied it, then poured another one. She rubbed her wrist over her brow which was showing some signs of perspiration. A moment later she unbuttoned four of the buttons that held the dress tightly under her chin.

"And I bet you make a lot of money in land speculation, Colt Smith." She frowned, drank from the second glass of wine. "Smith? Are you sure that's your right name? Lots of people use that when they don't want anyone to know their real name."

She sat on the bed and unbuttoned two more fasteners on the top of her dress. Something lacy showed through. Lila didn't seem to notice.

She turned toward him where he sat next to her on

the bed. Her room had no chair. He saw the sway and bounce of her breasts under the chemise. She didn't notice.

"Tell me about New York. I've never been to New York. Is it as big as everyone says?"

"Yes, it has almost a million people. It's the biggest city in the whole nation. But it's still made up of a lot of small communities. Different nationalities seem to gather in one place."

She blinked at him, yawned and emptied her wine glass.

"I really love this white wine." She filled her glass again.

"Now, Lila, I've told you about me. You tell me about Lila Pemberthy. Where were you born?"

She smiled, drained the glass of wine and hiccuped. "Pardon me, I love wine." She poured a fourth glass and watched him. "Me, where was I born? Lousiana. Down there outside of New Orleans a ways. I went to school and everything." She sipped on the wine.

"You might think I'm getting tipsy from strong drink." She giggled. "Not so. I am fortifying myself from the cold night air. Right, from the cold, cold night air. And . . . and . . . and because I have to sleep alone. I used to be married. Did I tell you that? The best part of being married is to have somebody to warm your feet on. Did you know that?"

"I've never been married," Spur said.

She blinked. Most of the aloofness was gone, the regal bearing had slumped into her wine glass, and now she unbuttoned the rest of her dress front down to the waist. It was as though he wasn't there, or that he was her husband or another woman.

It seemed to make no difference that he was sitting beside her on the edge of the bed, and that they were alone in her hotel room with the door locked. Her dress fell away on one side and showed a finely sewn lace chemise that covered her breasts but revealed a soft white wrapper under the chemise.

Spur stood. "Thanks for the wine. It looks like it's about time for me to go."

"I want to talk some more. Don't go." Her eyes pleaded with him. "I don't get to talk to nice men very often. Usually the men I meet don't want to talk. You talk nice." She stood and lifted the dress off over her head and tossed it on the bed.

"Getting too warm in here. Are you warm?" Without waiting for an answer she poured another glass of wine. She sat on the side of the bed, totally at ease. Now she wore her shoes and long stockings that vanished under knee length drawers that showed under a flounce of three petticoats from her waist down. The lace chemise was the most beautiful Spur had ever seen.

Lila wasn't aware that she was half undressed. The wine must have done it, Spur decided.

"Really, it's time I was going."

Her face slid into a sly little smile. "If I kiss you, will you talk some more?"

"No, then I'd have to leave right away." He caught her hands when she moved toward him on the edge of the bed. "Lila, it isn't that I don't appreciate a beautiful girl. And you're one of the most beautiful I've ever seen. But I do have rules about taking advantage of a lady when she's had too much to drink. You have had too much to drink."

"Not so, not so, not so. There, I said it twice. Just relaxing after a long hard day of work in the saloon." She giggled again. "Mama would lift my skirts and paddle me good she see me now. With a *man* in my room!"

She laughed softly. "Speaking of working in the saloon. Do you know those two girls who work there really don't sell drinks? They go upstairs with men and . . . and do it . . . and get paid for it! I've never known a woman who *did it for pay*. Now that is just terrible. Fallen women. They are sure as hell, fallen women."

She pushed closer to him, put her arms around his neck and pulled his face toward hers. Her lips were warm and inviting against his as she kissed him. He edged away and unlaced her hands from his neck.

Spur leaned back and when she opened her eyes, he caught her attention. "Lila do you realize that you have taken your dress off?"

"No, no, no. I just was a little warm." She looked down, saw her petticoat and chemise and laughed. "I'll be damned. I'm half undressed." She giggled again and fell backward on the bed.

A moment later, she giggled again, then gave a long sigh and went to sleep. Spur smiled and rolled her over to get the covers down, then arranged her under the light quilt and sheet and snuggled the covers up to her chin.

"You're going to have a headache in the morning," he told her, as he slipped out of the room. He used her key and locked the door from the outside, then took out the key and pushed it under the door and went down to his room.

Morning came much earlier than Spur was ready for it. He was out of bed with the sun and waited for the dining room to open at six-thirty. He had shaved closely, trimmed his sideburns and moustache, combed his hair and had a whore's bath in the cold water from the pitcher.

He felt ready to take on the world, but not before breakfast.

That daily ritual out of the way, Spur settled his low crowned, brown Stetson on his head and ambled out the front door of the hotel. He was halfway to the sheriff's office when he turned quickly away from the street and pretended to stare in the first window he found, the hardware store. He looked over his shoulder as a pair of riders passed close to his side of the dusty street. For a moment he couldn't believe it.

The two dusty and trail weary men riding into Greensburg were two of the most wanted bank robbers in the west: Tex Rogers, and "Little Boy" Harry Marcello. There could be only one reason they were in town They were here to rob the Greensburg State Bank.

4

McCoy watched the two riders moving down the street. Both looked bone weary. They pulled up to the hitching rail in front of the Lucky Chip Saloon, next to the other hotel and slowly eased out of their saddles.

They must have been riding a long time. One man took his saddlebags and they both banged on the saloon door. It wasn't open yet. They stood there a moment talking, then went into the hotel.

Spur walked past the hotel to the jail and found the sheriff having breakfast off a tray.

"Glad to see you looking so healthy, Sheriff Bjelland," Spur said, dropping into a chair beside the desk.

"Not half as happy as I am to be alive another day. Could you use some coffee?"

"Thanks, just ate. We've got some famous company in town. They just rode in. You've heard of them, Tex Rogers and 'Little Boy' Harry Marcello."

"Bankers, both of them!" the sheriff said, hardly missing a bite of the bacon, eggs and hashbrowns on his plate. "Them polecats team up and got only one project in mind and I don't like the idea attal."

"True, you best let the bank owner in town know what's happening. Rogers used to work with a gang of four. I didn't see anybody else who trailed them into town, and I been watching them for some time."

Bjelland's long face took on a toughness Spur was glad to see. "We had a bank man in town three four years ago. Nailed the son-of-a-bitch with a fifty-two caliber slug in his gut just as he stepped out of the bank with the loot. But he worked alone, at least that time."

"You could ask the bank to stay closed today, death in the family, maybe," Spur suggested.

"Can't. Merchants need change and want to make deposits. That's the only vault or safe we got in the whole town."

"I'll be glad to help," Spur said. "Can you get together six or eight men who know how to shoot straight? We'll set up a little reception committee for the banker specialists."

"Yep." The sheriff went to the front window and looked out. The bank was across the street and down half a block.

"Put a pair of riflemen across the way on top of the buildings," Spur suggested. "Maybe three to cover the front door of the bank. Does it have a back entrance?"

"Nope. Jesse built it that way so he'd just have one door to worry about. And it's brick, the only brick building in town. Can't burn it down."

"You get your posse, I'm going to find a chair

where I can watch the hotel and their horses. They didn't put the nags into the livery, so they must not plan on staying long. Probably not more than a few hours."

Spur checked the .45 at his hip, went down to the hardware and looked for a rifle. The store man had three, and Spur picked the Winchester 1866 model. It was an improvement on the basic Henry repeating rifle the North used so effectively during the big war.

It weighed a little over nine pounds, was 43 inches long with a 24-inch octagon barrel with six grooves. The best feature was a tubular magazine under the barrel that held twelve .44 rim fire rounds. It would shoot thirteen times as fast as you could work the lever. The Rebels used to say the Northerners loaded the Henry on Sunday and fired all week without reloading.

He bought the rifle for thirteen dollars and fifty cents, a little overpriced, but he needed it. Rim fire rounds were fifty-seven cents for a box of fifty. He took two boxes and slid them in his pockets.

Spur stopped at the front door and pushed one round into the chamber, and loaded the long magazine with twelve more. Then he left the store and found a spot to sit in the sun where he could watch the dusty, sweat streaked horses in front of the other hotel. Spur set the rifle behind him, out of sight and eased his Stetson down over his face so he could barely see out. He could have a long wait.

The bank opened at ten, right on schedule. Spur hoped that the sheriff had told only the bank owner or manager about the threat. No sense creating a panic.

A half hour after he sat down, Spur checked the roof lines of the false fronts behind him. He saw movement in two spots and as he watched closer, he could see a man changing positions where he sat in the shadows. Two men up, Spur just hoped they were from the sheriff and not a part of the robber gang.

Twenty minutes later Spur stood to stretch, just as the two robbers came out of the hotel. Both were picking their teeth. So it had been food they were after, not a bath or a bed. The two men checked their horses, tightened the saddle cinches which had been loosened and led their mounts down the street. They tied them at a hitching post down the alley next to the bank.

Then they sat in chairs in front of the bank and waited.

As Spur watched the street, he realized there weren't as many people moving around as usual. Only half a dozen rigs were parked on the block where the bank was. Now and then someone left a store, but it was usually to go a short distance to another store.

A rider came into town. His horse looked trail weary. The man wore two pistols and had a rifle in his saddle boot. He reined in across from the bank and fiddled with his horse and saddle.

The man was on the same side of the street as Spur was and he had trouble keeping an eye on him. A few minutes later, two more men rode in at a walk, also tied up on Spur's side of the street across from the bank. They were in no rush to leave their mounts. Both had pistols and Spur spotted rifles in their boots.

Now there was no one on the street. Spur couldn't see the sheriff's office from where he was. Rogers and Marcello lounged near the front of the bank, then stood and wandered into the front door of the money lender.

The men on his side of the street pulled out their rifles and spent a lot of time checking them and their saddles. They were stalling, staying in position ready to defend the robbers when they burst out of the bank.

There was a tension in the air. He was sure the men could feel it. They had to know something was wrong. Nobody moved on the street. Usually there would be half a dozen buggies and wagons driving up and down the dusty avenue and twenty or thirty townsfolk and ranchers walking around.

Spur had checked his pocket watch. The pair was in the bank for five minutes, then he heard a muffled shot. A moment later both men charged out of the bank. Rogers, the taller one, held a woman in front of him.

Spur dove to the boardwalk, lifted the Winchester and fired before the unprotected man could make a break for his horse. The heavy .44 slug caught Marcello in the shoulder and spun him around. He stumbled and fell, dropping a large canvas bag. He lifted his gun and fired wildly. Spur put a second round into his chest and he flopped over and lay still.

One of the robber gang on Spur's side of the street turned and snapped a pistol shot at Spur. McCoy returned fire, missed as the robber dove to the ground. But Spur's second shot caught the robber in the side of the head and silenced him forever.

In the few seconds Spur defended himself, Rogers had hoisted the small woman under one arm, sprinted to his horse and climbed on board.

Down the street Spur saw the sheriff and two deputies charge toward the horseman. A rifle barked from the rooftops and nicked Rogers' horse as he charged down the alley away from the guns. Another rifle snarled and Sheriff Bjelland went down with a bullet in his leg.

One of the horsemen on Spur's side of the street leaped aboard his mount and charged for the alley. Six shots barked and the horse and rider went down. The rider rolled and tried to run but the rooftop rifle cut him down.

A horse galloped down the other alley and suddenly the street was silent.

The doctor ran out to tend to Sheriff Bjelland. Spur checked the two riders who had been giving covering fire for the robbers. Both were dead. The bandit's horse in the middle of the street had to be put out of its misery.

In front of the bank Spur knelt by Marcello. He would never rob another bank again. Under his body was a sack filled with paper money, much of it stained with the robber's blood.

Spur ran over to the sheriff.

The bank owner was already there.

"He took Mindy Lou!" the man screamed. "We've got to get a posse to go after him. He kidnapped my Mindy Lou!"

"We move ahead until I can't make out the tracks anymore, then we spread out in a company front about fifty yards apart. It gives us a long line a quarter of a mile on each side of the trail. If he makes a fire tonight, one of us is going to smell it. When you spot him, get everybody together and we'll decide what to do."

Turner, the lead deputy agreed. "Yeah, let's do it. This gent has been on this kind of hunt before. None of the rest of us have, so we do it his way."

They spread out. Spur took the farthest position on the right side of the road. He was guessing. Most men were right handed. He figured Rogers would turn right when he wanted to find some cover. Along here the trail was on the left side of the stream.

They moved ahead at a walk, tried to keep in sight of one another, but Spur knew that would not happen. There was no moon as it got dark, and you could see only about fifty feet in any direction.

They covered a mile, maybe a mile and a half, and Spur wondered if he had guessed wrong.

Another half mile and he figured he had. He was riding up a small rise, with the stream well below and to the left. An owl hooted somewhere to his right. It was real, no Indians were left around in Kansas.

They moved through the countryside for a half hour. Now and then he heard or saw the man next to him toward the road. They rode and watched, sat and listened. Always they sniffed the clean, pure air for the taint of wood smoke.

For another fifteen minutes he saw nothing ahead but blackness. Then the slight breeze stirred and brought to him the thin, unmistakable smell of smoke.

Where?

He rode forward and the smoke was stronger. He rode, angled to the left and it decreased. He changed to the right and forward and lost it all together.

Spur backtracked and moved toward the stream. The smoke came to him again and this time he followed it upwind. He got off his mount, took the Winchester and moved slowly through the slightly downhill prairie.

He wondered if it were a rancher's cabin, or a sod-buster. They hadn't seen any habitation out this way for miles.

Ahead there was a clump of brush. Now he could see the soft glow of light. The fire!

Spur edged closer, moving like an Apache withut rustling a leaf, without breaking a twig. When he was twenty yards away he saw someone move.

Closer, he had to get closer. The brush here prevented any kind of sure shot.

He worked up slowly, not wanting to risk Rogers using his gun on the girl. No sense in that. Slow and easy. He had all night.

After another ten minutes he had moved around the pair to where there was almost no brush. He could see them now in the soft glow of the small cooking fire. The girl did not seem to be tied up.

He heard them talking, both softly. He must have warned her not to make any noise. Then he smelled the coffee, and the crisp, sharp odor of frying bacon. Rogers must be confident.

Spur angled closer, crawling on hands and knees

now until he was ten yards away. The girl must have been lying down. Now she lifted up and in the light of the fire he saw that she wore nothing above her waist. Her firm, young breasts swung out and bounced and jiggled as she moved. Mindy Lou did not look at all like a hostage. She smiled and held out both arms.

"Darling! It's been so long. I didn't think you were ever coming to get me out of that stuffy old bank. Let's make it just as good as we did the other time. I'm sure those men have gone home. We haven't heard anything from them. I've got your shoulder all bandaged up and the beans aren't ready yet. We can do a quick one now and then take our time on the next four or five."

Tex Rogers laughed delightedly and turned toward her.

"You're right, Mindy Lou, it's been too damned long."

5

The two bare bodies stretched out on the blanket in the faint firelight and Spur worked closer. There could be no mistakes. He wanted them dead to rights if either tried to pull a pistol off the blanket.

A minute later the pair coupled on the blanket were groaning and laughing and yelping with delight when Spur saw a visitor. He saw the twin coals of fire in the eyes of the animal first. Then as it crept closer on its belly, he knew what it was. A coyote, a rabid coyote or it never would get this close to humans.

Being rabid it was also half starved and would take on any prey it could find, even man. One bite from those saliva drooling teeth and the human would suffer a sure and painful death from rabies.

Spur moved his Winchester's muzzle to the left to cover the animal, saw it creep three feet closer to the couple and spring. Spur's follow shot caught the thin coyote as it hurtled through the air. The heavy slug cut a swath through its chest and heart and tore out through the other side of the coyote.

The report of the rifle brought a scream from Mindy Lou, a string of curses from Tex Rogers, and a new scream as the coyote landed at the very edge of the blanket.

Mindy Lou sat up, not trying to hide her breasts as she screamed again and again and stared at the dying coyote.

"Don't either of you move!" Spur bellowed. "You're both under arrest."

Spur did not show himself. Rogers had dropped out of sight and Spur was sure he was crawling for his guns.

"Come on, Rogers, give it up or you're dead."

Only silence answered him.

Mindy Lou finished screaming and edged away from the dead coyote. Then in a flurry of action, a six-gun cracked twice and Spur saw a figure wearing only pants and boots, leap up and scramble deeper into the brush and toward a big cottonwood. Spur snapped one shot at the darting figure, but he figured he missed.

"No way out, Rogers. We've got this camp surrounded and covered with ten guns. You saw us following you."

"Not a chance, asshole!" Rogers called from behind the cottonwood. "You stumbled on us and we got lucky with that damn coyote. Be a hero, rescue the girl. You'll never find me moving alone in the dark."

Spur fired the Winchester at the voice three times. It would act as a signal to the rest of the posse to join him here. He also might wing Rogers.

Then the night quieted. The girl rustled around, putting on her clothes. Spur listened but could hear no movement from Rogers.

Horse? Where had Rogers tied up his horse? Spur lifted up and moved through the brush with no attempt to be quiet. He circled the little camp and found nothing. He made a wider circle and reached a tributary to a small stream with the main trail to Wichita followed. He heard a horse snorting. He crashed that way only to hear saddle leather creak, and to see the backside of the bay charging into the darkness to the east.

Spur sent three shots after the rider, then walked back to the campfire and found Mindy Lou fully dressed sitting beside the blaze. She looked up at him, her dark eyes angry. She held a pistol that now pointed at him.

"This six-gun is for my protection and I know how to use it," she said simply.

"Doesn't look like your virtue needs much protection, Mindy Lou."

She lowered the weapon and pouted. He figured she was not more than eighteen.

"Just don't tell my uncle. He'd just die. Truth is, I've known Tex for two years. He came to town to rob the bank back then and I talked him out of it. We went to bed instead. He's been back every few months. But this time he said he needed the bank's money and this would be an ideal time for him to take me with him. He's been the only one. I've been in love with him since the first time I saw him."

Spur sat there watching her. Her hands fiddled with her dress, fed small sticks into the fire. She glanced up at him from time to time, her face softening.

"Miss, I'd say any problems you have with your uncle are your own business. Won't do any good for me to tell him about your little roll in the blankets out here." He stood. "Build up the fire, I've got a posse to find."

He fired three more shots, then called into the Kansas night, and after a half hour he had all but one of the posse in the fold.

"All right men. We nearly had Tex, but he got lucky and slipped away. Mindy Lou here is safe, and come dawn, I want most of you to head back to Greensburg and take her along. Missy Mindy Lou is your charge and I expect you to treat her like a lady. Anybody who doesn't will be reported to the sheriff."

He looked at them in the firelight. "Which one of you is the best shot?"

The cowboy spoke up when no one else did. "I've used a weapon now and then. Did three years as a sniper with the 27th Michigan Volunteers in the war."

"Fine, what's your name?"

"Froude, sir. Ken Froude."

"I'd like to take you with me now, tonight, to track Rogers. Are you volunteering?"

Froude grinned. "Sir, you know the rule, never volunteer for anything. Yeah, I'm with you."

Spur nodded. "The rest of you get some sleep and ride back to Greensburg in the morning. Might post a guard if you want, mostly to watch for rabid coyotes. Where there's one, there's bound to be others."

Ten minutes later Spur and Froude checked the main stage road toward Wichita. Spur found enough dry grass to twist into a torch and work back and forth across the road. He spotted the same looking horseshoe mark he had been tracking before. It was more square than most of the shoes in use. This mark had no insect tracks over it as most of the others did. No nighttime bug had crawled over this one, so it must have been made within the past hour or so.

"This has to be the one," Spur said. "Let's ride a half mile and check again."

The second time they made a torch and checked. They could not find the tracks.

"He's holed up somewhere waiting for morning. The girl told me his shoulder is hit pretty bad. He can't put his weight on it, and he didn't unsaddle his horse because he didn't think he could throw the saddle on come morning."

Spur looked into the blackness, and listened for any night birds. He could always go back for more men. He made his tactical decision the way he used to in the Army.

"Froude, I want you to lay low here until morning. If I flush him out, he'll come this way. If he does, pretend you're back in the Army and blast him out of the saddle. He's wanted for murder and bank robbery. You'll be doing the country a favor."

"Yeah, I can do that. You think he'll run?"

"First I have to find him. He won't make another fire, that's for damned sure. If nothing happens by noon, and you don't hear any shots, take off for town."

"I'll come hunting you, Smith."

"Might be too late. This is going to be one on one."

Spur turned and rode back down the stage trail for two hundred yards, made another torch and searched for the prints. Nothing. He repeated the procedure twice more before he found the hoofprints he wanted. They led on down the road for another fifty yards, then turned off into the trees along the small stream.

Spur stamped out the torch and jumped to one side, but there was no barrage of hot lead from the brush. If Rogers saw the torch he kept hidden, figuring he could stay out of sight until he and his horse were rested.

McCoy was counting on Rogers' horse to give away his hiding spot. If Rogers was down and sleeping, he wouldn't be able to hold his mount.

A horse has a fine sense of smell, and can sense another horse up to a quarter of a mile if the wind is right. The animals are curious and usually will whinny or wicker or make some other sound in communication. Mares talk a lot more than the stallions.

Spur hoped Tex's mount was feeling friendly and ready for some horse talk. He marked the trail where the tracks vanished, then rode slowly fifty yards each way listening carefully, but heard no contact.

Back at the mark he rode into the brush, which was only about twenty yards wide on both sides of the creek. He splashed through the water and walked his mount out the other side, then sat and listened.

Nothing.

He rode fifty yards up and back on the far side of the creek, but had no response. McCoy penetrated the brush at several points, but his mount did not respond. The other horse might be so worn out it was sleeping on its feet. Or Tex might have tied a bandanna around its muzzle so it couldn't make any sounds. Spur hoped that wasn't the case.

The Secret Agent moved into the brush every ten yards now, probing, examining, determined to find Rogers before he could run again. If he got on his horse and rode, this could turn into a two week chase. Spur didn't have time for that. This was a side trip. He was hunting a lawman killer.

On the sixth invasion of the brush from the far end, he paused again. This time he heard a snort and some horse talk. It came from dead ahead, not more than another ten yards. Spur slid off his mount, left the Winchester in the boot and worked ahead through the light brush and small willow and cottonwoods with all the stealth of a Chiricahua Apache.

He never put his weight on his foot until he was sure there was no branch or twig under it. No tree was scraped or green bough rustled. It took him five minutes to cover five yards. When he edged around the last thicket he saw the horse in the darkness. It was tied to a sapling on a grazing line and munching away on the spring grass.

Spur checked the surrounding area he could see without moving. Nowhere did he spot a blanket roll. He eased up to the horse, smoothed its flank, rubbed its neck, then untied the animal and led it downstream and, he hoped, away from the bank robber.

Ten minutes later, both horses were tied and hidden. He returned to the same spot and began searching for Tex. It was a grinding, slow, monotonous job. It was too dark to see his pocket watch. The trees and clouds hid the Big Dipper so he couldn't judge the time by that.

McCoy kept searching. He made two circles around the place where Tex's horse had been without finding him. Tex couldn't be more than twenty or thirty yards away. He had to be here somewhere.

He moved forward and a bramble bush raked his wrist bringing blood. He stopped.

Yeah! Slowly he moved around the six-foot high, twenty feet in diameter, impenetrable mound of thick growth with thorns on it that would make a rosebush blush with shame. He remembered that the bramble bushes were the favorite hiding spots for Indians on the run. They worked around the brushy bush until they found an opening at the bottom, and wormed their way in underneath, safely below the mass of thorns and thickets.

He had to go around the brambles twice before he found the right spot. There were no brambles to the ground and a small opening showed. He knelt at it and felt the ground. It had been disturbed. He found indentations and scrapes that could have been made by boots as someone crawled forward.

Spur moved back ten yards, found a good sized cottonwood and settled down. He had a perfect shot at the entrance and when Tex came crawling out, he would be in no position to defend himself.

Spur turned his back to the bramble bush, opened

the light jacket he wore and lit a match to check the time. Two-thirty A.M. He had a long wait ahead of him.

He dozed, then gave himself a wake up call at four-thirty and went to sleep. He woke promptly and checked the time with another match. Twenty-eight after four. Good.

He slid a sixth round into his .45 and hunkered down watching the bramble bush.

With the first streaks of dawn tingeing the east, Spur slid to a prone position to offer a smaller target and watched the bramble opening. Coyotes could have used the brambles as a den. If so, there should be plenty of room inside where the animals would have chewed off the dead branches so they could move around. Spur had seen one bramble bush that had a space four feet high inside. Some children at a small ranch had shown the bush to him one day. They had used clippers and cut out some of the dead wood and live shoots inside to make a playhouse.

Just as dawn came, and the light gave him a full view of the bramble bush, Spur was glad he had not tried to crawl in. The opening looked smaller now, less than a foot off the ground, but room enough to slip in.

Ten minutes later he heard someone cough. The sound came from the brambles.

Another five minutes went by before Spur saw movement at the opening. Tex Rogers crawled forward slowly, seemingly in pain. He let his left arm drag behind him, pulling himself outward with his right elbow digging in the dirt. Spur could tell that the man was hurting.

Spur hurried to one side before Tex could see and when the killer was half-way out, Spur planted his heavy boot on Tex's neck and pushed down.

"What the hell?"

"Morning, Tex. Have a good night's sleep?"

"Bastard!"

Spur moved his foot. "Come on out, but remember, I won't need more than a small excuse to put a slug right between your eyes. That would get my day off to a fine start."

Once Tex was out of the brambles, Spur stripped the .44 from his holster, took a hideout derringer from his pocket and two knives from his ankle.

His shoulder had a bandage of sorts around it made from cloth from a petticoat.

"You'll live until you hang," Spur said pushing him forward toward the spot where he had hidden the horses.

Back on the road, Spur tied Tex's hand in front of him and held the reins to his horse. Spur fired three times in the air, and a few minutes later, Ken Froude rode up, his rifle ready, his dark eyes curious.

"Damn, you got the bastard," he said.

"Yeah, and the only place he's going is to a hangman's trap. He's wanted in at least three states for bank robbery and murder."

They rode into town just before noon. Word spread quickly and before they got to the jail, half the town was in the street to see the killer. He wasn't much to look at, still dirty, bearded and with stringy, dirty hair.

One of the deputies who had been on the posse met them in front of the jail.

"Mr. Smith, I think you better come inside," the deputy said.

"Trouble?" Spur asked.

Inside Spur looked around. "Where's Sheriff Bjelland?" Spur asked.

"That's what I wanted to talk about. The sheriff is dead. Somebody shot him last night while we were gone. Gunned him down at the edge of town."

Spur's face tightened into a scowl. "He was killed with two .45 rounds, fired so close there were powder burns, right? And he was killed at night and there are no witnesses."

"Yeah, but how could you know all that?"

"Throw this bank robber in a cell, I want to see the sheriff's body!" Spur spat and rushed out the door. He had been here two days and now this happened the minute he was out of town. There had to be a tie in. Did the repetitive killer know that Spur was after him? Or was this all a coincidence? Spur McCoy was damned well going to find out!

6

McCoy knew he was right before he looked at the cold, waxy body of ex-sheriff Jon Bjelland. The first bluish hole with a ring of powder burn marks around it was a little lower than he might have guessed, but it did the job. It disabled the sheriff and made the second shot easy.

He wondered if this killing bastard talked to his victims during the time between the two slugs. Did he let the man last for an hour, sweating and screaming in pain? Did he make the sheriff listen to a diatribe about how terrible lawmen were and that they all should be shot once in the belly so they had to suffer for an hour before they died?

Spur slammed his hand against the table on which Bjelland lay in the back room of the barber shop. The barber was also the undertaker and the official county coroner. What churned in Spur's gut was the fact that Bjelland wouldn't be dead if Tex Rogers hadn't come to town.

One of the deputies said the sheriff must have been out rattling doors on the night shift and somebody got to him. Yeah, somebody, but who, and how, and when, and most importantly, why?

Spur pulled the sheet back over the body.

"I got to dress him up nice," Dorian, the barber-undertaker said. "Folks expect to see a body dressed nice."

"You do that!" Spur snarled. "All I have to do is find the guy who killed him." Spur slammed out the door and walked a half mile out of town and back. By then he was calmed down enough to think straight. At the sheriff's office he found out who discovered the body and went to talk to him.

The man's name was Nemo Nester, who ran the hardware store. He was up early to get a shipment of bolts and screws and nails put away before opening time. Spur talked to him in the store.

Nester was so farsighted he had glasses to check the invoices against the boxes of goods. He was almost entirely bald, but wore a full beard that was close clipped. His eyes were a soft blue.

"Got up early, Mr. Smith, to come in to the store and I seen this buggy over about two hundred yards from my place. We live out on the edge of town so I can see across the prairie. I like it out there. Nobody bothers us much.

"Anyways, I came out to walk down to the store and I saw the buggy. Wasn't sure whose it was, but right away I saw that the lines weren't tied, and the horse was moving along, grazing and pulling the buggy. That ain't normal. A body's got to figure that something is wrong when that's happening, especially at five in the morning.

"I ran over there, caught the lines which were

trailing and then looked inside. The sheriff lay against the seat, kind of spread out. I could see the powder burns on his shirt. His head was back and his eyes wide open but I could tell right away that he was dead. I took the reins and led the rig down to the sheriff's office and yelled at the deputy.

"But nobody was there. Two of them were out with the posse and the other one must have been home. He come fast when he heard about the killing. That's about it."

"You didn't see anything dropped inside or near the buggy? You didn't take anything out of it?"

"No sir! Wouldn't want to interfere."

"You already did, Mr. Nester. Would you take me out to the exact spot where you saw the rig this morning?"

He called to his clerk to mind the store and they walked out to the area. It was on the west side of town. The last street just ended in the prairie, half a block from the store owner's place. The buggy was another hundred yards into the country from there.

The hardware store man frowned a moment, then walked to where Spur could see buggy tracks turning around in the soft ground.

"Right here. See, that's where I turned the rig around and went back to town."

Spur thanked him and told him he was free to return to his store. Spur spent an hour going over the area. He followed the tracks of the rig back to the street. Saw where the horses had cropped down the grass on its leisurely feed.

He kept looking for footprints. Three or four days ago, there had been a rain in Greensburg and some of the ground was still soft. He checked the whole area from the street out to the turnarond but found no footprints other than those of the horse. Someone could have exited at the end of the hard packed street and left no prints at all.

Spur could find nothing at the end of the street, either. He hoped that something had been dropped or thrown away that could give him a clue. There was nothing at all.

It was the middle of the afternoon, after he had taken a bath in his hotel room in a portable tub, shaved and dressed in clean clothes, that he made the rounds of the saloons, talking with the barkeeps.

It soon became evident that Sheriff Bjelland had taken his usual tour the night he died. That would put him last at the Bar None Saloon.

Mike served Spur a cold tap beer and nodded.

"Yeah, sure, the sheriff was around as usual last night. We talked about his bum leg and the tight bandage the doctor had put on it. They decided it wasn't broke after all, just damn near broke. He was on crutches, but he figured he had to make the circuit."

"He stay long?"

"Oh, about a half hour, as usual. This is . . . was . . . his last stop before he turned in. Things quiet down around here just after midnight. Mostly working folks we have here in town."

"Mike, you remember anybody watching him? Anybody having an argument or a fight with him while he was here?"

"Not a chance. He only talked with me. We had one card game going that didn't end until a little after one. But outside of those four players, wasn't but one or two others in the whole place. I wanted to close up and git."

"The buggy. Any idea whose it was? I forgot to ask the deputy."

"Sure. Belonged to the livery. Some drummer rented it and left it parked in front of the Pride of the Plains Hotel. He left it all ready to go because of an early morning start. He was going to use it today to go out to Hemlock and Roundtree, north of here a ways. No stage goes up there, but there's these two nice little towns where he wanted to show his goods."

"So anybody could have walked along the street, stepped into the rig and driven off."

"Bout the size of it, Mr. Smith."

"Yeah, thanks, Mike." Spur finished his beer slowly, trying to figure it out. He went to the stage office and checked. Five people had left town that morning on the stage heading east. Three more had tickets to go on to Dodge City on the westbound rig that left about an hour ago.

Spur threw down his hat in the sheriff's office. Deputy Sheriff Turner seemed to be in charge. He showed Spur the map of the state. The next town of any size was Dodge City.

"A problem?" Turner asked.

"Somewhat. Let's say you are the killer I'm hunting. You've just killed the lawmen in the five towns behind us toward Wichita. What town would you pick for your next victim, moving on west?"

"No doubt. Dodge City. Nothing worthwhile between here and there. Not even a full time lawman. Some parttimers. One little place has a barber who is also town marshal. Another one has the mayor, who doubles as the town marshal and he's also the operator of the livery stable."

"My man is probably already on his way to Dodge City. I'll be out of here tomorrow. You turn up anything you wire me care of the sheriff in Dodge City."

Spur ate a large early dinner and showed up at the Bar None Saloon for some serious poker playing. He had fifty dollars that he hoped he might lose. Then he would feel a lot better about getting out of town tomorrow just after noon on the westbound stage.

He played poker and drank beer. Damn! He hated to be beaten by the killer. He killed Bjelland right under Spur's nose! It could even be someone he had seen in town. More likely the man held in the background, watched the routine of the sheriff and planned his strike. The bank robbery and two deputies gunning out of town had been made to order for him. Damn!

"Hey, mister, I just raised a dollar," a voice jabbed at him from across the poker table. "You in this pot or not?"

McCoy threw in a chip and stared at his cards. He won the pot and was twelve dollars ahead.

They stopped the game and Lila came on to sing. She had put in several new songs tonight and finished with a song Spur had never heard before, "Empty Arms And A Crying Heart."

By the time Lila came on to sing at the eleven o'clock show, Spur was ten dollars losers. He folded, kept his chair for the show and then waited for Lila.

She had seen him in his chair down front. He played solitaire as he waited.

"Red queen will play on your king of spades," a familiar voice said to him over his shoulder. He turned and stood.

"Lila, you were great tonight, as usual."

"Thank you. Going back to the hotel?" She seemed rather subdued as he nodded.

"Lost all my money, time to leave."

"You still have your horse, saddle and rifle."

"Not even that, rifle is all, I guess."

Outside she caught his arm and pulled close to him.

"This time of night still makes me shiver," she said. "I guess it goes back to my childhood. I always was afraid of the dark."

Then went up the stairs and straight to her room. She gave him the key, he opened the door and she waved him inside. As soon as Spur lit the lamp, she closed the door and locked it, then she put her arms around his neck and pulled his face down so she could kiss him.

The kiss was serious. Her lips parted and her tongue darted at his lips, then inside his mouth. She sighed and pressed against him. She broke it off and led him to the bed where she sat down.

"The other night, did you think I was drunk?"

"You did have several glasses of wine."

"I knew exactly what I was doing, even when I took off my dress. I never let it change the way I treated you. I'm sorry I was so tired. I really just went to sleep." She reached over and unbuttoned the soft leather vest he wore over his shirt.

"Right now I know exactly what I'm doing, too. I want you to stay in my bed tonight. I want us to make love together. Yes, together. Making love is a cooperating thing. Nobody assaults the other one. Together we explore and caress and then at last we come together to our mutual satisfaction."

She kissed him again where he sat beside her. Gently she pressed him back on the bed and leaned over on top of him.

"First we do a lot of kissing and petting, and then if we both are pleased, we will undress each other."

She leaned up to watch him carefully. "Is that way of making love all right with you?"

"Absolutely. It's a beautiful system, it's poetry."

"Maybe you won't like me naked."

"You were half-naked the other night, and I loved what I saw."

Lila giggled. "You didn't even start to love any of me, but before tonight's over we're going to love each other to pieces!"

She bent and kissed him again, lying fully on top of him, pressing her breasts against his chest. She caught one of his hands and put it between them covering a breast.

"They do love to be petted." She kissed him again, devouring his open mouth. "Oh, did I tell you? Tonight was my last night. I'm going to Dodge City tomorrow. It was all arranged weeks ago. A booking agent in St. Louis set it up for me by mail."

Spur's hand rubbed her breast through the fabric of her dress. He felt her nipple swell and the heat came through the cloth.

"I'm heading for Dodge City tomorrow, myself.

Perhaps we can sit together on the stage?"

"I'll count on it." She kissed him again. "But that won't be near the marvelous, wonderful experience that we're having now, and that we're going to have until morning!" She sat up and began to open the buttons down his shirt front. Her hand slipped inside and played with the black hair on his chest.

"I love a man with hair on his chest," she said then pressed back his shirt and kissed his chest, biting tenderly on his man nipples.

He sat up and opened the top buttons of her soft blue dress.

"Did I tell you that you're the prettiest lady I've seen in a dozen months of Sundays?" She shook her head. "You are, you have a marvelous smile, dancing eyes, a little nose that turns up just a smidgen, and a mouth that is delightful when open or closed."

She helped him slip the dress off her shoulders. He sucked in a quick breath. The chemise she wore over her binder was of soft blue lace, so delicate it looked as if it might blow away, yet sturdy and protective. He touched it and she smiled.

"You liked the white lace chemise the other night, too. It was interesting to watch you as I took off my dress. I wondered what you would do. I made a little bet with myself that you wouldn't 'take advantage of me' in my evidently tipsy situation."

"You won." He leaned in and breathed his hot breath through the lace and into the binder that covered her breasts.

"Oh, lordy but that is nice!" she said softly. Quickly she lifted up on her knees on the bed and pulled the dress over her head. His hands covered both her breasts and she slid toward him.

"You have no idea how wonderful that makes me feel."

He lifted the chemise and pushed his hand under it, sliding under the wrapper until his fingers closed around her bare left breast and he squeezed her pulsating nipple.

"Oh, glory! Colt, I want you to kiss me just ever so long!"

He did and she moved her hand down his bare chest to his crotch, found the swelling there and rubbed it through the trousers.

After several minutes she lifted up from him, pulled the chemise over her head and then quickly took off the wrapper letting her breasts swing free.

Spur sat there staring. "So beautiful! The wonder of a woman's breasts always amazes me. So perfectly sculptured, so wonderful!"

His hand moved toward one and she breathed deeply in anticipation. He barely touched her skin below her breasts, rubbed gently, then moved upward to the swell and tenderly traced a line around her mound.

Lila sighed and leaned toward him more, so her breasts hung nearly straight down. They were large, with heavy soft pink areolas and throbbing dark red nipples.

He caressed the breast, working slowly around it until he came to her nipple. Her eyes were closed. Spur bent and kissed the small bit of extended flesh, then licked it and at last pulled as much of her breast into his mouth as he could.

Her hips bucked convulsively and she jolted into a climax that rattled her and kept her hips pounding upward toward him for almost a minute. Her breath came in ragged gasps and the tremors slowed and then faded away.

Slowly her eyes opened and she pushed her arms around him and clung to him, her breasts against his bare chest.

"Oh, God, never . . . never in my life have I ever exploded that way before . . . before you were inside me. Marvelous!"

He kissed her other breast, then pulled at her petticoats. She took them off and then her stocking and shoes and sat there, proud in her bare top and white drawers that had small pink bows on them.

Spur stepped to the door, made sure it was locked and came back. He walked to the bed and she hugged his waist, then kissed the bulge in his pants.

"Show me," she said. She sat on the bed shivering, not knowing what to do with her hands. "I'm so nervous I can hardly wait," she said softly.

Spur opened the fly buttons and turned, pulled down his pants and short underwear and kicked them off. Then he turned.

His erection was full, ready. It stabbed out from him at a angle. Lila gave a small cry of delight and grabbed his shaft. She was so gentle he hardly knew she held him. Slowly and with her eyes wide, she lowered her head toward him and kissed the thick, purple head.

Lila shivered. "Sweet damn! sweet damn! sweet damn! I've never seen one so wonderful, and so big. Lordy, he'll never fit inside my little cunny." Lila giggled. "Lordy, lordy!"

She sat on the side of the bed and quickly unbuttoned her drawers and began to pull them down. He stopped her. Gently he pressed her back on the bed and moved his hands to the white material that was still at her waist.

He pulled down the material. Soon the gentle swell of her flat belly showed and after another inch he revealed the top of her pubic hair. Spur kissed the spot, moving the cloth down a little at a time, kissing it down her legs until her entire "V" of soft brown hair showed.

He pushed his face into the muff, found her moist spot and kissed it.

"Oh, God!" she screeched. She put her hand over her mouth, surprise on her face, a look of absolute worship wreathing her features.

"Lordy, nobody ever did that for me before!"

He took her drawers off and then lay beside her on the bed. At first they didn't touch, then her hand stretched out.

"Please, Colt Smith. Please love me!"

Spur touched her breasts, caressed them, leaned down and kissed them both, then turned her gently to her back. She shook her head.

"No, the other way." She lifted over him and lay on his stomach, kissing him all over his face, then at last on his open mouth.

Slowly he lifted her hips, moved her down, then adjusted his shaft and lowered her to meet him.

"Oh . . . oh . . . Colt . . . that's good . . . so . . . so . . ."

For a moment he thought she had passed out.

Then her face blossomed over his with a wonderful smile. "So wonderful!" She had been holding herself up. Now she lowered and Spur felt his lance penetrating deeply into her.

Lila moaned in joy, lifted and dropped suddenly impaling herself to the very last tenth of an inch.

"Oh, lord if I'm going to die soon anyway, let it be right now!"

Spur chuckled. "I've never heard it put that way before," he said.

She didn't bother to answer. She lifted up and came down. Her face showed the kind of pleasure that was beyond all measure. She repeated the movement and soon set up a rhythm that kept her rocking and riding over him like a jockey on a thundering race horse.

Perspiration beaded on her forehead and a salty drop hit Spur on the lip. He grinned, moved his hands so he could play with her bouncing, rocking big breasts. He felt a stirring deep within himself but knew he could control it, make it last for a long time.

After a dozen more strokes he wasn't so sure that he could last. Lila closed her eyes and growled, then the throbbing, thundering climax hit her and her whole body rattled like a rabbit in a dog's mouth. She shook and trembled as one series after another of spasms pulsated through her, making her hips dance and pound down on him a dozen times without any control.

She wailed softly, dropped her chest to his and kissed him furiously for the last half of the long climax.

Just as she was about to taper off, Spur's own floodgates opened and the river of molten lava flowed through the valve and jetted from his shaft like a liquid metal geyser, splashing into her, setting her off on another series of climaxes, even as he trembled and his whole body stiffened as he drove upward as high as he could, lifting her and himself off the bed, bowing up until the very last drop of seed shot from him and he collapsed on the bed, panting, trying to get in enough air to live on as the mini death claimed him.

She lifted up to look at him a moment. Lila snuggled on top of him, secure in her womanhood, glad that she could satisfy him, delighted that he was so gentle, so tender, that he had made love with her, not simply taken her.

She moved her hips gently, feeling him inside her, then to her sorrow she felt him shrinking. She gripped him with her muscles, trying to excite him again.

Spur laughed gently. "Don't worry, sexy little lady, there is lots more. We are only beginning a long, exciting night. I do need a ten minute recuperation time. Do you still have that bottle of wine?"

She was up and away from him in a second. She bounced all bare and delightful to the dresser and came back with two bottles.

Spur smiled. It was going to be a great night that would make up for a terrible day. Tomorrow. He would worry about catching a killer in Dodge City tomorrow.

7

Spur McCoy woke up in Lila's bed the next morning. It was just after daylight. She snuggled against his side, one arm across his chest. He caught one of her breasts and rubbed it gently. She stirred, smiled, but continued sleeping. He bent and kissed her bare breast and she came awake slowly.

"Once more!" Lila said with a savage snarl. "Once more quick—fast and mean!"

He rolled over her and thrust and she cried out. Then they began pounding against each other as though it was the first time and they both climaxed quickly, then lay together panting and laughing and grinning and talking.

"It's never been so good for me," Lila said. "Sure I like sex, I like to get fucked, but this has been something tremendously special for me. I know you'll be moving on, but I'll never forget you, Colt Smith."

He held her close. "How could I ever forget a lady who sings like a nightingale and makes love like a tiger!"

They had another nap, got up and dressed and went down to breakfast. After that Spur checked in at the sheriff's office but there wasn't much he could do. Absolutely no clues about who killed Sheriff Bjelland. Before he left, a rider came in. He was from south a ways, he said, from Coldwater.

The rider was lean, sunburned, all cowhand.

"Heading out to Montana where my uncle lives," the man said. "Yeah, pardon me. My name is Eugene Gregg and I work cattle. Rode up to sell my horse and catch the stage west and north. Don't know the best way."

He turned the well worn hat in his hands. "What I really want to tell you is that the sheriff down at Coldwater got himself killed couple of days ago. Don't know how it happened, but thought I should tell you, you being another sheriff and all that."

"How was he killed?" Spur asked, at once alert.

"Don't rightly know. Shot, I know that for sure. I was on the Bar Y spread and didn't hear about it until I got to town. Only about twenty miles down there. Guess that's another county, but I'm not too sure."

"But the sheriff was shot dead?"

"Right about that, I saw his body." The cowboy hesitated. "Well, I guess I better get to the stage and buy myself a ticket. Oh, where is the livery?"

The deputy pointed the way and the cowboy thanked them and headed for the livery barn to sell his horse. Spur rubbed his jaw. "There was time. Our man could have lit out on a horse the night he killed Sheriff Bjelland, had lots of time to get there and bushwhacked the sheriff down in Coldwater the next day. I've got to go down and check on it."

Spur looked at Deputy Turner. "Good luck here, and if you hear anything, send word to the sheriff in Dodge City."

They shook hands and Spur hurried out the door, his jaw set in a determined pose that was half anger, half frustration.

He found Lila in her room and only half dressed.

"Once more?" she said with a grin. Spur shook his head.

"Sorry, I won't be able to ride to Dodge City with you. I have to grab a horse and ride south." He told her about the problem and that he wanted to find out what happened.

"For being a land buyer, you seem terribly concerned about these lawmen."

"Curious, mostly. The stability of a town affects the price of land. A place like Dodge City with its strong lawmen, is much better for land speculation than say, Tombstone, Arizona, where there is hardly any law at all."

Spur wasn't sure he had convinced her. "I'll see you in our room in Dodge City." He kissed her, lingering over the task. "No sense in renting two rooms when we use just one."

She smiled, nodded and waved as he hurried out the door.

Spur packed his gear, went to the livery and rented a horse. He left his carpetbag at the hotel but took his rifle along. It was only twenty two miles to Coldwater. A little over four hours at a good canter. He'd try it.

The bay he rode was strong and steady and loved

to canter along at her natural gait eating up the miles. He stopped at what he figured was halfway and ate the two sandwiches he had had them make for him in the hotel kitchen. There was no time to boil coffee.

He arrived in the small community of Coldwater just after two o'clock. There couldn't be more than two hundred people in the town. It was ranching country.

He rode directly to the small courthouse and the sheriff's office. It was locked.

The county clerk came down the short hall.

"Yep, thought I heard somebody come in. Might be I can help a bit, I'm the county clerk."

"The sheriff. I heard he was shot."

"True, the Caruther Boys. Got a little rowdy and skunk drunk in the Silver Spur Saloon three nights ago and shot up the place. Sheriff Downing went in to calm things down and they shot him dead before he could say howdy."

"Did they escape?"

"Yep, for a day and a half. Then our posse tracked them down and did some shooting of themselves. Killed Jed and shot up Willy bad. If he lives, he'll be hanged in three days. Had the trial yesterday."

"No wasted time. I like that."

"Anything else? I'm the county staff today. The other two are off inspecting or something. Danged place is getting top heavy with workers."

Spur thought of the thousands and thousands of government employees in Washington, D.C., and he smiled. "Yes, sir, I guess it can do that. Thanks for the information."

Spur walked down the main street, which was called Gulch Lane, until he found a small restaurant. He knew he should start back. He might be able to catch the stage. One look at his pocket watch told him the stage was just leaving. He'd be on the one tomorrow.

He had two cups of coffee and treated himself to two pieces of homemade cherry pie. It was the best he'd had in months. Spur took a half mile walk, came back to his horse. He looked over his rig a minute, then stopped at the hardware store for a quart sized canteen with a carrying case. He filled the canteen from the public pump at the far end of town, and hit the trail. With any luck he should be into Greensburg just before dark.

It had been a wild goose chase coming down here. But he knew it might be that when he left. In his position he had to double check every possibility, run down every chance. That's why the killer always had the advantage. Spur felt he was getting closer. Maybe he could nail the bastard before he killed again.

When Spur arrived back in Greensburg that evening, he returned the horse, rented a room and enjoyed a long hot bath. Then he talked to Deputy Turner, found out there were no clues of any kind to the sheriff's death and turned in for an early bedtime. He had to recoup his strength from last night. Now that was a delightful kind of a problem to have.

McCoy smiled as he thought of the enthusiastic, inventive and insatiable way that Lila enjoyed making love. He looked forward to more of her love-making when he got to Dodge City and found the little songbird again.

The long stage ride did nothing for his bad mood when he stepped off the rig in Dodge City slightly after dark the next evening. He had thought of absolutely no new means to smoke out the killer. Spur had rejected the idea of setting up the sheriff as bait for the killer and then catching him just before he pulled the trigger. It was too risky.

He tried at two hotels before he found the one where Lila had registered. He took a room for two nights, paid the outrageous sum of two dollars for the two nights and went up to the second floor.

Lila was on the third, her favorite. She said she liked to look out over the lights of a town and discover how far into the plains she could see.

He put his gear in his room, washed up and shaved closely, then knocked on Lila's door. She wasn't in. It was just past 6:30. Maybe she was having a late supper downstairs in the hotel dining room.

Spur stood at the entrance to the dining room and looked over the supper crowd. The room was about half filled. He spotted Lila at a table for two in the far corner. Spur made a roundabout trip so she wouldn't see him come up.

He stood behind her chair.

"Miss, it's terribly crowded tonight, would you mind sharing your table with a hungry person?"

Lila looked up, beaming at him, her smile so genuine and fresh that he bent and kissed her cheek, then sat down. She reached for his hand.

"I missed you. What took you so long?"

"Slowing down in my old age. Do you sing tonight?"

She nodded. "At eight and ten at the Silver Dollar Gambling Emporium. I told him I would sing twice a night. He finally agreed. He had a letter from Mike telling him about his increase in business.

"I also raised my rate to twenty-five dollars a week! I'm making as much in a week as most cowboys make in a month!"

"You must have earned a lot more in the big music halls in the East."

"Yes, but that became boring after a while. I didn't want to join one of those traveling shows with singing and dancing. I don't dance at all, and I'm not an actress. So I decided to come out into the Wild West and see for myself what it's all about. You know, it isn't as scary as I thought it would be. Of course I haven't even seen an Indian or a buffalo."

"You're afraid of buffalos?"

"No, silly, but I want to see some, just so I can say I saw them out here."

"And are you learning lots out here in the big bad, Wild, Wild West?"

"Mostly from a man who was raised in New York City!"

She hadn't ordered. Here the menu was much broader than it had been in Greensburg and they took some time to figure out what they wanted.

After the meal Spur escorted her up to her room where she said she needed to lie down for a while before she sang. She always did.

Spur went down the street to the sheriff's office. He had been here before and knew the sheriff, Frank Johnson, a tough, smart lawman who had been in dozens of shooting scrapes and always came out of them.

"McCoy! Thought you might be around somewhere. Heard about Bjelland. Didn't know him, but I hate to see any lawman go down. Five in a row back toward Wichita?"

Johnson was a tall man with a paunch that turned into a beer belly, but his belt still held up his pants. He seldom wore a gun now, dealing out his toughest assignments to quick, young men who wore deputy badges.

They went into Johnson's small office.

"Frank, on this trip I'm Colt Smith. Be obliged if you could call me that. Trying to stay low key as a land buyer. You know of any good deals in land I can look at around here to help make me look legitimate?"

"But you're really working on this lawman killer, right? I can call you Colt for a spell. The important thing is that I'm probably next in line for that damn killer. From everything I can hear and from what the broadsides say, this killer is the sneaky kind. Not a stand up and shoot it out, but a sly, slick sneaker who always shoots his victims in the gut first from point blank range."

"That's about it. Try always to have a deputy with you wherever you go, even to the outhouse. The better your protection, the longer you're going to live. I hope we can get this guy caught in a day or two. I keep looking for some gunman I've seen in the towns before this one, but I can't spot anybody so far."

"Keep looking." The sheriff laughed nervously. "Keep a deputy with me all the time. You mean my deputy has to go to bed with me and Milly, too?"

Spur grinned. "Damn right, but he can sleep on your side and Milly on the other side." Spur paused. "Unless, of course, Milly wants to be in the middle!"

They both laughed, but each knew the importance of their talk. Spur left a few minutes later.

Just outside the sheriff's office he jolted to a stop. Across the street was a drummer he remembered seeing in two of the previous towns. Yes, the drummer would have a legitimate reason for being here, he had clients and customers to sell his line to, whatever it might be.

But that would also be a good cover-up for a murderous trail. Spur went across the street behind the man, and followed him. He did not have his sample case. He had even untied his string tie, but still had on his white shirt and his black businessman's suit.

The drummer was average height, a little bit on the well fed side and the brown hair on top of his head had thinned to the point of providing a palm-sized bald spot.

The drummer turned in at a saloon and Spur followed him. He had a beer, then sat in on a game of poker. It wasn't his game. He lost every hand and even though it was a dime limit, he quickly lost three dollars and shook his head. He pushed back from the table and bowed out.

The salesman went down the boardwalk, stared in

windows and stopped in the next saloon, a larger one with gambling and six fancy ladies who danced and served drinks and flipped on their backs in the cribs upstairs for "one dollar straight, and two dollars all fancy and wild."

Spur's target had two shots of whiskey, then grabbed the first girl who walked past and headed for the closed stairway that led to the cribs.

Spur waited. Actually he timed the drummer. He was gone exactly twenty-two minutes. He came down with a smile on his face, had another beer and settled in at a nickel limit poker game.

The salesman's luck had changed and before long he was winning. By midnight he had outlasted all the other players and asked for a cloth bag to put all the dimes, nickels, quarters and one and two dollar gold pieces in. No paper money was allowed on that table.

There were few people on the Dodge streets after midnight. Spur saw two patrolling sheriff deputies who tried store doors, urged drunks on their way home, and generally surveyed their domain.

The drummer ignored them. He had downed about four beers during the evening, but was not drunk. He walked steadily and went past the sheriff's office, stopped and looked in through the barred doors, then continued to a smaller hotel and went up the steps and vanished inside.

Spur saw a light come on in one of the second floor windows, then the drummer looked out the window for a moment and closed the curtains.

Good night, sweet prince.

Spur gave it up. If the man were going to do anything suspicious, it would have been after midnight. But he didn't even try to see the sheriff. The head lawman had agreed to stay in the jail for the next few nights, just to be on the safe side. No sense taking any chance. His wife's sister was staying with her and the kids.

The drummer had not made a false move. What else was there for a visiting salesman but beer, whiskey, a naked fancy lady and a little poker?

Spur went back to his room and tensed when he saw light coming from under his door. He touched the doorknob and turned it slowly, silently. It was not locked. He drew his long barreled .45 and thrust the door open in one quick move, his .45 covering the room.

The only person in the room was Lila Pemberthy. She sat on the bed wearing what looked like a pale yellow shift made entirely of expensive lace. She pouted like a spoiled little girl when she saw him.

"I hate you, Colt Smith!" Lila said. "You didn't even come and hear me sing tonight! I should never even talk to you again, let alone undress for you."

"Sorry, I was busy. I had to see several men on business. I'll listen tomorrow night."

"Then you don't hate me?"

"Of course not. Just the opposite." He closed the door, locked it and pushed the .45 back in leather.

"For really and truly?"

"Absolutely."

She lifted up on her knees on the bed. The yellow lace traced a shifting pattern over her surging breasts. As she lifted on her knees, the shift rose over her waist and revealed the soft brown "V" of hair.

"Then come and show me that you love me, right now!" She held out her arms.

Spur smiled and unbuckled his gunbelt and dropped it on the dresser as he walked toward her. He put his arms around her and bent her slowly backward on the bed, resting on top of her slender, sexy body.

"I know just how to prove to you that I don't hate you," McCoy said softly.

Lila kissed his nose and then his eyes and lastly his soft lips.

"You're going to have to prove that at least three times tonight," she said. Then she began kissing him again.

8

The next morning's stage brought in some mail from Kansas City for Spur McCoy, in care of the sheriff's office. Spur checked in with the law people just after breakfast. A big envelope contained eight wanted posters. Each one had a note on it fastened with a straight pin.

All eight of the men pictured had been arrested at one time or another by one or more of the five lawmen murdered in Kansas within the last six weeks.

Spur laid them out on the sheriff's desk and they went over the names. Spur had heard of all of them, had chased and not caught two.

Slowly Spur began to shake his head. "It just doesn't work, Frank. These men are wanted, some of them killers, and granted they might have hated some of the dead lawmen. But the fact remains that one man killed all six of the men. It's exactly the same method, the same kind of gun, the same placement of the shots, and the whole set of circumstances are almost identical."

Frank Johnson leaned back in his chair and scratched his thinning hair.

"Hadn't heard that, about the same method."

"Powder burns on every shot made. My guess is the first round is in the gut to put the man down and helpless. Then when the murderer is ready to finish the job, he puts the muzzle over the victim's heart and pulls the trigger again."

McCoy stared at the pictures. "All but one of these outlaws are stand up shooters. They'll go toe to toe with you with their six-guns, but they'd rather be away from you ten or fifteen feet."

"These flyers don't help a rat's ass, then, do they?" Sheriff Johnson asked.

"Afraid not."

The sheriff bunched the wanted posters and put them in a drawer with a hundred others.

"You know anything about one of the drummers in town, Sheriff? This one is average height, bald on top. I don't know what he's selling."

"We get half a dozen a week through here. They must sell something. Most of them give us no trouble at all. The trail crews are the ones we watch out for."

"I'll do some more checking. He's the one man I've seen in more than one of these towns where the lawman was killed. Oh, I'd say you're free as a bird during the day. It's nighttime when this killer strikes. After dark, I don't want you to wiggle out of the jail without at least one deputy guarding you."

Spur left the sheriff's office and checked the register at the Dodge House Hotel where he had seen the salesman go in last night. The desk clerk said they only had one salesman, a Mr. Jonas Kelly from St. Louis, who sold fine kitchen cutlery and sporting knives.

"How can I find him?"

"Beats me. Wait, he did say something about selling to his wholesale customers first. He just got in yesterday, so I'd guess he's at the stores. Hardware maybe."

Spur thanked the clerk and walked two blocks to the Dodge Hardware. It was a good sized establishment, with almost everything a farmer or rancher needed except food. But the drummer wasn't there. A clerk said he might be next door at the saddlery.

He was. Spur spotted him at once, went in and looked at a hand tooled saddle. It was a beauty. The saddlemaker was inlaying additional silver in it. It wasn't new. By now the silver in it alone must be worth a lot of money.

"I said I'll take two of those small knives," the saddlemaker said. "That's all I need. You know I don't sell retail."

"I can give you a real good price."

"Enough! You were here six months ago and loaded me up with more knives than I can use. If you don't want to sell me those two, forget it."

Spur wandered out. The drummer was a real salesman, and he had been here six months ago. Not a chance he could be the chain-linked murderer.

For an hour Spur wandered the town. Dodge was growing. Lots of new stores and houses had been built since he was there last. Many more people. Which made more problems for him. More people meant more individuals to watch, more places for the real killer to hide.

He stood in front of the hotel for half an hour, watching the citizens pass by. One man he followed for two blocks. The man seemed familiar, as if he had seen the same face before. He wore a suit, with proper vest, gold chain and watch fob. He also could be hiding a derringer.

Then the man took out a key and opened the door to a dry goods store. He was probably the owner—not the killer Spur searched for.

Spur bought a deck of playing cards at the Dodge Mercantile and went back to the hotel. He went directly to Lila's room and knocked. She opened the door a crack to see who it was, then swung it wide.

She held a pink dress in front of her as Spur closed the door.

"Colt, marvelous lover. Do you like me in this pink?" She tossed the dress aside and she wore nothing at all. She grinned and grabbed a blue dress and held it in front of her. "Or do I look better in the blue?"

"The blue," Spur said surprised at the sudden show of naked flesh. He went over to the window and looked out, then back at Lila who had let the dress fall and stood there deliciously topless, smiling at him.

"It was a special surprise for you," she said. "I was watching out the window and I saw you coming up the street with that determined, no nonsense stride. I knew you were coming here."

She cupped both her breasts and held them up toward him.

"Hungry?"

He went to her and took her in his arms and hugged her properly, then released her.

"Lila, you're beautiful, you're a marvelous lover, and I like to be with you. But right now we need to talk, and I can talk to you lots easier if your beautiful, sexy charms are covered with a dress."

Lila giggled and put on the blue dress, but buttoned up only a few of the front fasteners so her breasts peeked out as she moved.

He took out the cards and sat cross-legged on the bed.

"We're going to play gin rummy and talk. I want to know all about you, and I'll even tell you more about me. I need to get some things settled in my mind, and I like to play gin rummy as I'm thinking. Would that be all right?"

"Of course. But you have to kiss me first."

He did. She won five straight hands of gin rummy. Spur couldn't keep his mind on the game. It wandered to new and wild ways to catch the killer, but none of them seemed practical. Maybe he should ask the sheriff to pretend to be bait for the killer's trap. Set up some kind of lonely vigil.

No!

He could have the sheriff locked up in a jail cell every night! Yes, that would help. There were enough officers here so there was always one man at the jail during the evening hours. Another walked on patrol out in the streets. They changed places at midnight or some such hour. That might work.

Spur held the cards. "Now, the other day you told me you were born in Louisiana. How did you get started singing? Did you take lessons?"

"All right, I'll tell you," Lila said. "Nobody has ever been interested before. I sang in the church choir when I was in school, and one day I saw a traveling troupe of singers and dancers and I told my mother that's what I wanted to do. She ignored me. When I was sixteen, I ran away from home and worked in a small store in New Orleans and learned how to sing.

"I was married for a short time, and then I went back to singing, and got better and went to St. Louis and Chicago, and I've made a modest success. That's about all of it."

"How old were you when you were married?"

"Seventeen, but my husband was killed in an accident and since then I've concentrated on singing."

"You're good," Spur said. "You could sing in New York and Washington if you wanted to. I could give you a letter. . . ."

She shook her head. "No, I'm here now and I'll stay for a while. I've waited a long time to look at the West, so now I want to see all of it."

She jumped off the bed and let one breast pop through the half closed dress. Lila watched him, grinning.

Spur laughed. "You just never get enough, do you? I'd love to but you used me up this morning. Besides, it's noon and time to have a bite somewhere. Let's find a little restaurant out of the hotel."

She finished dressing and they went out to eat. It was a small cafe beside the Dodge Mercantile, with only six tables and the food had a decided German accent. They had big sausages smothered in sauerkraut, toast and jelly and coffee.

"That's the strangest meal I've ever eaten," Lila said. She told him it was time for her afternoon rest before she sang, and he walked her back to her room. She pulled him inside, kissed him deliciously and let him rub her breasts. Then she smiled.

"Now I think I can have a nap without dreaming that you are making love to me."

Spur went to the sheriff's office, but there was no report of any contact by a weird person with the sheriff. McCoy watched Frank Johnson for a minute, then plunged ahead.

"I have an idea. What would you think of having yourself locked up every night at ten in the evening, with strict instructions you don't get out of the cell unless the jailhouse is burning down."

"I hate the idea. I don't like to be locked up." Frank scowled and lit is pipe. "But I think it's a damn fine idea. If I can't get out in the dark, nobody is going to bushwhack me." The sheriff frowned. "We'll try it for five or six days, no more. If your killer hasn't made his play by then, I'm going to decide that he's done with his chain link killings of lawmen."

"Sounds fair to me, Sheriff. I had thought of displaying you in a black buggy as bait . . . ." He watched the lawman.

"That's what we'll do if this week of incarceration don't work. At least I can get my work done during the day."

Loud voices in the outer office brought both men

out of their chairs and through the door.

Two men stood arguing with a deputy. He turned and lifted a hand in resignation and turned to the sheriff.

"The matter of water rights again, I'm afraid, Sheriff. Scotty MacDougal is at it again."

"Sheriff, you told us the next time it happened you'd arrest that son-of-a-bitch," the taller of the two men said. They both looked like ranchers which they were. "Now is the time, Frank. He damned up Amber Creek again."

Sheriff Johnson stood there a minute. Then he brightened. "Yeah, I got a solution. Men, I'd like you to meet Colt Smith. Special deputy of mine. Colt, this is Dick Hendricks, and Horace Eagleton, ranchers out of town, a ways to the north.

"Gentlemen, I can't get out there right now, but I can send Smith here. He'll take care of the matter, work it out somehow. If he has to arrest Scotty, then so be it. I want this thing settled once and for all."

Spur pulled Sheriff Johnson back down the short hall.

"What the hell? I can't go chasing around the countryside. I got a killer to nail."

"If you don't go, I got to go. Take your pick. Me safe in jail here or out there in the dark where I might get bushwhacked and it would be all your fault."

Spur growled. He was boxed in with nowhere to retreat. "Three ranches on one stream and the top man is damming up the water?"

"Yep."

"Kansas have an irrigation rights law?"

"Yep, and Scotty knows all about it."

"Damn! This could take two or three days . . ."

"You should be back in time for supper. Only about six miles out to the top spread."

"Hell! Loan me a horse and a rifle. Might as well get it over with and get back to my main job."

9

Spur McCoy and the two ranchers were halfway to the Scotty MacDougal Ranch before the men calmed down. They were mad and they wanted some action. In two or thee days they would start to lose some of their cattle.

McCoy had stopped by at the hardware on their way and picked up six sticks of dynamite, detonators and fuses. That was in case there was a damn across the creek that needed blasting. They would take shovels from the Hendricks Ranch since it was closest to the suspected dam.

"He always does this," Horace Eagleton said. "Just because he was here first he thinks he owns God."

"About the size of it," Hendricks said. "This time we put him in his place for good, or he gets arrested!"

At the Hendricks place they stopped for a cold drink of water, took shovels and moved up through the trees along the stream so nobody from the MacDougal spread could see them.

Amber Creek here was just about that, maybe a foot deep and fifteen feet across. But now it was nearly dry, an occasional low spot still held pools of water. Normally it would have a good current and a lot of water would go down it.

"I get so mad I could spit every time I see the creek this way!" Hendricks snorted. "Damn his eyes!"

"This time we've got the old bastard," Eagleton said, grinning.

Spur wanted only to get this over with and ride back to Dodge City to catch his killer. But sometimes things got a little out of order. He wasn't quite sure what to do yet. When he saw exactly how the water was diverted, he could decide.

They rode another half hour, passed within a quarter mile of a spread the men said was MacDougal's. Then they came out at a natural little lake.

"So that's how he done it," Hendricks said. "Used to be an old lake here a hundred years ago. Good grazing. MacDougal must have cut a new channel, diverting the water from Amber Creek into the old lake bed. Damn thing is huge. He can take all of our water for the rest of the summer."

They rode faster then, along the side of Amber Creek and next to the filling lake.

"There it is!" Hendricks said.

They pulled to a stop at the top of the lake where it was at almost the same level as the stream. A two-foot-wide ditch had been dug through the bank for a distance of not over ten or twelve feet. From there the water found a natural course into the dry lake bed.

Spur eyed it for a minute.

"Glad we brought the spades," Spur said. "Let's fill in the ditch."

The three men dismounted and began throwing the dirt and rocks back into the ditch that had been dug out. The water washed most of them away in the current.

Spur stopped. "We need some brush or old logs to jam in there first," he said.

They found the brush easily, hacked off some more with belt knives, and then Spur discovered an old rotting log that he kicked to pieces and carried the two foot long sections to the ditch.

Now, with a foundation to hold the dirt, it was a much easier job to throw dirt in front of the logs and brush to start making a dam across the ditch.

After an hour of hard work, all but a trickle of water from Amber Creek was flowing downstream in its natural bed again. The men wiped brows.

"We better find a defensive position," Spur said. "My guess is that as soon as MacDougal sees the water coming down the creek again, he'll come storming up here with some help.

All three men had rifles with them. They went to the far side of the stream about fifty yards above, hid their horses in the brush out of the line of fire, and settled down to wait. Spur found a cottonwood tree that gave him fine protection. The other two used old logs and a small rise of ground for their fortifications.

"How long it going to take?" Spur asked.

"Old Scotty stays pretty close around his ranch

buildings lately," Eagleton said. "He'll spot the water coming down quick, I'd guess."

An hour later nothing had happened. Spur pulled his pocket watch and read the time. Almost three o'clock. At three-thirty Spur slapped his thigh.

"Hell, we better go down there and talk to Scotty," Spur said.

"Not a chance," Hendricks spat. "He'll shoot us as soon as he sees us."

"Not me," Spur said. "He doesn't know who I am. You two can stay in the brush."

"Worth a try," Eagleton said with a twinkle in his eye. "If he kills you we'll ride back and tell the sheriff."

Before they headed for their horses, Spur caught movement on a slope across the stream.

"Company," Spur said. The rider left the open rise and angled into the fringe of brush along the stream. Three minutes later he walked his roan up to edge of the filled in diversion ditch.

"That's Scotty," Hendricks said.

Spur stood up quickly.

"Mr. MacDougal. I'm with the sheriff's office and notifying you that the ditch you dug there is against the law, so I filled it in. You do not have irrigation rights to all the water from this creek. One third is yours, the rest goes downstream."

Spur didn't see the man draw his six-gun, but it thundered in the early afternoon. At once one of the men beside him fired a rifle and Scotty MacDougal screamed and rolled out of sight.

Spur stepped behind his tree.

"Who fired that shot? All he has is a pistol and

we're out of range."

"Seen a man killed once at a hundred yards with a six-gun slug," Hendricks said. "Taking no chances."

Spur called again. "Scotty, we have to talk. Are you hit bad?"

Four rounds answered Spur, the lead flying harmlessly into the ground well in front of them.

"Scotty, my name is Colt Smith. Sheriff Johnson sent me out here as an impartial observer to straighten this out. There'll be no charges against you if you throw out your six-gun and sit on the bank so I can come up there and talk."

"All right! Damn bushwhackers. Who was it shot me?"

"Throw out your gun, Scotty."

Spur saw a weapon come over the bank. He left his tree and with the rifle under his arm, walked slowly up to the small diversion ditch they had filled in.

Scotty MacDougal lay on the far side. He had just tied up the wound in his leg and glared at Spur.

"Got to be Hendricks and Eagleton, right? Them bastards!"

"MacDougal, you know I could arrest you right now and take you into jail for diverting this water. You know it's illegal, so why did you do it?"

"Damn fancy new laws. In my time a man owned the water on his spread."

"Still do if it's a lake with no outlet. A running stream is not property, MacDougal. It comes under the fair use irrigation law, which you know about."

MacDougal glared at Spur. "Tell me, Hendricks and Eagleton over there with you, right?"

"Yes, they are the complaining parties. Do I have to arrest you and toss you in jail for a few days?"

"Probably. Get Eagleton and Hendricks over here. I want them to accuse me face to face!"

"Reasonable." Spur called to the other two men to come over and talk. They were hesitant.

Hendricks stopped beside Spur. "Sure you got his gun? He's a sneaky old bastard."

"Hendricks, why did you shoot me?" Scotty asked.

"Two of my beef died today, no water. That's why."

Scotty turned half over where he lay on the ground, pulled a derringer and fired. The round smashed into Hendrick's leg and he bellowed in rage.

As soon as he saw the small gun, Spur dove at Scotty. He arrived just after the round ripped out of the barrel. He knocked the weapon out of Scotty's hand and grabbed it. He patted the smaller man down and made sure he had no more weapons.

"Now, you god-damned trio of jackasses. We're going to sit down and not move until we work out this problem. There is going to be no more shooting. Is that clear?"

Spur boomed the ultimatum at them in his best parade ground angry officer voice. All three wilted. For the first time, they realized that one or more of them could have been killed.

"You three don't look this stupid. You know right now I could arrest both of you on attempted murder charges. What would happen to your ranches while you sat in jail waiting for the trial? And then, if convicted, and with my testimony you damn well would be, you would get from three to five years in the Kansas State Prison. How does that sit with you?''

He waited for two minutes, letting them think it over.

"Fine. Now I'll tell you what is going to happen here. Scotty, you've got a fine dry lake bed here. You're right to use it to save water for a dry spell. But you can't save all the water. I'll mark the stream and show you where you can put in a diversion gate. Then you can divert one third of the water coming downstream and put it in the lake."

"Then he can't water his stock below, right?" Eagleton asked.

"Correct, Mr. Eagleton. According to the irrigation and water rights law, each of you has rights to one third of the runoff water. Is that perfectly clear?"

"No, damnit!" Scotty said. "How can I tell if I get all of my rightful one third?"

Spur helped him stand and showed him the stream. Spur stepped on rocks and then into the foot deep stream. "Right about here you drive in a stake. It's one third of the way across and the current is about the same all the way. You put your wooden diversion gate in here at an angle so it doesn't pile up the water.

"One third of the stream goes into your lake. The rest goes downstream. If your lake gets full, and there's plenty of water, you lift your diversion gate and let it all flow downstream. Clear?"

"Yeah. Damn, I hate these modern times. Like the

old days better."

"We get to inspect the gate? Check his lake?" Hendricks asked.

"Yes," Spur ruled. "Anytime these gentlemen wish to inspect the gate and your lake, you must grant them free access to the area."

"Hell, okay, okay. I understand. Now will somebody help me get back on my horse so I can ride to my place?"

They helped Scotty on his mount.

"One more thing, Mr. MacDougal. Your diversion ditch has been in place for about thirty days, I understand. You are enjoined from putting in your diversion gate for 60 days, to allow the downstream ranches their fair share of the past 30 days of water."

"Hell, you got anymore surprises for me?"

"One more. I'm filing attempted murder charges against both of you with the sheriff and leaving my legal deposition, detailing what happened. If either of you go back on this agreement, or violate the water rights in any way, these charges will be brought against both of you and you'll have to stand trial. In my business I call this a little insurance that you'll behave yourselves like adults."

Scotty rode off, mumbling to himself.

Hendricks scowled as he watched Spur. "That true about the attempted murder charge?"

"Absolutely. You fired first, I should just charge you, but this way I have a hold over Scotty as well. Now both of you grow up and start acting like adults."

They rode back just as the low sun started to

throw long shadows. Spur knew it would be dark before he got back to town. They dropped off Hendricks at his ranch and Eagleton invited him to stop by his place for supper. It was almost time.

Spur decided he might as well. The ranch house was smaller than he guessed. Eagleton said he'd only been there four years and was just starting to build up a good herd. He should have a thousand herd for sale later in the summer.

He met Mrs. Eagleton, a small woman who had gone to fat at forty, and their twenty-year-old daughter, Alice. She came in only when supper was ready, ate with no comments and glanced up at Spur only once. She smiled shyly, then looked away.

They had pheasant and rice and potatoes and vegetables with lots of homemade bread and fresh butter. The coffee was boiled to death but tasted good. Spur ate too much, then thanked Mrs. Eagleton who beamed.

"I love to see a man eat!" she told him as he was leaving.

A quarter of a mile down the road to town, Spur realized someone was coming up behind him. He stopped and looked back, wondering if he had forgotten his rifle or his hat. He hadn't.

A moment later a black horse materialized out of the darkness with Alice on board. She smiled and rode up until their legs almost touched.

"I wanted to thank you for having supper with us. We don't get many visitors."

"Quite all right, Miss Alice."

She hesitated. "Mr. Smith, would you kiss me? I don't get much chance to practice my kissing."

Spur laughed. "Might be arranged."

"Right here?" she asked. He nodded. She pushed her horse closer and leaned toward him. A moment later she fell off the horse and he caught her. One of his hands came to rest around her ample right breast.

She looked up at him and smiled. "Thanks for catching me, maybe we better try kissing off our horses."

Alice kicked off the mount and slid to the ground. Spur dropped beside her and she caught his hand and led him to the side of the trail where some fresh spring grass grew. She sat down and he sat beside her.

"Now, the kiss."

He bent toward her and her arms went around him locking fast. Her lips found his and then her teeth caught his lower lip and held on. She pressed hard against him. When she let loose with her teeth, she smiled and kissed his lips and his nose and then both of his eyes.

"I knew at supper I just had to fuck you. Would you mind? I just have to feel you big and hard inside my little cunny."

"Now this is a surprise," Spur said. "You barely looked at me at supper."

"I was busy rubbing myself under the table," she said. She pulled open her blouse and her breasts tumbled out, restricted by no other garment. "Please kiss them!"

Spur didn't need a second invitation. Her milky white breasts had small areolas and thumb sized nipples. Her hands found his crotch and tore at the fly buttons until they were open. She probed inside his pants with her hands, and squealed in joy when she pulled free his erection.

"Oh, wonderful!" she said. She dropped between his legs, sucking all of his shaft into her mouth, chewing him, pulling, then starting an up and down motion with her head that set him on fire.

A dozen strokes later, Spur exploded with a moan as he spurted his load into her willing mouth and she made small, happy noises as she sucked every drop from his planting tool. Slowly she came away from him. She kissed him.

"Did you like me doing you that way?"

"Oh, yes!"

"Good, now you do me!" She caught his head and pulled it down to her crotch. She pawed at her skirt and petticoats pulling them up over her chest. She wore thin drawers.

"Bite through the cloth over my cunny!" she ordered. Spur bent and bit the cloth, tearing it. He used his hands to tear more of it, then smelled her musk.

He kissed around her soft pubic hair, then her hands caught his head and pressed him forward to her heartland.

He was there. He kissed the pink lips, then licked them and she began to climax over him. He licked her and kissed her outer lips until she erupted in a grinding, moaning and flailing mass of arms and legs as she exploded around him.

She shook and vibrated and spasm after spasm tore into her body. Alice's breath came in great gulps to keep her alive and her whole body gyrated and shivered and her hips humped against his face until the climax paled and she lay in the grass panting and wheezing.

When her breathing quieted, he lay next to her and looked over at the shy ranch girl.

"My God! Are you still alive?"

"Barely. You were beautiful!"

"Is it always so wild for you?"

"Oh yes, especially when you go down below that way. I go wild for a few minutes."

"Your father know you're out here?"

"No! He'd shit his pants. Mom knows. She said she fooled around every chance she got starting about sixteen. She got pregnant when she was nineteen and then got married. I figure I can fuck for another year before somebody gets me with a kid. Plenty of time to get married then."

She rolled quickly on top of him and pumped her hips at his crotch. "Once more?"

Spur shook his head, kissed her and buttoned up his pants.

"You would kill me for sure if I tried again. Right now I have to get on my horse and get back to town."

"Can you come back out?"

"Probably not. I have some business in town."

"Jeeze you were good. It's been three months for me. I was ready."

"You certainly were."

They stood up and she arranged her clothes, then pulled Spur's hands inside her blouse.

"Sure you can't stay for one more?"

He kissed her and took his hands away.

"I'm sure." He helped her mount her horse, then swung up himself.

"One more kiss, and I promise not to fall off. That was all an act."

"I know." He kissed her, then rode away. When he looked back she was watching him and waving.

Spur rode hard for town then. He got back slightly before 8:30 and went straight to the sheriff's office. He told Sheriff Johnson what happened and about the attempted murder charges. He filled out a form, and then wrote up the charges, dated it and left it all with the sheriff.

"Now, has anything happened here?" Spur asked.

"Quiet as a grave," the sheriff said.

"You don't quite take this threat seriously, do you, Johnson?"

"Damn right I do, but I'm not going to let it make me into a recluse crying and whining all day long."

"Good. When do you get locked up?"

"Ten o'clock. I've been inside here since it got dark."

"Any good suspicious characters hanging around town waiting for it to get dark?"

"A few. There are always suspicious characters here in Dodge. You just have to take your pick."

"That's a lot of help. Everything quiet?"

"So far."

"What cell will you be in?"

"First one. It's closer to the outhouse."

Spur waved and headed out the door. He'd make a round of the saloons. Maybe he could turn up something interesting.

He did on the second stop. The kid's name was

Verner Archer. He was the top sheet on the list of flyers sent out. Verner had been wanted by the sheriff in Greensburg for murder and bank robbery.

Spur loosened his gun in the leather, and moved into the shadows of the saloon as he settled in to watch every move that Archer made. He might have his sights on the lawman killer. He damn sure wasn't going to let Archer slip through his fingers. One way or another, Archer was finished!

10

Vern Archer tipped the mug of beer and drank. A chill settled over him and he let the beer down slowly. He kept both hands on top of the bar.

Somebody was watching him. He'd felt it before. Once it happened just before some bushwhacker put a slug through his lung and almost killed him out of Tucson. Never was going to let that happen again.

He turned with his beer to watch the poker players, and as he did he surveyed the whole saloon, casually, not making it obvious.

Arthur saw no one he knew, nobody who looked like a lawman. He eased back to the bar and put his boot up on the brass rail. Maybe he was getting jumpy. He had a job to do in town and he would stay here until it was done. Nothing was going to change that. Once he made up his mind he was as bull-headed as an old buffalo charging down a line of flight. Nothing but death could budge him off that selected course.

He finished the beer, stood next to a poker game for a while, then meandered toward the saloon's front door. He hadn't lived this long by his wits and his .44 to get cut down from a dark alley by some bounty hunter or do-gooder. Not by a damn sight!

Archer walked through the front door of the saloon, then jumped to the street and sprinted silently for the closest alley. He got there two stores down on the same side of the street and edged into the blackness.

Automatically, he pulled the .44 from his hip and and held it ready, the heavy hammer cocked and ready. A man came out of the swinging doors of the same saloon he had just left, looked both ways, then ambled toward the hotel. Two more men came out laughing and telling bawdy stories. Three more men came out and left in various directions.

Archer pushed his six-gun back in leather. He rubbed the back of his neck with his right hand and frowned. Maybe the strain was telling on him. Maybe he should give it up and forget old angers and move on west somewhere, out of the hellhole of Kansas.

Vern Archer shook his head standing there in the dark. Damn no! He came to town to do a job and he fucking well was going to do it! He stomped up on the boardwalk and stalked back to the saloon he had just left.

If anybody wanted him, they would have to face him down in the lamplight of the saloon. That way he'd have a fair chance. And lately he'd been as good as anybody he'd met with a gun. Better, in fact, because he was still alive and several of the others weren't.

Spur McCoy had eased out of the saloon behind

two other men and wandered across the street. He faded into some shadows of a farm wagon and watched the area around the drinking and gambling establishment. Archer was out there somewhere.

Five minutes later, someone came from the alley two doors down from the saloon, looked around, then walked determinedly back to the card room and bar. In a flash of light at the door, Spur saw that the man was Vern Archer. He'd been scared by something and went outside to watch and wait.

Nobody was better at waiting than Spur McCoy. He eased his hat down a notch over his eyes and went back in the saloon. The Secret Service Agent picked up a beer at the bar and wandered around the poker tables, asking if he could sit in at tables that were full. He got waved away.

After moving halfway around the room, he spotted Archer again. He had joined a poker game at one of the dollar limit tables. Archer had never been a big gambler.

Spur leaned against the wall, sipped on his beer and watched the players and the three chippies who sold drinks as they bent over a lot to show off swinging breasts and round bottoms. One of the girls squealed and slapped a cowboy who got his hand under her skirt and rubbed her crotch.

She yelped but didn't move, knowing what she was doing. A minute later she kissed him, caught his arm and pulled him to the door that led to the cribs in back. His buddies at the table hooted him on and he couldn't turn back. The girl was a great little salesman.

Spur made sure Archer was still at the poker

table. He was losing. Spur didn't want simply to arrest Archer on an old charge. That was too easy. If Archer was the lawman killer, he wanted to catch him in the act—almost. It would be perfect to nail him just as he grabbed the sheriff, but before he had a chance to use his hideout derringer.

Yeah, but it wouldn't happen that way because Sheriff Johnson was safely locked up in his own jail. That was a problem, but if Archer was the serial killer, he'd figure out a way to get the sheriff out long enough to kill him. Spur had to be sitting there waiting for Archer's move and nail the bastard.

A half hour later, Spur began to feel obvious and self-conscious in his position. He sat in on a poker game where he could look at Archer's back. It was a quarter limit table, and using half of his attention, he won six dollars in the first four hands. Then he lost two by throwing in his hands on a five card draw.

When he checked Archer after the hand was over, the outlaw stood, scooped some change into his hat and headed for the door. Spur quit his game, left two dollars in the pot as compensation for his winnings, and left the saloon a few seconds after Archer. Another man went out the same time Spur did.

Archer was ahead of him, moving toward a cheap hotel. From the street, Spur watched him go inside, talk with the room clerk a minute, then slip him some money and examine the register. The man didn't live there, but he was interested in who did.

When Archer headed out the front door, Spur walked slowly toward the main part of town.

Wrong choice.

When Archer came out he headed the other way. He walked quickly now along the dirt streets, checking houses from time to time. He stopped in front of one that still had lights on. It was a modest frame structure, five or six rooms, one story, with a small picket fence around the front that had been whitewashed. There were even some flowers in the yard and two trimmed lilac bushes flourished.

He stood at the gate a moment, then he mumbled something, kicked the gate and spun on his boot and headed back toward town. Spur slid down a cross street and waited for his target to pass, then followed.

Vern Archer rushed into the first saloon he came to. It was the smallest one in town, had no girls and no poker games. It was for drinkers. He ordered three draft beers and drank them all before the head bubbled away on the last one.

Spur watched him through the window. Archer pulled his pistol and fired three times into the ceiling, then lurched out of the saloon, nearly knocking Spur down as the lawman had been charging inside.

Archer swore at him without seeing who he was, and continued down the boardwalk. Spur followed.

Half a block down, Archer saw something and waited in the shadows. A deputy sheriff walked his rounds, checking each merchant's front door along the boardwalk. Archer crouched behind a rain barrel in the darkness of the alley and waited. The deputy came closer.

In the moonlight, Spur saw Archer's six-gun come up as the deputy turned from the dry goods shop and walked forward.

"Look out, Deputy!" Spur bellowed. It was enough to make the lawman jump to the side. Archer's aim followed and he fired once. The round slammed through the deputy's side and dumped him on the boardwalk.

By that time Spur had sent two rounds at the shadow near the water barrel. Archer vanished down the alley away from main street and Spur charged forward. He checked the deputy.

"How bad are you hit?" Spur asked.

The deputy held his own pistol and recognized Spur. "Not bad, go get the bastard!"

Spur sprinted down the alley heard movement ahead and dove flat in the dirt as two rounds whispered three feet over his prone body. He saw the flashes ahead and fired twice, heard a gasp and then swearing as footsteps sounded out the other end of the alley.

Spur ran again. At the alley mouth he saw a street. Only a few businesses and a few houses. He saw no movement. Then from the side of the closest house he heard a horse snorting. McCoy charged across the street, down to the house and along the side of it until he could see a small shed at the back.

As he checked it, he heard more movement, and a rider raced from the shed on board a dark horse. Spur got off two shots at the rapidly vanishing target, then ran to the shed. One more horse stood there pawing the stall.

Spur grabbed a bridal and threw it over the horses' head, pushed the bit into the animal's mouth and vaulted on board bareback. He pulled the horse's head around and kicked it in the flanks.

For a moment Spur almost lost his seat as the animal spurted away after its stablemate.

Spur could still see the dim form of a rider pounding out the street that almost at once ended in the prairie. He stopped a moment and listened. There were faint sounds from ahead as the animal hit a harder spot and hoofbeats drifted back.

Spur rode again.

A half hour later he lost the trail where Archer had splashed through a small stream and come out on a hard rocky slope. He could have angled either way from there.

Nothing to do but stop and wait for dawn, which was then about five hours away.

Vern Archer could be half way to Wichita by dawn. Spur reconsidered. Archer could not make it quite that far, but with a good horse a five hour start could mean at least a twenty mile head start. If he kept going. He might stop and light a fire and go to sleep.

Spur snorted. Not Vern Archer. He had come out of the war and simply never stopped fighting the North. Nothing he loved more than a good fight, especially with some "damn bluebellies." Half the lawmen in the West knew Vern Archer. Catching him was another problem.

Several bits of evidence pointed toward Archer as the lawman killer. He was Southern, hated all Northerners. He had been arrested before by one of the dead lawmen, he had taken an unprovoked shot at a deputy who he could have mistaken for the sheriff.

A damn good suspect, Spur decided. Especially since right now Archer was the only suspect he had.

He put the horse on a long lead line to graze and settled down against a tree for some sleep. He had half convinced himself that Archer was not taking off for Denver or St. Louis. He must have come to town for a purpose, like killing Sheriff Johnson. That could mean Archer would make a wide circle and be back in town long before Spur could follow his tracks.

McCoy quit trying to second guess the outlaw and instructed his subconscious to wake him slightly before dawn. Then he went to sleep.

Spur was up and moving with the first streaks of light. He picked up the freshest tracks off the slabs of rock and found the outlaw had not turned back toward the city. Spur also found some drops of blood on the slick rock surface. His slugs had made contact with flesh and Archer must be hurting.

Would Archer go to ground or run? Head back to town later for some medical work, or gut it out with some homemade bandages out of his own shirt? He had no supplies for a long ride. There was little chance to live off the land out here in the Kansas prairie. Not even many ranches or farms to stop at for a friendly handout.

Spur worked his fast tracking technique. He judged where the trail would go, and rode quickly ahead to a pre-determined point or a half mile, and got off and inspected the ground for the continuing tracks. This worked best when a rider was lighting out for a long run over known terrain.

Here it was risky, but once the trail was lost, it

only involved backtracking to the last known point and working the tracks on foot.

Spur won the bet on the first three half mile contents, then the trail vanished. He went back to the small cottonwood near the bend in the creek where Archer had cut across. From there he looked all around. Slightly rolling ground, mostly flat. He stared each direction and then caught the first whiff of a fire. Campfire or wood stove?

He rode in a two hundred yard circle around the last spotted Archer hoofprints, and found the trail angling back toward town. It turned again, followed down a small draw and across an almost dry creek. A quarter of a mile down, Spur saw a cabin.

It was what was left of what had been a small farm. One cow still munched where she was tied to a stake near the stream. Smoke came slowly from the chimney. The house was no more than twelve by twelve. It was the kind with "minimum improvements" that had to be made on a homestead to "prove it up" and gain title.

Somebody was home.

Spur moved up on the cabin along the brush line of the creek. He left his horse two hundred yards from the cabin and rushed across an open space between trees and brush on the creek. He was halfway across when a rifle snarled from the back window of the cabin.

The slug dug up dirt at his feet and Spur darted the last ten feet before the gunman could aim and fire again.

Spotted.

Was Archer alone in the cabin or was there a

hostage?

The creek ran within twenty feet of the front of the cabin. As he got closer through the now denser brush, he could see that the place was occupied. A washstand had been built near the creek, and a string of pots hung in the sun on the back cabin wall. An axe stuck in a chopping block and two armloads of split wood lay nearby.

There was only one outbuilding, a shameful excuse for a barn. Evidently the cow would not live in it. Both the front poles that held up the roof were leaning to the left. The roof of shingles was in drastic need of repair.

Spur found a log, crawled behind it and lifted his hat just barely over the top of the log with a stick. A rifle bullet slammed into his hat, spinning it off the stick and ten yards away. He retrieved it without danger. So Archer had found a rifle inside. Who else was in there?

The Secret Service Agent edged through the brush again until he could see the front door. He sent one .45 round into the side of the frame house. There was no response.

What next? He had an idea, reversed his direction and got into the barn with only a short dash across ten yards of open space. He found the same horse he had seen charge away from the shed in Dodge last night. It still had its saddle on. Spur cinched the saddle, and rode out of the barn and behind the brush screen for a hundred yards upstream where he tied up the mount and jogged back to the barn.

He found some interesting items he might be able to use to smoke the killer out of the cabin without endangering anyone inside.

Spur checked again. Yes, the back side of the cabin had no window. It faced the excuse for a barn. Spur carried the heavy sheet of tin and a half dozen burlap gunny sacks as he ran from the barn to the back of the cabin. He went up the low back wall which had been dug three feet into the edge of a small slope and was soon on the roof.

Smoke came freely from the chimney now. The hostage could be cooking food for Archer. McCoy put the tin over the chimney and then bound the six gunny sacks over the tin to stop up the flue. He made sure the sacks were secure and looked over the front of the roof to see who would come out of the smoke choked cabin first.

They held out for nearly five minutes, then Archer came out, a wet cloth over his nose, and a woman clamped tightly to his chest with one arm as he backed away. He dropped the cloth once out in the open and drew his .44. Spur saw the bloody bandage on his left arm. The arm would need medical attention.

Archer's big gun touched the woman's head.

"Whoever you are, one wrong move and this lady gets her head blown off. You want that?"

"Go ahead, I don't even know who she is. You kill her and your shield is useless. I'd bet you won't do that, it's just a bluff."

Archer kept backing toward the barn.

"Might be a bluff, but you ain't shooting."

"Your horse isn't there. I know who you are. There isn't another horse there either. You might as well give up."

"Not while I'm breathing, whoever you are. I come to Dodge to do me a job, and I'm gonna do it. You stay outa my way, or I'll start my work by killing this woman and you."

"Big talker with a small brain," Spur snarled. "You got about one chance in a dozen of finding your horse before I ride you down and ventilate your worthless hide with six .45 rounds."

Archer kept backing up, heading for the brush. He was soon there and pulled the woman into it with him, then dropped her and ran north, upstream toward where Spur had hidden his horse. He would find it.

Spur leaped off the back of the house and hurried inside, he located the rifle, saw that it was functioning. A single shot carbine. He grabbed a dozen cartridges and took the rifle as he raced out the door toward the horse upstream. If he was lucky he could get there in time to kill the horse. Then he would have Archer on foot and a much easier quarry.

All he needed now was enough time and a little luck. He also would be thankful if Archer didn't figure out what his opponent in this little chess game might do.

Spur came around the barn and found Archer standing there waiting for him, the six-gun already up in a two-handed firing position. Spur heard the gun go off as he pulled up the just borrowed rifle.

11

The booming report of the six-gun overlapped a sudden jolting force as the slug smashed into the wooden stock of the carbine. The stock slammed into Spur's shoulder and powered him backward.

It happened in slow motion then for Spur McCoy. He was closer to death than he had been in a long time. He saw Archer thumbing back the hammer on his .44. Spur pivoted and tried to change directions in mid-air as he dove for the edge of the barn.

A slug thunked into the side of the barn and then McCoy was around the corner with the hard wood protecting him. He rolled to his feet and crouched at the edge of the barn, his Colt .45 in his hand.

He saw only a flash of green shirt as Archer ran into the heavy brush just beyond the barn. Spur sent three shots at him, paused to reload, putting in four rounds to load up with six in the cylinder.

Spur knew he had been damned lucky at the barn. The .44 slug from Archer should have gone through his chest where the outlaw had aimed. It had been mere chance when he moved up the rifle at exactly the right second and in precisely the right place to stop the death bringing bullet. That kind of luck ran out sooner or later.

Now he knew what he had to do. The rifle could misfire after the jolt it had taken. He couldn't chance it. He still had to get to the outlaw's horse before Archer found it. Spur had the advantage. He knew exactly where it was hidden.

The Secret Service Agent ran from the protection of the barn and into the virgin meadow that was well over a hundred yards wide. In the middle of the open space he turned and ran north, up stream. Even if Archer saw him he didn't have a weapon with enough range to reach him. Speed was the most essential right now.

Spur picked up his pace, holding the revolver in his right hand and pumping his arms. He had run a lot of foot races at Harvard, but never anything with boots on. Still he figured he was making good time.

At the spot where he had tied the mount, he turned and ran directly at the woods, his .45 leveled in front of him. Now was the critical point. If Archer stood just inside the cover behind a tree waiting for him, the chase would be over, and so would his life.

He tensed as he came closer. At twenty yards from the brush, he dodged one way and then the other to present a tougher target, and stormed forward.

It was almost a surprise when he swept into the brush and trees without being shot. Quickly he changed directions to get within ten yards of the horse, hunkered down behind an old willow and waited.

He heard Archer coming before he saw him. The man was jogging along, crashing through the brush, not trying to be quiet and watching behind him. He had stayed to the cover of the woods which meant slower going. Evidently he had no thought that Spur would dare move in the open ground.

Wait. Wait. Just like a military operation when you had the enemy walking into a trap. You had to wait for the right moment to spring it.

Archer was twenty yards from the horse. Now he saw it. He looked along his back trail and then ran forward. When he was less than five yards from Spur, the Agent leaned around the tree and cocked his pistol.

"Take another step, Archer, and you're breakfast for the buzzards!"

"Bastard!" Archer screamed. He let his .44 swing down, pointing at the ground and his shoulders slumped. Spur relaxed for a fraction of a second, and the outlaw sensed it. He angled up the six-gun and blasted a shot as he dove to the side and rolled into a smattering of small brush and a thicket of two inch trees.

Spur leaned out and fired three times. He saw two of the slugs bore into the small trees and the third hit a twig and whine away off target.

By then Archer had crawled to a substantial cottonwood tree that protected him.

"I'd say we have a standoff, lawman. Nobody else would know my name. You must have seen my advertising."

"The wanted posters. Lots of people have seen

them. How many men have you killed now, twelve or thirteen?"

"You're way behind the times, lawman. I hope you try for the horse."

"I'm in no hurry and you're not known for your patience."

"Don't matter, lawman. I got cover. I can get out of here and you'll never see me. But you're pinned down." Archer sent a slug zapping into Spur's willow tree.

"How many lawmen you killed now, Archer?"

"Who can count that high." He laughed. "Actually just one, beginner's luck about ten years ago. But I was fresh out of the Army, what did I know?"

Spur was figuring the odds. The gunman wouldn't miss if Spur made a surge for the horse. That was out. He didn't believe Archer's account of killed lawmen. He would never admit he was the serial killer.

Spur tried to breath softly so he could hear any movement by the outlaw ten yards away.

A meadowlark sang through his call in the edge of the grass. Spur heard nothing from Archer. The morning breeze rustled the tree leaves. No sound came from the outlaw.

Cat and mouse.

Was he there or not? There was no way to tell. Now Archer had the advantage. If he could make Spur think he had left and wait for a killing shot as the lawman moved, the game would all be over.

But, if Archer had left right after their last talk, he would be well on his way by now. No matter which guess was right, Spur McCoy knew he had to move.

Spur took a deep breath, picked out his first bit of protection, and dove to the left toward the horse. He rolled and stopped behind a decaying log that had fallen several years ago. It was barely a foot thick, but high enough.

There was no reaction from behind the cottonwood tree. Spur sucked in a pair of big breaths, then lifted up quickly with his eyes just over the log and stared at the cottonwood, then jerked his head down.

No shot. He was still alive. And he had not seen any sign of Archer behind the tree. The man could have moved around to the side to keep out of sight.

Somehow, Spur didn't think so. He was gone.

Spur checked his next burst. He had a dozen or so small trees growing five yards over. Not positive protection but it could be effective. He pulled his feet up under him, and surged to his feet and ran four long steps then dove to the ground behind the small trees, cradling the .45 to his chest but with the muzzle pointing away from his body.

No reaction.

He lifted up and stared at the cottonwood. The man was gone. He ran to the black with a saddle, untied her and stepped on board. Which way? Archer would stick to the screen of trees along the creek for cover. He would go downstream hoping to find Spur's horse. Then to the same little cabin.

Spur kicked the black into motion and charged through the brush into the meadow. There he raced upstream to where he had hidden his own mount.

The horse was still there. Good. He left the bareback horse there and rode back the way he had come toward the cabin. The woman who had been a hostage was still there. Her husband must have been on the range. The shots would have brought him back. Archer might have them both as hostages now if he went back to the cabin.

If he had gone back, it would be for food and the rifle, then he might run downstream to a ranch where he could steal a horse? Maybe.

As he rode easily, thinking about it, Spur heard three closely spaced pistol shots from downstream.

The signal for help, or to attract attention. Spur continued downstream toward the cabin. He came up around the same old barn and stayed out of sight as he dismounted and peered around the rotting siding.

Archer stood beside the door to the cabin. A man lay on the ground tied up. Archer held the same woman by the throat.

"Lawman, I know you're here somewhere. You make one bad move and the man here gets his head blown off. That clear? I know you can hear me."

Spur kept silent. Archer didn't know if his shots had pulled Spur back or not. He was playing a big bluff.

"You show yourself, lawman, or I'll start shooting these people in various, non fatal parts of their bodies."

Spur didn't respond.

"How about a nice little rape, you like that, lawman?" Archer caught the neck of the woman's dress and jerked downward. Her head snapped forward, then the cloth tore and seams parted and the whole front of her dress ripped to her waist. She wore only a thin petticoat top under the dess and now her breasts showed plainly. She tried to turn away. Arthur held her.

"Like that, lawman?"

Spur lay behind the barn and judged the distance. Almost forty yards. Too damn far! He needed another ten yards closer.

He hefted the Colt .45 with the ten-inch barrel and studied the scene again. If Archer stood to one side, there was a chance. His variation on longer shots was always up and down, never from side to side.

Spur brought up the .45 and steadied the long barrel on the pier block supporting the barn. He sighted in on Archer who had moved in front of the woman again and this time ripped off her petticoat top so her breasts were bare.

"Stop it!" the woman screamed.

Archer laughed.

"Women, they always want to get fucked, always beg for it. But most of them have a funny way of showing it." He stepped to one side, holding the woman by the wrist. "Look at her, lawman. Hell, you can have a turn after I leave. Just show yourself and lay down your iron and promise me you won't follow me."

Spur steadied the .45, aimed and made a slight elevation angle for the distance. He had only one chance, then the man would be dead and probably the woman too.

McCoy wiped sweat out of his eyes, and sighted in again. He aimed at the top of Archer's head, hoping that would be enough elevation to carry the slug into his chest.

"I can't wait all day. My old whip is getting hard as a baseball bat."

Spur fired. He could almost see the .45 slug fly through the air. A moment later Archer went down, clutching his right shoulder. The .44 in his right hand spun away and he moved toward it, away from the woman.

Spur fired twice more, then jumped around the barn and ran forward. One of Spur's shots had hit Archer in the belly. He tried to hold his shoulder now as he crawled toward his weapon. Spur fired at the six-gun but missed.

"Don't do it!" Spur bellowed.

"Hell, I'm a dead man either way." Archer crawled another two feet forward and looked at McCoy.

"Who the hell are you, anyway?"

"Spur McCoy, United States Secret Service."

"Figures. You weren't even looking for me, were you?"

"No. Have you been killing off the sheriffs down the stage line between here and Wichita?"

"Lawmen? Hell, no. I told you. Just that one when I was a fuzzy cheeked kid." He lunged for the weapon.

Spur fired again, the slug caught Archer in the side and angled downward into his gut. He screamed, tried to crawl forward, then held his belly.

Spur ran up and grabbed the six-gun off the ground and cut the cabin owner loose from his rope bounds. The man thanked Spur and hurried his hysterical wife into the cabin.

Spur sat on the grass beside Archer. The man was dying. There was no way to save him. The shot in the belly would do it in half an hour.

"Archer, you use a derringer?"

"Not usually. Don't own one."

"Did you just come from Greensburg?"

"Hell, no!" He cringed in pain. His face red. He screamed and screeched as the agony flooded through his whole body. Sweat beaded his forehead where he sat. Slowly he lay on his back.

The wave of hurt swept by and he shook his head. His anger came back. "Hell, no! I came here from McCook, Nebraska. There's a bank clerk up there who will testify to that. Still got most of the money in my hotel back in Dodge."

"Which one?"

"Dodge House. Under the name of Art Luther."

"I'll check it out. You know nothing about these lawmen killings?"

"Swear to God. Sounds like a good idea, but I'd rather just rob banks."

The lean, tall man came out of the cabin. He had the rifle, and a pistol.

"You need any help, I'll be more than willing," the man said.

"Thanks. Mr. Archer here is under control." The man went back inside. Soon smoke began to come from the chimney which had been cleared of its tin and burlap.

Archer doubled up in a spasm of pain, then stretched out swearing softly.

He looked up at Spur. "I'm dying, right? No way I

can live gut shot this way."

"Happens," Spur said. "You figured some day you'd go out this way, didn't you?"

"Never did. Never thought about that. Just wanted to get more money to spend and enjoy life."

"That part's about over."

"Maybe half an hour," Archer said. He blinked tears out of his eyes. "Damn! I haven't cried since I was ten. Came here to see my wife. She left me a year ago. Lives in Dodge. Never quite got up nerve enough to go talk to her."

"That where you went last night to that little house with the picket fence?"

"Yeah. You were following me even then?"

"True. You're a famous man."

He saw the woman come from the cabin. She had put on a different dress and carried a cup. She walked up to Spur and looked down at Archer.

"Would a cup of coffee help, or some whiskey?"

Spur shook his head. "Not with a wound in the belly, ma'am, but thanks."

"Yeah, I'd like some whiskey," Archer said. "Is it going to ruin my health? You got any good whiskey, lady?"

She nodded and went back to the cabin.

Spur stared at Archer. "Drinking something now will only speed up the end."

"I'm not complaining. I'd do it quick if you'd give me my six-gun and one round. But don't reckon you will do that."

"Don't reckon."

They looked at each other. Archer coughed, spit up blood and shook as another round of killing pains raced through his belly and out into every nerve ending in his body. He rode through it, then wiped sweat off his brow.

The woman came back with a bottle of whiskey and a cup. She poured the cup half full and gave it to Spur.

"You sure, Archer?"

He nodded. "Damn right. Last things I want is a good drink of whiskey and to watch a pretty woman. Ma'am, sorry about the way I tore your dress. Would you sit and let me look at you? I never knew many nice women."

She frowned a minute, looked back at the cabin, then sat sedately in the grass a few feet from Spur.

"My name is Lucinda," she said.

"Verner, ma'am," he said.

He lifted the cup and smiled at her, then drank. When the whiskey went down his throat it made him cough, and that set up another spasm as the terrible pains marched through his body like Sherman heading for the sea.

Archer started to swear, then looked over at Lucinda.

"Sorry, ma'am, a bad habit."

Lucinda's husband came out of the cabin with the rifle that had saved Spur's life. He watched the little scene, then sat down leaning against the cabin.

"You want me to notify any kin, Archer?" Spur asked.

"Most don't have no truck with me." Archer looked up. "Might tell my wife and my sister. She's up in Omaha. She understood me best of any. Her name and street is in my gear." His face twisted as the pains came again, engulfing him. "Oh, lord! Sweet Jesus!"

"Yes, Verner! Yes, pray to Jesus!" Lucinda said softly. "He'll help you. He'll lift up your soul for an eternal home in paradise. Pray to him, Verner, and everything will be glorious!"

She was on her knees now, hands folded, eyes closed, praying silently.

Vern Archer looked at her in surprise. He frowned for a moment, then the pain touched him and he lifted up from the ground as the billowing fire burned higher and higher until it reached his brain, then he slumped back down.

Verner Archer had ceased to exist.

An hour later, Spur McCoy had tied Archer across the back of the bareback horse, said goodbye to the couple at the cabin and ridden out for Dodge. It would be only a two hour ride back to town.

12

Spur rode directly to the back door of the undertakers and gave him the body. There was no need to cause a stir on Main Street with a dead body. Then he went and talked with the sheriff.

"So you don't think this Vern Archer is the lawman killer? Why not? He tried to do in my deputy." Sheriff Johnson stared at Spur with a troubled frown.

"We talked about that. He'd been down the street to go visit his wife, lost his nerve and went back and finished getting drunk. He was mad at the whole world, and deputy sheriffs are not high on his favorite people list. He shot him in a stupid, drunken rage."

"Maybe so, maybe so. At least he was a wanted man. Wanted for two killings and about a dozen bank jobs. I'll send out a flyer that he's been disposed of so all those sheriffs can clean out their wanted drawer of him."

"You also get to tell his wife that he's dead, which won't be bad news for her, from what he said. He also told me there's some McCook, Nebraska, bank robbery money in his room at the hotel under the name I told you."

"Yeah, we'll clean out his room, give his personal effects to his wife. Except the cash from the bank. that will go back to McCook, Nebraska."

Sheriff Johnson eased into his big chair behind his desk and leaned forward toward Spur.

"You think the killer is still in town? I was hoping like blazes that you had him on the run last night."

"He's still here. Just waiting his chance. This is a smart one, willing to wait. How long has it been now since Greensburg, six, seven days? He's in no rush."

"That gives him the advanrage."

"The man on the attack always has an advantage over the defensive position. You never know when he's coming, and he times his attack on you at the worst possible moment for you. We just have to stay calm, play it right and stay alert."

"Besides that, I get locked in a cell every night."

"Good for you. Maybe you'll put better mattresses in there for your guests."

Spur moved toward the door. "Next on my list is food. I missed breakfast and dinner. You look at Vern, fill out the paper and I'll sign it."

Spur ate and hurried upstairs. He wanted to change clothes, catch up on his sleep and be roaring ready when the sun went down to prowl Dodge City and nail the bastard who had been shooting all the lawmen. There had to be a familiar face here somewhere.

In the lobby he met Lila. He grinned and said hello, but she turned away and walked past him. She carried a big paper sack in her hands and headed up the stairs. He followed her a moment later, caught up with her on the steps up to the third floor.

"I thought I knew you, Miss. You look just like a beautiful singer I know called Lila. Maybe you aren't the same girl. I guess I was wrong."

She let a grin sparkle over her face before she frowned again.

"People who know Lila tell her when they are going to miss her performances. Somebody I know missed both of them last night."

They were at her door. She opened it and turned. "So?"

"I was out of town, getting shot at by a bank robber, and trying to figure out why I was there. Then I slept on the ground and was miserable and cold and wishing I had you to keep warm beside."

"Good, I hoped it was something like that."

A couple passed them in the hallway and went down the steps.

She stepped into her room, reached out and pulled him in by one arm, then closed her door. A second later she had her arms around him hugging him tightly and looking upward to be kissed.

Spur answered the request.

"Now, that's better," she said. Lila pointed at the sack she had tossed on the bed. "I bought a new dress and I want you to help me try it on."

Spur kissed her again, then put one hand over one of her breasts.

"Does this involve some removal of your current costume?"

"Yes."

"Good, I like you half dressed, and then undressed and all bare assed naked."

"Mr. Smith! What a naughty thing to say! I'm shocked. I'd rather be fucked, but I'm shocked." She laughed. "Now help me get out of this dress so I can try on the new one."

"My second most favorite sport, watching a pretty lady take off her dress." He unbuttoned the fasteners in back of the dress and spun her around.

"When I'm not helping, how do you get these things buttoned and unbuttoned?"

She smiled as she lifted the dress off over her head. She had on the soft blue chemise. Her breasts were delightfully half hidden. He bent and kissed them.

"Darling, not right now. Be patient. About the buttons, I get them fastened with a lot of swearing and stretching. Usually I don't buy dresses that fasten that way."

She stroked one hand up his crotch and felt the growing lump there.

"My, my, we are excitable today, aren't we?" She lifted one brow and smiled at him. "Poor baby has to wait." She took the new dress out of the box and held it up to her chest.

"Well?"

"Nice, but it covers up too much of the lady behind it. I like the naked look."

"Good." She held the dress and then slipped it over her head mussing her hair. She fastened three snaps in the front and adjusted it to her satisfaction looking in the wavy mirror over the dresser. She turned. The dress was beautiful. It was much lower cut than the other and the top of the lace chemise showed.

"Yes, I'll have to use different undergarments. But what do you think?"

"Nice, extremely nice. Too good for these country cowboys at the saloon where you sing."

"Good, I didn't buy it for them, I bought it to impress you!"

She walked over slowly, put out her arms and held him, then kissed his offered lips. The kiss lasted a long time.

"I like the dress, but right now I'd rip it off you for half a penny."

"Don't you dare. It's time for my afternoon nap. I need a lot of sleep and working late I never get to sleep until after midnight."

"I'll have a nap with you."

She giggled. "Now that would be fun, but neither of us would get any sleep."

"The sexy part would be fun, though."

"Tonight, after work. I'm at the Silver Dollar. You be there for the last show at eleven and then we'll come back here and make love until neither of us has the strength to wiggle and you can't get it up anymore!"

"Done!" Spur said. "I'll get out of here. I can't stand to see you take that dress off. I might attack you."

"Please!" She giggled. "Only do it tonight."

Spur kissed her nose goodbye and went down to his room. There was a note under his door when he went inside. It was written on a school tablet paper with lines on it.

"Mr. Smith. I must see you. Come to 142 Second Street before dark."

Spur washed up, shaved and changed clothes. That was what he was headed to do before he saw Lila. Feeling back in civilized society again after his wash and shave, he walked out of the hotel and tried to remember where Second Street was.

After a block's walk down Main Street he found it. Spur strolled two more blocks and came to a small house with a white picket fence.

The new widow's house, he decided. This was where Archer had kicked the gate last night. If he'd gone inside he'd probably still be alive.

Spur saw the curtain move at the window. He was spotted. He walked through the gate up to the front door. It opened just as he was about to knock.

"Mr. Smith?" a tall, blonde woman asked. She was at least five feet eight and slender.

"Yes. You must be Mrs. Archer."

"I was at one time. I took my maiden name when I discovered Verner. I understand that you're the man who killed my ex-husband."

"Yes, ma'am. We had a gunfight."

"You must be good with a gun because Verner was one of the best."

She stared at him a minute, then opened the door. "Please come in, we have to talk."

"Archer tried to come see you last night, but he changed his mind and left. That's when he got drunk and shot the deputy sheriff."

"He always tries to see me when he comes to Dodge. I never let him in the door. He just wants to . . ." She sighed. "He just wants to have his way with me and then leave. I never let him in the house anymore."

"I didn't try to kill him, Mrs. Archer."

"Mrs. Grenville. I took back my maiden name."

"Yes, Mrs. Grenville. It just happened. Sometimes it's the other man or me who gets hurt."

"Oh, I'm not blaming you. It's just that. . . ." She stopped. "I made a vow to myself, two years ago. I promised myself that if somebody did kill Verner or put him in prison, I'd be . . . I'd be extra special nice to that man."

"Not necessary, ma'am. I'm a law officer, so this is just a part of my regular job."

Mrs. Grenville opened the top button on her dress and kept at it until they were free all the way to her waist.

"No, I insist. This is a debt I need to pay. I need to give myself to you, as payment, to meet my promise to myself. I won't let you say no." She shrugged out of her dress top showing proud breasts surging forward. The areolas were brown tipped with heavy brown nipples centering them. He could see the nipples full of hot blood and throbbing.

"I want you to understand, Mr. Smith. I'm not a loose woman. I have not given myself to a man since Verner last raped me about four years ago. That's a long time to wait. . . ." She shook her head. "I don't mean that. It's a long time to be without the love of a good man."

She caught his hand and brought it over one of her breasts, then found his other hand and led him through two rooms into her bedroom.

"My son won't be home until supper time. We

have three hours, and I want to pleasure you just every way you can think of." She paused. "Mr. Smith, you do like women, don't you?"

"Oh, yes, especially remarkably attractive women such as yourself."

"Then this . . . this arrangement . . . is agreeable to you?"

They sat down on the edge of the bed and he took her hand and placed it at the large lump extending up from his crotch.

She grinned. "Mr. Smith, I think this is going to work out just fine."

She slipped the dress off over her head and, to Spur's surprise, she wore nothing under it. She had been ready and waiting for him. She lay on the bed for a moment, her legs spread and her knees raised.

Spur watched her for a moment, then slipped out of his vest and by that time she was on her knees on the bed unbuttoning his shirt. His pants came next and when he was as naked as she was, she knelt on her hands and knees over him, letting her breasts swing down to his face.

"Eat them, Mr. Smith! Damn, I haven't done this, or said anything like that for six years! But the feeling is just the same: delightful, marvelous!"

Spur lay there still a little surprised. He'd seen gratitude before, but this was the best kind. This woman was everything that Lila wasn't. She was tall, full boned, slender, strongly built, with long legs and a delightful softly blonde muff and wide hips for easy childbirth.

This was not going to be a quick pop and out the door. Mrs. Grenville was settled in for a full afternoon of lovemaking. When he sucked and chewed on her second breast, she collapsed on top of him in a quick climax that sent her into shrieks of delight and a passionate kiss that left him drained. She ended the climax and lifted away from him.

She flipped on her back, spread her legs and urged him to come between them. Then she lifted them high in the air and placed her deliciously long and slender legs on his shoulders.

"Just once this way," she said softly. "You go in so deep I don't want you ever to come out!"

He did, amazed at the long legs over his shoulders and what she did with her internal muscles, gripping his shaft and letting go and then grabbing him again. She slowed him down, making him last longer than he thought was possible.

At last she nodded and began coming up with her hips to meet him and they both exploded almost at the same time. She screeched in rapture again and kept pumping long after he was through. She opened her eyes.

"Like that one? I've got about a dozen more to try if you can hold out. Maybe we should cut it down to six more. You look like about a seven fucker to me."

She ducked her head as she said the taboo word. She was away from him as soon as he moved to the side of the bed. She came back with three bottles of cold beer, a plate of small sandwiches and pickles.

"Most men get hungry and thirsty when they make love. I want this to be one you'll remember. I always will. Is five minutes enough between times?"

Spur nodded. The beer was cold, the sandwiches delicious and the woman amazing. It looked like it was going to be a damned interesting afternoon.

Dusk had fallen when he put on his clothes. Spur had to admit that he was not used to being a "seven timer" he knew that was a record for an afternoon of lovemaking. He grinned as he slipped on his boots. The woman had not dressed and lay there in a sexy, provocative pose.

"Figured you might like one last sexy look before you left," she said.

She watched him dress. "You don't want to get married, do you? We could do this every week, on Thursday. That way you'd keep your pistol clear and I'd be able to settle down a little and maybe relax."

Spur laughed softly.

"No, I figured not. You're not ready to get married, not yet. Maybe I'll take a lover, it's been known to happen. Find some nice young man who needs a woman and we could get together once a week or so."

"On Thursdays," Spur said.

She laughed, sat up, her big breasts bouncing. "Yeah, on Thursday. Fucking on Thursday!"

Mrs. Grenville saw him to the door, had him kiss both her breasts before he left. He stepped into the late afternoon dusk, not really sure how this all had happened, but realizing that he had helped Mrs. Grenville close out one phase of her life, and maybe launched her in a new and more fulfilling direction.

Spur checked in at the sheriff's office. Sheriff Johnson was just having his dinner off a tray from the Town House Cafe. He had been using a different eatery every day so he wouldn't make any of them mad.

"Quiet?"

"Too damn quiet. I'm getting the jitters. I bet you a two dollar gold piece we never see this lawman killer here in Dodge. He heard I was here and you were here and he just bypassed Dodge and headed on to Garden City, fifty miles or so on down the stage line."

"As soon as I see a kill report on the sheriff over there, I'll believe it," Spur said. He sniffed the plate of fried chicken in front of the sheriff. "Supper time for me, too. I'll be back tonight. Try and stay healthy."

The sheriff looked up. "Smith, I been thinking. This damn killer could make it yet. Somehow. But I got my mind made up about one thing. If some son-of-a-bitch does catch me and kills me dead, I'm gonna do my damnedest to tell you before I cash out of the game, just who it is.

"I don't know how, and maybe I can't. But if I do show up dead one of these days, you go over everything on or near me, because I'm sure as hell going to be trying to tell you something, even as I'm lying there bleeding to death."

"I hear you, Frank. But that's one problem I'm not going to have. I've seen enough lawmen die. I don't relish seeing any more go down. If I do my job here right, we won't have any more problems that way.

"Now, enough of this morbid talk. You haven't eaten half that plate of chicken yet. Dig in. I don't want to see the county wasting food."

Spur grinned and walked out of the sheriff's office, but he had a deadly feeling somewhere in his gut. He was sure now that he hadn't seen the last dead lawman. He hated the idea, but it was there and he couldn't make it go away, no matter how hard he tried.

13

McCoy left the sheriff's office and headed down the Dodge City street. The small town had shown a remarkable growth in only a few years. It was like a magnet for half the gamblers and gunsharps in the west. A lot of fast gun reputations had been made and lost here, and usually for nothing but the glory of it and the resulting blood.

He ducked into the biggest gambling house in town, a saloon called the Last Drink. It had a fifty foot long bar, over thirty gambling tables, and layouts for faro, monte, seven up and roulette.

Spur was still watching faces, checking the stage whenever he could, looking for that face or even a swing of the shoulders he had seen before in Greensburg and back down the bloody line of dead lawmen toward Wichita.

So far it had not produced any results.

He had a short beer, walked around the gambling tables and gave up. Maybe at the next saloon.

Spur would work his way toward the hotel and supper, but on the way he could check half a dozen saloons. Damn, the hard work he did for the good of the cause!

At the Dice'n Cards Saloon and Gambling Emporium, he made his survey again. This time he skipped the beer. There were plenty of places at the gambling tables, but he slid past them. None of the cardsharks looked familiar. There were probably ten wanted men in both the saloons he had been through, but he couldn't keep up on all the wanted posters.

Spur decided he could do no good here and pushed open the saloon swinging doors and walked out on the street. The sun was a half hour from down. The air cooler now, with a touch of the light fragrance of peach blossoms. He hadn't seen a peach tree.

He walked toward the hotel.

"Spur McCoy!" It was an accusation that bellowed into the quiet street from behind him.

Spur stopped, kept his hands well away from his .45. Slowly he turned and saw the only man who could have called him. The man was dressed fancy like a gambler, black hat, sparkling vest and ruffled shirt front under a ribbon thin black string tie. He held a long, thin cigar in his teeth and a snarl on his face. He was short, maybe five-six.

"I figured it was you, no matter what name you're going by. Hear you're a fast draw."

"You heard wrong, stranger. I've never met you before."

"Not good enough, McCoy. Try Joplin, about two years ago. You were a lawman of some kind. You didn't take kindly to a little printing operation I had going."

"I never forget an outlaw's face, and I've never

met yours at Joplin or any other town."

"My good fortune. In Joplin I was the one who got away, clean, with more than twenty thousand in pretty good ten dollar bills."

"The Barnhart Plates. Yes, I remember. At least we got the counterfeiting plates and everyone but you."

"And the twenty thousand. You should know that I passed all but about a thousand of it. Most of it in high stakes poker games. Amazing how many phony bills you can slip through a game."

The short man in the gambler's clothes flexed his right hand where it hung next to a polished six-gun in a well worn holster.

"You remember what happened to Josh?"

"Yes. We told him to drop his weapon. He made a grandstand play and lost."

"Lost his life, but it was enough to let me get away. Promised myself, McCoy, that I was gonna kill you. Never have liked lawmen much."

"You use a .45 caliber derringer, right?"

"Hell, no. Sometimes I carry a derringer, but always a .22, smaller, scares as well as a .45 size and can be effective at close range. Never a .45 derringer. That's my serious weapon size. We've talked enough. Time for you to die. I always like to let my victims know why they're getting shot to death. Only seems right."

"As long as you win. You ever lost, Barnhart?"

"Only in Joplin when my gun hand got hit. But it's healed and well and faster than it was then."

The two men stood on the boardwalk in Dodge City. People coming out of stores and saloons stopped and listened, then backed off and got out of the line of fire. They had seen it happen many times before. Two men with old grudges meet in Dodge and settle the score.

Spur judged the distance as about forty yards. It was much farther than most gunsharps liked. Fifteen yards was the favorite, and ten yards better. Twenty the maximum and even then the six-gun's accuracy dropped off alarmingly.

"McCoy, I don't want this to string out any longer. Two years is plenty. Why don't we make it a Texas walk down?"

Spur heard and remembered two other walk down shootouts he had been in. They were no fun. Each man had one round in his six-gun. On a given signal each was free to walk forward and fire whenever he wanted to. If the first round missed, or only wounded the other man, the one who had not fired could then "walk down" the other man and shoot him from any range he wanted to, even point blank.

The Texas walk down meant that it was certain that one of the two men would die within the next two or three minutes.

"I don't like that kind of fool's game," Spur said evenly. "It's an excuse for a poor marksman. You really that bad with a six-gun that you need a walk down?"

"Hell no, but I want to be certain. Then you won't shoot me in the back the way you did my brother." Barnhart shouted the accusation. Half the town heard him. It was the worst kind of insult to a gunman, especially a lawman.

Spur nodded. "You got what you want, Barnhart.

This is the last day you'll pass counterfeit money." He looked over the growing crowd, picked out a deputy sheriff and waved him forward.

"Deputy Carson here will referee. He'll check the weapons for rounds," Spur called.

Barnhart bobbed his head in agreement.

The deputy, who Spur had talked to from time to time, came up and took Spur's gun. He held it up and punched out four rounds and let them fall in the dirt. He called another man from the crowd who came over and looked in the cylinder.

"Only one round left," the farmer said.

Spur took back the weapon and eased it into leather. This would not be a fast draw contest, not from forty yards, but the ten-inch barrel would be a factor. It meant he had a thirty percent better accuracy at this range than Barnhart did. But what if he missed? The forty yards would be gone in thirty seconds as Barnhard walked down the line and killed Spur McCoy.

Deputy Carson and the sodbuster walked to Barnhart and took his gun. Spur saw it was a standard .45, maybe a Peacemaker. Spur watched the four cartridges drop into the dust. Little boys would be scrambling for the souvenirs in a few minutes even before the blood stopped flowing.

"One round left," the farmer called. The deputy double checked, gave the weapon back to Barnhart butt first and watched him slide it into leather.

The men still stood forty yards apart. Barnhart didn't seem to be worried about the distance. He probably figured both of them would start walking toward each other.

Deputy Carson reached the sidewalk and looked at the two men standing in the middle of the dusty Dodge City street. The whole town seemed to have come to a standstill. More and more people crowded the boardwalks on both sides. Down the street drivers quickly pulled horses up close to the boardwalk to get out of the line of fire.

The deputy looked at both men who indicated they were ready.

"Begin!" Deputy Carson shouted.

Spur turned sideways, as in a formal duel of days gone by, to present a narrower side profile as a target. His right foot went out ahead toward his target but placed at a .45 degree angle and he used a two handed grip on the big .45 after he drew it from leather.

Barnhart had taken one step as he drew his weapon. He stopped and looked at Spur.

"You're bluffing, McCoy. Nobody would risk a shot at this distance. Not in a Texas walk down."

He took another step and stopped.

Spur blinked, sighted in over the groove and blade, then looked at Barnhart. He was standing stock still, facing forward. Now was the time, before he presented a moving target, before he could turn to the side.

Spur realized his life was on the line. This wasn't the usual gun fighting kind of call out. Then, if both men missed, it would be settled for the moment. But now, if either man fired first and missed, the first shooter was a dead man.

McCoy thought of his life so far. It had been full, he had done most of what he wanted to do. It had been a fine, exciting life. Today, as his Indian friends used to say, today was a good day to die.

He sighted in again on the fancy ruffled shirt and slightly to the left of center. Sweat threatened to roll into his right eye. He wiped it away.

"Having second thoughts about such a long try?" Barnhart chided. "Go ahead, waste your shot. Make it easy for me."

Spur took a deep breath, held it, sighted in again. His hands held the big gun rock solid, square on the target. Don't pull, not now, squeeze the trigger. Never know exactly when it's going off. Smooth, stroke it, squeeze, squeeze, squeeze . . . .

It was a surprise when the Colt, long barreled .45 went off. He let the recoil bring his hands upward and to the left as he watched Barnhart.

A thousand thoughts raced through his brain in the fraction of a second it took for the flight of the spinning .45 slug. Had he figured wind? Was there wind? He prayed the powder charge in that particular round had been well packed, was up to strength and was good powder. What if Barnhart moved at the last second? Was his aim true?

The gasp of the crowd came briefly through his mind. Most of them didn't think that he would fire at that range, figured he was bluffing, as did Barnhart.

There was a roar from the crowd of as many as two hundred people when the bullet struck Barnhart. Spur watched in a kind of detached interest as Barnhard staggered to the rear from the impact of the big bullet, then fell on his back in the dust.

"Hold your position, Mr. McCoy!" Deputy

Carson bellowed. Barnhard had dropped his weapon. He lay still for a moment. Someone ran toward him. He moved, rolled to his hands and knees and crawled to the weapon, then slowly, with extreme pain and care, he lifted to his feet.

Barnhard held his left hand over his chest where a growing red stain turned his shirt bright red.

He took two steps, wiped his left hand over his eyes to clear them.

The crowd gasped as his hand left a bloody streak across his forehead and his cheeks.

He took another step forward, lifted the six-gun to waist height, and managed another step. He was still thirty-eight yards away. He had only little more than made up for the distance he had been knocked backward by the heavy .45.

One more step came and the crowd rippled with talk about the man and the shootout. The heavy weapon dragged Barnhart's right hand down and he used both hands to lift the .45. Slowly, ever so slowly, he raised it to eye level and tried to aim.

Spur McCoy stood where he had been a second after he fired, the six-gun still aimed forward, his feet exactly where they had been. Sweat ran into his eyes. His arm ached from the weight of the big gun. Slowly he lowered his arms to his side, slid the weapon in his holster. It could do him no more good.

Now, Barnhart could walk up thirty more yards, put the Peacemaker against Spur's chest and blow his heart into pieces.

Thirty-five yards away, Barnhart shook his head and blinked rapidly, but couldn't seem to clear his eyes.

Barnhart bellowed in rage and tried to run forward. He took two steps, then fell forward in the dust and horse droppings. Furiously he brushed the dry manure aside, struggled to his hands and knees, then teetered as he pushed up to his feet.

Once more he tried to lift the gun. It took both hands. One woman on the boardwalk began to cry.

"My God! Look at him! How can he even move!" A hushed voice asked. In the ear-humming stillness the words flowed across the broad street.

Barnhart took one more step, lifted the weapon with both hands to his waist, and gave a soft cry of anger and fear. He struggled to lift the weapon higher, then he screamed, dropped the .45 and clutched at his chest as he crumpled to the dirt.

Doc Crenshaw ran from the boardwalk in front of the hardware and knelt over Barnhart.

Spur watched with only half his attention. He had thought his round had only scratched Barnhart. Closely, so closely he had almost given himself up for dead. Now with the other man down, Spur tried to relax. Slowly, he realized that this was not his day to die. He gave a shuddering little sigh, and worked out five rounds from his gunbelt and pushed them into the cylinder of his .45. Now was no time to get caught with an empty gun. He took another breath and watched the doctor.

The medic tried for a pulse, then listened to Barnhart's chest. He ripped open the ruffled shirt and saw where the bullet hit home, directly under the heart. It had sliced in half one of the main arteries leading from his heart. The doctor shook his head.

"He's dead," Doc Crenshaw said. He pointed to two men to carry the Barnhart to the undertaker.

Deputy Carson walked over to Spur, a small frown fighting with a grin. "You'll have to write out a report down at the office, Mr. McCoy, or Mr. Smith, whatever." He shook his head. "That shot was over forty yards! Dead center."

Spur felt nothing. He heard the deputy. "Lucky shot," he said.

The deputy laughed softly. "Not a chance. A man doesn't risk that kind of shot if he isn't dead sure he can make it. If you had missed, you'd be on your way now to the undertaker instead of the other guy. Barnhart you called him?"

"I tried to talk him out of it."

"I heard. Let's get the paperwork done. It's time for supper."

For the first time in a month, the thought of food made Spur feel like throwing up.

It took him ten minutes in the sheriff's office to write out a statement and sign it. Deputy Carson signed it as well.

Sheriff Johnson had been making some rounds while it was still daylight and had walked up on the gunfight just before the shot was fired.

"Glad you're on my side, McCoy. I know that's your real name and everybody in town knows about it now. I'd never have the nerve to do that. Never agree to a walk down in the first place. You know I hear folks down in Texas say that's really the Arizona walk down."

Spur mumbled something, got out of there and walked directly back to his room in the hotel. It looked down on the spot of the shootout.

When he caught the doorknob he saw that the panel was unlocked. He drew the .45 and pushed the door open slowly. Lila sat on the bed waiting for him. She was fully dressed and had a book in her hand. She gave a little cry of joy and rushed to him. He closed the door and held her. She had been crying. She lifted her tear stained face to his.

"I was so afraid you were going to be killed down there! I saw the whole thing."

He stroked her hair and led her back to the bed.

"Okay, it's over now, Lila. It's all over. No need for any more tears."

"You could have been killed!"

"Could have. Wasn't."

He was calm now, the reaction of the sudden emotional meeting with Barnhart over. Soon he would have to telegraph Washington that the last of the Barnhart gang was dead and the case should be closed. The twenty thousand in bogus tens was in circulation.

He got Lila's tears stopped and kissed her cheeks and then her nose and at last her lips. She smiled and blew her nose.

"Don't ever scare me that way again, please."

"I'll try. But, like this time, the option is never mine." He watched her and then walked to the window. The street was empty now, with darkness sneaking into the daylight.

"I didn't hear all of it. But your real name is Spur McCoy? Why did you lie to me?"

"I'm doing a job where some people would recognize my name. So I use a different one." He picked up her hand. "I'd bet a dollar your real name isn't Lila Pemberthy."

She looked at him quickly, a frown growing. "Why . . . why do you say that?"

"You're a performer. I knew a singer in Washington who changed her name twice a year so she could get more jobs."

"That's no way to build up a reputation, to keep demanding more money each time."

"This singer wasn't good enough to have a reputation." They both laughed and Spur felt a little better.

"Lila, I'm not in the mood for any supper tonight. You go down without me. I need to sit here and figure out things a little. Do you understand? I always hate it when I have to kill a man, and when I do I have a little bit of rationalization to do, some thinking to get figured out.

"I have to get things right again. Especially when the dead man is one like Barnhart. He wasn't a vicious man, a mad dog killer or a real outlaw. He was just a counterfeiter. Can you understand what I'm saying?"

She bobbed her head and kissed him. "I do. Taking a man's life must be hard on you. At least I'll never have to worry about that." She hesitated. "Oh, should I call you Spur McCoy now, if that's really your name?"

"Might as well, everyone else will."

She laughed softly and touched his crotch.

"Maybe later on you'll show me your spur, the way we had planned this afternoon?"

"I'm not sure. Maybe we should put off the fun and games until tomorrow."

"I understand."

She frowned again and he liked what it did to her pretty face. "Oh, are you still in land speculation?"

"I'm afraid so. A job to do. That's why people might know my name. If they do, they raise the price knowing I have to buy no matter the cost, if my employers tell me to."

"Oh." She sounded disappointed. "I'll stop by after supper before I go to sing at eight." She hugged him and went to the door. "Spur McCoy, you take care of yourself," she said, then grinned and went into the hall, closing his door firmly behind her.

14

McCoy dropped on the bed and lay with his fingers laced behind his head. There had been no way out of the shoot, he knew that, but when an old case came up to haunt him that way, he wondered how soon it would be that some angry man would storm up to him and gun him down without warning. It had happened before to other agents, to other lawmen.

He lay there half an hour thinking about his work with the agency. At last he kicked off the bed, checked his weapon, and filled the empty spaces in his cartridge loops on his belt. It was dark outside, time for him to be moving.

Maybe tonight would be the time he would catch the lawman killer.

It seemed that half of the town knew him now. It was impossible to slip into a saloon unnoticed now and look around. He spent an hour touring the twelve saloons. The barkeeps at most of the spots had seen him before and nodded. By now everyone in town knew that he was a lawman "of some kind" as Barnhart had screamed in the middle of the street.

Those few words had made his job that much harder. He studied every face in each saloon, but there was no twinge of recognition, no face that he hadn't seen once or twice before here in town, or that was new to him. None of the faces could be pegged in Greensburg or the death towns back the stage line toward Wichita.

On his second round of the saloons, Spur sat in on poker games. He had a five dollar limit at each table. If he lost or won five dollars at the quarter limit table, he bowed out and moved on.

It was not good poker on his part as he tried to watch the people in the saloon at the same time. The first place he lost his five dollars and walked across the street to the next saloon. He realized that he hadn't heard Lila sing yet, so he made sure he was at the Silver Dollar Saloon at eight.

He was surprised by the songs she sang. Most of them were sad songs, not the bright bouncy ones she usually used. He caught her eye but she did not come out to his table after she sang. She was down about something, and he decided it would be better to let her work it out.

On his way to the next saloon, the Dangerous Dog, he met Deputy Carson. They talked a minute.

"Today's gonna be one I won't ever forget," Carson said. "Damn, you stood out there forty damn yards and blasted that son-of-a-bitch right in the chest with one shot!"

Spur didn't want to talk about it. He nodded, but he young deputy pressed him.

"That ten-inch barrel, it hard to find a weapon like

that?" the deputy asked.

"Most any good gunsmith can put one on most any good weapon like a Colt, a Remington, or a Ruger .44 Old Army. You want one ready made get the Wyatt Earp Dixie. It's a .44 with a twelve inch octagon barrel." He paused. "Don't count on drawing the Wyatt Earp Dixie in a rush, though, the things hangs half way down your leg."

Deputy Carson laughed. "Won't count on it. Sure would be nice to have more range than twenty yards and hit something. Maybe I'll just cut down a small rifle to about twelve inches and carry that."

He held out his hand. "Mr. McCoy, sure as hell want to say I learned a lot from you today. Hope to be a better lawman because of it. Hell, I'll be telling my grandchildren about today so often they'll get tired of the story."

They shook hands.

"Well, I got to move. I'm off at nine-thirty. Then I got a special meeting. Not sure what it's all about, but it does sound interesting. Doubt if it has anything to do with the law though." Deputy Carson chuckled. "Hell, you never can tell these days. Thanks again for today." He touched his hat brim with his first finger and ambled on down the boardwalk checking each merchant's door as he went.

At the next saloon, Spur paid attention to his poker and was soon seven dollars ahead. He stood, put two dollars in the center of the table.

"Men, I got to leave, but I'll sweeten the next pot for those of you lucky enough to be staying in the game." Most of the men around the table smiled.

The biggest loser kept his frown in place but didn't comment.

At nine-thirty Spur noticed the time by his pocket watch. He was deep in the middle of a poker game at the Lonesome Garter Saloon and was two dollars down. He hoped the deputy had a good meeting whatever it was. Spur went back to his cards, but swept the room now and then. He saw no one he figured could be the lawman killer.

Deputy Vic Carson had a bounce to his step as he walked out past the last house on Main Street and waited by the elm tree the way they had agreed. Nothing like this had ever happened to him before. He wasn't exactly sure why it was happening now, but the invitation had been rather explicit.

Five minutes after he got off work they would meet at the elm tree. It was supposed to be secret so he had told nobody. He didn't even want to think about it. But there was the hint that there could be some information about the lawman killer.

If he could help find the gunman who had been cutting down lawmen in Kansas, he would be a hero. He might even get a raise, maybe be a sheriff in his own right somewhere.

He was dreaming dreams so grand that he barely heard the buggy coming down the street. Yes, it was supposed to be a black buggy with the front closed in. He waited. The horse stopped beside him and he opened the side curtain.

"I'm Deputy Carson, and we were to meet here, right?"

There was a low answer and he stepped inside the rig. Almost at once, a muffled report came from the buggy and Deputy Carson slammed against the back cushion, his eyes wide as he realized he had been shot.

It hurt so bad he couldn't think straight. A quick hand stripped the pistol out of his holster and threw it out the far side of the buggy.

His mind refused to believe it, even as the series of smashing pains ripped through him. His gut! He had been shot in the belly, just like all those other dead lawmen back the line toward Wichita! He had read the warnings. He had to tell somebody. He knew who the killer was!

But when he tried to move his legs, they felt like lead sticks. He could barely lift his hands. There was no strength in his arms. His belly burned. He saw the weapon then, a .45 but a derringer! The small little weapon packed a mighty wallop. The gloved hand that held it moved up to his chest directly over his heart.

Billowing pain blocked out his vision. His ears were engulfed with a roaring that wouldn't stop. Somewhere, there was a voice talking, patiently, explaining something, he wasn't sure just what. The voice droned on and on. Sometimes it was clear and words made sense, then his mind became a jumbled mass of visions and sounds and memories and nothing meant anything.

He had to do something or he would be dead soon. Maybe he could lunge at the killer. Smash into the hand holding the gun, grab it and turn it against the maniac.

At once Deputy Carson knew that was impossible. He could barely speak. His words came out jumbled and unreal. How had he gone to pieces so quickly?

What had happened to all of his dreams? He was only twenty-four years old. That was too young to die!

The voice had faded. Only a few of the words he heard made sense. "Have to die," he had heard those words several times. It couldn't be true! This couldn't be happening to him.

Slowly, his eyes focused again and he saw the small gun coming toward him out of the blackness.

"No!" he blurted. The word was firm, solid. "Don't kill me!"

The gun came closer. He tried to swing his wooden arm at it. Nothing moved. He tried to butt it with his head, but his chin only hit his chest.

His eyes widened as the muzzle came closer and closer. Then it touched his chest just over his heart.

He tried to scream, but only a babble of sounds came out. Again the pain boiled through his body, tearing him apart, dimming his vision, blocking his hearing. When his eyes cleared the weapon's muzzle pressed against his chest.

His mind heard the explosion a millisecond before the terrible pain stabbed through his chest, the .45 lead slug plowed through his heart and it was over. He didn't hurt anymore.

Deputy Carson couldn't smell his burning shirt or the charred flesh around the wound from the powder burns. He couldn't see the round black ring, nor could he feel the buggy move slightly as a figure stepped out of it and closed the side curtain.

Then the killer whacked the horse on the rump, sending her trotting down the road, the reins trailing along beside and under the buggy as the startled animal kept going for nearly half a mile before she stopped in the darkness and began nibbling at the few shoots of grass at the side of the trail.

Spur McCoy tired of the poker. He sat at the bar and watched the men in the room, drinking, gambling, and grabbing at the two dance hall girls who circulated around the tables selling drinks and offering anything and everything else for sale upstairs.

Tonight the price was a dollar for a quick one and two dollars for anything you could do in half an hour.

Spur went back to the jail and made sure the sheriff was safely tucked in his cell.

"Do a lot of Dodge City townfolks good to see you in there, Sheriff Johnson," Spur said keeping a straight face.

"So bring them through and charge them a dime a head to take a look," Johnson said. "A couple nights like that and I can retire and move to Denver. Never been there but that's where I'm going when I can. One of my big dreams is to live a mile in the sky. Can you imagine that?"

"It isn't like you can step off the edge of Denver and fall a mile down," Spur said.

"A man can always hope." The sheriff scowled at Spur. "It's too damn quiet around here. How long has it been since Sheriff Bjelland in Greensburg went down?"

"Eight, nine days, not sure. Time seems not to be a factor in these killings."

"Remember, I said I'd stay in here a week and that's it. Then I'm back on the town doing my job. My deputies are holding up well, but they're overworked."

"You make an appointment with the killer and I'll be glad to cut him up into pieces and serve him to you for breakfast," Spur said. "If you're bitching, you're all right. Keep your spirits up and keep that loaded six-gun handy."

"No doubt about that, city slicker. I didn't just get into town with a trail drive from Mexico."

Spur waved and checked with the deputy who came on at nine-thirty. Everything was quiet. Not even a gunfight tonight.

"Things will pick up about midnight," Spur said and ambled over to the Silver Dollar Saloon to catch Lila's eleven o'clock song fest.

She came out smiling and sassy, and Spur saw a much happier and interesting Lila than had sung at eight. All of her songs were upbeat and only one from the Civil War, "The Bloody Mongahela," made it into the show. She closed with "Jimmy Cracker" and "Rosie You are My Posy" and "The Girl I Left Behind." The applause was honest and continuous. She came back and sang one encore that had a touch of sadness: "My Love, My True Love Has Left Me."

Lila had spotted Spur during the last song and winked. After the applause died, she came out to his table and had a cup of coffee that the barkeep always provided her.

"Howdy, tall stranger, you new in these parts?" she asked with a try at a Western twang. She broke up laughing as she finished it.

"Shore am, Little Filly. Anybody got a halter on you yet?" Spur went along with the game. Soon they both were laughing.

"You really worked for a U.S. senator the way you told me? Or was that all gully washing raspberry juice just to confuse a poor lonesome, inexperienced virgin like me?"

"Really. He was an old family friend. Now Washington is a town where you can meet some strange people." He hesitated. "Oh, I bought a new bottle of white wine, want to test it out?"

"Yes. Now."

They walked out of the saloon as several of the men who had just heard her sing, called to thank her. She waved back at them and soon they were on the street heading for their hotel.

She held his arm tightly.

"Are you all right, Lila? You seem a little tense."

"No, no, I'm fine. I always get wound up as I perform. The energy keeps me going and then suddenly it's all over. I need to relax and let everything slow down."

"With some good wine."

"Or anything else you want to give me . . . or put to me."

She started walking faster, looking up at him. "I can almost feel your hands on me now, all over me!"

Spur chuckled. "Not right here on the street or in the lobby. Try to control yourself for a few more minutes."

"I'll try."

She held his arm as they went up the front steps.

"What's this talk I hear about people saying that

you're a law officer of some kind? Is that true?"

"I came here to buy land. If the people think I'm some kind of marshal or something, that will be a help to me."

"But they said the man who was killed was a counterfeiter, and he accused you of killing his brother and you said you got the engraving plates. You must have been a lawman."

They went up the steps toward the third floor.

"Yes, I was a law officer for a while, in Joplin. We helped some men from Washington get the plates back. That was it. I quit the job and moved to Chicago. I never expected this Barnhart ever to see me again."

She watched him a moment as he turned her key in the lock and swung open the door.

"All right, Spur McCoy. I can believe that. It sounds right, and I want to believe it." Her sober mood changed. She touched his crotch, then leaned up and kissed him. "Now, where is wine and where is that big sexy stick of yours?"

He held up his hand. "The wine is down in my room, I'll be right back."

She already had her dress unbuttoned down the front. These buttons went all the way to the hem of the dress, over fifty of them.

"I'll let you go if you swear on a stack of land deeds that you'll be right back."

"I so swear." He reached down and pushed his face past the dress buttons and kissed the very top of her bare breasts.

"Get out of here and hurry back!" she yelped.

Spur made it in record time. She sat on the bed,

naked, waiting for him when he opened the door.

"What took you so long?" she asked.

He worked the cork out of the bottle with a puller and poured the pale white wine in the two glasses she had set on the dresser. She sipped it, and nodded, then drained half the glass.

"Good," she said. "Now me."

Spur shook his head silently as he stared at her young, delightful, unmarked body. A woman was all curves and grace and perfect line and motion. Especially her breasts.

"Remember, I said this couldn't be an all night affair. I still have some thinking through things to do."

"Just once, then quickly before I explode. You don't even have to undress, kind of like you were forcing me to fuck you."

"It's not as good that way," he said.

"Sometimes it's better for me. Just this once, be rough with me . . . a little rough."

Before she finished talking he pushed her down on the bed, held her arms spread at the side over her head and rammed her legs widely apart. With one hand he opened his pants and wedged out his erection. With no preliminaries at all he bent and rammed at her.

He felt the dry skin burning, eased off, let her juices flow a little and then drove into her with one quick thrust that brought a cry of pain and delight from her that was all mixed up. He held her hands spread wide as he powered at her, feeling his pelvic bones grinding against hers, then coming out almost all the way and ramming back so hard he pushed her two inches up the bed with every thrust.

"Yes, yes!" she crooned.

Ten more powerful plunges and he was on fire. He didn't know if he could perform again that day or not. He exploded with a raging fury that he knew was part of his anger for the death in the afternoon, yet part was pure animal passion. He held the final thrust until every drop of fluid had jetted out of him and then he came away from her and buttoned his pants.

"You wanted fast and hard. Was that fast enough for you?" He bent and kissed her cheek. She rolled toward him. He slapped her soft botton twice and walked to the door.

"Enjoy the wine," he said and slipped into the hall. He had a few more pegs to put in the right holes before he could get to sleep that night.

There had been too many interruptions on this case, too many side problems to clear up. He had to pick out the killer damn soon, or the whole thing would dissolve into chaos and the lawman killer would probably fade into the landscape and never be found. Tomorrow. Tomorrow had to be the day.

15

Spur heard about Deputy Carson at breakfast. He left the rest of his food and ran directly to the sheriff's office.

Sheriff Johnson sat behind his desk. They had not moved the body. The buggy had not been missed until morning and when it was found, the owner came straight to the sheriff.

"What the hell is going on here? Has this crazy maniac started killing any lawman he can find?" Sheriff Johnson shuddered and wiped wetness away from his eyes.

"That boy was like a son to me. I brought him into this business, taught him everything I know. He was good. Smart, ambitious . . . damn!"

"Let's go out to the scene," Spur said gently. "There might be something we can find this time."

They rode out to the buggy. The reins had been tied by the owner before he came back. He sat along side the road waiting for them. He held a six-gun.

The man's name was Billy Earlly. He handed the weapon to the sheriff as soon as they dismounted.

"Found this back by the elm tree there just at the edge of town. Looks like the rig stopped there for a while. There's some droppings there and some footprints, but I couldn't make out much of it."

"Thanks, Bill," Sheriff Johnson said. "That's Carson's sidearm. He was proud of that piece. Sent to Chicago for it."

They walked over to the buggy. Both front curtains were closed. Deputy Carson lay sprawled in the rig. The smell of charred cloth clung in the air. Spur reached in and checked his chest, and his belly.

"Two shots, just like before, Sheriff. I'd say it's the same killer. Same method, even down to the stolen buggy." Spur looked over the body, the pockets, then the rest of the inside of the buggy. He could not find anything that would help. Nothing had been dropped or left. There was no sign who had sat in the other seat when Deputy Carson was killed.

The sheriff looked it all over as well. At last they had Bill Earlly lead the horse and rig back to the undertaker.

The two men rode back to the spot where the owner said he found the pistol.

Spur stopped ten yards away, let the reins down on his mount and walked up to the buggy tracks in the road dirt. The tracks were plain enough, and the droppings told where the horse had stood for at least a short time.

Footprints? He went over the dusty part again. There were prints on the right side of the rig, but on the other side the ground was harder, blown bare by the wind. He could make out only a few plain men's boot tracks on the far side. Nothing distinctive about them. They probably matched Carson's boots and a hundred others in town.

"The killer took Carson's gun away here and threw it out. He might even have killed Carson here, then chased the horse down the trail."

"Which left only a short walk back through town," Spur said. There was nothing more for them to do there. On the way back to the office they checked the undertaker. He confirmed that death was due to gunshot, probably a large caliber, .44 or .45 at muzzle-touching range.

A few minutes later behind his desk in his office, Sheriff Johnson sighed. "One deputy dead, another one shot up. I'm down to two deputies. Means I got to work the street tonight."

"Not a chance!" Spur said sharply. "The killer went for a deputy because you were safe and secure. He'd just trying to lure you out of your protection. Stay put one more night."

"Hell, I guess it's better than dead." He stood and paced around his office. "Christ! I feel so helpless. What the hell am I supposed to do, McCoy?"

"If I knew, I'd be doing it myself. I'm as frustrated as you are. No clues, no suspects, just bodies turning up. God damn! I'm going for a ride, try to blow some of the fuzzy thinking out of my brain." He stopped on his way to the door. "Frank, today and tonight, you be double damn careful, you hear?"

Frank waved. He was cleaning his pair of .44 six-guns.

Spur rented a horse and rode three miles out in the

prairie. He sat there staring into the endless plains, then turned around and rode hard for a mile toward town, then eased off and walked the bay toward the stable.

He had figured out exactly nothing on the ride, but it made him feel better. He put the horse back in the livery and went to the undertaker to see if he had cut out the bullet. He had found one of them. It was banged up a little, but there was no doubt, it was a .45. Why didn't a big powder charge like that drive the slug right on through his belly and out his back? Especially fired that close? Low powder charge? He'd met the same question before.

All day Spur walked the streets watching the people. He was on hand for the morning stage. The only people who left was one grandma and her teenage grandson, and a salesman heading back toward Wichita. He wasn't interested in the incoming passengers.

If the killer hadn't ridden out of town on his own horse, he was still around. All Spur had to do was find him out of Dodge City's two thousand people, and maybe those on the farms and ranches nearby.

In his whole career, Spur McCoy had never come up against a case like this. Bodies dropping all over the state and he had absolutely nothing solid to work with. Worse, he had no suspects. The killer could be anyone: a teenage boy trying to make a name for himself, an old drunk panhandling himself from town to town, a just out of prison bank robber taking his anger out on all lawmen.

He had dinner with Lila at the hotel that noon. She was bouncy and full of energy.

"Let's go for a ride down the little stream this afternoon in a buggy and have a picnic about four o'clock."

Spur shook his head automatically. "Sorry, I have some work to do."

"Land buying? You don't talk much about it."

"That's the way it is with secret negotiations."

Somehow, he didn't think that she believed his land scheme cover story any more. It didn't matter that much. He had a much larger problem.

That afternoon he checked the three stores that sold guns. No, there had been no unusual sale of a weapon to anyone. Just a couple of cowboys, a drummer who wanted a small derringer in a .22 caliber for protection, and a farmer getting a new shotgun to use on pheasants.

He stopped in the middle of the street as he was crossing to the next gunsmith. Why had he decided to stay here? Why not move on down the stage line. Why was Dodge different? Slowly it came to him.

In every other town, the killer had cut down the top lawman. Here it had been only a deputy. He was starting to think like the killer. The man wanted the sheriff, but he'd take a deputy, waiting his chance on Sheriff Johnson.

Made sense. Spur was counting on being right about that. He continued his rounds. He was going to be evident, out on the streets, walking, watching, checking parked buggies on Main Street or anywhere else he saw them where they seemed to be out of place. Spur was determined to walk Dodge City until dawn!

Lila Pemberthy sang beautifully at eight. She was in fine voice, and enjoyed her work. She thanked the barman for the cup of coffee and slipped out the back door of the Silver Dollar Saloon and walked quickly toward a small building she had selected that afternoon.

It was time. She had thought it through and knew it would work. She still wore her performing dress and carried a fancy reticule. There was time, lots of time.

She slipped on a hat that fit closely around her hair and sat low over her eyes, then edged out to the street from the alley. No one was in sight. She left the alley, turned down the street and walked two blocks.

She saw no one. Half a block ahead was the vacant four room house she had selected. She walked to it, looked up and down the dark street and saw no one, so moved confidently to the back of the structure and the small open porch. There she took out a quart of coal oil she had stolen from the saloon. They kept it for their dozens of lamps.

She tried the back door. It was open. Quickly she moved inside to the bedroom. There were still curtains up, and some furniture, including a bed and blankets. Without wasting any motions, she assembled some papers, a sheet from the bed, and a wooden chair. She set them against a wall and poured the coil oil over the whole thing, saturating the wall. Then from her reticule she took some matches and lit the stack on fire. It burned up well. There was only a tiny window in the room so no one would see the flames for some time.

Lila went out the back door, through the vacant lot behind the house and around to another street. She walked back to Main and waited in the shadows. No one saw her. Lila could be patient when she had to be, and this was one of those times.

It was nearly half an hour before she heard someone yell "Fire!" It was another five minutes before someone ran into the sheriff's office and reported the fire. The volunteer fire brigade assembled at the now furiously burning house, but there was little they could do.

As soon as the report came, the deputy sheriff rushed out of the office and ran down the street.

Lila moved quickly to the sheriff's office door and slipped inside. She looked around, then went straight to the desk and found the keys to the cells. She took the right one and put it in her reticule. Then she opened the door to the cell room.

Sheriff Johnson lay snoring softly on the double mattress in the first cell. The door was not even locked. Lila closed the door into the outer part of the office and threw a bolt. Then she moved in beside the sheriff and saw the pistols at his side.

Carefully she lifted them and slid them far under the bunk where he could not reach them. She put on thin black gloves, then took from her purse a derringer and pressed it against Sheriff Johnson's slightly paunchy belly.

She slapped his face firmly.

"What? What . . ." His eyes focused and he blinked. "The singer, Lila. What you doing here?"

She shot him. The bullet crashed into his belly tearing up essential organs and plowing upward, doing more damage than she had really intended.

Sheriff Johnson passed out.

She slapped him back to consciousness. He roused slowly, the pain coursing through his body evident on his face.

"Christ, you gut shot me! Damned derringer. Damned woman! You're the one who killed Carson, and the rest!"

"Sheriff, I don't know what you're talking about. You killed my Robert, and I swore an oath to myself that I would repay you. I told myself that someday I'd come back to this Kansas town and I'd kill you. To even the scales of justice because you killed my Robert."

"Lila, I never met you before last week when you come to town to sing!" He said it over the grinding, wrenching pain that gushed into his brain and set his whole torso on fire.

"Liar! You are all liars! If I must I'll remind you what happened. Been several years ago now, six or seven, I lose track. Robert and me just come in from Texas in our little wagon ahunting a place to farm. You folks in Kansas didn't treat us right good.

"You kept hitting Robert and knocking him down. I didn't know why. I said: Why you doing that, Sheriff? He ain't hurtin' you. I was little more than a girl then, just seventeen, and married only two months with a Texas sunbonnet hiding most of my long brown hair. I wore a cheap calico dress that covered me from wrists to neck to shoe soles. I was only five feet tall but I could get right mad.

"Then you slammed your revolver down across Robert's face, driving him to his knees. Blood gushed from scrapes on his forehead and check and when Robert tried to talk, his jaw didn't work right.

" 'Stop it, stop it!' I shouted.

"You said: 'Shut up, you little poon. I'll take care of you later.' You was a big one, over six feet, with a week's growth of beard and a shiny sheriff's star pinned to your shirt pocket.

"You glared at Robert and told us nobody sassed the sheriff there in Willow. You said you had laws about that sort of thing. You called Robert a scrawny little snot and said lots of unkind things about him. Told him he'd know better next time. 'We call it teaching Texas no-counts to be proper,' is the way you said it that day.

"I screamed at you that he didn't hurt you none. But I moved away a little as I said it, cause you scared me something terrible. You just glared at Robert on the ground.

"You yelled at Robert. 'You gonna hold your tongue now you damn Texas Rebel?'

"Poor Robert got to his knees, then struggled to stand. He was weaving, working hard just to stand up. But he stared hard at you, Sheriff.

"He said: 'Suh, ah don't apologize to white trash like you!'

"Then you went crazy. Your big fist lashed out, hit poor Robert's chin and snapped his head back. He fell in the dirt in front of the hardware store. You bellowed something about him being a rebel. 'My kid brother got shot to death by bastards just like you in the war.' Then you kicked Robert in the side with your heavy boot. Robert curled in a ball.

"You dragged him to his feet, held his shirt front

and pounded your fist into Robert's face again and again. Robert's nose spurted blood. You laughed. You closed one of his eyes and tore his ear. Robert's head flopped from side to side each time you hit him.

"I kept yelling at you to stop. Yelling for somebody to help us. But nobody came. A man and a woman on the boardwalk hurried past. A cowboy walking his horse down the street went to the far side and rode on quickly.

" 'Why won't somebody help us?' I screamed.

"Then you slammed a hard punch into Robert's jaw and he slumped to the ground. You glared at me and yelled. 'Woman, you shut your mouth or I'm gonna pitch you right in jail!'

"Then you kicked Robert again. You called him an ugly little Texas Rebel bastard. 'I'll teach you damn Rebs not to come into my town and insult anybody!' You kicked him hard in the stomach, then aimed for his crotch but missed, so you slammed your boot into Robert's head. When Robert brought his hands up to protect his head, you kicked him in the side again, breaking a rib.

" "Stop it! Stop it! Stop it!' I screamed. 'Won't somebody help Robert?' I watched five or six people on the boardwalk who could hear me. They turned away. So I jumped up and I raced at you, my hands clawing at your face. Before you got your arms up, my right hand finger nails scratched down your cheek leaving three deep marks that filled with blood.

"You bellowed at me, grabbed me and threw me into the dirt. 'Your turn is coming, you southern cunt! You're next, just as soon as I finish with this little bastard!' You turned back to Robert and kicked him again where he lay in the dust. You kicked him twice more in the head.

"All I could do was sob where I lay in the street. I had fallen on fresh horse droppings, but I didn't have the strength to move away from them.

"Remember? You felt your cheek and swore at me. You said we made a good pair, a rebel and his bitch. You told us to get out of town before dark, that you didn't want Texas rabble in your town. Then you spit on Robert and walked into a saloon.

"I crawled over to Robert, saw the ugly bruises on his face and head. So I cradled his head in my lap. I figured he'd come around in a few minutes, and we'd get into the wagon and drive out of your terrible town.

"I sat there for half an hour and Robert didn't move. Wagons went around us in the street. People passing on the boardwalk slowed and looked, but nobody came to help us.

"I told Robert he'd feel better soon, and we'd move on to a friendly little town where we could start farming.

"Then pretty soon a man knelt down beside us. He had a black bag and said he was Doc Smathers. He touched Robert and pinched his nose, then felt of his wrist, and at last put his ear down on Robert's chest.

"I asked the doctor if Robert was hurt bad and he nodded. Said he was hurt as bad as a body can be. He said he was sorry, but that . . . that . . . that Robert was dead! I screamed and wailed and fell on Robert and wouldn't let the doctor touch him again.

I screeched that the doctor was wrong. But somehow I knew he must be right.

"I told him the sheriff killed him, kicked him in the head. But the doctor said that was just the way things were. Said it would get better. But you, as sheriff, was running things. Said your term ended a year ago, but you wouldn't let anybody run for office. Nobody in town would stand up to you."

Lila sighed. She shook her head and frowned at the lawman who had killed her Robert. She was positive this was the man. Lila waved the little gun at Sheriff Johnson who shook his head.

"That ain't me you're talking about. I never met you before last week. You're all confused about it, Lila. Run and get Doc for me and we'll all be friends here. We love you here in Dodge City."

It was a long speech for him. Sheriff Johnson sagged against the mattress. He didn't know where his strength went. He could hardly move his hand. He should be slapping away that funny little derringer and locking her up for the murder of six lawmen. Or was it seven or eight now? He wanted to close his eyes. He was tired. Damn, but it hurt!

"You're trying to trick me. I've seen others try it. Deny that they even knew me. I saw you kick my husband to death! You can't deny anything. Right now we even up the score. I might be from Texas, but I can pull a trigger good as any stinking damn Yankee!"

She put the muzzle of the derringer against Sheriff Johnson's chest, over his heart, and pulled the trigger. The second round from the derringer blasted through shirt and ribs and tore into his heart, killing him instantly.

Lila hummed softly as she put the derringer in her reticule, closed it and walked calmly to the back of the jail and opened the bolt on the back door. She looked out cautiously, then walked into the alley and back to the rear door of the Silver Dollar Saloon.

She went in and slipped in to the small room the owner let her use while she sang there. It held a cot where she could rest between her performances.

She put her reticule under the cot and lay down. A soft smile crept over her face. She would have no trouble sleeping now.

"Good night, dearest Robert," she said softly.

That night at eleven, Lila Pemberthy gave the best performance of her career. She sang two encores and told the cheering group that she could stay only two more days in Dodge, then she had to return to St. Louis for an engagement in the opera house. She invited all of them to come see her the next two nights.

Lila left the saloon looking everywhere, but she could not find that nice Mr. Spur McCoy. She wondered what he was up to tonight.

16

Spur had rushed to the site of the fire as soon as he saw the flames and heard the fire bell which boomed out three times. He had soon learned in the West that it was the duty of every able bodied man to assist in a fire call.

Often it was only a bucket brigade but every man helped. Spur got there in time to see the roof cave in. It had been a small one story house, but the fire must have burned half of it out before anyone saw the flames break through to the outside.

By that time all they could do was wet down the shingle roof of a house fifty feet away, and watch down wind for any sparks that might catch something else on fire.

Spur found out that no one had been living in the house. The woman who lived closest said she thought she had seen a figure come out of the place a half hour before she saw the fire, but she couldn't be sure.

If no one lived there, how could a fire start? Soon the theory surfaced that a drifter must have been there, maybe started a fire by a lighted cigarette. No one had seen smoke coming from the chimney.

The head of the Dodge City Volunteer Firemen was Ivan Lane, who ran the hardware. He had the situation well in hand. He used a short bucket brigade of twenty men to pass buckets of water from the closest pump and had managed to wet down the outside walls and pushed one into the fire after it weakened.

Spur left it up to him and walked back toward the sheriff's office with a deputy and Galloway.

"Somebody told me about the fire and I rushed right down here," Deputy Galloway said. "We don't have a fire too often. I guess it's sort of a social affair. My dad used to say you saw friends you never saw anywhere else except at a fire or a funeral."

"Who else is on duty tonight with you?" Spur asked.

"Who else? Just me and the sheriff sleeping in the jail. Hell, we're down to two deputies now with . . ." Deputy Galloway looked in surprise as Spur began to run. The deputy caught up with him.

"You left the sheriff *alone in the jail!*" Spur growled at him. "Don't you have any sense at all?"

"You mean someone might try to . . . to hurt the sheriff, right there in the jail?"

"Damn right that's what I mean! How long you been gone from the jail?"

"Fifteen, maybe twenty minutes. At the most twenty-five." The deputy had to rush to keep up with Spur.

"How long would it take to fire two .45 rounds?" Spur asked and ran faster as he rounded the corner and sprinted for the front of the sheriff's office and jail six doors down.

Inside the office it all looked normal.

Spur breathed a sigh of relief. Then he tried the door into the jail cells.

"This usually locked?" Spur asked.

"Not when I've been here," Deputy Galloway said. "I think it has a bolt or a bar inside."

"The back door!" Spur bellowed. They both ran out the front and down to the end of the block and raced through the alley to where the jail backed up to the service drive.

The back door was closed. It just might be all right, Spur hoped as he reached for the doorknob. There was no lock on the outside. He turned the knob and pulled the door open. One lamp near the front through a storage room and past the four cells gave off a faint light.

Spur ran to it and turned up the wick. He looked in the first cell where he could see the double mattress the sheriff always used.

"Damnit, no!" Spur bellowed with such hurt and pain that the deputy sheriff rushed forward. Spur bolted into the cell. He saw the sheriff lying on the mattress as if he were asleep. But etched on his body were the familiar powder burns and Spur knew there was no need to check for signs of life. Somebody had murdered the sheriff in his own jail!

"The fire!" Spur bellowed. "The damn fire was a diversion to draw you out of here!" Spur yelled at the deputy. "Whoever it was knew the sheriff was in here, and got rid of you the easy way. Otherwise you'd be dead right now, too."

He opened the bolt on the door into the sheriff's office, went through the door and slumped in a chair. Spur bounced to his feet a minute later.

"You're in charge here now, Galloway. Close that back door to the cells and lock it, then close this one and don't tell anybody about this until morning and I give you the word. I'm a government lawman, with the Secret Service. I'm in town to try to find out who has been killing all the lawmen in Kansas. You've got to help me. Do you understand?"

Galloway sat down in a chair and nodded. "Damn, why did I run out to the fire?"

"It's what you would normally do. It's done now and that we can't change. Help me find out who did it. You just stay here, and don't tell anyone what happened. Do you understand?"

"Yes, sir."

Spur trotted back to the fire. Most of the flames were out. He talked to the head volunteer fire chief, Ivan Lane.

"Notice anything funny about the fire?" Spur asked.

Lane was a square set man, no nonsense, honest as a twenty dollar gold piece. He shook his head.

"Can't right say. Why?"

"I think it was deliberately set. You ever smelled a coal oil set fire?"

"Yep. Smell never does burn out."

"Get your nose warmed up, let's see what we can smell around the edges."

It took them half an hour as the bucket men kept throwing water on the dying fire. Then on the far side, Lane yelled at Spur.

When Spur went around to where Lane was, he had both hands on his hips. "Damn, McCoy, I think we've got something. Not very strong, like maybe less than a gallon, quart maybe. But it's there. Coal oil for damned sure. The smell don't go away."

"Maybe there was a lamp inside," Spur said.

"Not so. Woman next door said a family moved out and took what they could. They showed her through to see if she wanted anything left. She said there wasn't a lamp or a stove or anything like that left to start a fire."

"Show me," Spur said.

They went as close as they could to the still hot skeleton of one wall and sniffed. Spur put his head between the framing and sniffed some more.

"Yes, it's there. You sell coal oil at your store?"

"Of course. Pump it out of a barrel off the back dock. Been doing that for fifteen years."

"You sell any today to someone who might not ordinarily use it?"

Lane thought a minute. "Nope. Sold a gallon to a saloon owner, and another gallon to Mrs. Burdock. Known her for thirty years. She buys a gallon about twice a year for her lamp. She is a thrifty person."

"The barrel is outside your store in back. So someone could pump themselves a gallon or a quart after hours and you'd never know it?"

"Could happen. Don't think it did. I leave the pump in a certain position. It was that way when I used it this morning and when I left tonight."

"Thanks, Mr. Lane. I'm grasping at straws in the tornado here. Don't mention this to anyone else, all right?"

Spur walked rapidly back to the jail.

Deputy Galloway was unravelling like a half knit sweater. He shook and wouldn't look Spur in the eye.

"Galloway, go home. Get out of here and forget what happened and go to sleep. Come in tomorrow when you feel like it. We'll simply close up the jail tonight. When does the other deputy come on board?"

"Eight in the morning."

"Fine. Get out of here."

Galloway looked at the closed door leading to the cells. He shuddered then bolted for the front door. He had forgotten to take his six-gun with him.

Spur let him go. He went in and searched the cell around the body. He spent an hour doing it, going over every inch of the place.

There was nothing there, only a dead body with the usual powder burns on the clothing and flesh. Spur sat on the mattress beside the bed.

"Who?" he said, as if fully expecting the sheriff to answer him. Then he remembered that Frank Johnson said he would try to tell Spur who it was who had killed him if at all possible. He looked over everything again.

Spur studied the body more closely. How could Frank have left a message? By writing something! How could he do that? There was no paper or pencil there. With blood!

Spur checked Frank's clothes in detail. He had seen blood on his shirt. Only a flicker of blood showed on his chest over his heart. Below at his belly there was a much larger red stain.

He had been belly shot first, and bled for several minutes. McCoy checked every inch of Frank's shirt front, then his pants. McCoy's eyes widened. On Frank's right leg he saw what looked like letters. He moved so he could see it from Frank's viewpoint and looked again. There was a strong "L" written in blood, what looked like another letter and then what could be a "B."

They could be the initials of someone's name. L.B. meant nothing to him. L.D. produced little as well. Lane, Ivan Lane was the fire chief. He hardly seemed like a suspect. Spur could think of Larry, Lester, Lewis or Lawrence. He blew out the lamp and closed the door into the cells. He turned out all but one lamp, which he set low in the office, and went out the front door, making sure the night lock clicked into place behind him.

It was too much for him to batter through tonight. What he needed was a good night's sleep and a fresh start in the morning. He had to figure it out right here. There was a good chance that the sheriff knew his killer and he had tried to tell him. The man had dipped his finger in his own belly wound for blood to write down the letters! He must have been positive of the name of the killer.

At the hotel, Spur went up the steps and down to his room where he checked his door silently. Unlocked. He drew his gun, even though he guessed who was inside.

Spur edged the door open and saw the light, turned low, then the brown head of hair on his pillow and the shapely form of his favorite songbird sleeping naked on his bed. He slid into the room, locked the door and slipped out of his pants and shirt. Gently Spur edged over one of Lila's legs so he could lay beside her.

As soon as he stretched out, she rolled over on top of him and kissed his lips. Then leaning up she watched him, her eyes bright.

"So you thought you could sneak in on me and take advantage of me while I was sleeping? No such luck." She kissed him again. "Why didn't you tell me you were with the United States Secret Service and that you were trying to find the man who has been killing all of those lawmen? I found your orders. You are a naughty boy for lying to me."

Spur sat up and turned the wick higher in the lamp. The room filled with light.

"So spank me or something for being naughty," he said. "You were a bad girl yourself."

She frowned, looked at him quickly. "Whatever do you mean by that, Secret Service Agent Spur McCoy?"

"You changed your name, and you don't tell all these Yankees that you're from New Orleans."

The tenseness went out of her face and she relaxed. Lila giggled, then leaned over and kissed him.

"Okay, we're even. I don't care if you're a detective or a lawman or a butcher or saddlemaker. I'm falling in love with you and if you're not careful you're going to wind up getting married. There, I said it."

He held up his hand. "There is always that delicious problem to worry about." He stared at her more serious now. "You know that I hid my orders and my credentials. You had to dig pretty deep in my gear to find them. Why was it so important that you find out for sure what I do?"

She caught one of his hands and used it to cover a breast.

"I was just curious. You seem to be at the sheriff's office a lot. And I've not seen you talking with any local landowners. Then that man said you were a lawmen. I just kind of figured he'd know what he was talking about before he risked his life in a gun fight against you. It made me more curious."

"What if I get mad and throw you out in the hall all bare assed the way you are?"

"I'd start knocking on doors until I found some lonesome man who would take care of me."

Spur had to grin. It was exactly what she would do. He let the frown fall away.

"All right. I'm not angry with you any more, but I've got another problem. Sheriff Johnson was murdered tonight. I have to find out who did it before the guy gets out of town."

"You'll check the stage and the livery stable."

"Already covered. I've got to play detective and do it damn good and damn fast."

"Let me help!"

"No, that could put you in danger. This is my job and I have to do it. Now, you mentioned something about marriage. Let's pretend that we're married."

"Oh, yes, that's what I've been waiting for!"

"Good." Spur snuggled down in the pillow without touching her.

"Hey, we're married, let's see how many times we can make love tonight," she cooed.

"Not tonight, Lila, I told you that I have a hard day at work tomorrow."

She swung a pillow and hit him in the face. He swung one back and for five minutes they had a pillow fight that left them both gasping and laughing and in each other's arms.

The kiss was long and flaming and when it ended he caught her breasts and petted them tenderly.

"But just once. I really do have a lot of work to do tomorrow."

"Whatever you say, lover, whatever you say."

He pushed her on her back and suckled at her mounds. She stroked his hair and found his crotch and petted him.

"Maybe we could make it three times?" she asked.

"Questions, always questions." He rolled over hugging her so she stayed on top and kept licking her breasts.

"Standing up," she said.

"What?"

"Make love to me standing up! I've never been able to. Show me how!"

"This is not a classroom."

"More the pity. Come on, let's fuck standing up!"

She bounced out of bed and grabbed his hand pulling him with her. Spur groaned and followed. He pushed her against the wall.

"Now jump up and put your legs around me and lock them together in back."

"You're joshing me."

"No, not at all, try it."

She did and leaned her back against the wall.

Lila giggled. "This is starting to feel strange."

"It gets better." He loosened her legs a little, holding her bare bottom, then lifted her and bent backwards until his shaft matched her slot and he edged forward.

Lila shrieked in surprise and delight.

"My God! We can do it!"

Spur drove into her until they were firmly locked together pelvic bone to pelvic bone. Her legs were locked behind him and she leaned against the wall with her arms fast around his neck.

"Of course, it helps if one or the other of us has good balance."

She ignored his jibe and leaned close to his ear. "That feels so wonderful! I don't know how you did it, but please do it now, fuck me so hard I'll never forget this time tonight!"

Spur growled at her, kissed her soft lips, then her nose and thrust, came almost out and jammed into her again with such sudden force that she gasped and flattened against the wall.

"Jesus!" she breathed.

Spur made the same slow withdrawal and then the pile driver thrust again and again, gradually increasing the tempo. After five deep penetrations she billowed into a climax that sent her into spasms of unending gasping and moaning and soft little kitten noises deep in her throat.

Her hips got into the act, punching hard against his and rotating as her vaginal muscles gripped him in a shattering series of motions that pushed him almost over the edge. He slowed his stroke and stayed with her, then when she at last tapered off and hugged him so tight he thought he would collapse, he picked up the tempo.

"Yes! Yes! Yes! Yes!" Lila crooned. "Do it again, again. I love it this way. Promise me we can always fuck this way, just forever and forever!"

Then he couldn't respond. He was over the edge, roaring and racing down with an avalanche of power and drive and surging thrusts that jolted his hips harder and harder until he vaporized and the stars and the moon went sliding past him as he shot into the space around them and circled the sun and came back with one final thrust of his hips hard against her.

Slowly he sagged toward the floor. First his knees bent and she slid down a foot. Then another foot and he went down on his knees. She unhooked her legs from behind him and he leaned backwards, then went flat on the floor, still mated with her, and she held on as if he was a lifeline.

He couldn't talk for a moment. She sighed and curled on top of him, holding him deep inside of her. At last he stirred and his eyes opened and he stared up at her.

She grinned, kissed his nose, her eyes sparkling with an unusual fire.

"You have any more surprises like that one, ex-cowboy now boy detective and Secret Service Agent?"

"Dozens, but I can only show you one a month. There have to be a few surprises down the line."

"You mean we have a 'down the line' to consider?" she asked looking at him quickly.

"Who knows. You might lose your voice tomorrow and I'd have to dump you."

She hit him in the side with her fist.

"Well, you might get called to Washington to take over the agency."

"Not a chance, there are six good men ahead of me."

"My tonsils are strong and my voice smooth. I'll still be singing this well in twenty years."

"Will you be making love this well?"

She smiled at him. "Why don't you hang around in my bed and see for yourself?"

"Always a chance," he said half seriously. Suddenly he grabbed her around the waist and lifted her body straight up off him and they slipped apart.

"Wine?" she asked.

"It's in your room. Want me to run up there bare assed and bring it back?"

She shook her head. "I'd rather have your bare ass in my bed."

They got off the floor and back in bed. He kissed her softly, then pushed her away.

"I wasn't kidding about one time only. I do have a damned tough job tomorrow, and I want to be ready for it."

"Oh, damn! Who can tell what's going to happen tomorrow? Maybe . . ." she stopped. "If I can't go to sleep, I might start to seduce you in your sleep."

"Fair enough," Spur said. He put one arm under the pillow under his head and put his other hand on his chest. It was his sleep position. In two minutes he was sleeping soundly.

Lila lay there for a while, then slid out of bed silently and lifted the big, heavy .45 six-gun from his holster. She held it for a minute. She carried it over to the bed and aimed the weapon at Spur's naked belly. She cocked the hammer back on a live round, then hesitated. Lila grinned as she remembered the marvelous way they had just made love and slid the big gun back in the holster where it hung over the wooden backed chair.

Maybe tomorrow they could make love again. What difference would another day make? She moved back into bed gently so she wouldn't wake him, reached over and put her hand over his genitals and soon drifted off to sleep.

Sometime during the night, Spur had a dream. He was running down a tunnel but couldn't see the end. Someone chased him with a dog on a leash that had a foaming mouth and huge teeth. The dog almost caught him and he turned and tried to fire his .45 at the dog, but a beautiful girl kept getting in the way and he never could fire.

He sat up, sweat wet on his forehead. Now what the hell was that all about? It had seemed so real. McCoy turned over, trying not to think about the dream. Tomorrow was going to be some of the toughest work he had ever done. He had to wrap up this case tomorrow, or he might never solve it!

"Sorry. I tried every trick I knew to protect him. I was simply outgunned." Spur went through the door into the cells and looked down at Frank. He concentrated on the letters crudely sketched on Frank's dark pants. Spur walked out to the office and brought back a pad of paper and a pencil. He copied down the writing as closely as he could.

It still came out a strong "L" and then from there on he wasn't sure. Best he could make out of it was a "D" or maybe an "E". The hand that had printed the letter in blood was shaky by that time. Frank had probably done it without looking down. Damn!

Deputy Oberlin came to the door and looked in.

"Christ, right in his bed! Who in hell . . . ?"

"That's what I'm going to find out, right now. How many men do you know who have the first initials of 'L' and either 'D' or 'E' for the last name? Make a list of them, right now. Your only job."

Spur turned back to the body. Again he went over the cell. There was no clue there, nothing had been dropped, no shell casing, no scrap of cloth or dropped cigarette or anything. He went out, closed the cell block door and headed to the street.

"I'm going to get the undertaker. His job now."

A half hour later the body had been taken out the back way and Spur looked over a list of names the deputy had made. There were only eight. Six of them were long time residents who hadn't been out of the county in years. The last two were possible, but one was a new Baptist preacher and the other one was the new owner of the struggling newspaper.

"Far as I know both those last two guys been in town the last few weeks. Both are real busy."

Nowhere, the initials had led him exactly nowhere. He stared down at the printing that he had copied from Frank's pants leg. What else could he make from it? Spur stared at the paper so long his vision blurred. He went out and walked the street, winding up at the undertaker. He walked inside.

The man was in back with the body. Spur went through the door and saw the man lifting something from Frank's belly wound. The undertaker turned and smiled.

"By damn, I found it!"

His name was Oliver. Spur didn't know if it was first or last or only. He held up something in bloody tweezers.

"Bullet that hurt him bad," Oliver said. "We used to call this a punishment round. Hurts like hell and will kill a man eventually, but makes him suffer for an hour to three hours. The worst kind of horrendous pain any human ever can stand."

Oliver wiped the lead slug off on a cloth, then washed it in a basin of water and dried it.

"I kept wondering why a belly shot with a big slug wouldn't go right through the body and out the back somewhere. Had a hunch, but now I got your answer. See this little cupping on the back of the slug?"

Spur looked closer and saw it. "Yeah."

Oliver took a .45 round off the table and with two pair of pliers carefully twisted the slug away from the copper casing. He turned it around so Spur could look at it.

"Same kind of cupping, right."

"True. What does that prove?"

Oliver tossed Spur another round from the table. It also was a .45 cartridge.

"That's a special load .45 round made especially for a weapon called the Aldrich. Actually a minor change in the standard derringer, but enough so it took a slightly shorter cartridge. They cupped the slug so they could get a little more powder in the charge. But it never was as powerful as the standard .45 round."

"A derringer? You're telling me that Frank Johnson was killed by a derringer slug?"

"Not sure. But this belly shot sure was. If I could find the other slug in one chunk it might prove it. But what killer is going to gut shoot his victim, then change guns for the heart shot?"

"A derringer. Now it makes sense. In a couple others I wondered why a muzzle blast like that wouldn't go right through a man and exit. They all were the same, and all derringer shots!" Spur leaned back against the wall. "This sets it up in a whole new light. It doesn't have to be a crazy outlaw who just got out of prison."

"Could be anybody," Oliver said. "Hell, I know a couple of women who carry little derringers for protection."

"A woman?" Spur asked himself. "Oh, my God!" Suddenly things tumbled into place, like the last few pieces of a giant jigsaw puzzle.

A woman. What person had been in the last two or three towns where lawmen were killed? What person had the opportunity to do the killings late at night? He thought of the initials again and took out the folded piece of paper from his pocket. What person he knew had a name that began with an "L"? He looked at the last wiggly lines he had copied. Damn! the last initial could have been not a "D" or an "E" but a "P."

Lila Pemberthy!

He shook his head and looked at the piece of paper again. There was no doubt, the first initial was plain, and the last one could be a "P." She had the opportunity. He had been with her at the last two towns!

"Don't tell anybody what you've found, Oliver. We might need this kind of evidence for a trial. I've got an idea who the killer is. Don't tell a soul!"

Spur walked quickly out of the death room and straight to the hotel. Lila was not in his room. He went up to her room and knocked. There was no response. She could be sleeping or having breakfast.

Spur used his pocket knife and pushed back the sliding bolt on the lock and slipped the door open. He swung it wide and stepped inside. She wasn't there. The bed was a mess and clothes were strewn everywhere. On the bed sat her large reticule. She had two or three of them.

Spur picked it up and noticed that it was heavy. He opened it and looked inside. The first thing he found was a derringer. He sniffed the barrels. It had been fired recently, he could still smell the cordite. Slowly he turned the weapon over and saw on the side the fancy scrolled name, "Aldrich."

He dropped down on the edge of the bed. He had never heard of the Aldrich. There might not be more than a hundred of them made. The coincidence was too great.

He smelled something. The weapon had another

odor on it but he couldn't place it. He opened the reticule again and lifted it to his nose.

The smell was unmistakable. Coal oil. A quart jar would fit neatly into the reticule. Just enough to get a house fire going so hot and fast burning that a local fire brigade couldn't put it out, and form the perfect diversion for a murder.

Spur put the reticule down and stared at the little gun. The shell casings were probably still in place. It was almost enough to charge her with murder, but not quite. All circumstantial. A jury liked to have an eye witness or a confession, or a lot more proof than he had.

"Good morning."

Spur looked up and saw Lila standing in the doorway. He hadn't thought to close it. "I see you've found my protection. A girl shouldn't be walking around a wild Western town like Dodge at night without some powerful personal protection."

Spur sighed. She was cool, cold, almost detached. She could do it. She had done it!

"This derringer isn't for protection, Lila, it's a murder weapon."

"Whatever do you mean?" She closed the door but stayed there leaning against it as she began to unbutton her dress top.

"Lila, why did you kill Sheriff Johnson?"

Her face flushed, her eyes blazed. "Because he killed my Robert!" The words screamed at him, rolling out of her mouth with ten years of pain and torment and anger and hatred. "Killed Robert and my Robert didn't do a thing to him. Kicked him in the head . . ." Her words had moderated, become normal speech tone, then faded to a whisper at the end.

She blinked and her face returned to its normal expression.

"Whatever do you mean the sheriff is dead?"

"This gun killed him, Lila, and I can prove it. It's a special weapon, not many were made. Takes a different kind of .45 round you can get only on order from the factory. And in your reticule are some spots of coal oil where the jar leaked. You used the coal oil to start the first last night, just before you slipped in and shot the sheriff to death."

"I don't understand . . ." The words trailed off, then her face changed, her eyes blazed and her hand darted into her reticule that hung from her wrist.

"See, Mr. Lawman. I have another derringer. They aren't so rare, I have two. And this one is loaded with two rounds. Oh, yes, I can use it. And keep your hand away from your weapon. I saw you kick my Robert to death. *I saw you!* Right there in the street! Half the town saw but they wouldn't lift a finger to help. Afraid of you. Everyone afraid!

"My Robert stood up to you and you called him a Texas Rebel bastard and you kicked him again. My Robert wasn't real strong. He was a prisoner during the war and he never was well after that. So you kicked him in the head! But that's the last good man you're ever gonna kill! You bastard!"

She rushed toward him. Spur knew the little derringers with its two-inch barrel was useless at more than two or three feet. He dove off the bed to the left as he heard the shot fire. It missed. He threw the derringer he held at her, saw her swing the weapon toward him again and fire as he hit the floor and rolled.

He felt the slug slam into the floor an inch from his side and wood splinters stabbed into his flesh. He rolled, came to his feet and caught Lila as she stumbled and fell on the bed. She still held the derringer.

She swept brown hair back out of her eyes and glared at him.

"Mr. Lawman, you done kicked my husband to death, and because of that I am going to have to kill you."

She put the still smoking derringer to Spur's belly and pulled the trigger. The firing pin fell on the spent round.

Her eyes were bright. "Now I'm going to remind you what you did to me and to my Robert.

"You slammed your gun down on his head and Robert fell into the dust. Poor Robert got to his knees, then struggled to stand. He was weaving, working hard just to stand up. But he stared hard at you, sheriff.

"He said, 'Suh, ah don't apologize to white trash like you!'

"Then you went crazy. Your big fist lashed out, hit poor Robert's chin and snapped his head back. He fell in the dirt in front of the hardware store. You bellowed something bout him being a Rebel. 'My kid brother got shot to death by bastards just like you in the war.' Then you kicked Robert in the side with your heavy boot. Robert curled in a ball.

"You dragged him to his feet, held his shirt front and pounded your fists into Robert's face again and again. Robert's nose spurted blood. You laughed. You closed one of his eyes and tore his ear. Robert's head flipped from side to side each time you hit him.

"I kept yelling at you to stop. Yelling for somebody to help us. But nobody came. A man and a woman on the boardwalk hurried past. A cowboy walking his horse down the street went to the far side and rode by quickly."

Spur held her as she screeched and roared at him. He sat there holding her from hitting him or hurting herself. She kept talking for five minutes. Telling him the story of how her Robert had been brutally killed by a Kansas sheriff in a street.

He had the idea that she gut shot her victims, made them listen to the story, then used the second round in the little gun to shoot them dead through the heart when they were helpless and half dead already.

Lila finished her story. She lifted her derringer and put it over Spur's heart, then she pulled the trigger. Again the firing pin struck a spent round.

She sat up then, put the derringer in her reticule and straightened her dress.

Lila Pemberthy looked at Spur and smiled.

"Hey, what are you doing in my bedroom? I didn't expect to see you until later today. You told me last night you had a lot of work to do."

She put her arms around his neck and kissed him tenderly, slowly, deliciously. Spur simply could not respond. He took her arms away.

"I have someone I want you to meet," he said.

She pushed against him, her breasts hard against his chest.

"We must have time for just once before we go. Please? You kind of promised last night."

Spur half relented. She was going to be in an institution somewhere for a long, long time.

"Maybe just one time." She grinned and straddled him, then moved to his right side and before he could react, she jerked his Colt .45 from the holster and tried to back away. He swept his heavy boot at her ankles, hitting them, tripping her. He saw her cocking the hammer as she fell. He dove on top of her, smashing her small body to the floor. Almost at the same instant the .45 roared.

Her eyes went wide and Lila gasped, then shuddered.

"Oh, God!" she said. "Oh, God, I shot myself!"

He rolled her over gently. Both her hands held her flat belly where a crimson stain already showed. The Colt lay to one side. Spur shoved it across the floor.

Somebody knocked on the door.

"Come in!" Spur shouted. A cowboy looked in.

"Thought I heard a shot . . . My God!"

"Run and get the doctor!" Spur bellowed.

The cowboy raced away and Spur could hear him tromping down the steps.

Lila looked up at him through the pain and the waves of nausea.

"Spur McCoy?"

"Yes, Lila. I'm right here." He held her head in his lap, and now bent and kissed her cheek.

"Did I tell you I'm going to Chicago next? I've got a job singing there at an opera house and the manager said they sometimes had a thousand people in the audience!" She coughed and blood tinged her lips.

"He said I could stay there two or three weeks. Isn't that great?"

"Yes. Robert would have been proud of you."

She frowned. "Robert? I don't know any Robert." Her face changed then and she bleated in pain and terror. "Spur, I hurt myself bad. I don't know even why I had a gun. I don't like guns. Why did I do that, Spur?"

"An accident, Lila. Just an accident. Nobody's to blame. I'll tell the deputy sheriff just what happened."

"Is a doctor coming?" She screamed then, a cry of pain and anger and fear, a wail of anguish that she had heard before from the string of gut shot lawmen she had watched die.

"It hurts so bad!"

"The doctor is coming, he'll help you get well."

Slowly she shook her head. She lifted her right hand. The whole hand dripped with blood.

"No. I understand how badly hurt I am. I'm . . . I'm going to be dead in less than an hour."

"You'll find Robert again," Spur said.

For a moment her face worked, then she smiled. "Yes, Robert. My first love, my husband. I was so young, only seventeen, but he was a war hero and so good to me. He defended me to the very last. Somewhere in Kansas he died. A terrible sheriff kicked him when he went down. And . . . and Robert never woke up." She sobbed.

The pain charged through her slender body again and she cried out in terror.

"I don't want to die!"

Three people came to the open door and looked in. Spur waved them away. The doctor hurried in and knelt beside her. He frowned when he saw the wound. He took her hand away and put a pad of cloth on her wound and pressed it tightly.

He shook his head at Spur when Lila couldn't see him.

"You just rest easy now, Miss. I've got something that will make you feel much better."

"No. Never feel better again. I understand, Doc. Go to somebody you can help. Not even laudanum would have time to make me feel better. Go on."

The doctor stood, then nodded. "You're a brave lady," he said and went out the door closing it behind him.

"Not brave, terrified!" she said.

"You'll see Robert again."

"Robert? I told you before, I don't know any Robert. I've never been religious. Dead is dead. I've never seen anybody come back to life. No proof there is anything more than what we have right here on the good earth. I tried to make it a happier place for those I sang for."

"You did that, Lila. You certainly did."

She gasped, closed her eyes as pain distorted her pretty face. In a moment it was over and she relaxed.

"Spur McCoy, kiss me."

He leaned down and pressed his lips to hers. When he lifted away he heard a long gush of air from her lungs. The lady avenger with the deadly derringer was dead.

Two days later Spur had completed all of his reports, filed all the proper papers with the county, and had his ticket on the morning stage east. He had named Lila as the sheriff's killer, told the whole story, and paid for her burial. Then he sent a long telegram to Washington giving the story in detail and closing out the deaths of the Kansas lawmen. That case was at last ended.

He was heading back to St. Louis. It had been more than six months since he had checked into his "office" there. He figured it was about time that he found out what the place looked like.

General Wilton Halleck, his boss in Washington and the second in command of the Secret Service Agency, had indicated there was a case coming up that would be bigger and wilder and more dangerous than anything he had ever tackled. The general would come to St. Louis in person to give Spur the assignment. He was to be well rested and ready before the general arrived.

Spur looked at the calendar on the wall. It was June 4. In three days he would be in St. Louis. The General was arriving on June 13. He would try his damnedest to be rested and ready by then. Curiousity billowed in him. He would just have to wait and see what this giant of an assignment was.

LARAMIE LOVERS

1

The snarling, deadly sound of the heavy rifle shot blasted into Spur McCoy's consciousness at almost the same fraction of a second that a whispering lead bullet ripped through the warm Wyoming air not a foot from his head.

Spur dove off his roan gelding, hit the hard ground on his hands and left shoulder, and rolled behind a boulder big enough to protect him for the moment. His horse pranced a few nervous steps away, then stopped to nibble on some early spring grass.

McCoy huddled behind the rock waiting for the attack to continue. He had no idea who was gunning for him. He had arrived in Laramie late the night before on the Southern Pacific train, found a room at the little village's only hotel and dropped onto the hard bed exhausted.

This morning he had rented the roan for a look-around the area before he settled down to dig into the reason he came to Laramie.

Now the priorities had changed. Number one now was staying alive.

A voice came from a scattering of higher rocks to his left. "What the hell you doing riding in here, stranger?"

"He's trying to get hisself kilt, that's what he's doing!" a second, younger voice brayed with an answer.

"Naw, he's just plain shit dumb, that's all. Bet I can wing him 'fore he runs ten yards." It was a third voice that sounded heavier, older.

Spur had only his pistol. He had borrowed a Spencer rifle that morning from the livery man, not really expecting to need one so quickly. Now the repeating weapon nestled in the saddle boot on the horse five yards away.

Spur McCoy was six-two and in fighting trim at a hundred and ninety-five pounds of solid muscle and bone. He was thirty-two years old, top agent for the U.S. Government's Secret Service, and responsible for all the states and territories west of the Mississippi river.

"Hell, he ain't gonna try to run!" a new voice called from the same general area.

"Bet I can encourage him," the younger voice shrilled. A rifle shot slammed into the silence of the Wyoming high prairie. The round caught the roan in the head and she went down with a scream of protest. The beast rolled half over, then shrilled a scream again and died.

"We coulda sold that animal, you bastard!" a voice screeched.

"Don't fret about it, Blade. You get the saddle."

Blade, Spur would remember the name. He lay there trying to figure it out. Four or five men in good positions. Whoever fired at him the first time had missed on purpose. Nobody toting a rifle in Wyoming would miss at thirty yards unless he wanted to.

Why? Spur gave up trying to figure it out. The big question was how could he get out of here without a dozen holes in his hide? In front there was no chance. Behind him was another boulder, then a few more. He might make it to the rim of broad-leafed cottonwood in the low spot. Once there he could at least defend himself. With a pistol?

First the rifle. The roan had rolled toward him. That would help a yard or two. When she went down the Spencer had fallen out of the boot and slid toward him. It was still ten feet away. He made up his mind at once. Surprise.

Spur bunched his powerful legs under him, then in one swift move he surged away from the rock in a bent-over position, took three strides, grabbed the Spencer and dove for the bulk of the roan for protection.

Two rifle rounds needled through the air around him as he dove. One more slapped into the dead body of the saddle horse. Spur was untouched so far. Now all he had to do was get back.

He levered a round into the Spencer, a dandy 7-shot repeating rifle that had been his favorite for years. He peered over the horse a second, then dropped down. Best spot for a bushwhacking was the rocks dead ahead. He'd give them some return fire.

Spur pushed the Spencer muzzle over the roan and cranked off a round, then surged to his feet, fired again, dove and rolled toward the rock.

A rifle round slammed into the heel of his boot and tore the heavy leather buildup half way off. Two more shots missed. Then he was behind his rock again.

He studied the enemy around the far end of the boulder. He had been lucky so far. Down there were three notches which formed perfect firing spots. He bent around the rock and pounded two shots into the slots of the rock, heard a shouted curse, then he pulled back.

A dozen rifle rounds shattered on the granite boulder. Spur grinned. He'd made them mad. As soon as the surge of firing was over, he judged the distance to the next safe cover. Twelve, maybe fifteen feet. Four good running steps—if he had time and was lucky.

He had no choice. To stay where he was would invite circling by one or two of the bushwhackers. They would have an open shot and for him it would be sudden death.

Spur fired once more at the enemy, mindful of his ammunition supply. As he often did, he had shaken out twenty rounds for the Spencer from the box he got from the livery and put them in his jacket pocket. Still, that was damn few.

He jolted away from the rock without thinking about it. Spur darted one way, then cut back and dove for the safety of the next boulder big enough for cover. He felt the slug tear into his upper leg but before it hurt, he was behind the rock and safe.

He pulled up his left leg and saw the blood. There were two holes in his jeans. The round had slashed through two inches of his leg, missing the bone. He'd have to care for it later. He could hear the men behind the rocks talking. Now and then a round came his way to keep him honest.

From here his route to the trees was easier. The next rock was only six feet away, then he had cover the rest of the way. Without giving them a lot of time to plan anything, he jumped to the cover of the next bigger rock. A round hit the granite but too late to find any flesh.

From there Spur bent over and ran into the screening trees. The cottonwood was sturdy and big, gaining its life's water from the now dry creek that must run full in spring thaw.

Spur was about five miles north of town. He could use a horse but it was't necessary. He had more need to return some angry lead against the bushwhackers. Also, he wanted to know who they were and why they attacked a stranger without warning.

McCoy had come to Laramie to talk to the sheriff about a problem he had with a big rancher who had vanished two months ago. That job would have to wait.

It was still morning, the sun was warm, but not overly hot. He worked forward, downstream on the dry creek bed. He kept out of sight of the rocks where the shooters were. Spur had learned to move through brush from the Indians. He never took a step without making sure his weight would not break a dry stick or rustle a leaf.

Fifty feet down the stream bed he came to a larger broad leafed cottonwood. By standing on the first low crotch he could see the back side of the rocks that were his objective. Two men remained there, rifles over the top, waiting.

Spur wanted to gun down the two men, but he knew he couldn't, even if they had shot at him first. He leveled the Spencer in on the pair. First he had reloaded the tube so he had eight shots, seven in the tube and one in the chamber. Then he called, knowing his voice would distort through the trees and make his location hard to figure.

"Why did you men shoot at me?"

The two on the rocks looked around. Before he could react three rifles from another location fired toward him. They had no target but figured on the tree. One round came close, chipping wood beside him.

The two men he could see pointed at him and turned. Spur fired. The first man screamed and slammed backwards off the rock.

The second man scurried behind the rock.

"Bastard!" he bellowed. "You done kilt poor old Ned! Now you get it for certain. We was just funnin' with you. Now we show you what Circle S riders do to trespassers and bastards who gun down our riders!"

Spur dropped off the crotch and crouched behind the tree. The Circle S. At least he knew who they were. Someone crashed brush behind and to his left. Spur froze against the tree knowing that a moving figure is easy to distinguish in brush. However, a target that remains motionless is ten times as hard to find. Like a pheasant that crouches down when threatened and will fly only when kicked out of the hiding spot.

The sound came again and he saw movement. Automatically, Spur lifted the Spencer and sent three rounds into the light brush where he saw the motion.

A scream, then cursing followed quickly. All was quiet for a few moments. Then a piercing bellow of pain.

"Come help me, you bastards! He done shot me bad. Gut shot me. Come get me out of here."

A voice came from the rocks again.

"Dreek, you know better'n that. Rules say every man for hisself. Rules say no prisoners. Hell, you remember that."

"Yeah, Dreek, you got yourself shot. You get back to the ranch. I ain't about to come under his gun. Who is that guy, anyway?"

"Fuckers! You can't leave me here! All I need is my horse. Bring me my horse, damn you!"

"The old wheel spins around and around, Dreek. Just wasn't your turn to win. We're getting out of here. Seems I remember asking you for some help about six months ago, over in Kansas. Remember, Dreek? Hell, you didn't even answer me."

A pistol fired four times. None of the rounds were aimed at Spur.

"Bastards! Fucking bastards!"

The small stretch of woods was quiet for a few

minutes. Then Spur heard leather squeak, and horses move away.

"Bastards!"

Spur moved up slowly on the man they called Dreek. He still had at least his pistol.

It took McCoy twenty minutes moving cautiously through the growth to get to the man. By then Dreek was so weak he couldn't hold up his gun. Spur sat down beside the bushwhacker, pushed away his six-gun and looked at the wound. One of the rifle rounds had hit Dreek in the gut and come out his back. He was bleeding to death inside and outside.

Dreek was about forty, with a beard. He wasn't a big man. He snorted when he saw Spur.

"You my damn executioner?"

"Looks like it. What was this all about?"

"You're on Circle S land. We was just having some sport with you."

"A strange kind of entertainment."

"Hell, it was all in fun, until you got that rifle and splattered some lead into Willy. He got damn mad."

"You men riders for the Circle S?"

"Oh, hell yes. We're riders." Dreek tried to laugh, but spit up blood. He shook his head. "Damn, not long now."

"Tell me about the Circle S. What happened out there?"

"Happened? Not much. Just a ranch. Gonna sell off the steers, get our payroll up again. Kind of slack for a while there. Especially in Sixty-Seven and Sixty-Eight."

Spur frowned. "I don't understand. What was bad about those two years?"

Dreek laughed softly. His color was bad, too much blood was draining from his veins.

"Hell, we all went our own ways. Then we got Cameron back. He told us he could make it like old times, the good times. Hell yes, he did, too. Last few years . . . great!"

Dreek coughed then. Blood spewed out of his mouth gushing over his shirt and pants in a red froth.

"Like old times? I don't understand. Are you talking about an outlaw band? I've never heard of a Cameron who's wanted."

"Damn right!" Dreek said. "Never will." He shook his head. "Nobody never will."

Dreek grinned at Spur, blood surged out of his mouth again and he fell back against the small tree never to take another breath.

Spur searched the man for some papers, but found only a pocket knife, a plug of chewing tobacco, and two double eagles in a small purse. He left it all there. His friends would come back for his body.

Spur took time out and checked his leg again. Most of the bleeding had stopped where the rifle round had lanced through the back of his left thigh. He pulled down his pants, cut the tail off the blue shirt and made an effective bandage with the shirt strips and his neckerchief. Then he pulled up his pants and started hunting a horse to ride.

Spur found Dreek's mount after a fifteen minute search. It was a big black, a fine animal and easy to identify. It even had a new looking Circle S brand on its left hip. The black munched on the shoots of grass and snorted when Spur took the reins.

"Easy, boy . . . easy does it. You'll be getting a new rider now. Just settle down."

Spur's easy way of talking and his confident tone calmed the big animal. McCoy had been good with animals since his first pet puppy in the New York town house. He hefted the Spencer rifle and lifted into the saddle.

It was western style, a little shorter than Spur liked but easy enough to sit. The ride back to town seemed shorter, but still he kept watching over his shoulder. There was no pursuit. He made up his mind about the big black well before he came to the livery.

He would turn the mount in. He would be found and recognized by men from the Circle S. At least that way Spur could isolate the killers who had come after him. It might be a place to start.

At the big barn on the edge of town, he turned the horse in, gave his name and said he'd ridden out that morning. There was a different wrangler on duty and he accepted the animal, then scowled.

"Don't never remember seeing a mount that good around this place. Old man Dowd must have spent some money."

Spur left the livery and went on down the street. As he walked he was aware of the pain in his left leg. He'd have to get it checked, but not before he talked to the sheriff.

Laramie couldn't be called a town yet. Three years ago there was nothing on the spot except an Overland stage swing station and what had once been a Pony Express stop back in 1862.

The railroad had changed all of that. When the mighty Union Pacific came blasting into the area, it brought with it a whole menagerie of camp followers, fast buck sharpies, prostitutes and gamblers.

The surveyors went through first and hardly ruffled the landscape. Then the engineers came to form up the grade and somewhere behind them were the track layers.

"Hell on Wheels" was what the railroad construction camps were often called. These mushrooming communities sprang up every few miles as the railroad moved along, ever westward. Often they died as soon as the rails moved ten miles away and a new site was picked up for the next tent city.

Spur could remember some of them; North Platte, Julesburg, Cheyenne, Laramie and Corinne. They began with a big tent that some enterprising merchant-gambler put up. The tents were stocked with the cheapest whiskey available, the best prostitutes they could wrangle into coming along, and cards and wheels of chance.

As many as four-hundred rust-eaters worked the railhead with the "perpetual train" that pushed a long flatcar to the very end of the tracks to make it easier for workers to get rails, tools, ties and use the rolling blacksmith shop.

The four hundred men lived in 85-foot long boxcars with bunks slung three or four high. They worked hard and played, gambled and whored just as hard. Most quickly lost their thirty-five dollars a month in wages before the tent stakes were firmly in place.

Spur had watched one of the rail head tent cities when it was roaring back in Sixty-Eight. There had been gamblers, saloonkeepers, pimps, whores, con men and every other shade of fast buck man in the West. The whores walked around the camp with derringers strapped to their waists. He'd heard they were deadly accurate with the close-in weapons.

The code of Western chivalry toward women prevented anyone from taking action against the prostitutes even when they robbed and shot up the men they serviced.

Now, almost three years after the tracks went through, Laramie was still here. It had not faded away with the camp followers. Fifteen or twenty frame buildings made up the business section of town. Maybe forty or forty-five small houses completed the settlement. Beef and the stock yards were almost the only reason that Laramie had survived.

It was a start. In another ten years Laramie would

be ten times as big . . . or would have faded into history.

Spur had dressed in worn jeans, an old blue shirt and a lightweight black vest when he had left on his ride that morning. He wanted to melt into the landscape as a cowboy.

Now he fit right in as he walked down the short main street. The sheriff's office was in the small frame building that boasted it was the court house for Albany county.

Somebody told him there were only four counties in all of Wyoming. That made it easier to get organized for territorial status. As the population grew, new counties would be carved out of the four.

Sheriff Stan Dryer looked up from his desk in back of a low railing that separated the outer section of the office from the inside.

"I'm hunting the sheriff," Spur said.

"Found him," Dryer said. "Business?"

"For damn sure, Sheriff. Can we talk private?"

Sheriff Dryer nodded and waved Spur into a small office to one side.

"Usually, I'm in here," Dryer said. He settled in a rocking chair behind a small desk and rubbed his chin that had a day's growth of stubble on it. At least half of the bristles were white.

Spur closed the door and sat in the chair across the inexpensive desk.

The sheriff held out his hand. "Name's Dryer, like it says on the sign." Spur took the hand.

"McCoy, Spur McCoy is my name." He took out his wallet, removed a tintype and unfolded a piece of paper stuck to the back of it.

"Sheriff, I'm a United States Federal Secret Service officer here on official business. That card grants me police powers in any of the states or territories, and instructs all law enforcement agencies to cooperate with me."

The sheriff took out a pair of spectacles, adjusted them on his nose and read the folded paper. He grunted.

"Never heard of no Secret Service before. But this sure looks like the genuine article." He handed the paper back. Spur folded it and pressed it against the tintype, then stuck a second thin metal picture to the back covering the identification.

"Sheriff Dryer, I want to keep my official capacity here a secret. I came in response to a message from the county clerk, I believe. Your name was mentioned."

"Yep. I told the clerk to write the letter. My hand ain't too steady since my fainting spell. Doc said it was a minor stroke. Anyway, it's all true, what Will told you in the letter. This big rancher's whole family and crew just vanished. Over night there was a new outfit running the place. Owner, boss, crew, the works."

"A big spread?"

"They claim about ten thousand acres, but must work over forty thousand with their stock. Out here property lines ain't what they are back East."

"The letter said something about a change of ownership being recorded by the county clerk." Spur said.

"Yep. That was first time anybody knew about the change. A gent by the name of Curt Cameron showed up with the grant deed signed over, and a bill of sale signed by the former owner. Receipt was for thirty-thousand dollars cash and a home in Illinois."

"Nobody in town saw the family or any of the crew after the sale?"

"Not a hide nor hair of them. The Circle S men used Laramie a lot while they was there. Can't fancy them just riding away without a by-your leave."

"Does seem odd. What did this Cameron say?"

"Some wild story about old man Shuntington getting called back to Missouri where his people lived to take over a family business. He had to sell quick and ride for Cheyenne to catch the train."

"But the train runs right through Laramie," Spur said, interrupting. "Why would he ride an extra fifty miles?"

"Exactly what the clerk asked this Cameron. He just shrugged, and said Shuntington was a crazy old coot who might do anything."

"How old was he?"

"Ollie Shuntington was about forty-five. His wife was a couple of years younger. They had two kids but both were away at some kind of college or finishing school."

"Foreman? He still there?"

"Not far as I can tell," Sheriff Dryer said. "Looks like the whole crew got laid off and replaced." The lawman scratched his thinning hair. "Funny about that, too. This new owner didn't hire a single man from town. Always half a dozen hands looking for some riding work. Damn strange."

"How big is the usual crew out there?"

"Right now, before roundup? Probably about forty hands, give or take a handful."

"About right. Sheriff, I took a ride out that direction this morning. Got about four or five miles up the river and five or six riders bushwhacked me. Killed my horse, tried to kill me. Two of them wound up dead along the river."

"Damn! You don't say! Heard they could get mean about strangers riding their land."

"Two of them won't bother anyone again. You write up a report and I'll sign it. Line of duty."

Sheriff Dryer stared at Spur. His long face went slack and he sighed. " 'Fraid I can't even go check the bodies. Me and my one deputy got warned off the place."

"You're the law in this county. You can go anywhere you want to."

"If I want to get shot. I ain't as young or as good with weapons as you must be. The Circle S will take care of the burying themselves. Happened once before, two weeks ago."

"And you let them get away with it?"

"Damn right. Cameron's got an army out there. I don't. That's why I sent a letter for you."

Spur walked over to the window and looked out at the side street. "What do you think happened to the Shuntingtons?"

"Both must have been killed. I knew them. Good church people, every Sunday morning. Belinda wouldn't miss church for any reason. They're both dead all right. The big puzzle is I just can't figure out what happened to a crew of forty cowboys."

Spur scowled at the lawman, then a shiver straightened him up in the chair.

"You suggesting there might be forty more bodies out on that ranch?"

"I hope to God there ain't."

"What we need now is some evidence. No chance now that I can sign on as a hand out there. I want to stay unofficial here. I'll be able to find out more that way. Remember, I'm just another out of work cowhand."

The sheriff nodded and Spur walked out the door and down the boardwalk. His first stop would be the doctor's office he had seen last night on the way to the hotel. Was it down this way, or back the other? He wasn't sure.

The little town was wide open and roaring. A pistol snarled behind him. Spur heard the round shatter a window in the saloon beside him and he darted into the nearby alley mouth. Who the hell was shooting at him this time?

2

Spur hit the shiplap side of the bar five feet down the alley and worked his way back toward the boardwalk. As he came to the corner he dropped to a crouch. Just at that moment a pistol fired from the other direction down the street. The round slammed into the shiplap splintering off a piece.

Two gunmen!

Spur spun, his Colt .44 snapping around to a new target. The man was a cowboy. As if in slow motion, Spur saw the man's big six-gun moving down to aim at his new position. The rider was in his late thirties, bearded, a dark brown hat and a tan leather vest.

Spur fired once, saw the bullet jolt into the man's chest, then he turned and looked for the second man across the street. A figure near a vanishing puff of blue smoke faded into a half dozen people around a saloon.

The secret agent watched the scene, glanced back at the first attacker. He was down on the boardwalk, his six-gun three feet from his extended hand. He wasn't moving. Spur turned and looked for the second bushwhacker across the way.

One man broke free of the others and charged across the street, a gun in each hand. He fired as he ran. Spur ducked as the first round chipped raw wood over his head. He edged lower, saw the gunman grab a horseman riding by and used the horse as a shield walking the mount closer and closer to the alley mouth.

No chance to hit the attacker, and big odds that he would wound the rider or mount if he fired.

Spur saw he was shielded from the gunman's view. He stepped around the corner and ran down the boardwalk past the saloon and darted into the next store.

Too late he saw it was a seamstress, with fancy women's goods and clothes on racks and two dress forms with garments being made on them.

"Sorry, ma'am, gent out there is trying to kill me," Spur said to a blur of a woman sitting at a sewing machine.

He slid to the floor near the door and peered out the glass panel. The bushwhacker had left the horse and stared at the empty alley. The man swore, ran into the mouth of the opening, then came out, his gun still ready.

He looked at the drinking den's open door beside the alley, swore again, angled across the street and vanished into the Tumbleweed Saloon.

"Was that man in the white hat the one who shot at you?"

Spur turned and for the first time looked at the woman sitting behind a sewing table. She was about thirty, he estimated, a little heavy with a pretty face and sharp, penetrating eyes.

"Yes, ma'am, that's him. Know who he is?"

"I thought you might. He's a stranger so that probably means he's one of the riders from the Circle S ranch outside of town." She hesitated and her eyes softened as she watched him. "You're new in town as well, aren't you?"

"Train, last night. So far I've been shot at by two different groups. This is not a friendly place."

"Oh, but it is!" she burst out quickly. Then she laughed. "I mean, I like Laramie. It's going to be a fine little city some day."

"Let's hope so. Pardon my manners. My name is Spur McCoy."

She smiled and a touch of a blush colored her neck. "Pleased to meet you. I'm Amy York. I don't imagine you need any dresses made."

Spur laughed. "Afraid not. But I thank you for letting me hide from that killer over there."

"I heard the shots." She shook her head in dismay. "I just don't understand you men and your guns."

"Way it's supposed to be, Miss York. I certainly don't understand hemstitching or blind button-holes."

She nodded. One hand twisted a strand of her long brown hair. Amy looked up at him once, then quickly away. Spur waited, smiling.

"Mr. McCoy, would you . . . that is . . . I mean, it's almost noon. Would you like to have a bite to eat with me?" She stormed ahead quickly so she wouldn't stop and run. "I live in back and I have some fresh fruit that came in on the train, and I'd make you a sandwich or whatever."

She closed her eyes and lowered her head. "Goodness! I don't know when I've been so forward!" She glanced up at him warily. "I'm sorry, Mr. McCoy. It was rude of me to ask. You really don't have to answer at all. I'm sorry."

"Amy, I'd love to have lunch with you. I'll know for sure that nobody is going to shoot me, right? And I want to ask you some questions."

"You will?" Amy's eyes widened. "Oh, my goodness! My kitchen isn't cleaned up at all! I'll need at least a half hour! Could you wait here? Oh, no. My goodness!"

Spur walked over to where she still sat.

"Miss York, there's no cause to fuss. I'm just common people, and you're doing me a favor. Besides, it's not every day I have a chance to eat with a pretty lady."

Amy looked up, some of her shyness gone. She watched him a minute, then smiled. "Mr. McCoy, that's the nicest thing anyone has said to me for a long time. Since the last time I saw Mr. and Mrs. Shuntington, I guess."

She went to the front of the small shop, locked the door and pulled a shade down over the glass. Many such window shades on businesses had been hand lettered like this one on the outside to say, "Closed."

Amy smiled again. "Right back this way, Mr. McCoy. And welcome to my humble home, such as it is."

Spur had noted her remark about the Shuntingtons. She might have made a dress for the woman. He would probe it later.

The rear of the shop had been made into a small apartment. There was a living room, tiny kitchen and what looked like two bedrooms opening off the main room.

"This is it," she said. "It suits me fine and with no more business than I do, it certainly is all I can afford." She led him into the kitchen and pointed to a chair.

"Sit down and read the weekly newspaper from Cheyenne. I don't know why I take it. Cheyenne is a long ways off and I don't get any business from there."

The meal was delicious. She made roast beef sandwiches for them, thin slicing a roast she said she had cooked last night and kept in her ice box.

"Yes, of course I have an ice box. It's just a home made affair, but ice is inexpensive here, and I can keep milk and meat fresh for four or five days without it spoiling. A friend made the ice box for me. We have plenty of ice here in the winter and the men cut it out of a pond from the river and put it in our town ice house, packing it down with straw. It lasts most of the summer, at least through August. Then the weather starts to get cold again."

Spur took a bite of the sandwich. She had found some lettuce, used a home made mayonnaise, and even put on a dill pickle.

"Sorry, I don't usually run on at the mouth that way."

"The sandwich is wonderful. You could start up a small cafe on the side."

She blushed lightly and looked down at her own sandwich. They had coffee and some of the fruit for dessert. When they finished they stood and she hesitated.

"Thanks for the meal, it was really good. Oh, you mentioned the Shuntingtons. Did you work for them?"

"Yes, I made three dresses for the Mrs. She was a wonderful lady."

"Did she say anything about leaving town, selling their big ranch?"

Amy shook her head, her face worked for a moment but she beat back sudden tears.

"No! not a word. That's why I'm afraid . . . why I'm afraid something bad happened to them."

"Were you working on a dress for her when they left?"

"Yes! It was almost done. I still have it. She had been in town a week before for a final fitting. She said she'd be in to pick it up the next Saturday when the men came to town. She even paid me for it in advance. What a nice lady."

"Good, Miss York. You've helped me." He turned toward the door into the store.

"Oh, Mr. McCoy. There is something else. A small

problem maybe you could help me with."

"Of course, you've been the one helping me all morning."

"Good. It's in the other room." She led the way through a door that opened into a bedroom. Amy turned and faced him, her features alive, flushed. She gripped his vest and pulled his head down and kissed his lips. She held the kiss a long time, then her tongue probed his lips. At last she released him.

"Mr. McCoy, I used to be married. My man died in the big war. I loved him dearly. But he's gone. I—" she blushed again, then stormed ahead. "I ain't had a man for five years, Mr. McCoy. I wondered if you might do me good and proper right now."

"Miss York—"

"Don't say no, right off. Let it simmer a minute." She kissed him again, her breasts pressed hard against his chest, her hips pushed against his crotch and she began a slow grinding. His mouth came open this time and she probed inside.

When she let go of him her hands tore open the buttons down her dress front. She pushed the bodice open and lifted her chemise so one large breast showed.

"I'd be ever so grateful, Mr. McCoy. No demands, no strings, just a good bedding so I don't close up into a virgin again. I really need your loving!"

Before he could react, she pushed the dress off her shoulders and lifted the pink chemise over her head. Her breasts hung heavy, with large pink areolas and small, intensely red nipples that stood tall now with warm blood.

"Amy, I don't want to take advantage of you. Is this really and truly what you want to do?"

As he asked, she pulled the dress off over her head and wiggled out of some fancy new style drawers with elastic in the waist. She stood in front of him naked, her arms out.

"Mr. McCoy, for five years I've been waiting for you to come into my shop. Yes, it's what I really and truly want to do. Please, right now and for the rest of the day!"

"Amy, there's no argument in the world like a beautiful lady standing naked in front of me. Not a chance you can lose that contest."

She smiled and stepped up to him, catching both his hands and putting them over her breasts. She leaned in close and whispered. "Spur McCoy, I need you to fuck me good about six times!"

He chuckled. "Six? I'm not seventeen anymore. But we sure as hell can give it a good try!"

Spur picked her up and carried her to the bed, put her down softly, and kissed her lips.

"I want to . . . Spur, can I? Let me undress you!"

She did, first his boots and socks, then his vest and slowly his shirt. It was as if this were a happening of great consequence and she wanted to be able to remember it for years.

When she had his clothes off she frowned at the makeshift bandage and checked his leg. "You've been shot!" At once she ran to the kitchen and brought back dressing and salve and alcohol. She went to work cleaning the two wounds, treating the punctures and bandaging his leg skillfully. "That should hold you for a day or two." He thanked her with a kiss.

Spur fondled her breasts. They were heavy and he could feel blood pulsating through her growing nipples.

"Spur, lover, do me quick the first time. Been so . . . so long. Put it inside me right now. I'm ready, lord knows I've been ready for five years!"

Amy turned on her back and spread her legs and lifted her knees. She was ready, Spur decided as his lance slid into her sheath with almost no resistance.

"Wonderful!" Amy whispered. Then she shrieked

and her whole body trembled and vibrated. She shrieked again and again as a climax slammed its way through her entire body. She whimpered at the last and her eyes came open. Spur would never forget the smile on her face.

"Oh, goodness! Five years! I tried to do it by myself, lots of times, but just never works. Oh, goodness!"

Spur began to stroke into her and at once Amy climaxed again. This time Spur went with her and blasted his own satisfaction deep into her sheath as she faded on her second climax.

When she opened her eyes this time, Spur had recovered and lay over her resting.

"Tell me about Spur McCoy," Amy said. "Where do you come from? What are you doing in Laramie?"

"Not a lot to tell. I grew up in New York City where my father has three or four stores. I went to school there and then on to college. When I graduated I worked in dad's businesses for a couple of years, then joined the army as a second lieutenant."

"You were in the war then. My Ned was killed at Bull Run."

"I was in the infantry. Served for two years and came out a Captain. Then I went to Washington D.C. where I was asked by an old family friend to be a military liaison for the United States senator from New York. I was with him until just after the war ended."

"Land sakes! You're a celebrity. Worked in the U.S. Senate with a senator, and a war hero and all."

"Not much of a hero. I survived. I think all of the heroes were the men like your husband who died. I was lucky." He looked around.

"Amy, would you have anything to drink in the place?"

"Brandy!" she said. "Yes, I got some for cooking, but never used much. Yes, some brandy."

As she left the bed and hurried out into the kitchen it was more obvious that Amy was more than a little heavy, but she was good in bed. Spur tried to remember any of the women he had made love to who were not good in bed. Yes, there had been one or two, but it was only because they had worked at not enjoying it and had not let him enjoy it either. But they were few and with many states between them.

Amy came back with the bottle of brandy and two water glasses. She poured and they toasted.

"To your health, and to a good man in your life soon," Spur said.

Amy blinked back a tear and nodded. "That would make me truly happy. Almost as happy as I am right now, standing here naked in front of a man I met only an hour ago, still glowing with the delight of making love, and expecting a lot more. I'm just glad as all get out that you ran into my store."

"So am I, Amy. This is excellent brandy."

While he was getting his strength back he probed about the Shuntingtons. "Do you remember Mrs. Shuntington saying anything at all about selling the ranch? Was she the kind of person who would tell you if anything important was coming up?"

Amy put her chin in her palm, her forearm flattening her breast. "Nope, Mrs. Shuntington never said a single word about moving, about selling the ranch, about anything out of the ordinary happening. I've been making dresses for her for almost four years now, and we were good friends. She and I talked about just about everything, even about bedding our men.

"We were good friends. She'd come in once or twice a week sometimes, just to talk. I'm dead sure,

Spur, that she didn't know nothing about moving or selling the ranch."

She watched him a moment. "Spur, you from some insurance company, or a private detective like them Pinkertons, and you come here to find out what happened to the Shuntingtons?"

"Something like that, Amy, but you can't tell anyone. I'm supposed to be just another out of work cowhand."

Amy grinned. "I like knowing a secret about you. Makes me feel all warm and good inside." She giggled. "Course, just getting fucked better than I ever been done in my whole life might have something to do with it, too. Do me again, good fucker! Do me again before I start begging you!"

She jumped on the bed and Spur was close behind. This time he rolled her over and put her on top.

"Really? Will it work this way? I mean, can we fit?" She giggled and saw that indeed it would work.

"Guess you know I never done it this way before."

"Figured that out," Spur said.

Then they both were lost in the lust of the moment and Amy quickly picked up the motion and before long was riding Spur like he was a stud horse.

"My goodness, I've never felt anything like this before," she said. Then her time came and she yelped and screeched and cried and wailed as the action brought her to another surging climax.

When the fury died Spur had reached his peak as well, and they clung together for ten minutes before rolling apart.

She pushed up on one elbow and stared down his long pale white and starkly brown form.

"Pretty Spur McCoy, why don't you just stay here in Laramie? I'll support you. Open that restaurant. We'll make a living and you can make love to me twice a day for the rest of our natural lives!"

"Twice a day and I'd be dead in six months!"

"All right, once a day so you can live two years. Best two years of your life."

Spur reached over and played with her breasts. "Tempting, but I'm afraid I better pass. I'm a fiddlefoot, never stay in one place very long. Got to keep moving. Not that you don't have everything it takes to keep a man happy. And you sure as hell know how to use it."

She giggled and blushed.

"Besides, my work moves me around. You couldn't trust me out on the job with all the pretty women I meet."

"With you, McCoy, I'd be willing to share. Just so you came back to my bed every couple of weeks."

"You have the rest of the afternoon to convince me. Hey, have you ever made love standing up?"

"Can't be done."

"Give me another ten minutes and I'll prove to you that it can be done."

It can. He proved it. Amy never did believe it.

3

Spur pulled on his clothes in the back room of Amy York's dress shop about three that afternoon. Amy hummed softly as she watched him. She sat on the bed grandly naked and teasing him with various suggestive poses.

"Now you be careful, Spur McCoy. The whole crew of fifty men from the Circle S is going to be gunning for you. I've seen it happen before here once. They hounded the blacksmith until he challenged one of them. As soon as he pulled out his gun, four of them shot him down without saying a word. Then they went to a saloon and bought drinks for everyone."

She scowled. "Spur, be careful and come back to me."

Spur hugged her tightly, kissed her lips and walked out the front door. He hurried directly to the sheriff's office where he gave a verbal report on the death of the cowboy in the street just before noon.

"Figured you in the fracas somewhere," Sheriff Dryer said putting on his spectacles to read a paper. "Had three witnesses who testified at least two men tried to gun you down. I got a report all made out. Just read it over and sign it. Both the bushwhackers were circle S riders, we're sure."

The sheriff looked at Spur, a frown growing on his face. "Just hope to hell this don't mean all fifty of them riders are going to storm into town and shoot up the place. We don't have that many guns in all of Laramie."

"I'll try to keep it on a more personal level than that, Sheriff Dryer. Soon as it gets dark, I'm going to pay a social call on the Circle S spread."

Dryer looked up, his thin face puzzled. "You gonna walk right into the damn lion's den when you know they'll shoot you on sight and then get nasty?"

"The lion will never know that I'm there, Sheriff. If someone spots me, I'll leave a calling card so they'll be sure. Without some direct information, we're stymied on this case. I simply need to see the lay of the land, investigate as much as I can as soon as I can."

Sheriff Dryer stoked his pipe "Damn glad it's you going out there to the Circle S and not me. Good luck."

Spur moved to the Johnson Dry Goods store and found the owner, Dick Johnson, a man who knew weapons and repaired them on the side. He sold new and used guns and repaired weapons of all kinds. Spur bought a used Spencer carbine the man had reworked.

Dick grinned. "Damn good piece. Wanted to keep it myself, but if you need it, welcome. Got to charge you seven dollars for it. But I'll throw in a box of fifty rounds. Damn fine weapon, that Spencer. Sometimes I wish it had more range, but hell, it's good for six hundred yards. I can't rightly see much further than that anyway."

Spur hefted the weapon. It measured 39-inches long overall, much shorter than the Spencer rifle that reached out to 47-inches. It used the same .52 caliber bullet and had the seven round magazine that loaded through the butt of the stock. The thin magazines could be carried in a small box holding ten, giving a man 70 shots in a rush.

"Carbine's lots easier to use, if'n you riding a lot," the storekeeper said eyeing Spur's cowboy clothes.

"I tend to do that, yes," Spur commented. He paid the man, bought another box of 50 rounds for his Colt .44 six-gun and went out to the street.

He saw a group of four riders churn into town and pull up at the Tumbleweed Saloon. They looked like they could be from the Circle S, so Spur turned into an alley off the main street and went the long way to the livery. If he challenged a batch of Circle S riders it would be on his terms and on his timing.

In ten minutes he had picked out a horse, bought it for thirty dollars and paid another five for a used saddle and halter.

"You the gent who rode in this morning with that big black stallion, ain't you?"

"Might have been. Why?"

"Some Circle S riders came in here snorting fire. Said somebody stole the horse from Dreek, one of their riders. They pointed out the new brand and just took him right out of the stable. Not even a thank you."

Spur pulled a double eagle from his pocket and flipped it to the livery man.

"Had a small misunderstanding with Dreek. He shot my horse so I traded him for his, since he wasn't going to be needing it anymore. No reason you should take a loss on the mount you rented to me."

The livery man grabbed the twenty dollar gold piece and grinned.

"Now, that's right neighborly of you, friend. I thank you. No way to reason with this new batch of Circle S riders. Just no way a'tall."

Spur rode out of town to the south so he wouldn't

have to move down the Laramie main street. Someone had put up a sign and called it First Street. He curved across the Union Pacific tracks, rode out of town, and soon hit the Laramie river to the west. He forded the river at the shallowest point he could find, got his legs wet and then rode north beyond the trees and out of sight of the town.

But he didn't go far. He stopped in some thick brush of young cottonwood and box elder along the stream and moved into the thicket until he couldn't be seen. There he'd wait for darkness.

Spur ground tied the mount, a strong, steady looking gelding about five years old that had a pretty roan coat. The dark red glistened in the sunlight and Spur wished he had a curry comb and brush to give the animal a grooming.

Instead he drank from a small side stream that came into the Laramie river, then settled down against a log and pulled his hat down over his eyes. He didn't expect any visitors and he would be alert to anyone riding by on the trail north.

Since he was going on a night patrol, some shuteye now would come in handy. Spur relaxed and in a few moments, he slept.

He roused to the chatter of a squirrel who was surprised to find a human in his favorite hunting ground. Spur pushed up his hat and looked around. It was approaching dusk. He made sure his horse had all he wanted to drink, then mounted and took the trail north.

He had learned his lesson and would swing off the track and move north parallel to the stream which he discovered he was moving along downstream. It grew larger the farther north he rode. Evidently it emptied into the North Platte river, which then ran south into the Platte in Nebraska, then on to the Iowa line and into the mighty Missouri.

His left thigh hurt some, but not as much as he

had expected. The rifle round had punched through in an instant without distorting much, leaving a clean exit wound. Amy had done a good job bandaging and treating it. Tomorrow he'd go see the local sawbones and have him take a look at it. Right now it didn't slow him up a bit.

It was soon dark, and there was no moon that night, so Spur rode slowly, working his way north. At one point he heard some singing and laughing, saw a campfire, and skirted it by another quarter mile. It sounded like the Circle S guards were having a small party instead of tending to business. For a moment the sound and the situation reminded him of off duty soldiers. But these riders were certainly not soldiers and out here they should be acting as lookouts, doing their job.

Another three miles along the Laramie river, he topped a small rise and looked across the high plateau and saw lights. He moved ahead slowly, testing the lay of the land, watching for any campfires, any sounds that could reveal a ring of guards set out. There might be none. The Circle S riders were over confident. They felt their reputation for violence protected them so no one would try to slip in. He was counting on that arrogance to help him.

By the time Spur had walked his mount within a hundred yards of the first barn and corral of the spread, he had not heard nor seen any guards. He tied his roan's muzzle shut with his kerchief so he would not horse-talk, and left him tied to a tough small shrub.

Spur felt as though he were back in the war. He had slipped up on a lot of farms and ranches and patches of woods and draws and hillsides back then only to find them come alive with Rebel forces.

Now he had no idea what kind of a force he faced. Were they simply rabble gathered up to rustle a whole ranch, cattle, crew, owner even the chuck wagon cook? Or was it totally innocent, the result of massive bad planning and bad luck on the former owner's part?

He had to find out.

Spur slid to the ground twenty yards from the rear of the nearest barn. He spotted a lookout after only a few minutes of waiting. The man coughed, then swore silently and lit a cigarette. A few moments later the lonesome notes of a harmonica drifted from the position.

"Red! You play another note and I'll cut your guts out!" a voice called from somewhere near the middle of the barnyard.

The harmonica music stopped.

Spur crept silently to his left around the musician until he could edge into the far side of the barn. Inside he found what he expected: a few stalls for milk cows, several stalls for favorite horses, a mow of cured hay with room for lots more. To one side sat a feedbox with a lift top that held bins of feed grain.

It was a working ranch barn. Nothing unusual or out of the ordinary—unless there were forty-five bodies buried under the hay somewhere. That simply could not have happened. He hoped. How else did you get rid of a crew of men and the owners and not leave a trace?

Spur climbed a ladder to the hayloft and watched out the open haymow door. There was just enough light to see across the barnyard. The main house was forty yards away. A well stood in the middle of the area with the gentle slope of the land running downhill to the barns. A bunkhouse showed to the left, now blazing with coal oil lamps.

He saw no other guards for a while, then spotted one more with a rifle over his shoulder like a soldier, walking around the main house. Was he protecting someone inside, or keeping someone inside a prisoner? The Shuntingtons could be held prisoner in there.

Maybe. No. Not logical. Why steal their ranch and let them live? No prisoners, that would be neater, smarter. And whoever worked a plan like this had to be smart.

A pair of men wandered out of the bunkhouse, lit ciarettes and came toward the barn. They stopped directly below Spur and talked. They had been in some kind of a discussion.

"Hell, I say we hang right here. Where we got to go? Besides, this is a good outfit. We get fed good, dry place to sleep every night, not one hell of a lot of work to do."

"Not much to do right now, that is. You ever done any roundup work or trail driving? When does Curt plan to ship the rest of these damn cattle?"

"Christ, but you are dumb, Doffler. We can't just ship them, got to be a buyer in Laramie to buy them first. You want to give away all your shares in this operation?"

"Naw, guess not." The man threw down his smoke and stamped it out. "Still, I like the old days better. Always something going on. Usual some woman around we could flip on her back."

"Them good old days is gone forever, Doffler. We take what we can get now, and this is a sweet deal."

"Better be."

The two walked back toward the bunkhouse.

Spur learned little by listening to the men. Obviously they were going to sell the cattle. But shares? What good old days were the men talking about?

Spur turned and looked around. His main interest now centered on the ranchhouse. He went down the ladder, slipped out of the barn and silently worked around the long way until he came up in back of the main house. Four rooms showed lights that he could see.

He lay in the weeds for ten minutes watching the house and the guard who circled it. The man came by every four minutes, regular as the Waterbury ticking in his pocket.

Spur waited unitl the guard made his pass behind the house, then Spur worked his way forward slowly on his belly, crawling within ten feet of the route the guard took. The man came again, but didn't even glance toward where Spur lay hidden in the high weeds. When the guard passed the edge of the house, Spur surged up in a run and charged to the lighted window on the ground floor twenty-feet away.

The shade was up. Spur looked inside. A woman stood in front of a bed and slowly took off her dress. She flung it aside, ground her hips and laughed at a man who sat on the bed. Spur couldn't hear what she said, but the wild squeal was plain enough to understand.

She ripped off clothes, throwing them one way and then the other. When she was naked she rushed at the man sitting on the bed, toppled him over and then sat on his face screaming in delight.

Spur hurried away from the window and back into the darkness just before the guard came around the house. The watchman paused and looked inside, then shook his head, rubbed his crotch and kept on marching around his post.

Spur lay in the brush trying to figure it out. He had used several military terms since he got on the ranch: post, marching, sentry. Why? As he thought it through, the whole place seemed to have a slightly out of focus military atmosphere. There was nothing concrete he could put his finger on to explain it.

Even with the military flavor, he had found

nothing to cause concern for the missing family. What if they had simply tired of the area, picked up and left without any notice? People probably did that every day in New York. Why not here?

The barn floor. It would be an ideal burial ground if you didn't want the bodies found. In a stall or an indoor corral for a half dozen horses, new dirt would not be evident. Nobody would think to look there for a body, or a pair of bodies—even forty-five corpses.

He took the same route into the barn as before, found a pitchfork and began pushing it into the ground floor everywhere he found the earth exposed. The stalls yielded only the acrid stench of ammonia from the urine. The three stiff tines of the fork dug into the soft ground an inch and stopped. Not here.

He tried the other spots, then went to the edge of the small corral built inside the barn. Again he found no soft spots around the sides. He was just ready to step through the doorway into the corral when someone jumped him from behind.

"What the hell you doing, stranger?" A voice screeched just as the body hit Spur. He had no time to grab for his six-gun. Instead he swung around, slammed the sturdy fork handle against the man's side, drew it back like a rifle with bayonette and rammed the three tines into the attacker's chest.

Only when the man blurted in pain and fell to his knees did Spur see the ten-inch knife he held. Another second or two and Spur would have been impaled on the big blade.

Spur watched the ranch hand's eyes go wide, then he bleeted in pain and toppled to one side. The man didn't have a chance in hell of living for ten minutes.

Spur worked his way to the same door he had used to get in before and cautiously stepped through it.

He heard a six-gun cocking, then a second one. His hand darted for his holster as he dove away from the sound, hit the dirt and rolled. His weapon was out as he came to his stomach, pushed up and raced into the blackness away from the barn.

Two guns blazed at him. The lead was wide. He darted in the opposite direction to confuse their sound-oriented target but kept pumping his legs. The two men behind him cursed and fired until their weapons were empty.

More lights bloomed in the ranch yard. A rifle spoke sharply and with authority but the bullet came nowhere near Spur. He ran steadily now, arms pumping, the Spencer Carbine in one hand.

Somewhere behind he heard horses calling to each other as men evidently saddled up. Someone shouted an order for six men to move out.

By then Spur found his roan, undid her muzzle and stepped on board. He rode away due south at a canter, waiting to see what the pursuit would be before he tested the speed of the big red. Chances were that some of the riders would come this way.

The sounds faded behind him.

Spur stopped and turned his ear toward the north. A light breeze stirred the grass on the plains, but he heard nothing. He resumed his ride, moving generally south, staying in the Laramie valley with the Medicine Bow Mountains to the south and west.

A half hour later he stabled the roan in the livery and walked up to the Medicine Bow Hotel where he had a room. It was on the second floor front. He picked up his key at the desk, noticed the strange look the night clerk gave him, then went up the stairs.

He had determined not to stay in his room that night. Too many people were interested in his whereabouts. He went down the hallway, paused at his door and then turned sharply as a door opened behind him. His hand lifted the Colt .44 from leather as he pivoted.

He saw only a large blonde woman who waved

him forward. She caught his arm and pulled him into her room, closing the door quietly. She held a finger over her lips.

"Your room ain't overly healthy for you tonight, Mister," she whispered. "I overheard two gents who were making a bet which one could kill you first. Later on I saw them in the lobby waiting for you to come back from wherever you went for a ride. Yep, they know about your horse and rifle, everything."

Spur saw the woman clearly now in the light of two coal oil lamps. She was taller than most women, probably five-six, with long wheat straw colored hair that came to her waist. She wore a robe over a full figure and stared at him now with a faint smile.

"You look like you're not used to getting rescued by a woman," she said with a soft laugh.

McCoy nodded. "True, especially one so beautiful."

"Save the blarney, you'll need it. From what I hear there are at least fifteen Circle S men in town wanting to punch holes all over your body with their six-guns slugs."

"People have tried that before," Spur said. "That's why I have no plans on taking advantage of your hospitality here in your room. Too dangerous for you."

"Take advantage?," she asked surprised. "Just how did you mean that?"

Before Spur could answer there was an explosion that blasted in the hallway, jolting the woman's locked door open. Spur looked through the inch-opening and saw his room directly across the hall had its door blasted off its hinges, hanging in splinters, and his room was filled with smoke and flames.

He closed the blonde woman's door gently.

"Maybe it would be a good idea if I stayed here for a while after all," he said.

"Timing," she said softly. "It's all in the timing."

4

Curt Cameron forked a load of scrambled eggs into his mouth and chewed quickly before he burst out laughing. Lucia had just finished serving him his breakfast and vanished for a moment. When she stepped back into the kitchen at the Circle S ranch house, she was as bare as she had been last night in the small bathtub.

"Ain't I a gorgeous, sexy pile of woman?" she said, throwing her chest out in a provocative pose. "Curt, you big cock, you better just finish eaten' up them eggs quick so you can start nibblin' on me in just any old place you want."

Curt had more eggs, then a bite of toast and home made jam, and a long drink of coffee.

"Lucia, you wild woman, what if the men look in the window?"

"None of them gonna see any part of me he probably ain't seen before, only then it was probably involved in some sexy action. Come on, Curt, I need a morning wake up poking."

"Woman, you tryin' to kill me off at an early age so you can get at my bank account? Twice a day is once too much for a man of my advanced years."

"You talk about money, honey. But you never showed me none. Just some figures in a little old blue book about as big as a nickel."

"They call them bank passbooks, Lucia. But don't worry your pretty titties about that. You get dressed so I don't get all excited here and drop you right on the kitchen floor. You'd get splinters in your backside down there on the boards."

"Wouldn't mind," she said, thrusting her hips out in a series of three quick little bumps.

Curt swatted at her and she yelped and hurried out of the kitchen.

Curt had something more important to worry about this morning. One of the lookouts from last night was found dead, run through with a three tined pitchfork. Damn tough way to die. Curt scowled as he finished the coffee.

Who killed the man? More important, why? If it was a fight among the men, that was acceptable. Curt hoped it was an old grudge or a new one and a fair fight.

The alternative was what worried him. If there hadn't been a fight last night, it could mean they had an outsider snooping around, got himself caught and then turned the tables and killed the catcher. Damn, that really worried him. Things moving along smooth as Tennessee sippin' whiskey. Now this.

Lucia came back in, hugged him over the back of the chair and pushed her big breasts against his shoulders.

"Hey that feels good, my titties all snuggled up against you that way."

"Better, cause if you don't get the kitchen cleaned up I'm gonna have them ground up into sausages!"

She bit his ear lightly and went to the table.

Curt ambled outside to talk to his second-in-command, the foreman of the ranch.

Joel shook his head as he watched his boss. "Don't rightly reckon, Major. None of the men say they even heard an argument or scuffle last night. We got five or six guys in town looking for that skunk we missed yesterday. I'd say the killing happened by somebody from the outside."

"Got past our sentries?"

"Hell, a little old grandmother on a mule could do that. We ain't expecting any trouble. Said yourself we didn't have to have tight security around the ranch."

"Yeah, true. But now this." Curt kicked at the desert dry high plateau Wyoming dirt. It was a light sandy loam with lots of small rocks mixed in. "Get me Blade. I want him to see if he can find any tracks."

"He's in town looking for that skunk who killed Joe and Willy yesterday down by the breaks."

"Yeah, right. Get out the next best tracker we got and have him do a double circle about a hundred yards out, looking for any boot tracks or fresh horse prints from last night."

"Yes sir, you got it," Joel said and walked off toward the bunk house.

It was less than half an hour later when Joel and Curt knelt in the prairie south of the ranch house and stared at the tracks.

"Looks like the horse was ground tied or on this little brush. Critter was here some time considering the droppings. The boot tracks lead toward the ranch, and back toward the horse."

"Shit! We did have a visitor last night."

"Same one who rode onto the place yesterday?" Joel asked.

"Could have been. Find out in town everything you can about him. Who he is, what his name is, and why he's here snooping around."

"Maybe Blade will wipe him out first and we won't need to bother," Joel said.

"Maybe, but we have to make sure. Do it. Send

another man to town, now. One who can speak good English without a heavy accent."

Joel nodded and ran for the bunkhouse.

Curt walked slowly back to the ranch house and let the screen door slam as he went in.

Lucia meandered in drying her hair with a towel. When she swung her long dark hair over her head with the towel wrapped around it, he saw that she was topless.

"You promised me St. Louis this Spring, remember?" Lucia said. "When the hell we going to St. Louis?"

"After you learn to wear clothes."

"I can wear clothes in the city. Let me show you. You'll like St. Louis."

"I've been there before. I'm busting bigger problems. We're needing to sell about five thousand head of steers. That means getting them into a pen somewhere. Most of these damn riders we have never threw a rope in their lives."

"So hire some cowboys."

Curt snorted. "Oh, hell yes. And so much as admit that we ain't what we say we are. Not a bloody chance of my doing that. I might not be a college graduate, but I know better than that."

Lucia flounced around, her breasts swinging. "Never said I graduated, just that I went for a while, 'cause this boy was going and I and him was gonna get married."

"You thought you were, thought it with your crotch. Get out of here."

Curt walked to the veranda and watched Joel striding toward him.

"He gone?"

"Yeah, sent a good man, Walters. He's a great talker, he'll find out who the polecat is."

"Anything else?"

"Yeah, Major. The boys are getting restless.

Nothing to do for too long. They get to thinking too much. Some of them say we still owe them a hundred dollars from that last job we did."

Curt looked up sharply. "You kept the company records, we owe anybody or don't we?"

"One or two, maybe six."

"So tell them after this score we'll settle up. We need to get two-thousand head of cattle in that lower pasture where we got that smooth wire fence across. Time we talk with Elliot Parker and find out how we sell these critters. When we have two-thousand rounded up and in that pen, we'll be ready. Take thirty men out and start moving them steers into the pen. Must have some cowboys in the bunch."

"Damn few, but we'll manage." Joel turned and walked smartly toward the bunk house. Curt called after him.

"When you get them on their way, come back. I've got another job for you."

Joel nodded. "Yes sir," he said.

Inside the ranch house, Curt found Lucia sprawled on the big bed combing her long dark hair. She had pulled off her blouse again and now sat up shaking her breasts at him.

"Just stay right where you are and get ready for a party," Curt said. He tossed her a pint bottle of whiskey.

"For me?" she asked.

"For you and Joel. He's due."

"No!" she shrieked. "I don't do that no more with them, just you. You promised me!" She screamed at him again.

"You hurt me!"

"Not half as bad as I'm gonna if you don't treat Joel right when he gets in here."

"You said I didn't have to service nobody but you no more! You promised me in Kansas!"

"So I changed my mind. He gonna use up your

pussy or something? Hell, you serviced half the damn company for the last two years. Why you bitching?"

"Because you said—"

She stopped when he drew back his hand.

"Things change. Getting harder to hold the company together. Six damn years we been a group now. That takes a lot of planning and a lot of work. You're part of it. Your part is to shut up your mouth and be nice to Joel. You act sexy and appreciate him. I'll be watching from the hall. You sex him up good and proper at least three times, or I'll wash your little pussy out with coal oil and you won't even piss for a week!"

Joel came back to the porch a few minutes later and knocked. Curt talked to him a minute, Joel grinned and walked into the living room, then cautiously down the hall to the bedroom. He left the door open a foot when he went inside.

Joel stood beside the bed. Lucia sat on it topless, frozen in place. When he looked at her, she smiled and shook her shoulders so her breasts bounced and swayed.

"My god but you're beautiful!" Joel said. He sat beside her and caught her breasts. "Look good enough to eat!" he said.

"Then eat them, Joel," she said. She reached for his shirt and began unbuttoning it.

From the hallway Curt watched a moment more. He waited until Joel had stripped off her skirt and dropped her on the bed. Joel kicked off his boots and rolled on top of her.

Curt walked down to the back of the house to what had been a laundry room. There was a single bed set up there. He locked the door behind him and looked at the bed.

On it sat a kid no more than seventeen. Curt had taken him on at the last ranch as an amusement.

The boy was naked, his stiff penis in his hand.

"You said to come after Joel got in the house," the boy said.

Curt nodded. Then a slow grin spread over his face. "Something different, son, a little change of pace. And I know that you like it.

"Anytime, anywhere, anyplace," the youth said. He left the bed and walked up to Curt and unbuckled his belt and began tugging down his pants.

Spur McCoy left the room across the hall from his blasted one about nine the next morning. The tall blonde lady's name was Etta, and she had been more than kind to share her bed with him, a poor soul under a vicious attack. He promised that he would see her again.

Now he viewed the remains of his former room. The door was still hanging on wounded hinges. He picked through the rubble, was glad it had not been a feather ticking or mattress, and soon found what was left of his suitcase. It had been under the bed and shielded from most of the blast. Still, it had six holes in it and the latch wouldn't work.

He picked up everything he owned, held the suitcase under his arm and walked slowly down the back steps to the alley. He peered around the doorway but saw nobody there.

After five minutes of working from alley to alley, he came to the Sheriff's office and slipped inside.

"Heard your room got dynamited last night," Sheriff Dryer said. "They know you're bad news for them." He tapped the dregs out of his pipe, scraped it and filled it with fresh tobacco but didn't light it. "Peers they don't want you to stay in town."

"Peers they don't. Care if I bunk in an empty jail cell tonight? You don't even have to lock the cell door."

The sheriff nodded and Spur put his suitcase in the cell nearest the door.

"Have some news for you," Sheriff Dryer said. "Morning train brought in a former resident, Rutger Shuntington. He's twenty-one, and has been in St. Louis going to school. I wired him when it was clear something was wrong, and he's just getting here. He's at the Medicine Bow Hotel."

"I better have a talk with him," Spur said. "How did you find out he came in?"

"He registered that way at the hotel and the room clerk sent me a message. He thinks it might be dangerous for the kid to be running around shouting his name."

"Agree. I'll go track him down, get him moved to an easier to defend room, maybe."

Spur found Rutger on the second floor. When he answered the knock on the door, he opened it wide at once.

Spur scowled.

"Rutger Shuntington, my name is Spur McCoy. I'm a United States law enforcement officer here to find out what happened to your parents. You could be in a lot of danger. Never open the door that way again until we have this cleared up."

"Oh, sorry. Come in. I've got a gun."

Rutger was five-ten, solidly built with dark hair, a moustache and long side burns and he wore eyeglasses.

"Pack up anything you unpacked," Spur said. "We're finding you a better room. One on the third floor in the corner at the end of a hall. Easier to defend."

"I don't think that will be necess—"

He stopped when Spur glared at him.

"It doesn't matter what you think right now, Rutger. I want you alive for a few more hours so we can talk. Let's start as you pack. Did your parents say anything to you about selling the ranch?"

"No."

"Did they say anything about moving anywhere for any reason?"

"Not once. I'm sure something terrible has happened to them. Mother would never—" He choked it off.

"Would they have told you if they were going to visit relatives, or if relatives were in trouble and needed their help?"

"Yes, we talked about everything. Finances, weather, the way the meat prices were, how we could run the ranch better. I went to school so I could do it better. Learning business and government and I even took some animal husbandry courses."

Spur picked up the bag that Rutger finished packing and opened the door. He looked both ways, waited a minute, then hurried the young man down the hallway and up the steps to the third floor. There was only one stairway, a central one. Spur checked the end room on floor three one way. It was locked and occupied.

The end room the other way down the hall was open and not used. He put Rutger in there, gave him the key and told him to lock the door. Then Spur went down to the room clerk. For five dollars the room clerk made a notation that room 313 was out of service, needing repairs.

Back upstairs Spur knocked on the door.

"Who is it?" Rutger asked.

Spur responded and the youth opened the door. Spur showed him how to put the straight backed chair under the door knob as an added protective measure.

They talked for a half hour. Slowly Spur impressed on the young man the danger he was in. He was never to go to the dining room, but have his meals brought up to his room. He was not to go on the street or to wear a gun.

"No gun? I don't understand?"

"The Circle S riders are not the ones you know. All the old hands have vanished and new ones are out there. Yesterday they tried three times to kill me, and my last name isn't even Shuntington. Whoever rustled your whole ranch doesn't want you showing up to cause trouble. Their best plan will be to kill you as soon as they know you're in town."

"I understand. I'm certain that dad would never sell the ranch, at least not without calling me home and explaining to me why and what else we were planning. He told me time and time again that the ranch would be mine to run when I grow up. He said when I came home from college we'd run it together, make it the biggest and best cattle ranch in all of Wyoming and then of the whole West!"

"I hope you still get the chance. Now, I understand you have a sister away at school. Would she come dashing back here if she heard about this?"

"Yes, I'm sure she would. Priscilla is a level headed young woman. She's just a year younger than I am. She wanted to go to college, too. She's in Denver."

"Who was your father's closest friend in town?"

"Easy, the banker, Ira Villary. A good man. Always fair in his dealings with us."

"Anybody else?"

"We had a lawyer, Elliot Parker. Dad used him because he said he was the only one of the three lawyers in town who knew anything about the law. Requirements aren't very strict yet in the territory for lawyers to practice. Dad sort of wanted me to go read for the law, but I wanted a better, broader education."

"What about the doctor?"

"That would be old Doctor Asamore. He's the only one in town and I guess he's all right. Delivers babies and sets broken arms, but he isn't much for cutting people open."

"How is he on bullet wounds?"

"Dad said he was good at that. He gets enough practice."

"What I was waiting to hear. I've got a shot up leg I need to have checked. First thing we're going to do is see the banker, then the lawyer, and if we have time, the doctor.

"Get a hat to cover up your face, then we'll stick to the alleys and try to stay alive. Ready?"

For a moment a flicker of fear crossed the young man's face. Then he scowled and nodded. Rutger Shuntington was going to do all right, Spur decided.

5

As soon as Rutger Shuntington entered the bank by the side door right behind Spur McCoy, the bank owner saw him and motioned to the back. They went through a door into a private room near the vault and the rather tall banker with black hair pasted across a bald spot and horn rimmed glasses shook his head.

"Rutger Shuntington, as I live and breathe. Never thought I'd see hide nor hair of you again. I do hope you have some word about your parents. We're all extremely worried about them around Laramie."

Rutger frowned and then lifted his brows. "Mr. Villary, I'm afraid I came here hoping you could give me some idea of what happened to my parents. I know nothing."

"Oh, dear!" Ira Villary's eyes bulged in despair, then he motioned to a seat beside a big desk and dropped into the fancy, padded chair behind it. "I was hoping. . . ." He looked away. "Well, I guess we'll just have to. . . ." Villary shook his head again and stared out a small window fronted on a brick wall next door. The bank building evidently had been put up first when the window had a worthwhile view.

"Do the Shuntingtons still have an account at

your bank, Mr. Villary," Spur asked.

The man looked up coldly.

"I'm afraid I don't know who you are. I've heard that a stranger came to town asking a lot of questions and getting shot at. Are you that individual?"

"Yes, Spur McCoy is my name. Is there still a Shuntington account here?"

"No, I'm afraid not. As soon as I heard that Rutger came to town I checked that file time and time again." He tapped a manila folder on his desk. "The record shows that a check was drawn against the Circle S Ranch account, signed by Oliver Shuntington for the sum of six-hundred and forty-seven dollars. Two days later a man who identified himself with letters as one Archibald Pumetter, cashed the instrument here at the bank. The signature of Oliver Shuntington matched my records, the gentleman's papers were in order, so of necessity and a matter of law, I paid out the check."

"How much was in the account at that time?" Rutger asked.

"Six-hundred and fifty-seven dollars," the banker answered. "That left ten dollars as the balance."

Rutger walked to the door and came back. His face was sullen and angry, but when he looked up, his features softened.

"Mr. Villary, I'm not blaming you. But I'd say we have been swindled by someone, the family bank account emptied, and the family ranch rustled—not just the cattle, the whole thing!"

"At the time there wasn't a hint of anything devious or illegal," the banker said.

"I'm sure there wasn't, Mr. Villary," Rutger said. "I'm not blaming you. They planned it that way. All I can hope is that this is their last crime and that they soon step onto a gallows and feel the bite of a rope."

"Mr. Villary, I'm with the United States Secret Service sent here by Washington D.C. to investigate this matter. Could I look at the check and the signature card, please?"

"The Secret Service? I thought you were supposed to prevent counterfeiting." He blinked. "Yes, yes, right away."

A few minutes later Spur and Rutger left the bank and walked slowly down the street.

"It doesn't look good, does it, Mr. McCoy?"

"No. The more I see, the more worried I become that your parents are in terrible danger."

"Not danger, Mr. McCoy. I'm afraid they both must be dead. My father would never stand for this sort of a sale of what he has called the family's home place. He planned on this ranch staying in the Shuntington family for five-hundred years. The check proves it to me. My father would never let anyone else write a check on his bank account. Not even mother. And that was not his writing on the check. I'm positive of that. He might have to write twenty drafts, but he always did it himself. He learned to read and write late in life and he was proud of his accomplishment. It meant a lot to him."

"Who is the lawyer you mentioned?"

"Elliot Parker. Dad knew him for four or five years, I guess. He came out to the ranch every so often. Dad signed papers and they talked about new land and buying more land along the river.

"Whoever controls the Laramie river around here, controls all the grazing land in this section of Wyoming. Dad wanted to own land on both sides of the Laramie river, right up to the North Platte."

"That's a big spread."

"Yeah, big enough for somebody to spend a lot of time figuring out how to steal it. Somebody rustled not only our cattle but our land deed and the whole damn Circle S ranch!"

"If that's true, Rutger, we need to find out how they did it, who they are, and come up with the best way to win back your rights to the Circle S."

"Can't be an easy job. They've been here two months now. That's an old trail to follow."

"I've followed lots harder trails. Where is the lawyer?"

The law office perched on the second floor over the dress shop. A wag once told Spur that lawyers roosted on one floor off the street so no drunks would stagger in the door and ask to be represented. If a client could climb the steps, he should be sober enough to have saved some cash money for legal fees.

Spur turned the doorknob and the two men walked inside. It was a man's room. The office was only ten-feet square, but it was entirely paneled with some dark varnished wood. Around three sides were hunting trophy heads.

Spur recognized the shaggy head of a buffalo, a moose with its thick webbed antlers, and a prong horn antelope. On the far wall all to itself the white head of a mountain sheep stared down at Spur.

Across the room a man sat behind a solid oak desk. He looked up and rose at once. His vest was open showing a white shirt. A black suit coat hung on a hook behind him. Deep, dark eyes flared in a sudden reaction and his face showed worry.

"Rutger Shuntington! I'm surprised to see you here."

He came forward and gripped Rutger's hand. "I hope you can explain to me about your parents and the Circle S."

Rutger shook his head. "I thought you would be the only one in town who knew what happened. I understand someone says he bought the ranch. Is that right?"

"I'm as much in the dark as everyone else. I even had an appointment with your father on a Friday. I started to ride out to the ranch and someone stopped me at gunpoint, turned me around and said the ranch was now owned by someone else."

"Oh, Elliot Parker, this is Spur McCoy, a friend of mine. I don't think you've met."

The men shook hands briefly, Parker's glance resting too long on Spur. He looked back at Rutger.

"Is it true then, that you have no idea why your parents sold the Circle S, and especially why they pulled up and left the state in the dead of night?"

"Yes, Mr. Parker. I don't know now, but you can bet that I'm going to find out before too damn long. That ranch was the only reason I went away to college. I was coming back and planning on making the Circle S into the biggest spread in the whole state of Wyoming!"

Spur moved into the conversation quickly.

"Mr. Parker, didn't Mr. Shuntington say anything at all about moving? Maybe about some family problems back east. I understand you were the family lawyer. Did he make out a will or change any legal papers? How about his coming to you to raise some money by selling some land?"

"Yes, there was that about some money a week or so before. But I never thought much about it. Oliver was always getting together three or four thousand dollars to buy up a homestead of some little rancher or some creek bottom farmer who gave up and wanted to get back to Chicago or even Nebraska."

"How much was he trying to raise last you knew?" Rutger asked.

"I think it was eight-thousand dollars. He figured he'd sell off eight-hundred head of steers and have plenty."

"Ten dollars a head?" Spur asked.

"Been the going price lately. Railroad's made a

glut of beef on the Chicago market so the price came down."

Rutger stood and walked around the room. "You're still my lawyer, Mr. Parker. I'll pay you somehow. I want you to try to find any chinks in the papers that were filed on the ranch. Any way at all that I could sue this new owner. After that we'll think of some other way to get at him."

"Well, you sound determined, young Shuntington."

"It's my ranch. If Dad is gone, then it's my responsibility. I know dad would never walk away from his dream, not a chance in hell! Somebody might have driven him off, shot at him, something. You can be damn certain that I'm going to find out, and take care of the situation."

He walked around the room again. "Your first job is to check those legal papers, and the deed. See if it's really my father's signature or if it's a forgery. I'll be in touch."

Rutger walked out of the room and Spur followed. Spur caught up with him on the steps.

"You laid it on pretty hard in there, Rutger."

"True, I wanted to see his reaction. Also, I want to see what he will do. I've never liked the man. I caught him fondling my sister when she was sixteen. I wouldn't trust him to file his own death certificate."

They went across the street and into the Johnson Dry Goods store.

"I want to watch out the window and see if Parker leaves his place."

"Is there a back stairs?" Spur asked.

"Oh, yeah."

"I'll cover it." Spur walked out the front door, hurried across the street to a saloon and went through it and into the alley. He stepped behind a pile of pasteboard boxes just as Elliot Parker strode out the back door of his office, down wooden steps and marched down the alley away from Spur.

The lawyer went into the back door next to the brick building down the way. Spur checked it. Second establishment from the corner. He walked around to main street and saw that the second business was the Tumbleweed Saloon. Interesting. The lawyer suddenly had a big thirst. Or did he?

Spur leaned against the store across the street with a sign that identified it as: "I. J. Locklear, Dentistry." He pulled his hat down to shade his eyes and hide most of his face.

Five minutes later a man came out of the Tumbleweed Saloon, jumped on a horse and moved out of town to the north. Spur saw the fresh Circle S brand on the nag's hip. He wished he knew exactly why this Circle S rider came out of the saloon so quickly after Elliot Parker went in the back door.

Elliot Parker swore as soon as the door closed to his office on the second floor and Rutger Shuntington walked out. The kid was giving the orders now? Christ, there was gonna be shit flying over this! The kid wasn't even supposed to come back home until school was over at the end of the summer. Curt was going to shit green and puke purple.

Parker locked the front door, grabbed his hat and jammed it on as he went out the back door making sure it locked. He charged down the steps to the alley and up six doors to the Tumbleweed Saloon.

Once inside he turned left and took the steps three at a time. His key opened a lock and he slumped down behind an old desk in a chair with a feather pillow.

"Zeke!" he bellowed.

A razor blade thin man walked in with a small bar towel over his arm.

"Yeah, boss?"

"A cold beer and get Terry up here pronto."

Zeke had seen Parker in this mood before. He vanished, grabbed a bottle of cold beer from the ice box and waved at Terry who stood at the bar.

"Boss wants you upstairs, right now."

"He look mad?"

"Damn mad, if'n you ask me. Take the cold beer up to him, that might cool him down a mite."

Terry grabbed the bottle of beer and hurried up the steps. He pushed into the small office and looked at Parker, then took a step backward.

"Give me the damn beer!" Parker bellowed. He had written a note and now folded it and put it in an envelope. In it he had told Curt Cameron exactly what was going on in town, including the sudden appearance of the son of the former Circle S owner. They both knew the trouble that made.

They both knew the trouble that made.

"Now we are in a hell of a mess. Get those cattle rounded up at once so we can sell them and get moving!"

Parker didn't sign the note. Just pushed it in the envelope, sealed it and folded the white protector once. He looked up at Zeke and scowled.

"You get this into Curt's hand, and no other, or I'll cut your whang off, you understand me, Zeke?"

"Yeah, right. Got it. You want me to ride straight out there or meander around a little?"

"Straight as a rifle bullet, and just as fast. Move!" The sudden shouted word rolled Zeke out of the office and sent him running down the steps. He didn't even take time to grab a cold bottle of beer before he hurried out to the street and climbed on board his old dun gelding and spurred him out of town to the north.

Parker watched him go, then went down the stairs and checked the poker tables. The man he wanted wasn't there. It took Parker a half hour to find Weldon. Only name he'd ever known the man by. Parker pulled out a chair at a penny ante game in a saloon down the street and tossed a dime in the pot. The dealer dealt him a hand of five card stud.

"Weldon, the Circle S has five-thousand head of prime beef. You buying?"

"Sometimes. Not when I'm card playing."

"It's penny ante, for Christ sakes."

"Poker is poker. After the game."

When the hand was over, Weldon nodded. "Got a wire this morning. Chicago is stuffed with beef. You got any sheep or hogs?"

"Hell, no."

"Can't buy any steers for three days. No cattle cars to get out this far. Used them up in Dodge and the rest of Kansas. You get me a hundred box cars and I'll buy every steer you can beg, borrow or rustle."

"Three days?"

"At least three days."

"Can you ship five-thousand?"

"Can you round up five-thousand?"

"Yes."

"Get them here, I'll buy them. Now, let's play some real poker. Nickel a bump."

Elliot Parker stood up and snorted in disgust. He didn't want to play poker. He had much bigger game to stalk. He went out the back door and down to his law office.

Spur had watched Elliot Parker go from saloon to saloon. At last the lawyer failed to leave one drinking emporium, and Spur found Rutger still in Johnson Dry Goods pacing up and down and showing his anger and impatience.

"Dinner time back at the hotel," Spur said. "I'll bring it up to your room."

Spur had just brought the plates back down to the dining room when he saw an old friend.

"Frank Weldon, you old shyster gone bad. Is this your territory now?"

The cattle buyer stared at Spur for a moment, then stuck out his big hand. "McCoy, be damned. Ain't seen you since Dodge. You still working the lawman angle?"

"Seem to be. You been here long?"

"Two years."

"Then you knew the Shuntingtons."

"Much as anybody. Kept to themselves a bit."

"What happened to them?"

"Damned if I know. One day they were here, next day gone and a new man running things. His name is Curt Cameron. Fact is, I just made a deal for five-thousand head of his steers soon as he can get them to the stock yard."

Rutger Shuntington had come up behind where the men were speaking.

"No! It can't be! If he sells off five-thousand head, that will bring our level of good breeding stock too low. He's got to be cutting into the breeding stock to sell that many this time of the year!"

Frank Weldon looked up surprised.

"Rutger Shuntington, Frank. He's the man who should know about his father's herd."

Rutger set his jaw. "I was hoping you could tell us what happened to my parents, Mr. Weldon. Dad and mom both gone, and this wild man selling off the herd! He's looting the ranch of everything we own. I won't stand for it!

"McCoy, we've got to figure out how to stop this bastard before he ruins the Circle S!"

6

Blade Gunnison sat naked on the edge of the bed and cleaned his fingernails with his eight-inch hunting knife. The blade glistened from honing and Gunnison claimed he could shave with it. He only proved it on a bet.

Blade belched and wiped a dribble of saliva from his mouth. The woman on the bed beside him yawned.

"When the hell you gonna get to it, Blade? I ain't got all day for a fucking two dollars."

"Shut up your face, Petite, or I'll slap it shut!" Gunnison took a swing at her but the woman fell back away from the blow.

"Come on, Blade, you ain't got your money's worth yet. You got it in you for a second time or you done blew your whole wad with one fuck?"

"Day I can't cum twice, bitch, is the day I try for three."

"Show me," La Petite growled at him. She spread her legs and lifted her knees and grinned. La Petite had named herself when she first came to The Sewing Circle whorehouse two years ago when they were still in a tent. She stood a little over five-feet eleven, was big boned and slightly chunky, weighing a sturdy one-hundred and seventy pounds. Her breasts billowed out like ripe melons even when she lay flat on her back.

"Show me, little man."

He slapped her breast, his face purple. "Don't you ever call me that again!" he roared. At once he dropped between her heavy thighs and jabbed at her crotch. When he plunged in he snorted.

"Damn, La Petite, you're half cunt, you know that? Half cunt and the rest tits and mouth,"

"Whatever you say, Blade. Now show me what a big man you really are."

Blade grunted, drew up his knees outside of her thighs and pounded against her. By that time he was so angry at her that it didn't take long.

Ten ramming hard strokes and he went off like a premature dynamite charge.

La Petite brushed back dark hair from her face and laughed. "Oh, hell yes, Blade, you're a big fucking man. You must be at least seven-feet tall!" Her laugh roared out again and Blade reached over the side of the bed for his belt.

His hand came back with his eight-inch knife and he laid the razorlike edge of it against her throat.

"You got to do one more thing for me, whore. I always wanted to kill a fucking whore while I was inside her. Know what I mean? I think now is the right time. Whole territory of Wyoming be hell of a lot better off without you around."

La Petite lay totally still. Only her eyes moved. She watched his sadistic, leering face.

"Come on, Blade, just a little joke. A girl's got feelings too, you know."

"You feel with your crotch and think with your pussy." He stared at her a moment, then snorted. "Hell no. I'm not wasting my great idea on some big horse like you. I want me a small little pretty thing with a lot to live for. Horses like you just fuck and breed and get sent out to pasture or turned into soap."

He moved the knife down to her breasts and sliced a three-inch line a quarter-inch deep across one. Blood flowed at once and La Petite lunged away and screamed louder than any woman he had ever heard.

Blade jerked out of her, pulled on his pants and jammed on his boots. The whore on the bed continued to scream. Before he had on his shirt, Blade saw the door edge open.

Barney stood there staring. Barney was slow witted. He looked at the blood, then at Blade.

"Barney, kill the bastard!" La Petite screamed. "He cut me bad! Kill the fucking bastard! Take out that six-gun and give it to me if you won't use it!"

Blade moved toward Barney shaking his head.

"Don't do anything, Barney. Not your fight. Just turn around and go tell that old bitch downstairs it's no problem. Go on, get out of here!"

Barney loomed a foot over the five-foot four enforcer for the Circle S ranch. Barney shook his head.

"Blood," he said. "No hurt girls, no blood."

"Get out of here you halfwit. Move, damnit!"

Blade got his shirt on and slammed his fist into Barney's gut. The man was slow mentally, but not physically. He was as strong as a big draft horse. Blade's fist felt like he had hit an iron wall.

Slowly Barney stepped toward Blade. "You come," he said.

Blade snorted, swiped his knife toward the big man who didn't even try to dodge. The keen edge sliced a wound a half-inch deep across Barney's thick forearm.

Barney looked at the blood on his arm. He growled. His eyes went wide for a moment, then he walked toward Blade. The big knife rammed forward, Blade's wrist and arm forming a straight line with the weapon as it grated off a rib and plunged deep into Barney's chest.

Blade jerked it out and reversed the motion and before La Petite could scream again, the razor-edge sliced across Barney's throat, severing both carotid arteries. Blood spurted from the tubes, splashing across the room from the intense pressure in the slow witted man's blood lines. His eyes went wide again, he looked at Blade, then at La Petite. His hand started to come up, then ten seconds after his throat slash, Barney crumpled to the floor in a pile of lifeless bone and muscle.

La Petite forgot her wound. She darted around both men and ran down the hall, naked and screaming.

Blade looked at her a minute, then glanced out the window. If the sheriff came he'd have to explain. Instead of the sheriff, Blade saw Spur McCoy walk out of a store and turn into the seamstress lady's shop. Why in hell was he heading in there? Blade caught at his rifle that stood beside the door, but by the time he got it aimed, the doorway to the shop stood empty.

Blade snarled, cleaned the knife off on the dead man's shirt and ran for the stairs. He met the old whore herself, Wanda, as she charged up the steps from the first floor.

"What you been doing, Blade?" she shrilled.

Blade slapped her to one side and ran down the stairs, out the front door and headed for the seamstress shop. He hesitated before he went in. He'd never been in such an establishment before.

Then he thought of his quarry just inside and slammed the door open as he bolted in, his six-gun raised and cocked.

Blade stopped just past the door and looked

around. Bolts of cloth, strange looking half women forms with no heads standing on wire devices, some with part of a fancy dress on them. At the side he saw a head bob up from her lock stitch Singer sewing machine.

Fear flared across Amy York's face as she saw the gun.

She stood slowly, her face nearly white now. "Yes?" she asked in a soft voice.

Blade ignored her, stared around at the small shop, trying to find out where Spur hid. He found no possible location. A door at the back stood half open. Blade charged it, came into an empty room another forty-feet deep that had a door in the rear.

No spot showed where the man could be hiding, so Blade rushed to the door and stared out cautiously. No one showed in the alley. Blade swore, went back in the shop and stood in front of the seamstress.

"Where the hell is he?"

"I beg your pardon?"

"That man who just came in here. Where the fu—Where did he go?"

"Out the back, the same way you went. Why?"

"None of your business. It ain't healthy in this town to know that gent. See that you don't."

"I don't know who you are, sir," Amy said, her color coming back and rising to a red surge, "but I'll be friends with anyone I wish to. The likes of you will never tell me what to do."

"Damn uppity female! I've had enough of your kind today!" Blade whirled and stormed out the front door. The force of his exit jerked two screws out of wood that held the bottom of the screen door in place.

Amy sighed and looked after him as he marched down the boardwalk.

Blade fumed as he walked. What the hell? He

could have had a shot at the bastard if he hadn't been fucking around with that damn halfwit! Blade slid into a chair outside of the Tumbleweed Saloon, tipped back against the wall and watched the street. The fucker had to come out sometime and go into the hotel. That would be his last mistake!

Blade growled at anyone who approached him. Two riders from the Circle S tried to talk to him and he waved them away with insults. He had a job to do and so far he hadn't got it done. Who would have guessed the asshole would have stayed in somebody else's room the other night when the dynamite went off? Damn lucky for him.

Blade spent half the day watching the street, checking everyone on the boardwalk, and viewing the front and side doors of the Medicine Bow Hotel, but Spur McCoy had not shown up. Just like the bastard to get a room on the ground floor back so he could go in and out the window into the alley.

Blade belched. He was hungry. He sat there on the chair for a minute more, looked across at the small cafe on the other side of the street and at last gave in. As he walked across the dusty, horse-dropping littered avenue, he spotted four more Circle S riders spaced down the boardwalk. They were all hunting for Spur McCoy. The man who brought McCoy's head to Curt earned a fifty-dollar bounty.

Good hunting.

There were at least five more men in town. Not even Blade knew where they hid. In case of a shoot, there would be plenty of friendly guns from the company.

Blade ate a steak, three vegetables and four slices of thick cut bread. He sopped up the gravy with the last slab of bread and looked at the kitchen.

Enough. He had to be able to walk, even run if he found McCoy. He paid and left the eatery. Two more of the Circle S riders drifted into the cafe. Nobody spoke to anybody else.

Blade Gunnison belched again, grinned and settled down on the bench outside the hardware store. It was almost in the center of town and he could see both ways a block and a half to the end of the three-year-old village. Not one hell of a lot here yet. Might be some day.

He pulled the big knife out and cleaned his fingernails again, then he stabbed the blade into the inch-thick boards that formed the walkway. Hell, he might have to wait until dark . . . again.

Spur McCoy had made three quick trips to the town section that afternoon. Each was short, and he kept to the alleys and stores as much as possible. Twice he had left the jail by the back door. On the last trip he went to the hotel and discovered that Rutger Shuntington had left his room. So far Spur hadn't found him. He just hoped that he ran down the young man before some Circle S rider figured out who he was.

At least all of the Circle S riders were strangers, and didn't know Rutger. That could explain why the young man was still alive. Spur came through the alley and up to the street where the bank stood. He peered around the corner and down the boardwalk. It was still light, maybe six-thirty.

A look east proved unproductive. He glanced the other way and spotted Rutger coming out of the gun shop. The lean young man settled a new gunbelt on his hips, adjusted the feel of the holster with its load of a six-gun.

Spur walked out of the alley, strode down the boardwalk close to the buildings and caught Rutger around the shoulder and propelled him on down the street. They walked straight for the hardware store.

Too late Spur saw Blade Gunnison let his chair drop to the boardwalk and come up with a fist full of iron as he stood.

Spur pushed Rutger out of the way and drew. His thumb cocked the hammer as he grabbed the weapon and in one smooth almost effortless move brought it upward, out of leather. The split second the muzzle cleared the holster he swung it up and his finger caressed the trigger.

Spur's .44 round caught Gunnison in the left shoulder and drove him back against the wall.

Two more men down the street ran forward, six-guns in their hands.

Blade twisted around, lifted his pistol again, but before he could fire, Spur grabbed Rutger and jerked him into Johnson's Dry Good store. They ran through the store and out the back into the alley.

Two men were already down the alley waiting for them. Both lifted guns and Spur and Rutger's irons snarled at about the same time. One of the men went down, the other dodged behind a pile of cordwood.

Spur dove in back of a corner of building and Rutger crouched behind a garbage barrel.

"I'm hit, Jessie Bob! Give me a hand." The voice came with a wail of pain.

The other man fired twice into the barrel, then darted for another cover. Spur fired once and the running Circle S rider went down as a .44 slug slammed through his spinal column.

For a moment it was quiet. Then from behind them a man snarled and Rutger sprinted for the safety of the building.

"The other direction," Rutger whispered. "Another one of them."

"Might be eight or ten Circle S riders in town," Spur said. "Part of the reason I wanted you inside and out of sight."

"Couldn't stand it any longer cooped up that way."

"Better than shot dead."

Spur leaned around the building and fired twice down the alley, then reloaded the empty rounds to put six in the chambers.

A rifle snarled a shot down the alley from the direction of the dead man. Spur pulled back farther. Rutger leaned out to fire down the alley at the six-gun man when a round jolted into his shoulder and tumbled him backward.

Spur grabbed him and pulled him to safety before the marksman could fire again. Spur checked the wound. The lead slug had only grazed Rutger's upper arm. Spur wrapped his kerchief around the wound tightly and tied the ends.

"That will hold it for a while."

"Hurt like hell. I don't want to get shot again."

Spur eyed their situation. No way out, gunmen on both ends. He saw at once that there was no back door in the building they were backed up against. Like rats in a trap.

Almost. Spur spotted the ladder at the end of the building. They could go up and over the roof without either man seeing them. Spur pointed at the ladder and asked Rutger if he could do it with one arm. The young man gritted his teeth from the pain in his arm.

"I can . . . got to or die." He ran for the ladder.

Spur sent a bullet each way every two or three minutes. Soon there were two guns on each end of the alley. He let more time go between rounds. Then when he was sure Rutger was up the ladder, he fired once more and ran for the boards nailed up the side of the building.

Spur climbed. He was almost at the top when someone shouted below and behind him. He whirled almost at the roof line. A six-gun fired once from below. Spur drew and kicked out two rounds at the Circle S man, knocked him down with the second, and rolled over the parapet to the roof.

Thirty-feet across the roof, Rutger stood at the open door that led downward. Spur joined him and they soon were in the second floor over the General store. The stairs were inside, and they stayed in the store for a half hour. Spur and Rutger both bought new shirts and hats and left their old ones in the store. A little change in appearance right now might work. They left separately, ambling up the street toward the first alley.

Spur had insisted that Rutger come to the jail to stay that night. He offered little objection.

"Hell, don't worry about your shoulder. We'll stop by at that doctor friend of yours, Asamore. I hope he's good."

They made it to the first alley, slipped in and watched. Two men ran down the street and talked with a short man who had a new bandanna bandage around his upper left arm. Three of them talked a bit, then scattered, after reloading their six-guns.

Rutger led Spur to the back door of the doctor's office. Just as they came out of the alley, a gunman laughed and stepped out from some shrubs, his gun coming up.

Spur shot him before he could fire. The round drilled through his chest and heart, missed his back bone and lodged in the side of the house next to him.

Spur pushed open the door and moved into the doctor's back room. Rutger's color was fading. His new shirt sleeve was soaked with blood even after the quick repair job in the General Store.

A man came in wearing a suit and a frown. He was medium sized, lots of gray hair, a paunch and a frown.

"Figured somebody broke in back here." He looked back at Rutger. "It is you, the Shuntington boy, Rutger, right? Hope to hell you can tell us what happened to your parents."

"First let's see what you can do for his fresh gunshot wound. It's not serious. Then if you've got time, I want you to check over some amateur nurse's work on another bullet hole, mine."

Doc Asamore took off Rutger's shirt and frowned.

"Wish you'd quit playing with guns. Never helped a soul a bit. Give me too much work to do." He doused the wound with alcohol and Rutger whimpered, then passed out where he sat in a chair.

Doc grunted and then probed the graze wound in Rutger's upper arm.

"Guess the lead is all out. Sliced up some skin. About all." He worked on the wound, and watched Spur.

"You're the stranger in town who's trying to find out what happened to Ollie Shuntington, I reckon. They didn't leave town of their own accord, I can vouch for that. Guess I can tell now. Mrs. Shuntington had a tumor, bad one. Couldn't do nothing but make her more comfortable. She was on laudanum."

He looked up. "You know that's just watered down opium. I don't like to use it because a patient can get to depend on it. Terrible stuff, but it does make a body forget about the pain, and Mrs. Shuntington was in constant pain. Only way we could relieve it. Nobody in town knew. She was getting a new dress made for a party they had planned. I think she figured it might be her last party."

"Did either of them say anything about moving, selling out, going away?" Spur asked.

"Not a single word. I'm certain Ollie wouldn't

have made his wife suffer that way. Nope, they're either prisoners out there or they're both dead. Goldarnit, you can bank on that."

A few minutes later Doc had Rutger's wound bandaged and the young man had regained consciousness. Dr. Asamore looked at Spur's thigh wound, scraped off a little dead skin and put on some salve and rebandaged it.

"Whoever did that the first time knew what he was doing," Doc said. "You was lucky it was a clean through shot." When he finished he took the pair of greenback dollar bills Spur gave him.

"I could get spoiled, getting paid for my services. Come back every time you get shot," he snorted. "Actually, I'd rather not see you again in that the case." Doc Asamore sobered. "McCoy, do what you can to find out about Ollie and his missus. They was good folks. I'm just feared we won't see them again."

Rutger was a little woozy but he stood and he could walk. They went round about and it was just getting dark when they walked into the back door of the jail.

"Sheriff, have a new customer for you. He was firing his pistol in the city limits."

Sheriff Dryer grunted. He pushed a paper over to Spur. "Sign it, you got to be in on this last shooting, right? In the alley in back of the General Store. Kid was from the Circle S. Never did get his name. The other Circle S riders tied him over a horse and lit out. Figured it had to be you."

"One more gun we won't have to face when we charge the Circle S," Spur said.

Sheriff Dryer looked up quickly as if trying to figure out if Spur were serious or not.

Spur never told him.

7

Priscilla Shuntington sniffed daintily and moved away from the man who sat beside her on the Union Pacific railroad passenger coach. Her journey was almost over and she was looking forward to seeing her brother.

The letter that had finally arrived with the telegram in it from Sheriff Dryer was most unsettling. She had heard from her parents a month before. They were fine, the Spring roundup was getting started and everything was progressing nicely.

Then the letter came from the sheriff. She had taken a stage coach from Denver up to Cheyenne, then boarded the train. This trip numbered only her second ride and she enjoyed the fifty-mile run to Laramie. Even if one man had been more than friendly. At last she had taken a pair of scissors from her purse and laid them in her lap as she pretended to sew a button on.

Every time the man tried to talk to her, she picked up the scissors holding them like a knife. The man had soon moved to another seat. This current swain seemed not so easily discouraged.

"Now, miss. You don't have to hold those scissors like you're about to run me through. We both know you won't do that, because I'm just a friendly gent who likes to talk to beautiful girls. And you're about the prettiest thing I've seen in a month of Saturdays."

She turned and looked out the window trying to hide a small smile of pleasure at his compliment. "Sir, I am not speaking with you. I made that clear."

He grinned. He appeared to be about twenty-five, wore a suit, white shirt and tie and carried a case. Some kind of a drummer. He even sounded like a salesman.

"All that wonderful blonde hair and the way it's curled so nice is certainly your crowning glory, Miss. Are you traveling far? I noticed that you got on at Cheyenne."

She stared out the window, but the faint smile was still there.

"Fact is, what a beautiful lady like you needs is somebody to protect her on a trip like this. I'll be glad to volunteer for the position without any compensation whatsoever."

She turned and pointed the scissors at him. "Then you won't mind being my bodyguard from across the aisle. I need that space to lay out my sewing."

"Sewing? All I see is a bunch of buttons."

"Please let me lay out my things." Priscilla hesitated. "We can even talk."

"Great!" He moved across the aisle, she covered the seat beside her with some sewing and talked with him the last ten miles. He was a salesman heading for Laramie and points west.

When Priscilla detrained at Laramie, she lost the young man who had to find his sample cases. Priscilla had brought with her only a small carpet bag. She could get her other clothes at the ranch.

Priscilla pulled her bag from under the seat and hurried off the train and over to the Medicine Bow

Hotel. She would stay there until she talked with the sheriff and the lawyer. The family counselor must know something about all this.

She told the room clerk to register her on the second floor, left her bag with him and marched straight over to the lawyer's office. She remembered it was on the second level. Parker, that was his name.

Elliot Parker looked up warily when Priscilla came in the door of his office. When he saw her, he jumped to his feet at once. There weren't any girls as pretty as this one in half the state. He recognized Priscilla Shuntington at once. He'd been smitten with her for the past four years.

"Miss Shuntington! Priscilla! How nice to see you!"

She colored slightly. Priscilla remembered the day at the ranch by the well house when he had kissed her lips and then fondled her breasts. Priscilla had been young and curious. The incident still embarrassed her.

"Yes, Mr. Parker, it's good to see you too. Now what is this all about that my parents have sold the ranch and moved?"

"I thought you knew all about it. Your father never consulted me. One day a new owner came in and said he wanted me to make sure the deed was signed correctly and to get it filed with the county clerk along with the bill of sale."

"What did Daddy tell you?"

"Nothing. I hadn't seen him for a week or two before that, and then the new owners came and your parents were gone. Somebody told me they went back to Kentucky to be with relatives."

"Our people live in Ohio."

"Maybe it was Ohio. It was such a surprise to everyone. I figured you and your brother would be the first ones to know about it."

"I don't. I want to hire you to find out exactly what is going on. I have money in a bank in Denver."

"Well, I don't know. Are you of legal age?"

"I'm twenty years old. I don't have to be twenty-one to hire you."

"Let's talk about it. First, are you set up in the hotel?"

"I left my bag there."

"Good. You'll have to stay there until this is settled. These new owners are at the Circle S ranch house. Let me take you over and get you settled in the hotel."

"I can handle that."

"No, no, I insist. It's the least I can do. Room clerks can be a bit difficult at times."

"Not Charley. I've known him for ten years."

Parker would not be dissuaded. He shut up his office, held her arm and guided her across the street past the strings and clumps of horse droppings, and to the boardwalk on the far side. She lifted her skirt to step up to the walk and she saw Parker watching for a flash of ankle.

At the hotel he made sure the room was right with the clerk, then took her bag and walked her down to it. It was on the second floor in back. Parker opened the door and let her go in.

"This will be quiet for you and not a lot of people dashing by your door." At once he closed the door and locked it.

Priscilla looked up at him in surprise. She was more shocked than anything. "Mr. Parker! This is not proper, you being in my hotel room this way with the door closed."

Before she could say another word, Parker pulled her into his arms and kissed her lips. His mouth devoured her, pressed her to him tightly so she could hardly breathe.

When she pulled her lips from his, she screamed. His hand came over her mouth quickly.

"No!" he said roughly. "No more damn screaming or teasing me. You're nothing but a cock tease and today you get what you deserve!"

He picked her up and threw her on the bed. Before she could recover from her surprise he had fallen on top of her, crushing her into the mattress, his hands ripping at the bodice of her dress until it tore apart and he pushed up her chemise revealing her breasts.

"Yes, great tits, I knew it. It's been four years since I've had my hands on them!"

Priscilla screamed again but his hand cut her off. He pulled a large handkerchief from his pocket and tied it around her head and across her open mouth.

"Now, no more screaming. Remember how it felt when I played with your tits in the well house? It's going to feel ten times as good now. Just relax, let it go. Enjoy it, because there is no way in hell that you can stop me."

He pulled off her dress, ripping it nearly in half to get it off her hips. Then he unbuttoned her regular drawers and pulled them down over her feet. He had pressed her hands under her back so she couldn't claw at him. She pulled one loose and scratched his cheek.

Parker slapped her hard, making her head swim for a moment. Then she realized he was right. She couldn't stop him, and he could beat her if she resisted. So she would go limp, not help him, not let him know she felt a thing. She would be like a wet dishcloth.

He spread her legs and at once realized she wasn't fighting him any more.

"Well, so you've come to your senses. Good. This

is what a woman is made for. And such a pretty one as you will enjoy it more and more." He took the gag from her mouth and she swallowed twice to get some moisture back in her mouth.

"Fucking is fun, Priscilla, remember that. Such great tits! Sit up and let me play with them."

He pulled her to a sitting position and marveled at the orbs that were full, with bright pink areolas and nipples. He sucked on them until he groaned with his own passion.

His lips strayed lower, then he pushed her flat and spread her legs.

"Beautiful!" His head dropped into her crotch and he kissed her sweet lips and groaned.

Then he pulled open his pants.

Priscilla couldn't look. Then she did and saw his long "thing" and her eyes widened in amazement. She'd never seen one before, not an erect, hard penis like his! So big. That huge, long thing couldn't possibly enter her!

She knew for sure. She had trouble sometimes getting just one of her fingers up her tight little pussy.

Before she knew it he was over her and his big cock pressing at her opening. She knew it wouldn't go in!

Then he spit in his hand and rubbed it on his long stick. How disgusting! It was the grossest thing she had ever seen!

But this time when he probed there was an opening. She felt a sharp pain and screeched. Then the pain was gone and a soft warm glow replaced it. She felt him sliding into her. It had happened! A man was making love to her! She had dreamed about being with a man, but never thought it would be like this!

She hated him.

She had to hate him because he was raping her. Yes, she hated him.

The soft, warm glow built and built. Her breasts warmed and then felt so hot she knew they were burning. He touched her nipples and they exploded. Her whole body shook and rattled and she humped her hips upward as fast as she could as the spasms drilled through her again and again.

The feeling intensified, becoming the most wonderful, the most thrilling and tremendous experience of her whole life! She wanted it to go on and on.

Three more times the spasms tore through her, setting her on fire, exploding all the old wives tales she had ever heard about sex. It was wonderful!

Still she hated him. It hadn't been her choice. He was good looking enough, it wasn't that. He wasn't her husband. Sex was for married people.

What if she got pregnant?

She refused to think about it. She noticed that Parker was pounding harder now, sweat dripped off his nose and hit her breasts. He humped her faster and faster until he groaned and snorted and brayed in delight as he thrust harder and she felt something hot jetting into her depths.

Suddenly he was done and pulled out of her. He sat on the bed beside her.

"Priscilla, I bet that was your first time, right?" She stared at the ceiling. She had to hate him.

"Don't worry, the next one will be better. We can make love a couple times a day if you want to. I know you'll be going back to school, but when this is all over about your parents, we can slip away and live together."

She sat up and slapped him hard on the face. He swayed to one side and when he came back, she slapped him again.

"Get out of my room, you bastard! As soon as I dress I'm going to the sheriff and charge you with rape."

He looked at her for a minute. "No, I don't think you will. It would ruin you in town. None of the women would ever speak to you again. The men would all try to seduce you knowing you had been had and were now public property, a kind of community chest. No, you won't even tell the sheriff about this, much less charge me with anything."

He stood and pulled his clothes around straight and buttoned up his fly.

"Besides, you'd never be able to prove it. I can find a dozen men who will swear I played cards with them all afternoon. I saw you to the desk clerk, made sure you had a good room, but I never went up the steps with you. Even the room clerk will swear to that for twenty-five dollars."

She slapped him again but he caught her hand before it hit. He pushed her back down on the bed and kissed her. She didn't help or stop him. He fondled her breasts again, then went to the door.

She lay there naked and spent on the bed and looked at him.

"Oh, yes, but you are a good fuck. Now you know it, too. I knew you would be great when I first played with your titties three, four years ago."

"Get out!" Priscilla shouted. "You try to touch me again and I'll kill you!"

"Not true, sweet pussy. Not true because I might be able to help you find your parents, and that's important to you. Just be careful who you tell about this little fuck. Certainly not your brother who might have some sense of chivalry and try to hurt me. Then I'd have to kill him."

He grinned and went to the door. "Take care of that great little body, especially that sweet, juicy pussy!" He slipped out the door and Priscilla lay there naked, spent, sexually satisfied as she had never been before in her life.

She didn't know whether to laugh or to cry. Instead she hugged herself, then sat up and looked in her bag for a dress. She had just one other one. The ripped one might be saved if it had torn apart at the seams. She could take it to Amy, the seamstress.

Yes, that would work.

Priscilla sat there a moment thinking about her experience. The first time! She hadn't wanted it to be that way, but it had been thrilling, frightening, shocking, yet tremendously satisfying as well. Had she really been raped, or just roughly seduced? She hadn't fought him very hard.

At last she slipped into her dress and decided not to worry about it. Now she was more interested in the next time, by a man who would be gentle and giving and who would talk to her and explain things as he went along. Yes, the Next Time!

It was still morning. The A.M. train had been right on time, hitting the station at 9:05. Now it was slightly after ten. She would go see the sheriff and ask about her parents. Then she had no idea what she would do.

Would she hire an investigator? Her father had put three-thousand dollars in a Denver bank for her when she decided to go to college there. Most of it was left. She could write a draft on the Denver account and cash it at Mr. Villary's bank here in town. But who would she hire?

After dressing she looked at her hair. It hadn't been mussed up much. Priscilla combed it thoughtfully, patted it in place. It swirled around her shoulders now in a luxurious blonde sheath, bounced on her forehead with bangs and flounced down each side of her head with masses of curls.

Ready.

Strange, she had just been seduced/raped in one of the most terrifying/satisfying experiences of her life. Now she calmly combed her hair, adjusted her dress and got ready to go see the sheriff about her parents. Damn! She was growing up a little!

Sheriff Dryer shook his head at the pretty girl across his desk. "I'm sorry Miss Shuntington, I haven't been able to find a shred of evidence that your parents are still in the county. I wish I could. Your brother is in town, did you know that? He stayed in a cell here last night because the Circle S men are trying to shoot him."

"I guessed Rutger would come. Tell him I'm in the hotel." She stared at the law man. "Isn't there something we can do? Anything legally?"

"Not that I know of, Miss Shuntington. So far I have no evidence that a crime has been committed. the man has a legal bill of sale, the grant deed on the land has been signed over and registered with the county clerk. The ranch is his. Not a single reason for me to barge in there and demand to know what happened."

"But you knew my parents. They were your friends. How can you just let them vanish without a trace that way? Don't you wonder why they never came into town? Isn't it possible that the man who claimed he bought the ranch is really a killer who stole it and murdered my parents? Isn't that possible?"

Stan Dryer stood and walked around the room. He hated this part of his job. He stopped and watched the girl. She was strong, determined. She could get herself killed.

"Yes, Miss Shuntington, that is entirely possible. The chances are it's more than possible. The way the

Circle S men are rampaging around town, I'd say what you described is probably what has happened. The only problem is, there has to be some PROOF that it happened. Law depends on proving things. Right now I can't prove a single thing illegal took place."

He waggled a finger at her. "And I don't want you to start messing in the picture. A government man is in town trying to figure it out. He got himself shot at three times the first day he was here.

"There has been at least one try to gun down your brother. These men are not playing games. So far half a dozen men have been killed. Most of them from the other side. I want you to be damned sure that you understand that this is a deadly affair."

"Yes, I understand that. I'd like to talk to this government man. Where is he staying?"

"The only safe place in town right now for him. Here at the jail."

'You mean it?"

"Of course. They dynamited his hotel room the first night. He got away."

Spur McCoy stepped into the sheriff's office, then saw Priscilla.

"Oh, sorry, Sheriff. Didn't know you had a visitor."

"Come in, McCoy. This is a lady you need to meet. Her name is Priscilla Shuntington."

Spur held his hat in one hand as he came in. He nodded to the woman. "I've been expecting you, Miss Shuntington. We're trying to sort out exactly what happened here."

"Do you think my parents are dead?"

Spur smiled, turned his hat. "You seem to be a very straight forward person, Miss Shuntington. There is a good chance that this is an outlaw band of some kind who conspired to take over the ranch.

Your parents may have been eliminated in the process. These cowboys on your ranch seem more like outlaws than range hands. They all shoot exceptionally well, and are not afraid of a fight. We're still trying to piece together what happened."

"Mr. McCoy, I want to know everything you do about the problem. Can we have something to eat at the hotel dining room and talk?"

"That's a little public for me, Miss Shuntington. But there is a small restaurant down the street where I've been eating in a back room. If that's all right with you."

"Of course. Right now my job is to find out about my parents. Sheriff, if my brother comes in, send him to the same resturant, would you please?"

Sheriff Dryer nodded.

They ate and talked. Soon Spur had her up to date on developments including his suspicions about the lawyer. Priscilla seemed uncomfortable as he described their talk with Parker.

"Yes, I know Mr. Parker. I never have trusted him and never will. Would the outlaws have needed a person here in town to do all of the paperwork for them? If so, I wouldn't put it past Parker."

"Possible. He's on my list to watch. Right after we talked to him yesterday a rider rushed out for the ranch."

Spur stared at her. "How are we going to keep you safe? There is no chance you can stay in the jail."

"Won't I be safe in the hotel?"

"Not if they decide that you'll be in the way, or a threat to them." Spur shrugged. "Looks like you'll have to move out of your room without telling the clerk, and move into the room Rutger rented on the third floor. No, we'll put you next door someplace and I'll get the room beside you."

"You could stay in my room," she said quickly. Then put her hand over her mouth. "I mean, I could sleep in a chair and you could. . . ." She stopped and laughed. "Oh dear. I shouldn't have said that. I don't want you to think. . . ."

Spur laughed and shook his head. "I'm not thinking anything about what you said. But, it might be better if I had the adjoining room on the third floor."

When the meal was over he sent her into the hotel by the side door, and five minutes later he slipped in the same way and went to the third floor. She was in Rutger's room. He moved her bag to the room next door, and then he occupied the one next to hers.

Spur pushed the heavy dresser in front of the window. The tall model covered most of the glass and would prevent anyone from breaking in that way. He showed her how to set the chair under the locked door.

"What you're telling me is you're not going to be here for a while?"

"That's right. When it gets dark, I want to be halfway out to the Circle S ranch. A little scouting trip to see what I can find out."

"Be careful. May I call you Spur?"

"Yes, of course."

"You call me Priscilla." She hesitated. "Do you need to run the risk of going out there?"

"Yes. I'll be back. Nobody has killed me yet."

Priscilla smiled boldly. "Spur, I'll be just terribly mad if somebody does now. I want to get to know you better."

"That sounds interesting. When I get back."

He went out the door, waited until he heard her slide the chair under the knob, then slipped down the stairs and headed for the livery stable by the

8

Spur McCoy eased out the side door of the hotel. He had scanned the side street both ways and left only when he was certain that there were no prowling gunmen or idlers who could be Circle S hands. He hurried down to the alley and headed for the back door of the hardware store.

Ten minutes later he left the establishment with six-feet of dynamite fuse, a dozen detonator caps and twenty sticks of dynamite. Stumps that needed blowing out, he had told the clerk.

Spur used his roundabout route to get to the livery stables at the edge of town, and saddled up his roan. He paid the livery man for the board and room and rode out to the south so he wouldn't go through town. He had a two hour wait before dark. This far north the sun stayed up a lot longer than it did in New Mexico.

Spur knew the stable hand was watching him. He skirted some brush near a small stream and when he rode out of sight, turned west toward the strip of green trees. He crossed the Union Pacific tracks and angled northwest toward the Laramie river.

It was a strange waterway. Headwaters were far to the south in Colorado. It ran north into Wyoming, then north through Laramie and angled northeast at last into the North Platte River.

McCoy found a section he could ford and walked his roan through knee deep water to the far side.

Once behind the brush and cottonwoods along the stream, he felt more at ease. Spur took his time moving north. All of Laramie was now nearly a half mile on the far side of the river where it had built up around the railroad tracks.

He idled along, enjoying the coolness of the rushing water, a green ribbon in a semi-desert of high Wyoming plateau and the rolling start of the great range of mountains to the west.

Time would be slow to change this land. There was no reason to draw great numbers of people here. But Laramie would continue because it was a railroad town. The Southern Pacific had created Laramie to meet its fifty mile mandate from the government, and had left shops and workers here to service the rails and the trains. Each fifty miles of track meant the railroad had to put up a town. Some lasted, most didn't.

Idly, Spur wondered what the country and the town would look like in a hundred years, say 1971. He pondered on it a moment, shrugged and moved on. He had enough to worry about with the present, let alone the future.

He had not been thinking Indians. When he saw rail tracks he just discounted the idea of Indians being around, but he knew that was an over simplification.

There could be Oglala, Arapaho and Cheyenne in the area. It was mainly Cheyenne territory, but the other tribes were wandering more and more these days with all the white settlers surging into what were once reserved Indian hunting grounds.

A half hour later he had left the northern edges of Laramie far behind and was approaching the Circle

S ranch lands. He found a small rise and stared ahead into the vast territory controlled by the Circle S.

He could see no men riding guard duty. He sniffed carefully but could detect no hint of wood smoke. McCoy ground-tied his roan, sat down in the green grass near the river and watched the water. Soon he stretched out for a quick nap.

When he woke he sat up quickly. It was deep dusk, and would be fully dark in another ten minutes. Spur rode north. Once on the Circle S lands, he moved cautiously, but saw nor heard any riders.

Two-thirds of the way to the ranch house he heard cattle. He didn't have to wonder what caused the sounds. Spur had been on enough cattle trail drives to recognize the clues. The lowing and bawling came from a sizeable herd being contained and circled and bedded down for the night.

Hopefully.

The toughest job a cowboy has to do is try to bed down and control a herd that is not tired out, and has a touch of spookiness about it. This herd seemed to be of that type.

He found them just over a small hump of land to the left. Spur sat his roan near the river and saw that the cowboys had used the treeline as one boundary and were herding the critters into a semblance of a circle for the night. They were late. The bedding down should have been done well before dark.

Spur watched them a moment. The beef obviously were Circle S cattle that the new owner had decided to sell. He remembered what the cattle buyer had said and Rutger Shuntington's immediate anger at the idea.

This was one herd that would never reach the rail line. Spur moved back a quarter of a mile, dismounted and cut the dynamite fuse he had brought into six-inch lengths and made a dozen bombs by pushing the detonator cap into a hole in the stick of powder, and inserting the burnable fuse into the hollow on the other end of the cap. The burning fuse had enough punch to set off the delicate dynamite detonator and that in turn exploded the powder.

Spur tested one of the sulphur matches he had in a packet and lit a piece of six-inch long fuse. It burned for a slow count of thirty. Most dynamite fuse burned a foot a minute, but some kinds went a lot faster than that. It paid to know which kind of fuse you were using.

Spur carried ten of the dynamite bombs inside his shirt, and two in his hands. He rode up near the herd in the thick darkness, dismounted and studied the cattle. Many were still up, turning, lowing, trying to move. Others had bedded down. A kind of nervous excitement seemed to run through the steers, cows and heifers.

It was a motley gathering, looking more like a roundup herd than a drive to the stockyards. But why else would there be a herd this size so close to the edge of the ranch and headed toward town?

Spur made up his mind. He left his horse and crawled as close to the herd as he felt he could get without being seen. He was still thirty yards from the stock. Then he waited for the night herder to make his round on horseback.

When the horseman was out of sight, Spur lit two fuses and threw the twin bombs within twenty feet of the steers. Then he pulled back and circled around the herd for fifty yards and started to light another fuse.

The first two dynamite bombs went off with a cracking roar that stick powder exploding in the open produces. At once the herd of about two-thousand cattle came on its feet, lowing and bawling. Spur bit the next fuse in half, lit it and threw the bomb.

He pitched four more of the short fused bombs before the next one exploded.

Now he pulled his six gun and began firing over the heads of the confused and frightened animals.

As the last of the bombs exploded, the whole herd began rushing away from the sound, away from the expected danger.

The cattle stampeded into the small camp the drovers had put up. In a few seconds hundreds of cattle had pushed over a chuck wagon, trampled the supplies into mush, destroyed everything in their path as they stampeded away from the danger.

Spur watched them go. Most of them wouldn't stop running for an hour. They would spread out in half a circle from the danger and it would take the poorly trained cow hands three or four days to find them all again in the plains and gullies of southern Wyoming.

Spur grinned as he watched.

But soon his grin faded. He heard riders coming toward him. A man shouted as if he were a cavalry sergeant, and the men on horseback seemed to be following his orders. What kind of a bunch of range hands were these, anyway?

Spur found his horse, jumped on board and whirled just as one of the riders spotted him.

The U.S. Secret Agent sat rock still on his mount as the lone rider bore down on him. At thirty yards, Spur lifted his six-gun and pounded off two quick shots. The close-by rider screamed as he jolted backwards off the saddle and rolled into a broken, dead mass of bones and flesh as he hit the ground.

Spur whirled his roan and raced away to the west. He heard shouted commands behind him and the riders seemed to track him to the west. He stopped and listened. At least four riders were coming his way.

He walked his gelding silently at right angles to his former line of flight, now heading due south.

It took the Circle S riders three or four minutes to pound across the prairie toward him. By that time Spur had covered nearly a hundred yards south and melted into the maw of the skinny moon darkness.

An outrider to the main force took Spur by surprise. The first he knew of the enemy was a blast of a .44 and the whistling of hot lead past his shoulder. Spur spun, his big .44 tracking the hard riding cowboy. The man had flattened out along the neck of his horse to leave a smaller target.

Spur fired once and the cowboy screeched. The round had slammed into his hip, half unseating him. He dropped his six-gun and swore as he whipped his mount around and charged away from Spur.

McCoy rode hard to the south now, depending on the gelding's good lungs and strong legs to move him away from the Circle S men. They would know exactly where he was by the gunshots. It was run or be overwhelmed.

Twenty minutes of hard riding and Spur could feel the sweat and foam on the big gelding. A moment later he saw the lights of Laramie. He doubted if the Circle S riders would chase him all the way into the little town. Spur stopped and listened. He could hear no hoofbeats behind him. The closest saloon was easy to hear, however. First there was laughter and yelps of pleasure, then the deadly ring of a pistol round and a lot of quiet following it.

Another typical night in a wild railroad town.

Spur looked for Rutger in his hotel room but the room stood empty. The saloons were the next best choice. After checking in four, Spur at last found Rutger Shuntington confronting Elliot Parker. Both men had been drinking, but neither was drunk.

McCoy pushed through the crowd and stood near the men but neither looked at him.

"Then you don't deny it?" Rutger challenged.

"I took what she offered. I did not force myself on her. I don't need to do that with any woman."

There were cheers and cat calls from the crowd of men.

"And I say you raped her! If you're any kind of a man at all you'll belt on a gun and meet me outside in five minutes. If you're not out there, I'll hunt you down like the raping, mad dog that you are!"

Rutger turned and downed the last of his whiskey, then walked out the door. A pistol came up by an unseen hand near Spur and the secret agent's fist slashed down where the gunman's wrist should be. It hit flesh and there was a crack as bones snapped.

A Circle S rider screeched, dropped his six-gun and bellowed in pain about his broken wrist. The crowd parted enough to show who the man was holding his broken wrist. Spur plowed his left fist into the cowboy's belly and when he bent over with the sudden new pain, Spur's right knee rammed upward into the man's chin snapping his head back. He crashed to the floor to the rear and Spur hurried out the door after Rutger.

The son of the former owner of the Circle S stood with his back against the ship lap siding of the hardware store watching everyone. He saw Spur and nodded.

"This is a strange place to find you after we decided you should stay out of sight for a few days."

"The bastard raped Priscilla a half hour after she got off the train. He's wanted her for years. I couldn't just stand by."

"Guess not. But you know it's dark out. In five minutes there'll be ten hidden Circle S guns waiting for you out here. All Parker has to do is walk out of a saloon door, draw his gun and you'll have ten rounds in you from ambush."

"Dumb, all right. What I did was dumb. What's next?"

"Something smart. All we have to do is figure out something smart."

"But I *am* meeting him. Not a chance I'll back down on this!"

"I was afraid you'd say something like that. I saw Priscilla a few hours ago. She did not look in dire straights to me."

"She was covering it up."

"So what do we do smart?"

Rutger shrugged. "First, get off the street. Then you come up with an idea. You're the gunman."

Spur nodded and they walked quickly back toward the hotel.

"There's a lightning struck cottonwood a half mile out of town north. I'll try to get Parker to be there in half an hour. We'll go out early and wait. We'll walk. You have a gun?"

Rutger patted his holster.

Spur found Parker still at the saloon bar where he had left him. He was about to take another whiskey when Spur knocked it off the bar.

"No time for that, Parker. I'm second for Rutger. He's calling you out at the lightning struck tree a half mile north of town. You be there in half an hour or ride out of town. You savvy?"

Parker stared at him. His eyebrows lifted, then his mouth twisted. "Why the hell not? I used to be pretty good with a six-gun. I even have one in my office. Half an hour, I'll be there."

As Spur turned he came face to face with Blade Gunnison. The five-foot, four-inch killer had to look up to see the lawman's face. Before he could even reach for his weapon, Spur's Colt was out and tapping the bad-ass on the chest.

"If I see you anywhere around this shootout, you'll be dead meat waiting for the buzzards tomorrow morning. You understand me?"

Gunnison blanched from embarrassment, slowly nodded, then reached up and brushed the muzzle off his chest.

"Hell yes, you I can get anytime, anytime at all."

Spur's eyes hooded. "No, small gunman, not anytime. You've missed at least four times in the past. Your next try will be your last one, so make it good. I'll be ready."

Spur kept his weapon out as he backed toward the door. He slammed through it and darted to one side. As he did he heard the roar of a six-gun behind him and lead smash into the wooden batwing door as it swung back in place.

Rutger was waiting for Spur in the alley next to the Medicine Bow Hotel and they used an Indian trot to move north to the old cottonwood.

"Indians can run at this pace for six hours without stopping and be ready to fight when they get there," Spur said.

Rutger panted like a steam engine on a siding. "Then they're in much better condition than I am."

They got to the old cottonwood and Spur told Rutger to stand behind it and not move until Parker came, no matter what happened.

"You expect visitors?"

"Yes, two or three to help out Parker. He might not even know about it."

Spur vanished into the darkness moving back toward town fifty yards. Spur wished he'd brought a rope, but that good idea came a little too late. He heard a horse coming down the trail.

The odds were that the man would stop short of the tree. Spur stood near the river behind some brush as the hoofbeats came closer. Then the mount angled into the brush where Spur stood. He waited until the last possible split second, then jumped out as the rider walked the horse past Spur.

Spur caught the rider's right arm and jerked him off the horse.

"What the hell?" was all the man could say before Spur slammed his .44 down hard on the black hatted head. The bushwhacker crumpled and Spur tied his hands and feet, then used the rider's neckerchief to gag him.

Spur caught the horse, mounted it and found a lariat hung around the horn. He shook it out, formed a loop. It was a good rope. He nosed the black mare out to the trail and waited. Three or four minutes later a man rode hard for the big tree, pulled up when he made it just past Spur and angled into a patch of small cottonwoods on the other side of the trail.

Spur dismounted, took the rope and worked across the trail and through the woods. He spotted the man checking a rifle and looking for a good field of fire at the cottonwood.

McCoy formed a loop in the rope and twirled it, hit a small tree and trailed the loop as he moved toward his prey. In an open spot, the bushwhacker found a downed log to fire over. The same opening also gave Spur room to throw his loop and after two circles over his head, he threw the rope and saw it settle neatly over the rifleman.

Spur jerked backward with the rope wrapped around both arms, and the gunman spilled into the dirt, lost his rifle and found his arms pinned tightly against his sides.

It took Spur only a moment to relax the pressure on the rope. He darted forward twenty feet and rammed one foot down on the gunman's chest.

"Well shuck my hide, look what I caught in my loop," Spur drawled.

"Let me out of here!"

"Afraid not, bushwhacker. You was aiming to do a bad thing. Grown men been known to get themselves killed for trying what you're getting ready to try. You also ready to die, stranger?"

The man shrugged. "Shit yes. Been ready since the Wilderness."

"So you were in the war?"

"Hell, yes. Most men our age was in the war."

"And now you work for Curt Cameron. I've heard he's not really a rancher, true?"

The man laughed. "I might get sloppy on assignments like this, but I don't run off at the mouth. Forget it."

Spur put more pressure on his boot until the man wheezed.

"Go ahead, stomp me. Told you I was ready. One way or another, don't matter a damn bit to me."

The secret agent growled and tied up the man with the rope and made sure his horse was tied. Then he gagged the man and went back to the trail.

Ten minutes later, another rider came up the trail, his horse at a walk. He sat upright, his left hand holding the reins and his right on his six-gun on his right hip. He stared at the brush on both sides.

Spur let him pass. The man was Elliot Parker. Spur followed him on foot. Parker got to the old cottonwood and dismounted, drew his gun a few times and then looked around.

"I'm here, Rutger, where the hell are you?"

Spur moved around through the brush until he could see Rutger, then he slid up beside him without a sound.

"Oh God! you scared me!" Rutger whispered.

"It's time. If you're determined."

"I've got to. I made a public call out. He raped Priscilla. There's no other way."

Spur sighed. "All right. You have six rounds in your weapon?"

"No. Oh, sure, I might need them. I'm not what you'd mistake for a crack shot."

Rutger took a round from his belt and pushed it in the empty chamber, then let the hammer down cautiously on the round. He straightened his shoulders. He walked out from the cottonwood.

Parker stood thirty feet away.

"Parker, you rapist! Are you ready to apologize to Priscilla and stand trial for rape?"

Parker whirled, his hand on his gun. He saw in the sliver of moonlight that Rutger had not drawn.

"Not guilty. Sure she protested a little, they all do the first few times. Or are you still a virgin yourself, Shuntington?"

Rutger drew his six-gun and fired. He didn't aim, it was an automatic reaction. Then he shivered, lifted the weapon and tried to aim at the other man.

Parker had been jolted by the shot and drew as fast as he could. He hadn't fired a pistol in two years. Now he stood facing Rutger, his feet spread wide. Too late he realized he made a larger target that way.

Then Rutger walked deliberately forward. He fired twice more and missed.

Parker fired once and the round hit the ground ten feet in front of him. He swore and tried to aim. He fired again and missed.

Then in a hazy, dark scene, Parker realized that Rutger was running, running straight at him! The Shuntington pistol fired again and again, but missed. Parker wanted to turn and run, but he couldn't. He couldn't even move. He hated death more than anything, and now he stared at it in the face of a twenty-one year old angry young man!

Rutger counted his rounds. He had fired five times. He had one round left. He ran faster, saw Parker frozen in place and this time he lifted his arm higher, pointed his whole arm at Parker's chest and fired.

If he missed he was dead, because Parker must have three or four rounds left.

The old Remington pistol belched smoke and sound and sent a .44 round spiraling toward its target. The lead shattered the fourth button on Elliot Parker's shirt front, blasted through skin and tissue, sliced through the far side of one lung and chopped up a dozen medium sized arteries before it lodged near his spine.

Parker felt the blow in his chest, dropped his own gun and staggered backward from the force of the heavy slug. He sat down, then fell on his back and to his surprise found that he couldn't roll over or even try to get up.

His chest felt warm, but it didn't hurt. He couldn't have been hit badly. His arms wouldn't move. He lifted his head and saw Rutger walking toward him. Then the other man, the one from the saloon came up. The two talked a moment, then one kicked away Parker's gun and they squatted beside him.

Parker felt fingers open his shirt, then dark eyes winced and head shook.

"Parker, you're hit bad, almost gut shot. Can you move?"

"No," Parker said, surprised that he could still talk. "Guess I ain't dead yet."

"Not yet," Spur said.

"But soon, right?" Parker asked.

"Be my guess," McCoy said.

"Tell us about the ranch," Rutger said.

"I helped on the papers, the legal work. Hell, this guy comes in one day and says I can be one-third owner of the Circle S within a month. That had to be thirty, forty-thousand dollars for me! A fortune! I never make more than about five-hundred a year."

Parker coughed, spit some blood out on his white shirt, but didn't notice it.

"Hell, I took the deal. I fixed up the papers, they come back all signed and looked legal. I never asked how this Cameron arranged it."

"Murder and forgery, most likely," Spur said.

"I got five-thousand cash," Parker said. He coughed again and almost couldn't stop. More blood came out.

"The money is all in my desk drawer. Couldn't put it in the bank, that would cause suspicion. It's there. Guess I owe it to Priscilla and Rutger here. Damn, I'll never spend a dollar of it!"

He wheezed a moment.

"What happened to Rutger's mother and father out at the ranch, and the 35 to 45 ranch hands?"

"Not sure, just some hints. My guess is that. . . ." This time when Parker coughed he never stopped. Blood spouted from his mouth and then he sighed and his head turned to one side.

"Dead," Spur said.

They tied the lawyer over his saddle and headed back for town. On the way Spur untied the two Circle S riders he had bound before.

"You show your face in town again, I'll kill you!" Spur bristled at them. "You get on those nags and you ride for Cheyenne and don't ever come back here again!"

Both men nodded and rode out hard to the east.

"Come on, Rutger. We know part of the story about what happened to your ranch. Now we have to find out the rest of it."

9

Even though it was dark when they walked the lawyer's horse back to town that night, a trail of curious people followed them to the sheriff's office.

The people could tell the man was dead, but they couldn't see who it was, and neither Spur nor Rutger said a word.

At the sheriff's office, Spur stayed with the body as Rutger went inside and came back with the law man. The thin faced man lit his pipe as he walked, checked the face of the corpse and straightened.

"All right, people," Sheriff Dryer boomed. "This body is our former town lawyer, Elliot Parker. He came upon some misfortune. Now everybody get out of here, nothing more to look at. Scoot! All of you, unless you want to spend a night rent free in county jail!"

The crowd of about twenty people slowly faded away, but new faces came to take their places.

"Tell me about it tomorrow," Sheriff Dryer said to Spur. "I'll get his bones down to the undertaker and out of sight. Hear you sent two Circle S crooks down the trail. Good. Watch your hindside. Still a batch of gunmen in town."

Spur and Rutger went part way with the body, ducked into an alley and soon made their way by alleys and side streets to the back door of lawyer Elliot Parker's office. Spur held up the keys he had removed from the legal man's body. He found the one to fit the rear door and they slipped inside.

Neither man said a word. Spur waved Rutger forward. He walked to the big desk and pulled out drawers until he found an envelope and a leather bag. The envelope had a stack of fifty dollar bills in it, and the bag contained twenty dollar-gold pieces.

"Must be it," Spur said. We can count it later. Should be five-thousand dollars there. You want me to keep it for you?"

"Most of it," Rutger said. He took out four of the fifty dollar bills and they went out the back door. No light had shown inside the office, no one would know they had been there.

"It ain't like we're stealing," Rutger protested without any cause. "I'm just getting back what's legal and by rights, mine."

"Agreed," Spur said.

They kept to the alleys until they came to the side door of the Medicine Bow Hotel. Upstairs, Priscilla opened her door when she recognized Rutger's voice. She threw her arms around his, tears of joy in her eyes.

"I was terrified! I thought for certain he'd kill you. You were never any good with a six-gun. Remember when daddy finally let me learn to shoot and I beat you that time."

Rutger grinned and ushered Priscilla inside her room. "I'll sleep on the floor here tonight, and Mr. McCoy will be right next door. I don't think anybody is going to be after us, but you never can tell.

That night no one tried to get in either room.

The next morning, Rutger hired a guard to sit in front of Priscilla's door with a shotgun loaded with double-ought buck rounds. The extra long shells had thirteen .32 caliber slugs in each load and would blow a grown man in half at twenty feet.

Spur sat outside the side door of the bank early. the next morning and as soon as Ira Villary unlocked the door, Spur asked if he could come inside.

"You have those new fangled lock boxes a person can rent and lock up in your safe?"

"Indeed we do, Mr. McCoy. We call them safe deposit boxes. New York started them six years ago, so we're not far behind them. We have two sizes." He looked at the leather bag Spur took out of a folded copy of the newspaper.

"I'd say you'll need the large size. Rents for six dollars a year . . . unless this is official business of the U.S. Government."

"We're told to pay our way, Mr. Villary. Be glad to pay. Just set it up now, I've got some rather pressing business to take care of."

Villary made out a form, had Spur sign it, then smiled. "Hear you were involved in bringing in a dead body last night."

"True," McCoy said.

"Hear it was Elliot Parker."

"Right. He was involved with the takeover of the Shuntington ranch, but don't tell anyone."

Spur took the key Villary gave to him, put it on a new pocket watch chain and key ring, and dropped it into his pocket. "Thanks for accommodating me before banking hours, Mr. Villary."

"Oh, quite all right. In a small town, the bank is open whenever I'm here. Common courtesy to my friends."

Spur left quickly, had a fast stack of hot cakes smothered with four sunnyside-up eggs and six slices of sausage. What he needed now was more information.

A hour hour later, Spur sat on his roan a quarter of a mile north of town on the trail that led to the

Circle S ranch. He figured there would be a messenger or a pair of Circle S riders coming to town this morning.

By eight-thirty he found out he was half right. One rider with a new Circle S brand on his sorrel's hip rode out from town and headed for the ranch. He looked like he had been through a rough night with a pair of large bottles and a tireless woman.

Spur waited until the rider hit the fringe of trees where it was darker and sent a round from his pistol over the cowboy's head.

"Stand and deliver!" Spur bellowed. The traditional call of the robber and highwayman had the desired effect. The cowboy meekly raised his hands.

"Ain't got but a fifty-cent piece on me, stranger," the cowboy said. "That whore Vetta she done me out of every last dollar I had and woulda got the rest 'ceptin she missed it. She was half as drunk as I was, reckon."

"Get down, my side, and drop your iron in the dust. Move slow or you're dinner for some turkey buzzard."

The man moved cautiously, and soon had dropped his weapon and stood on the ground.

"Now, unbelt your pants and let them down to your ankles," Spur demanded.

"What'n hell?"

"Drop your pants, now!" Spur roared.

The cowboy shrugged, let his pants fall down and it became evident he wore no underwear.

Spur eased out of his saddle. He looped the bridle rein over the roan's head so it fell to the ground. The horse was ground-tied and wouldn't move more than a foot or two.

"You work the Circle S?" Spur asked.

"Yeah."

"You don't seem to be much of a cowboy."

"Ain't one, usual."

"What are you, usually?"

"Can't say."

Spur drew his Colt .44 smoothly, fast and put a slug between the rider's feet. The round cut through two layers of pants where they had fallen.

"Hey!"

"I asked what you do regular?"

The rider didn't answer.

"I can start putting a slug in your knee caps until you remember," Spur said.

"Cripple me?"

"Before I kill you. If you won't talk, what good are you to me?"

"You kill me I never can talk," the rider said smugly.

Spur slammed his fist into the rider's nose which erupted with a gush of blood that ran down his mouth and dripped off his chin.

"Goddamn!"

"What's your usual occupation?"

"Ain't done much since the war. I was a corporal."

"For the south?"

"Yes sir. Hell, most men our age was in the big war. Bet you was yourself."

"What is Curt Cameron? He sure isn't a rancher."

"Can't say."

Spur shot him in the shoulder. The heavy slug jolted through flesh, missed the bone, but slammed the rider backwards three feet and dropped him on his knees.

"You bastard! You shot me!"

"Soldiers get shot all the time. You've been shot before. I asked you who your boss is. He's no cattleman. He took over the ranch illegally by using forged deeds and bills of sale. Where does he come from and what's his racket here?"

"He'd kill me, sure."

"Maybe, if he found out. I'm the one who will kill you for sure, and I'm running out of time."

One of the horses skittered to one side and Spur looked up to find a three-foot long rattlesnake slithering away from the mount's hind feet. Spur grabbed a stick and caught up with the big diamondback and held its head to the ground with the stick.

He grabbed the writhing creature directly behind the triangular shaped head and carried it back to where the Circle S man stood ground tied by his trousers around his ankles.

"I hear you southern boys like to milk rattlesnakes like this frisky little critter," Spur said, waving the hissing snake a foot from the rider.

The man stumbled backward.

"Get that damned thing away from me!"

Spur grinned. "What, you don't like rattlers? He's going to be in your pocket for the rest of our little chat, you'll get to be good friends—if he doesn't bite you too many times. I've heard the average man can take two rattler bites, but after that he's bound to be dead before long. It's the swelling and the burning that's the most painful, they say, but one or two fang punctures isn't so bad."

The cowboy's face had paled to flour white.

"What's your name?" Spur barked at him.

"Seth Felson." The word came softly.

"You work for Curt Cameron?"

"Yes sir."

"He runs some kind of outlaw gang?"

"Yes sir."

"And you're stealing the Shuntington ranch from its lawful owners?"

"We did, yes."

Spur moved the snake closer. "The couple that

lived there, the Shuntingtons. What happened to them?"

"Swear I don't know. They was gone when I rode in. A dozen of us come in late. We had . . . had another job we was on. Curt said it was all right."

"You ever see fresh graves around the farmyard?"

"No sir. Don't know what happened to them."

"What about the crew? Thirty-five men just vanished. Where did they go to?"

"They was all gone, too, when I rode in."

Spur pushed the diamondback up until its darting tongue almost touched the hated human animal. Seth stumbled backward and sat down hard when he tripped over his dropped pants. He held his shoulder and blood seeped through his fingers.

Spur knelt in front of him still holding the snake.

"Why is Curt selling off the cattle?"

"We always do. I guess he wants the money. Cattle are hard to spend."

"What happens when you sell off all the cattle?"

"Curt sells the ranch and we move on."

"To another ranch where you kill the owners, forge the papers and take over the spread?"

"Hell, I don't know. It's all done before most of us get there. The Captain knows what he's doing. He treats us right."

"Captain?"

"He . . . he must have been an officer in the war."

"But you still call him Captain?"

"Yeah . . . so what?"

"You have sergeants, too?"

"Course not. We ain't in the army no more."

"Everyone in your gang was in the Rebel army?"

"Hell, I don't know . . . some of them."

Spur used a length of rawhide and tied it around a stake, then drove the stake in the ground. He tied the other end of the three foot rawhide strip to the tail of the snake. The reptile hissed and crawled away from them as far as it could.

"What you doing?"

Spur whittled two more stakes sharp and pounded them into the ground with a rock. Then he tied one of Fesler's wrists to the stake and reached for the other one. The outlaw jerked his hand away.

"You tying me here? What if that diamondback comes this way?"

"Spit in his eye. Hear diamondback rattlers hate that."

"He'll kill me, sure as hell! That's a damn mad snake!"

"Tell me what happened to the ranch owners and the crew."

"Christ! I would if I knew. Curt, he don't tell his men everything. He says we don't need to know. He says what we don't know, we can't tell."

"Like now," Spur said. "Only that way you wind up getting yourself killed, slowly."

"Christ sakes. I told you all I know."

"You've done this ranch stealing before?"

Fesler hesitated. "Yeah. Three or four times, takes six months sometimes. This one was gonna be quicker. Curt, he wants to get to St. Louis and meet this woman. . . ."

Spur reached down and sliced the rawhide with his knife. It had a six inch blade, honed sharp enough to cut hair.

"Pull up your pants."

"Thanks."

When Seth Fesler had his pants up and buttoned, he looked at Spur.

"Take out all but five rounds from your gunbelt loops."

"What?"

"Pull out the rounds and give them to me. Now!"

Seth did as directed. Spur walked over and picked

up the man's six-gun, drained out the live rounds, caught them and put them in his pocket. Spur checked the man's saddle. He had no rifle. In the saddlebags were chewing tobacco and a pint of whiskey. Nothing else.

"Fesler, you want to live to see the noonday sun?"

"Damn right!"

"You just resigned from Curt Cameron's outfit. You quit his little army, you understand?"

"I guess."

"You damn well better. I'm going to take him down, and his gang. Half of them are going to hang. You'll be first on my list if I find you out at the ranch when we take it. You get on that nag, turn her head west and ride the tracks for fifty miles and you'll come to a train town."

"You want me to run?"

"Damn right, Fesler. Run or die. Take your pick."

"I'm running. I get my iron?"

Spur tossed him the empty weapon. "Don't load it until you're ten miles from here. I see that weasel-ugly face of yours again, I'll put two .44 slugs into it. Now ride!"

Spur watched the man run to his horse, flip up the reins and mount, then spur the animal due west with a slight angle south to pick up the Union Pacific tracks.

Spur nodded grimly as the outlaw rode away. He threw rocks into the Laramie river and scowled at the ripples. Something still didn't ring true. How could Curt Cameron have such a vice-like hold on so many men? And they called him Captain. So maybe some of them had even served with him in gray uniforms during the war.

The fight had been over for six years! How could Curt hold them together for one swindle like this every six months? Of course, if they cleared enough money . . . If they sold five-thousand head of steer at twenty-dollars each that would be . . . He hesitated. A hundred-thousand dollars! Enough to keep forty men loyal for a while.

Spur rode back toward town trying to fill in the pieces of the puzzle. The biggest was what happened to the ranch owners and the thirty-five members of the crew. Men didn't just vanish into thin air, not even in Wyoming.

Curt Cameron looked out across the ranch from the bedroom window. It would take them three days to round up the cattle that someone spooked last night. It had to be Spur McCoy. Why wouldn't he die?

The dynamite charges and the pistol shots had spooked an already nervous bunch of cattle. His men had not been able to hold them and some had run twenty miles before they stopped. Now he had to rely on the best cowmen in his group, and there weren't many of them.

Real cowboys could do the job in a day and a half. It might take his men four or five days.

Damnit! That meant four or five days more until he could sell the first batch of two-thousand head. Then he'd have to do another roundup. Why was this one being so difficult, so damned hard?

He knew at once. Spur McCoy. He had increased the price on the man's head, but none of his hotshots in town had come with the man's topknot in a bucket. Curt snorted. He might have to ride into town and take care of the matter himself.

His basic plan still held. He would sell off every available steer and half to three-quarters of the breeding stock. He'd strip the place and try to come up with five or six-thousand head of cattle to market. Then he'd sell the real estate for ten or fifteen thousand, whatever the market would allow, and they would ride out of there for a long break in

St. Louis. Yeah, and he'd see Wanda again!

Just thinking about her gave him a hot feeling.

But before Wanda, they would put a new twist to this one. They could not simply ride away innocent as doves this time. That damned McCoy made it impossible. And the owner's son and daughter had complicated it beyond belief.

Now he heard that the lawyer, Elliot Parker, had got himself killed over the girl by her brother. Damn fool. He was in line to clear ten to fifteen-thousand dollars. He'd been worth it.

So the situation had changed. After they sold the ranch, they would sweep into town, clean out the bank, rob every store in sight, gun down the sheriff and anybody else who objected, and ride out with more cash money than his men had ever seen before!

Hell, they would also stop the train outside of town and blow open the express car safe and see if any gold was going out to the mint in San Francisco! They might pick up another twenty, thirty-thousand in gold bullion!

Damn, he was getting a hard-on, just thinking about it.

"Lucia! Lucia you tight little twat, get in here!" He bellowed it once more and she slid around the doorframe with her blouse half open and wearing nothing under it.

"You called me, big daddy dick?"

Shit! she did get his fires burning hot.

"Take that blouse off, now!" he said, his voice growing thick with emotion and desire. Christ, she knew how to get him worked up.

The blouse slid off her arms and she turned, letting one breast after the other swing out toward him. She shook her shoulders slowly making her twin peaks jiggle and bounce and swing in small circles.

She stayed barely out of his reach. At last he

lunged out, grabbed one breast and pulled her to him. He caught her other pink-tipped breast in his mouth and munched on it until she groaned with her own desire.

She pushed away from where they stood by the big bed. Slowly she slid down her skirt and he watched in amazement. She wore nothing under the heavy skirt. Not a fucking thing!

Curt growled, grabbed her naked body and threw it on the bed. Then he leaped on top of her writhing form.

She laughed and squealed as she pulled his clothes off. When he was naked she turned soft and gentle, stroking his penis, cupping his heavy balls, rubbing her breasts across his chest until he wailed and spread her legs.

"Damn, but you know how to get me moving. You sure you've never been a whore in some saloon?"

"You taught me everything I know about fucking!" she whispered in his ear. "You sweet cock, that's why I'm so fucking good at it!"

He wailed in delight, dropped between her legs and in one swift, searing stroke lanced into her.

Lucia screeched in sudden pain, then was lost in the rapture at the end of the stroke and the delight of his presence. She gripped him with her muscles and stroked him as he plunged forward, thinking now only of his own need and his urgency.

He was always so damn fast. Once a day satisfied him. She usually found one of the men who could treat her soft and gentle the way a lady should be treated. Then she demanded her own pleasure first, and if the man could last, he would get his chance to enter her. Ladies first, she told them, and they were so glad just to see her naked that it worked every time. If Curt knew, he said nothing. He was getting more than he could handle as it was.

She smiled at the man over her plunging and

snorting, sweating and rutting at her. Once they got back to St. Louis she had promised herself it would be payoff time. Curt didn't know it but she had found one of his bank passbooks and could forge his name perfectly.

Once in St. Louis she would get everything she could from him and vanish down the Mississippi on a river boat. Back to New Orleans where the living was easy—especially with fifteen or twenty-thousand dollars he had in that one account.

Lucia encouraged him to climax quickly, knowing he would roll away then at once, his mind on new matters, his loins drained, and his brain busy with some new swindle.

Just wait until St. Louis, Curt Cameron! Then they would find out who was the best swindler after all. Lucia had no doubt who would win on that score. She had ways, and she had the fucking little passbook that was the answer to all of her dreams for the rest of her life!

10

The sun stood directly overhead when Spur rode back into town after counseling with the Circle S hand and his pet rattlesnake. He had cut the rawhide off the critter and let it slither away into the brush. That was the snake's home range and he had a perfect right to be there.

Spur came into town from the east, rode down the alley to the back door of the jail and slid inside. He knew that several of the Circle S men were still in town hunting him. They had been more cautious lately since several of them had wound up in boot hill under six-feet of Wyoming soil.

Sheriff Dryer grunted when he saw Spur.

"How the hell is the United States Secret Service doing on our case?"

Spur laughed and dropped into the captain's chair beside the sheriff's scarred desk.

"Better than expected, Sheriff Dryer. But not as good as hoped for. From what the lawyer told us, and what I've just gleaned from a reluctant Circle S witness staring eyeball to eyeball with a diamond-back rattler, this outfit is an outlaw gang, straight and simple."

"But we can't arrest them without some proof."

"True, but we can harass the hell out of them and

hope they show their hand, or play the wrong card."

"I don't follow you."

"The boss of this gang moves in, takes over a ranch, then he sells off all the cattle he can, sells the ranch at a bargain price and moves on. The whole thing looks legitimate. It stands that way unless somebody can prove the takeover was a fraud or swindle or done with the help of murder and forgery."

"Yeah, but we got to prove it."

"Not if we get them scared, make them do something stupid so we'll have the break we need."

"How can we do that?"

"I'm working on it."

"You say they plan on stripping the spread of all the steers and probably most of the breeding stock?"

"Been the pattern in the past," Spur said.

"So maybe we can slow down the sales."

"They've already contacted a buyer. I stampeded about two-thousand head last night, so it'll take them a day or two to round them up."

"So what good is a day or two?"

"We try to make them nervous. Is there another lawyer in town?"

"One more. He's not all that good."

"Doesn't matter, I know the law well enough. We're going to have Rutger Shuntington challenge the sale of the ranch, challenge the signature on the grant deed and on the bill of sale. We'll declare both to be forgeries and try to get the assets of the ranch tied up in a lawsuit. Then Cameron can't sell the cattle."

Sheriff Dryer shook his head. "Nice plan . . ." He sucked on his pipe and blew out a blue cloud of smoke, "But it won't work. Circuit court judge was through town last week, and he won't be back for a month. Could take the train to Cheyenne and get a special court order, that would take three to four weeks for all the legal mumbo jumbo. Sorry."

Spur paced the office, hands behind his back, his scowl firmly in place.

"Damn! So we try something else." He grinned and dropped into the chair. "So we do it home grown style. From what I hear there has been a hell of a lot of cattle rustling going on in this county lately. And as sheriff, it's your responsibility to see that none of those cattle get sold and out of state before you inspect them."

Sheriff Dryer laughed. "And so I have to examine every brand on every critter before it can be shipped. Take two or three days for a big herd."

"Yeah, good thinking. And just maybe your brand inspector is in Cheyenne at the funeral of a close relative and won't be back for a week. He's the best brand man in the state and you won't move on clearing the herds until he checks them. Still you'll get the job done just as fast as possible."

Sheriff Dryer grinned. "I think we've got a way to hold up any cattle sale. The buyer will go along with it. He's got more stock now than he really wants. Nobody else around here has many steers to sell anyway so we won't hurt the other ranchers."

Spur stood. "We have our stopper in place. Now I want to get a lawsuit started, at least. We'll draw up some legal looking papers and have them served on the first Circle S rider you can find. Order him to take them directly to Mr. Cameron or his ass will get burned. It'll be another good scare for Mr. Cameron. The more barbs we can jab him with, the more nervous he's going to get."

Spur went out the front door of the sheriff's office, straight across the street and down a few doors to Amy York's seamstress establishment. He hadn't seen her for a few days, and she might have heard some news he could use.

She smiled when he walked in. He saw that she had on an attractive dress, and her hair was done up in a new way.

"My, my, my, but you're looking just as pretty as a bouncing long-haired kitten this afternoon, Amy."

She smiled. "Thank you, kind sir." She laughed and her eyes traveled down his body, stopping at his crotch. "You're looking extremely good yourself."

Before either of them could say another word, a man burst through the front door pulling at a six-gun in his holster. The trigger hung up or he would have killed them both.

Spur drew his .44 smoothly and blasted a round just as Blade Gunnison jerked out the weapon and dodged to one side. The lead slug slammed into the cylinder on the other weapon, smashing it out of Blade's hand.

The short man charged Spur in a surprise move. The two had been only eight-feet apart and before Spur could fire again, Gunnison had jolted him backwards, knocked the weapon from Spur's hand and they fell over a clothes dummy and rolled on the floor.

Spur was a head taller than the short, thickset man, but the Circle S enforcer was tough as old buffalo hide. He squirmed and kicked and dug his elbow into Spur's midsection, then clawed at a six-inch knife on his belt.

Spur got a hand lose and blasted a solid fist into Blade's jaw jolting him to the side. They rolled on the floor and Spur jumped up looking for his six-gun. He had no hideout. The small man got out his knife but Spur surprised him with a sudden kick that slanted off Blade's wrist and spun the knife away. It fell and stuck in the wooden floor.

Blade charged like a rampaging bull. He lowered his head and bellowed as he stormed forward. Spur had no place to dodge hemmed in on one side by bolts of cloth and on the other by a sewing table. Blade's strong, thick arms wrapped around Spur as they slammed against the wall and slid to the floor.

Spur got his hand under Blade's chin and rammed his head upward until the smaller man's eyes bulged. Blade released the bear hug grip and his fingers clawed for Spur's face. One fingernail drew a bloody line down Spur's cheek but missed his eye.

Spur changed his hands on Blade's chin grabbing his throat in a strangle hold. Just as he was tightening it to cut off all breath to the man, Spur felt Blade shift his position. Then his knee came crashing upward, skidded off Spur's thigh and barely touched Spur's scrotum before it smashed into his belly.

McCoy could do little but hold on. A flood of sudden pain and bile flooded his system. His testicles felt crushed, but he knew they were only grazed. A direct blow would have disabled him and Blade would have killed him quickly.

The outlaw saw his advantage and pushed away from Spur and scrambled to his feet. He darted to his still quivering knife, jerked it from the floor and sprang to the side grabbing Amy by one breast.

"You want me to slice her tit off?" the outlaw demanded.

Spur rolled over and came to his feet. He looked more threatening than he felt. His balls still ached, sending wave after wave of nausea through his system.

"No . . . this isn't her fight. Leave her out of it."

Blade waved the knife. "Move over there by the wall, face it, hands high on the wall, your legs spread." Blade's eyes searched the room looking for Spur's gun. His own must be jammed. He'd seen a pistol hit by a bullet before.

Spur watched him. If the outlaw found the gun, both he and Amy were dead. He tried to get that thought to her as he stared at her, but he wasn't sure she understood. She shivered, her hands at her side. Then Spur saw that she held a pair of big scissors she had been using. He looked down at them, then at her, then down at them again.

She understood.

"You'll never find my gun," Spur said sharply.

Blade looked up, uncertainty showing on his face.

"Now!" Spur bellowed.

Amy had changed her hand on the scissors, holding them now like a stabbing knife. She thrust the sharp points of the scissors upward. Spur saw she had closed her eyes. There was no way she could miss hitting the man standing directly in front of her.

As she moved, Spur blasted away from the wall, pushing with both hands and one foot. It all happened in a few seconds. Spur hurtled across the six-feet of space toward the pair. Amy's scissors flashed upward driven by desperation and fear. The point hit Blade's sagging belly, penetrated two inches and brought a scream of rage from the outlaw.

By the time he realized he had been wounded and he reacted with the knife on Amy's breast, he was too late. McCoy was in front of him, his big fist hammering down on Blade's right wrist like a pile driver, smashing the bone, spinning the knife away harmlessly.

Spur followed through with a crashing left fist to Blade's jaw, driving him backwards away from Amy.

"Get outside!" Spur roared at Amy. She darted for the door, made it and ran outside screaming at the top of her voice, still carrying the bloody scissors.

"That bitch stuck me!" Blade bellowed. "You're a dead man, McCoy!"

The knife lay on the floor between them.

Blade looked at it. Spur saw the glance.

"Go ahead, try for it!" Spur said.

Blade hesitated. Spur got there first, his big boot slamming down on the blade, putting it out of the contest.

Blade ran for the front door. Spur could not get there in time to stop him. They both stormed into the street a moment later. Spur had only his own sheath knife on his belt.

He knew what Blade was looking for—a gun. Blade was ten-feet ahead when he spotted a cowboy with a gunbelt. He charged the man, grabbing at the six-gun. The cowboy lunged away from him and got free.

Blade came up behind another man with a gun-belt. He pulled the six-gun out of the holster before the victim knew Blade was behind him.

Blade turned with the gun coming up, his thumb dragging back the hammer to half cock. Spur knew he had to do something quickly. Ten feet!

He charged forward, digging at the snap on his sheath knife scabbard. The knife came out.

A pistol blasted from across the street. Spur felt the slug tear into his left shoulder at the same instant he heard the shot. That shot was followed by another from a distance, then he felt himself being driven to the left by the force of the heavy pistol round.

Directly in front of him the stolen pistol fired and he felt the hot breath of the round. The shot from across the street had saved his life. But for how long?

As he fell he used the fractions of a second to throw his knife. One turn, throw hard!

The six-inch knife spun once and the sharp blade drove into Gunnison's right biceps. Gunnison screamed. He dropped the gun. The cowboy who had lost his weapon grabbed Gunnison from behind in an arm lock around his throat and held the smaller man.

Spur fell and rolled trying to take the force of the ground on his right shoulder instead of the injured one. He came to his feet with the pain seeping from between clenched teeth. He had no weapon at all now. Through a haze of anger and agony, he saw Blade held tightly by the man behind him.

The next moment Blade jerked forward, threw the cowboy over his head and dumped him on the ground, then rushed down the street to an alley and ran into the darkness.

Spur picked up the dropped gun and charged after him. His left arm hung almost useless. He hoped the gun he held still had four rounds in it.

It was a short alley. Spur saw no one in it as he looked into the daylight shadows. He ran hard to the end of the building and peered around it. Blade jumped back behind a stack of wooden crates fifty-feet down the connecting alley near the hardware store's back door.

Spur walked forward slowly, a calm had dropped over him. He knew where the man was, the man deserved killing, Spur McCoy was going to do society's job.

Gunnison threw a two-by-four at Spur. The two-foot long missile landed short.

There were no handy weapons to steal back here. It was one-on-one and Spur had the borrowed .44.

"Give it up!" Spur bellowed. "You come out now with your hands pushing sky and you get to live to stand trial."

"No damned trial!" Gunnison screeched.

Spur saw him two rungs up a ladder, nailed to the side of the building. His right arm was useless. It's tough to climb a vertical ladder with one hand, Spur knew.

"Down!" Spur demanded as he walked up to Gunnison.

"Don't shoot, damnit! I'm helpless. Bastard! I should have killed you six times!"

"But you missed. And there won't be a next time."

Gunnison hung there by his one hand, four-feet off the ground. He couldn't go up.

"Help me down."

Spur laughed. "Hell, you climbed up there, you can get down, hurt arm or no."

Spur heard something at the other end of the alley. It could be some of Gunnison's buddies. His shoulder throbbed where he had been shot. Blood oozed and dripped down his side staining his shirt. He glanced down the alley.

It had been what Blade had been waiting for. He pushed away from the ladder, his feet aimed at Spur's chest. One of his boots smashed the six-gun from Spur's hand, the other hit him in the chest and sprawled him backwards in the dust. Spur was on his feet before Gunnison.

They faced each other. Spur could only think of a weapon. What did he have? Not even a pen knife. In his shirt pocket he had a new lead pencil he had sharpened that morning in the Sheriff's office.

Yes! He pulled it out, put it between his two middle fingers after forming a fist. The eraser was against his palm and the point sticking six-inches out of the other side of his fist. All he had to do was keep the pencil straight with his forearm and he had a deadly weapon.

Blade laughed. "You gonna hurt me with a damn lead pencil?"

Spur didn't reply. He moved to his left. Gunnison moved the other way. They stood four-feet apart. Spur knew if the fight lasted much longer Gunnison's friends would find them. They all had six-guns and would use them with delight.

Spur dodged sharply to the left, then back to the right and then to the left again. The movement made his shot shoulder scream with pain, but Spur moved in spite of it.

He caught Gunnison trying to change directions. Spur sprang forward, lunging with all his two-hundred pounds behind his thrust with the pencil. His wounded left arm hung useless at his side. The pencil was firm and steady, straight out from his hand like an extension of his forearm.

Gunnison had time only to stare down at the sharp point as it slammed forward toward his chest. He twisted but the pencil point needled through his shirt, met flesh and won the battle.

The pencil plunged into Blade's chest, missed his heart but ruptured a big artery coming out of it.

Blade Gunnison fell backwards into the dust and horse droppings of the alley. He stared at Spur in shock, surprise and deadly disbelief.

"Can't be!" he rumbled. "Hell, can't be! I ain't gonna die from being hurt by a damn lead pencil!"

Spur had let go of the pencil when it impaled the outlaw. Now Gunnison touched the two-inches of the pencil that stuck out of his chest.

"Don't move it!" Spur said quickly.

"Hell, I know that much," Gunnison said. "You by god killed me with a fucking pencil!"

"Tell me about Curt Cameron. He was a Rebel Captain of cavalry in the war?"

"Yeah."

"And he got some of the men together to form an outlaw gang?"

"Shit yes! We done good for years."

"Until now." Spur watched his color fade as blood pumped from ruptured veins inside his body.

"What happened to the Shuntington's?"

"Damned if I know. One day they was there, and

the next day nobody heard nothing more about them. Left for back East, I hear."

"You know better. Tell me what happened. They're both dead, right?"

"You tell me. Men of the Twenty-Seventh don't talk out of school."

"What was that?"

Blade Gunnison smiled, shook his head and gave one long last gush of air from his dead lungs. His eyes stared at Spur, but they only saw eternity.

Spur lifted off the ground and walked down the alley to Dr. Asamore's office.

"Heard some shots, wondered if it would be good for business," the old doctor drawled with a grin.

"Not good on shoulders. How bad is it, Doc?"

"Tolerable. Tolerable that is for a body with as many scars and slashes and bullet holes in it as yours has. How many times you been shot?"

"Twenty, maybe, maybe twice that many. I lost count. It still hurts just as bad every time."

"You know about alcohol on an open wound then?"

"Yeah. Do it. I've still got work to get done."

Spur McCoy passed out when the alcohol hit the open flesh on his shoulder. The bullet had done more surface damage than internal. It slashed across the shoulder, bounced off the bone and angled down into the bicep and exited. Nasty, lots of blood but not totally debilitating.

A half hour later Spur sat in the sheriff's office.

"So it was you who saved my scalp this time," Spur said.

"Saw the Circle S man watching you come boiling out of the dress shop. He followed and gunned you before I could get there, so I put him down with a shot. Then I lost you."

The sheriff watched Spur a minute.

"You killed Blade Gunnison with a lead pencil?"

"A man can get desperate at times, Sheriff. Lots of common items can be used as weapons. You ever put a fist sized rock in a stocking and use it as a swinging club? Deadly, a dandy head buster."

They talked a few minutes. Some of the Circle S riders had been drifting out of town. The word was out that Gunnison had died and they were not as eager for the reward money on Spur's head now.

"I better check with Amy York. I don't imagine she ever stabbed anyone with a pair of scissors before."

When Spur knocked on the dressmaking shop door, he found it locked. He knocked again, then a third time. At last the shade over the door moved, a cautious eye looked out and then the door opened.

As soon as the door closed she was in his arms.

"Oh, glory! I'm so glad you're not killed. I didn't hurt your shoulder, did I? Did he shoot you? I hope I did what you wanted me to with the scissors."

Amy stopped suddenly. "Here I am running off at the mouth when I should be helping you to sit down and see how I can be a good nurse to you. Did you get shot again? I'm so sorry. Well, you're going to stay with me here tonight. I'll take care of you. That shoulder must hurt just terribly.

"I have a secret home remedy I make myself that will fix you up in no time. It's whiskey cut with some lemon juice." She grinned. "Might not be good medicine, but at least after three or four you won't feel much pain."

"Yes, thanks, I can use some of that medicine of yours."

She smiled and let out a long held breath. "Oh, good! I was afraid . . . I mean, you know I'm going to do my best to seduce you before the night is over."

Spur grinned. "Be right disappointed if you didn't, Amy. Be my pleasure, I can assure you."

She kept the shop closed, led Spur into the back to her apartment, and mixed a tall whiskey for him with lemon and a chunk of river ice.

"Most folks say you can eat our winter river ice. Some say it's tainted, but with enough whiskey to kill any bugs, I'm game if you are."

He pulled at the drink and felt the warmth hit his belly, then move outward. Spur sat on a big stuffed chair and relaxed. Things were moving better. The town was safer, the plan in motion to stop Cameron from selling off the stock. Time to take some time out and relax for a minute.

Amy came back in with some small sandwiches and another drink mixed for him. She had changed clothes and wore a softly clinging blouse. The way it outlined her large breasts, he was sure she wore nothing under it. She sat next to him on the arm of the big chair and leaned over and kissed his cheek. The blouse billowed open at the low neck and he could see all of one pink-tipped breast.

She moved back and smiled. "Spur McCoy, maybe we could give you the rest of your medicine later. Right now we should see if we remember how to make love."

Spur took a final drink from the glass and put it on a small table outside the chair. "Sounds like the best plan I've had all day." He held out his good arm. She kissed his lips, then took off the blouse and brought one of her breasts down to his mouth.

Spur McCoy moaned in delight and accepted the offering.

11

Spur McCoy relaxed on the soft bed. He lay propped up on two pillows and smoked a long black cigar as thin as his little finger. He deserved a short break from his rigorous schedule. The set pieces were in place to begin the harassment of Curt Cameron and his outlaw crew. Tomorrow or the next day the confrontation would begin.

Amy scurried into the room, all smiles and naked as was possible. Their first lovemaking had been fast and furious as she extracted her pound of flesh and raced him to a mutual climax.

The second time had been soft and lazy, with Amy on top pounding away like she was riding a fucking bucking bronco. When she had at last cooled down to a slow boil, she pulled away from him and kissed him.

"Time for the cook to get her big cock here some supper. Don't you go away!" She bent and kissed his softening penis.

"Christ, I haven't been fucked this good for five years," she laughed, "do you realize that! Frankly, I'd forgotten how good a man's prick jammed up my pussy feels. You can take it as gospel I sure as hell ain't waiting no damned five years again to get me a good fucking man."

She looked at him, her big breasts bouncing as she turned.

"You good for at least six times, right, on an all night fuck-out?"

Spur laughed, patted her breasts and then ran his hand down between her legs.

"At least six. What's for dinner?"

"Pussy!" she said and shrieked with laughter as she hurried out of the bedroom to the small kitchen. Rubens, the Flemish master portrait painter, would have loved Amy. She was all curves and solid heft with large breasts, a rounded tummy, a more than generous ass and thick arms and legs. Yes, Rubens would have loved painting Amy in the nude.

Spur pulled on his pants and went to the small kitchen. Amy was still naked, frying potatoes, onions and green peppers to go with the steak that was just turning medium rare in a heavy skillet on the wood burning kitchen range.

"Love to cook," Amy said. "Guess my size shows it, but I always say if a little is good, a lot of girl is better." She turned and watched him. "You got any complaints about the service in the bedroom so far?"

"None whatsoever," Spur said patting her fat fanny.

They ate quickly and hurried back to the bedroom.

"Something different," Amy said eyeing him as Spur slid out of his pants. His penis was flaccid now.

"You don't really like my fucking!" Amy screeched. "Look at your god damned shriveled up little worm of a prick! He's all soft. If you loved my screw you'd be hard again and ready to come in my face!"

He slapped her bottom and she bent over to give him a better target.

"Yes, spank me good. But I still say you don't like my kind of pussy if you go soft."

"A man can't stay hard all the time, or he'd pass out."

"Not so. My brother used to have a stiff dick for fourteen hours a day. He was fourteen years old at the time and I was a damned sexy sixteen. He'd show his stiff cock to me in the morning, and I'd see the bulge in his pants all day. We lived on a farm, and every chance he got when the folks weren't around, he'd flip his prick out and try to get into me.

"He got his first hard on when he was thirteen. He came into the outhouse when I had my skirt down and was bent over. He saw pussy for the first time that day and he screeched and grabbed his cock and instantly he was as hard as a pitchfork handle. He tried to jump me right there. I didn't let him, little prick.

"I made him wait until we got in the barn and I could really look at his dick. His balls were still almost hairless, but his dick hardened up to four-inches long. He played with my tits, which was as big when I was fifteen as they are now. I'd never had a hard prick to mess around with so I turned and pushed and pumped him a couple of times."

Amy laughed. "He touched my titties three times and he squirted cum all over my skirt. Then he wanted to play with my pussy too, but I said next time. Tell you the truth, I'd seen so many pregnant girls, I didn't want to get knocked up."

"What do you want to do different this time?" Spur asked.

"Something really strange, wild . . . sinful! She got on the bed on her hands and knees and looked at him.

"Like that?" Spur asked.

She took a deep breath and nodded.

"Which spot?"

"Oh, shit! Both of them!"

Spur moved behind her and spread some saliva

around her tight little bung and pushed.

"Jeeeeeeeeeeeeeesus!" Amy howled as he slid past the restriction and lanced inside. "Oh, damn but that is low down and dirty! It's so strange, so fucking wild!" she fell down on her elbows on the bed, her big bottom still high and throbbing.

"You sure this is all right?" Spur asked.

"You stop now and I'll kill you!" she brayed as her voice went wierd and she climaxed so many times in a row that Spur lost track. He felt his own juices flowing and banged against her round bottom as hard as he could. Then she caved forward as he exploded inside and they lay there, both panting, sucking for breath.

Spur started to move.

"Stay put!" Amy shrilled. "I want him to go all soft right there. You take a little nap, you want to. I want this one to last as long as it will. Might not get a cock down my shit alley again for a long spell."

Spur laughed softly and took a nap on her soft buttocks and creamy back. She moved a short time later and he roused. He rolled away from her and she grinned.

"So fucking wonderful! So pussy fucking, cock fucking wonderful!" She looked over at him. "I never swear or talk dirty except in bed, have you noticed that? It just seems right. If we're fucking up an all night storm, might as well call a fuck a fuck and a pussy a pussy."

She got up and led him out to the kitchen and the wash basin. She poured out some water, took a wash cloth and sudsed his limp prick off well. Then she washed it again and rinsed him. By that time he was hard again.

"Christ, just like my brother. Once at Sunday dinner we had company and us kids had to sit close together. He was fourteen then and first thing he did was put his hand under the table where nobody could see it and reached over to my crotch. I left his hand there. It felt kind of good. When he tried to get me to spread my legs, I did.

"Damn that was wild, getting pussy-felt right there at the table with the whole family in sight and not knowing a damn thing 'bout it! Then he pulled on my arm and I put my hand down in my lap under the table and he brought it over to his crotch. He already had his stiff prick out of his pants. He cupped my fingers around it and pumped my hand up and down.

"By the time the main course came he groaned and pushed his finger right up my pussy. I was jacking him off like crazy and he shot his cum all over the underside of the living room table. I guess I yelped some too, because my father looked at me.

" 'Amy, did you have something to say'?" he asked me. "I shook my head, sure my voice would be all crazy. Father nodded. " 'Good, because little girls should be seen and not heard.'

"We both sat up a little straighter then and ate our dinner. While we waited for dessert we played with each other again. I think that was the first time I really climaxed. Will had his two longest fingers stuck all the way up my cunny!"

Amy led Spur back to the big bed and they sat there all naked and flushed and warm and sexy and stared at each other.

"Spur, sweet prick, I want to suck you off. I want to take you all the way until you squirt your juice down my throat. Would you mind?"

Spur laughed softly and shook his head. "It's your night, Amy, whatever you want, wherever, and as many times as I can get it up."

She did. Spur couldn't remember the last time he'd been able to climax that way, but he sure did this time. Amy sucked and gulped and he fired his load.

It was nearly dawn when they at last stretched out on the bed and fell asleep. The only thing that woke them about nine the next morning was someone rattling the door.

"Oh, good gracious!" Amy said contritely. "I forgot I have a fitting for Mrs. Asamore this morning for that new dress. Spur McCoy, you dress your wonderful body and get it out the alley door. If Mrs. Asamore even suspects that I've had a man in my bed last night, she'd absolutely ruin my business. Now scoot!"

Spur got dressed and out the back door without being seen. He made his way to the hotel, found his shaving gear and scraped off two days of growth. Then he checked with the Shuntingtons and found them both up and edgy.

He told them about filing charges against Curt Cameron.

"Yes, about time we figured that out," Rutger said. "Might not work, but it should slow him down some."

"Spur McCoy, I need to talk to you," Priscilla said. "Am I free to do some shopping yet?"

"A few more days. Anyway, I like that dress. You look like a princess."

Spur left after a short visit to talk to the lawyer who said he would draw up the papers in the proper legal form right away.

He then went the long way to the back door of the jail and walked inside.

"Been looking for you, McCoy," Sheriff Dryer said. "Circle S has a thousand head of stock outside of town waiting to put them into the railroad stock yards. I talked to the buyer last night and he told the trail boss he would have to talk to me. He's due here in about half an hour. I'm certain that he won't come alone."

They talked it over and Sheriff Dryer deputized six extra men, issued them shotguns and placed them as obvious guards around the front of the sheriff's office. Each double barreled whammer held three and a half inch double-ought buck rounds.

"The trail boss said he was sure Mr. Cameron himself would be here for the meeting," Sheriff Dryer said. "The man was fit to be roped and tied. Said he's never heard of no such thing as a brand check at a loading chute. I told him he hadn't been in my county very long, then."

Spur checked outside. The guards were in position, not hiding, in plain sight and positioned to give them a deadly cross fire and not endanger the other guards.

The Circle S men came right on schedule at 10:30. The man leading the ten riders could only be Curt Cameron. He was tall, broad shouldered and wore an expensive jacket over a gambler's vest and fancy frilly shirt hung with two gold chains and a diamond stick pin in his tie. The diamond was big enough to make every woman in town envious.

Cameron swung down from his mount, looped the lines around the hitching rail and waited for his nine men to do the same. All the riders were armed with pistols.

Spur walked outside the office with the Sheriff and waited. The ten moved between the shotgun guards, and some of the Circle S riders were starting to frown.

Sheriff Dryer held up his hand. "Cameron, that's far enough. The only thing we have to talk about is the herd you brought in to the edge of town. You can't ship them. There hasn't been a general roundup in the valley yet and there isn't a brand inspector in town. Soon as Harry gets back from Cheyenne, I'll have him check over your critters."

"Won't do, Sheriff," Cameron said, his voice strong, sure. "I've got approval of the cattle buyer to ship. If I don't get them on this train, I lose my cars."

"Talked with the buyer. He says he'll have more cars in a week or ten days. My advice is take this herd back to grass and fatten them up for ten days, then we'll be set up to check your brands and get them out of town."

"Won't do, Sheriff," Cameron said. "My close in range is near gone. I'd just run the fat off them if I went to a higher range and back. Won't do at all."

"Sorry, Cameron. As long as this is my county, we run it according to the law. No general roundup and brand checks, no shipment unless every head passes the brand inspector. You have some argument with that, contact your Wyoming Territorial legislator with a complaint."

Spur McCoy leaned against the front of the sheriff's office watching. Twice Cameron's glance took him in. Both times his eye twitched until he reached up and rubbed it with his hand. Now he turned to McCoy.

"This has to be your doing, McCoy. The ranch is mine, bought and paid for. The cattle are mine, the brands are mine. Nothing you can do will stop me from selling what I want to sell, and when I want to."

"Cameron, you aren't a captain of cavalry in the Confederate any more. Here we live by the law, not the power of a company of army riders. You'll do well to listen to what the sheriff has to say. He's the law here, you aren't."

Cameron started to say something, then stopped. He wheeled around, motioned to his men and they walked back to their horses.

"Oh, Cameron. I guess it's time I told you." The sheriff waited until the big man looked around.

"I'm enforcing a new law in Laramie. No gunfire allowed within the city limits. Anyone firing a weapon in town will be fined a hundred-dollars and put in jail for three months. You might let your men know about the new law. It's being enforced as of now. Noticed a lot of your men in town looking for a gun fight. You'd be doing them a favor to pull them out. They'll just get themselves in trouble or killed here in Laramie. Everyone be better off that way. Now, Mr. Cameron, you have a nice ride back to your ranch."

The shotgun guards had the weapons angled over their arms, pointing at the ground, ready to pull them up at a second's notice if needed. The ten riders from the Circle S watched the guards a moment. Curt swore at everyone he could see, but did so softly. Then he turned and walked back to the street and his horses.

Spur waited until the ten men were mounted and moved off to the north. Then he relaxed. When the men were almost out of town it sounded as if all ten emptied their revolvers into the air.

Spur grinned. "New law you have on the books, Sheriff?"

"Thinking about it, just thinking about it," he snorted. "The big talker had to swallow my slow-down. He figured on blowing me away with his army behind him. But he sure as hell changed his mind about that. You called him Captain. He really used to be in the war?"

"True. Somewhere, somehow. I haven't figured out exactly what he did, but we'll find out. Wonder what he'll do next?"

"He better drive that herd back to Circle S land or

he's going to have a visit from me and my new deputies out there. My guess is that he'll take them back. He'll work on some new plan, some better idea."

"I'll probably hear about it. Right now I need to check with that lawyer, then go see the kids."

Spur looked up and down the main street that some were calling Third Street. He didn't see any of the Circle S loafers he had spotted before. Most of them had cleared out. But it only took one, and one lucky shot.

He went through the alley to the hotel and up to the third floor rooms. Priscilla let him in.

"Rutger said he wanted to talk to that lawyer you mentioned. He's down there now. He promised me that he would be extremely careful."

Spur closed the door and told her about how they made Cameron back down at the sheriff's office.

"Then it really is true?" Priscilla asked. "Do we have a chance of getting the ranch back?"

She wore a pretty dress that set off her complexion, and now she perched primly on the edge of the bed.

"More than a chance, a good chance," Spur said.

She stood and walked to him. She was just over five-feet-four, and she smiled up at him proudly.

"I'm sure that between you and my brother you can save the ranch. I . . . I just don't know what's happened to mother and father. We'll find out though."

She hesitated. For a moment he didn't think she was going to go on. Then she seemed to plunge ahead. "Mr. McCoy, you know about Mr. Parker . . . what he did. I . . . I shouldn't be talking this way. It was terrible, yet not all of it. I mean, he forced me, and that was bad. But—"

She turned to the window and looked outside,

then went on without looking at Spur. "Well, after a while, when he had ripped my clothes off and there was nothing more I could do, then I rather . . . no, not that, but I wasn't terrified. After a while it seemed, I don't know, kind of natural I guess. What I'm wondering now. . . ."

She took a deep breath and turned to him, walked up and put her arms around his neck. Priscilla reached up on tip toes and kissed Spur on the lips.

"There. That wasn't so hard." She smiled. "Mr. McCoy, I really am curious now. I want to know what it feels like to have someone I know and respect make love to me. Would you help me?"

Spur took her arms from around his neck, walked her to the bed and sat her down. Then he stood in front of her.

"Priscilla, you're a beautiful young lady. Any man would be lucky to make love to you. But that's a job you should leave for your husband. Now, just hold on. You're young, you have years and years ahead of you.

"Right now we have to use every waking minute trying to figure out how to get the ranch back for the Shuntington family, and finding your father and mother."

"If I took off my blouse, would that persuade you?" she asked, unbuttoning the top two fasteners.

"No, Priscilla. My job is to get your ranch back, and I need to get working on that right now." He bent and kissed her cheek, then moved and kissed her lips. Her eyes were still closed when he straightened up.

"You stay right here in your room for the rest of the day, and tonight we'll all have supper together in the dining room."

Her eyes opened slowly and she nodded. Spur slipped out the door and heard her walk to it and

12

Spur went back to the lawyer's place. His name was Hascomb Bernard, a balding man in his sixties with a pince-nez, watery eyes and an egg sized goiter that hung like a bell on his throat below his right ear. Spur tried not to look at it.

Bernard and Rutger sat near his desk working over a pencilled draft. Both looked up as Spur came in.

"Afternoon," Spur said. "How is it going?"

"You know the judge won't be through for a month or more," Bernard said, a small frown growing.

"We know that," Rutger said. 'You just draft the papers and file them with the sheriff, or the district attorney, or whoever you have to, and make sure that a copy goes out to the Circle S ranch."

"That I can do. Hate to do all the work and not expect to go to trial."

"Do it," Spur said. "You'll get paid for your time."

Spur motioned Rutger to one side. "Looks like most of the Circle S men have left town. I think it's safe to have a civilized dinner tonight in the dining room at the hotel. About six. I'll meet you and Priscilla there."

Rutger nodded. "I'll be there. Now, what was that confrontation with Cameron all about and why wasn't I invited to the bloodletting?"

"Didn't want you to get killed. It came within a mare's whinny of being a shoot-out. We had more guns, six double-barreled shotguns with double-ought buck. I could almost hear Cameron figuring the odds. But we stopped him cold. He can't sell any cattle here in town, and he won't drive them to Cheyenne. He's not the type to work that hard."

"So he'll give up? That doesn't sound like a man who has done all this work and then walk away empty handed."

"Yeah, that's what bothers me. He gave up too easily today. Have to do some recon work tonight."

"Meaning you're riding to the ranch. I'm going with you."

"Might be good for you to get your feet wet in this thing. It isn't all fun and frolic out there. Somebody could get killed."

"I think Cameron has already killed my parents. I owe the bastard."

Spur took a long breath. If he were in Rutger's position, nothing could keep him away. "All right, Rutger. We'll go just before it gets dark. You still have that shotgun guard in front of Priscilla's door?"

Rutger said he did.

Spur and one of the Sheriff's special shotgun toting guards roamed the town for an hour after that but could find no Circle S brands on any of the horses at the hitching rails. They saw none of the loungers who Spur had suspected were Circle S riders looking for an extra bonus for Spur's head.

He got to the dining room at the Medicine Bow Hotel just as Priscilla and Rutger came in. Priscilla had slipped out and bought a new dress and she looked as pretty as a fresh bunch of spring flowers.

Her smile dazzled Spur as he took her arm and led her into the dining room.

"Prettiest girl in sixteen counties," Spur whispered in her ear, then kissed her cheek.

"It was all worth it!" Priscilla whispered back, her smile reserved just for him.

They all had steak, the house specialty, with family style bowls of vegetables, potatoes, a salad and tall glasses of brisk, iced tea. Spur ate his quickly, as was his fashion. Rutger ate about half of his pound-and-a-half sized steak, but Priscilla only nibbled on hers. Most of the time she spent watching Spur.

Once she reached out and touched his arm. "Spur, are you really going to ride out to the ranch tonight? Won't that be terribly dangerous? I mean, if we have Mr. Cameron and his men on the run now, shouldn't we just wait and see what they do? See what happens?"

"Priscilla, most things we do are dangerous. Right now it's important we know what's going on out there so we can get ready for it. If they get packed up and move on, we'll know about that too. Dangerous doesn't mean we're going to get hurt."

Her pretty, young face pouted for a moment. "If you do get hurt I'll never forgive myself. Please don't go."

"We need to go, Priscilla. We're not doing it just to keep busy. I'll be with Rutger so we'll protect each other. It's your job to smile as pretty as you can and send us out with your good wishes."

She smiled with an effort leaning toward him. She touched his hand and gripped it tightly.

"All right. But you be careful of your hurt shoulder. Now, you have my good wishes and a smile, but I'm going to need a reassuring hug before you go."

Spur nodded. "I think we can oblige you on that. I just don't want you to starve yourself to death."

"Oh, I'm not a big eater."

They left a few minutes later and Rutger insisted on paying for the meal. He caused a flurry when he gave the cashier one of the fifty-dollar bills. At last they found change.

Upstairs, Priscilla stood in front of Spur until he reached out and hugged her. She came to him openly, pushing her whole body against his in a needing embrace. He felt her breasts crushing against him and she sighed.

She looked up. "A goodbye kiss on the cheek for luck?" she asked.

He pecked her cheek and hugged her again with his good right arm and stepped back.

"Riding time," Rutger said. He wore a pair of old jeans, shirt and leather vest and his gun belt hung low on his right hip.

Full darkness ate up the tentative dusk by the time the pair of riders trotted onto Circle S land. Rutger stopped and stared around him.

"First time I've been on the home place since I left last fall," he said. "It feels good. This is my land, and I want it back!"

"Do what we can," Spur said.

They rode harder for fifteen minutes and stopped and listened for patrols. They sniffed the air for wood smoke from some lookout's campfire. They did not hear or smell anything. Twenty minutes later they came through open range from the north and down toward the Circle S ranch buildings.

Lights blazed in several windows. They had left their horses a quarter of a mile back tied to some brush near the Laramie river. Now they bellied up to a small rise less than fifty yards from the first corral. Spur's shoulder hurt like fire from the motion, but he settled down on the ground and the pain eased. They could see a large camp fire blazing up in the middle of the ranch yard.

Spur spotted more than a dozen men around the fire. As they watched, thirty more men came from the bunkhouse and the screen door on the ranch house slammed.

Spur touched Rutger and they lifted up and moved forward without making a sound. Spur recognized Cameron as he came into the firelight. He held up his hands and the men quieted their chatter.

Rutger slid to the ground and Spur followed. They were near the corral and beyond one of the barns. Spur figured they could hear what was going on from their vantage point.

"How about a little dance?" Cameron called to the crowd of men that had grown to nearly fifty.

"Yeah, Captain!" someone yelled.

"Lucia, Lucia, Lucia!" the men chanted.

A woman stepped out of the darkness into the light and the men pushed back from one side of the fire to give her a stage. She danced to the picking of a Spanish guitar and her movements were slow and sensual. Then the tempo increased and the dance became more erotic until at last she began a strip tease, tearing off clothes and throwing them behind her.

The men whistled and stamped and shouted, and when the last binder came off her breasts, Lucia was bare to the waist and the men screamed in delight. She danced topless for several minutes, ending in a simulated sexual encounter in the dust before the men. Then she jumped up and vanished into the darkness to a screaming, cheering response.

Cameron stood up in the light and waited for the cheering to stop. When it tailed off he waved his hands.

"Now to business. We've got a complication. The

sheriff has gone sour on us. He suddenly is demanding a brand inspection because there hasn't been a general roundup and brand sorting. Says his inspector is out of town for ten days."

"Bastard must be wise to us," somebody called.

"Damn close. Or McCoy is prodding him. We could wait the ten days and protect our investment here. But my feeling is that then there would be some new problem. We're not going to score the way we hoped here."

A wave of chatter rumbled over the crowd.

"But we still have a damned good chance to make some big money. Way I figured it, we slip out of our legal operation this time. There's a dandy little bank in town that usually has a good sized amount of cash on hand in the vault. We take the vault, we strip every cash register in town, and then we crack open the safe on the Union Pacific express car when it rolls into Laramie."

"Yeah! Just like old times, Captain!" one of the men shouted.

There were three cheers for the captain. The men stood and shrieked their pleasure. A dozen rebel yells pierced the dark night air.

"Now we're really going to live again!" one voice boomed.

Cameron got them calmed down. "It ain't gonna be no walkover," he called over the voices. "We've got to plan it out and do it right."

"Damn, we're gonna ride hard again!" a voice shrilled.

Everyone cheered.

Cameron grinned and calmed them down. "Don't know for sure just how soon we'll go. You'll know in time to pack your saddle bags. That's all you're supposed to own, right?"

"Hey, damn it to hell, Captain. We gonna be able to get us some women this time?"

Cameron scowled. "That gets tricky. Sometimes a man will chase you to hell and back if you poke into his pretty. We might have to hold off this time."

"Christ, Captain, we been holding off for three years." Half the men jeered the response and Cameron listened.

He threw up his hands. "Hell, why not? We'll bust this little town wide open and take anything and everything and any pretty woman we want!"

The men cheered for five minutes and Cameron at last waved at them, rolled out a keg of beer, and walked back toward the ranch house.

Spur looked over at Rutger. Even in the darkness he could see the grim lines on the young man's face.

"At least they're moving on," Rutger said.

"But they could burn down Laramie and all your ranch buildings before they go."

"We can't let them do that," Rutger said, his voice tight. "They could also kill a lot of people, rape a lot of our women."

"We won't let that happen. We'll be ready for them in town. About the ranch—"

"Yeah, I know. Nothing we can do about it if they decide to torch it before they leave. What else can we do here?"

"I want to check the smaller barn back there."

"You're looking for graves, aren't you, Spur?"

"Yes. Two graves, or thirty-five, I don't know how many. You must have known some of the hands on your ranch. Would they just have packed up and left without talking to anyone in town?"

"Not unless there was a mighty potent threat hanging over their heads . . . like getting their guts blown out by a shotgun."

"Way I figure, too. Let's check that barn."

They eased away from the ranch yard, circled around a corral, but saw no guards. At the smaller barn they found no livestock, only hay and some feed grain stored in sacks and some in bins. Spur used a pitchfork and probed the floor under the hay and in the open areas, but could find no soft spots where there could be a grave. It was awkward work with his wounded left arm, but he made it.

Rutger stood by the door watching the bonfire. "Sure wish to hell you had some more of that dynamite you used to stampede that herd. I'd throw about a dozen sticks around that fire."

"Not sure we want them to know we're here," Spur said. "We want to surprise them when they ride in to take the town."

"How about their horses?" Rutger asked. "We could open the gate and they'd never know how it happened!"

Spur chuckled. "Why not?"

They moved cautiously to the main corral where about forty head of horses milled around. The gate was a swing type with a wire loop holding the top and the bottom pole in another wire loop. Spur lifted the top loop off, pulled the gate pole out of the lower loop and dragged the gate open six feet.

He went around one side of the corral and Rutger moved the other way, gently urging the horses toward the opening. The nags wandered out. A stampede would have alerted the outlaws. It took them five minutes but by then all but one horse was out the gate heading for the open range at a walk.

Spur and Rutger moved along after them, then cut to the north where they had left their horses.

The pair had mounted and ridden around the ranch and were well south before they heard the shouts of alarm from the men around the bonfire. Somebody must have checked the corral or found a wandering horse.

Spur and Rutger rode faster for a while until they were well away from the ranch.

"What did the men mean, just like old times?"

Rutger asked Spur as they rode through the softly cool darkness toward town.

"Not sure. These men don't impress me as being soldiers, but they were. You ever heard of Quantrill?"

"Sure. He was a Confederate officer who led a gang of murderers, robbers and rapists along the border during the war. He was supposed to raid the north and send the money and loot to the southern treasury. Most folks think he kept most of it for himself."

"Right you are. In 1863 he raided Lawrence, Kansas with four-hundred fifty men. They burned and pillaged the whole town and killed over one-hundred and fifty men, women and children. He turned into a scavengering outlaw after the war until he was hunted down by a federal force in Sixty-Five. He was wounded and died a month later. Cameron could have had the same kind of outfit near the end of the war. That would explain all the military jargon."

"You mean he's held a group like that together for six or seven years?"

"Could be. At least we have a better idea now what we're up against, a military force that's going to attack Laramie in the next day or so. We have to get to the sheriff and organize some form of defense, put out some outposts, the whole damn thing!"

"Lots of the men in town were in the war," Rutger said. "At least they know how to shoot a gun."

"Good. What we need is to get organized. We'll ride straight to the sheriff and see what he has to say."

"You were in the war, weren't you, Spur? You'd be the man I'd pick to put the whole thing together. I mean, you know what we need to do."

"We'll see," Spur said.

An hour later they sat in the sheriff's office. He

glowered at them and puffed on his pipe. The room was a blue pall of tobacco smoke.

"You're telling me we're going to have a damn Confederate army unit come boiling into town shooting us up?"

"Exactly what I mean, Sheriff. We finally put it all together. My suspicions are that Cameron operated a raider unit near the end of the war, something like Quantrill. After the war he kept them together and they operated as an outlaw band. Whatever, there's gonna be about fifty soldiers heavily armed come storming into Laramie in the next couple of days."

"Damn, we'll meet army with army. We got Ft. Sanders a mile outside of town. They should be able to throw up a hundred mounted troopers to meet any such attack."

Spur shook his head. "Wish they could, Sheriff. Remember that law Congress passed a few years ago. It prevents the military from taking part in any civilian law or policing operation. The congress was afraid we were heading toward martial law."

"The hell, you say? You mean if the Indians were attacking us, the army could help. But if it's just a bunch of white rabble they can't lift a saber?"

"Afraid so. But there may be one glimmer of hope. I can show the army my credentials and then if I can prove to the Fort commander that this is a unit of the Confederate army, I just might have a chance. I'll ride out there first thing in the morning. In the meantime, we better get our own troops together. How many deputies you got, including those six from today?"

"Nine."

"That's a start. How many able bodied men in town who own rifles?"

"Hell, maybe fifty or sixty. We had a sight more

before the Union Pacific moved so many of its people down the line."

"How do we get them organized?"

"Not me. You're the expert, McCoy. I'll turn the whole damn thing over to you. I never was in the army."

Spur nodded. "Fine. Here's what I want you to do. Tomorrow morning send your deputies into every store and to every house in town. Tell them what's happening, and ask the men to volunteer with their rifles and pistols. Probably won't happen tomorrow, but we need to be ready by noon.

"Have all the men report to your office here and I'll have a defense plan set up and position everyone. We'll put out three men as lookouts to spot the Cameron raiders before they get here. In the meantime, I'll be heading for the fort and try to make my case. If it doesn't work, we still have a way to defend ourselves."

"Sounds good. What about the women and children?" the sheriff asked.

"We'll keep them barricaded in their homes. Better than grouping them all at one spot."

Spur paced the floor a minute, then grabbed his hat. "Right now I want to look over the town. They probably will come from the north, all in one bunch, since they won't know that we found out they're coming." He waved and went out the door with Rutger close behind.

They walked to the hotel, got a big tablet and three pencils from the room clerk, then made a rough map of the town starting at the northern trail outskirts.

Spur's arm still bothered him. He could move it, and he had his shirt on, but still the shoulder was stiff and it hurt to lift his arm. He was in no shape for a fistfight.

Back at the hotel in Spur's room, they checked the sketches and Spur began to make a plan. He would need at least three scouts out two miles from town. They would be his forward observers and would race for town the moment they saw the Cameron Raiders coming. Then the placement of the men.

He hesitated. It was late. He would think better in the morning. Maybe the army would help them do the job. Maybe. Spur said good night to Rutger and lay on his bed thinking about it. He had to use the best arguments he could at Fort Sanders, and his rank of full colonel. Even that might not be enough.

It took Spur two hours to get to sleep.

13

Spur found the leaflet under his hotel room door when he woke up. The page sized warning had this headline:

RAIDERS TO HIT LARAMIE!

Below it told concisely what the sheriff expected to happen to Laramie in the next twenty-four hours and asked all able bodied men to report with their weapons at the sheriff's office at noon.

The sheriff had been busy last night. Spur dressed, had a quick breakfast and rode out of the livery stable on his roan heading south. He hadn't been to the fort, mainly because he did not expect to need any help. But now he had a handle on the outlaws, and he was sure that the town needed the army's help.

When he rode into the familiar looking fort with the buildings and large parade grounds in the center, Spur almost felt like he was back in the army. It had been a tremendously important and terrifying and maturing part of his life.

He gave his horse to an orderly who directed him to the fort commander's office. The smell of the room when he opened the door gushed back memories: leather and paper, lots of raw wood and more leather and the smell of polish and gun oil.

A sergeant with a full beard met him. "Yes sir, what can we do for you, sir?"

Spur handed the sergeant the usually concealed identification form that certified that Spur McCoy was a full colonel in the United States Army on special assignment and should be accorded all proper respect.

The sergeant saluted at once. Spur returned the salute.

"I'd like to see the Fort Commander," Spur said.

"Yes sir. Let me tell him you're here." The sergeant took the identification form with him and hurried through a door into the adjacent office.

He returned almost at once.

"Major Patrick O'Reilly will see you, sir. Right this way."

Again the memories: a big U.S. flag on the wall, a picture of President Ulysses S. Grant behind his desk, two chairs and a bench, two rifles on the wall, a spittoon at the side of the battle scarred work place.

At the corner of the desk stood a man ramrod straight in his carefully tailored blue army uniform. He saluted smartly and Spur returned the formal greeting. Major O'Reilly was stubby, square, solid, and looked like the ideal mold of a perfect cavalryman. His face was sunburned but a white line around his forehead showed where his campaign hat usually protected his head from wind, sun, rain and weather. Piercing gray eyes stared at Spur a moment. He had a moustache but no beard.

"Colonel McCoy, good to meet you. Have a seat. We have few visitors out this way."

"Major, I have an urgent problem and I need your help. I'm in Laramie on a delicate mission and now I find the remnants of a Confederate force of some fifty men. I suspect they were Quantrill type raiders near the end of the war. They've taken over the Circle S, the biggest ranch in the Bull Pen Valley, and now they are threatening to sack Laramie the way Quantrill did to Lawrence, Kansas back in Sixty-Three, I think it was."

"Confederate raiders? That's hard to believe, Colonel. It's been six years since the war was over."

"True, but this man, Curt Cameron, seems to have turned the trick."

"They wear uniforms?"

"No."

"Then what leads you to believe they are men of the Gray?"

"I've questioned one when he lay near death. Death bed confessions are seldom lies."

Major O'Rielly stood and walked around. He offered Spur a cigar, then lit one himself. He walked and puffed. After half a dozen circles of the office he stopped and tapped off the ash in the spittoon, hitting it dead center.

"Sir, if you say they are Confederate renegades, I'll have to accept your evaluation. However, that doesn't give me the right, under the new law Congress passed, to engage inforce of arms against them."

Spur started to say something but the Major held up his hand.

"Sir, if you would permit me to finish. The Congress was specific in its regulations. The army may engage in battle with nations and peoples the United States is in a state of war with. We no longer are in that state against the former Confederacy or its soldiers. Therefore, my troopers can't help you."

Spur blew smoke in the major's direction.

"But if the Cheyenne were preparing the same kind of a raid against Laramie, the army would ride to its defense?"

"Absolutely. The army is in a state of war against all hostile Indians within the boundaries of the United States and its territories."

"But, damnit, O'Reilly. I know these are rebs. I've heard their rebel calls. I heard them say it would be just 'like old times during the war' to raid and rape. . . ."

"I understand your dilemma, Colonel, indeed I do. But you can understand mine. There is no absolute evidence that these are rebel renegades. If there was I would bend the law a little and engage. But on the evidence you've given me, I'd be court martialed within two weeks."

Spur looked out the window at a company of cavalry drilling on the parade ground.

"Major, I was afraid that you might be a book soldier. We are now in the process of gathering up every rifle and pistol in Laramie and preparing for the assault. We'll do the best we can with the manpower and guns available. The matter is closed.

"Now, on to a more interesting subject. My orders instruct you to cooperate in every legal and proper way possible. I believe that's the wording."

"Yes, sir. As long as it's legal, I'll be glad to cooperate."

Spur smiled. "Good, Major. I'd like to have a review and inspection of two companies of your troops. I want to see a field bivouac with tents a quarter mile north of Laramie. Your people are to set up their camp there at one P.M. today and remain in place until tomorrow evening, at which time I will inspect the troops." He looked over at the major who was smiling.

"During this period of time, Major, your men should be engaging in drills including rifle target practice aimed to the north. Have I made my request and my instructions clear to you, Major O'Reilly?"

"Absolutely clear, sir. I see no problem with your request. We'll be glad to put on a show of strength. However, you must understand—"

"I know, Major. If the bluff does not work, you will not be expected to engage in any action against the rebels."

Spur looked out the window.

"Major, there is one section of army regulations I'm sure you are familiar with."

Major O'Reilly looked up quickly, a questioning expression on his face.

"If any unit of the United States Army is attacked or fired upon by any force, that unit is permitted to return fire and to defend itself at the discretion of the unit commander and to engage in direct action against such a force."

"Goddamn! You're right! Be more than glad to wait for the first shot from those damned rebel renegades!"

"If you have any problem in channels with your report, I'll be glad to send along a letter. If that doesn't help, the President will be more than happy to add his congratulations to your efforts which should negate any general problems you may have."

Major O'Reilly held out his hand. "You're a damned good man to have in his corner. We'll see you in Laramie about noon time."

Spur returned a friendly salute and hurried out to his horse. It had been rubbed down and curried and was ready for him at the door. Word travels fast when a visiting full colonel is on any army post.

Back in Laramie, Spur talked to the sheriff.

"Telegraphed Cheyenne to send the territorial militia. Turns out Wyoming doesn't have any, not yet. Also told the Union Pacific to stop its train outside of town if they heard any shooting in here."

Spur filled in the sheriff about what the army would do.

"That might solve our problem. Curt might see all those blue uniforms and turn tail."

"Might, but I've seen lots of men killed on a might. We keep doing all we can to get ready for a fight. How many men we have signed up?"

"Don't know until noon."

Spur went out and with his sketch of the town, picked out the places he wanted his best shots. Some on rooftops, some behind corners of buildings, some in wagon boxes.

At one o'clock they had forty-five men with rifles and pistols milling around outside the sheriff's office. Spur divided the men into those with military experience and those without. He took the ex-soldiers and spotted them at his selected spots. Then he filled in the north part of town with the rest of the twenty men who could shoot but hadn't been soldiers. Most of these men had never even shot at another human being, let alone killed one.

When the men were in place he told them to memorize their position. They would ring the school bell when the lookouts spotted the rebels coming.

Spur had kept three men for the lookouts. All appeared to be tough and self assured. He led them a mile north out of town, found no suitable spots and moved another mile. There he placed one at the river, another one each side about a half mile apart.

He told each the same thing. "If you see a troop coming, make damn sure it's forty or fifty men, then ride like hell for town. Fire your pistol twice as a signal. I want all three of you into town and then you mix with the other defenders."

Spur left the lookouts in place, telling them he would replace them at dusk or have them come in. He didn't expect a night attack by the raiders.

Back in town, Spur released the men from their defensive positions and put everyone to work boarding up store windows. Some of the merchants had already started. Windows were not big on most of the stores, but glass had to be brought in all the way from Chicago or St. Louis and it was expensive.

By two o'clock all was ready. Spur rode out of town to the north and saw about eighty cavalrymen setting up a bivouac. Major O'Reilly was with the men and he saw that the small tents were set up so they crossed the main trail to the north.

Spur rode up and took the salute.

"Progressing nicely, Colonel." O'Reilly said. "Camp will be set up in another five minutes. Then we will engage in drills and hold our target practice until your scouts return with word of hostiles. Each of my men has a hundred and twenty rounds.

"Oh, I took the liberty of sending out three scouts to watch and observe and learn from your men."

Both old soldiers laughed.

"Thanks. Not even sure Curt Cameron will come when he sees all of this spit and polish and blue uniforms. Hope to hell they don't. Then again, I hope they do. That murdering mob can't just be turned lose to ply their dirty trade somewhere else."

"Exactly why we're here, Colonel McCoy. About time their renegade raiding days were cut short, damn short, and deep, at least six-feet underground."

Spur nodded, turned and rode back into town.

Sheriff Dryer had been grinning ear to ear when he saw the army setting up tents.

"Curt will never have the nerve to come into town past that many U.S. Army regulars," Dryer said.

"Let's hope. Oh damn! What about ammo? I want every man to have at least fifty rounds of ammunition." Spur ran out to the street and began to spread the word. Fifty rounds. Men scattered to get more rounds from home, and from stores. The hardware man and the general store man brought out their entire stock and doled it out to whoever needed it.

"No charge, damn right no charge!" the hardware man said. "What good are cartridges going to do me if them Rebs put a couple of rounds through my skill? Help yourself." He hesitated. "Course, after this is all over, if you got any rounds left over, I'd appreciate having them back."

Spur checked with the sheriff. Both men were on their horses to get around town faster. "When is the train due?"

"We usually have a four-thirty. Curt knows that. He might time his hit to catch the train here."

"I would if I was in his boots," Spur said. As the minutes slipped by, more and more of the men moved back to their assigned guard positions without being told.

Spur tipped a cold glass of lemonade the hotel handed out. He made one more ride around the town to check the men. Out north of the Markham house he could see the blue troopers doing company horsemanship drills. Damn, they looked good! Just seeing all those blue shirts and pants and soft brown campaign hats gave Spur more confidence than he had been able to work up before.

He knew what a trained company of raiders could do. They would shoot up the town, burn it down, rape the women, kill every man they could find. It could be devastation!

But with the Pony Soldier troopers . . . would they be fired at by Curt's men? All it would take was one hot headed rebel. Pray for that one to lose his nerve and shoot. Just one!

At three-fifteen, Spur rode to the north end of town where Third Avenue emptied into the trail north. He could see his men on rooftops and behind fences and in wagons. If Curt and his men came through the troopers and into town, and if they stayed bunched as they charged forward. . . .

Damnit! Too many IF's!

Far off Spur thought he heard the sound of two shots.

The signal? Were they coming? Was it his imagination?

He stood in the saddle and looked where he had left the first man. A thin trail of dust rose into the air. A man was coming! Then two more thin trails, and two more pistol shots.

"They're coming!" Spur bellowed. "The scouts are coming in which means the rebels must be heading our way. Every man get ready. Fifty rounds. Don't fire at the rebels until you hear my command. Does everyone understand?"

He saw heads nod. Saw men's nervous faces. A few responded with a yea, then all vanished back into their hiding places.

Spur rode north to the troopers. They had heard the shots, their own scouts were riding hell-bent-for-breakfast toward the troop.

Major O'Reilly cantered up and saluted.

"I'd say your renegades are on the way. We'll do our duty here. We either help you or we don't. It's up to the rebels."

"Understood. Good luck!"

Spur galloped forward and met the first scout.

"Coming, Mr. McCoy! Must be at least fifty of them. They all got rifles and pistols and they're riding hard!"

"Fine. We're ready. Get up on the roof, over there. Don't shoot until I give the order. Go!"

He talked to the other two lookouts who gave him the same story.

Spur moved his horse behind a house, climbed the ladder nailed to the rear and stepped out on the second floor porch roof. He carried his Spencer rifle with him and now lay down and peered over the wooden parapet.

He could see the cloud of dust from the two hundred hooves as they charged toward town. Out maybe two miles.

The army had drawn up in a double company front, with eighty men on horseback side by side looking north and stretched across the trail for forty yards on each side. It made a formidable sight and Spur was sure it would have an effect on the rebels.

He watched them come. Spur turned to the town from his high point.

"They are coming!" he bellowed. "Women and children inside. Rifles on the roofs and pistols in the open windows. Make every shot count. Nobody fires until I give the signal. We'll suck them in as far as possible, then let go."

He watched the dust. A mile out. Then a half mile. The front riders could see the blue line of troopers drawn up across the trail now no more than four-hundred yards from the rebels.

Spur bellied down on the roof. He hadn't even felt his hurt shoulder as he climbed the ladder putting his weight on the arm. Now it throbbed, but he knew once the action started the hurt would be forgotten. He held the rifle muzzle at the very edge of the gingerbread on the roof line and waited.

Curt Cameron scowled as what he thought he saw turned out to be the real thing. Eighty, maybe a hundred blue shirted Yankee soldiers had camped outside Laramie and now were stretched in a company front across the trail blocking it!

What the hell, the war was over. The Bluebellies couldn't mess in civilian police work. Congress had passed the law. He knew all about that law.

So what were the troopers doing?

He held up his hand and slowed the gallop.

A trap. It could be some kind of a trap.

"No firing until my command!" Curt barked and heard the orders repeated to the rear of the herd of horsemen. He thought about it again. Yeah, a trap.

"No man fires at the Yankee Bluebellies or he gets his head blown off by me!" Curt bellowed. Again the words were passed back until every man heard.

Curt slowed the riders again, then at last when they were within fifty yards, he walked the men forward. Twenty yards from the line he halted the riders and moved out five steps.

"Who is in command here?" he yelled.

Major O'Reilly kicked his sorrel forward three steps and stopped.

"Major O'Reilly, sir, and are you Captain Cameron?"

"Curt Cameron, the war is over. Give way for my party to pass. You're blocking a public roadway."

"Not so, Captain. We're in a mock battle defending this roadway in an entirely legal war exercise against a simulated attack by a force of five-hundred Cheyenne. I'll have to ask you to go around if you want to proceed."

Curt felt his temper flaring. He held it in check, tried to calm himself. He whipped his horse around, and in spite of himself gave a cavalry hand signal to his men to turn and follow him.

Damn! He had been tricked. They knew, somehow they knew. He'd give a hundred dollars to gun down that Bluebelly Major!

The men behind him grumbled.

"Stand steady!" he bellowed as they rode to the left. Curt had turned the lead men around the last Yankee and headed for the north end of town when he sensed trouble. The men at the end of his ragged cluster of men were grumbling. He picked up the pace and soon the last of his men had cleared the last Yankee. Then he swore as he heard a single pistol shot.

The last Yankee in the line crumpled and fell off his horse.

"Return hostile fire!" Major O'Reilly bellowed.

Curt's force galloped toward the town. The Pony Soldiers swung their horses around in a moment of confusion, then the line steadied and eighty rifles lifted and the roar of shots deafened the men for a moment. A third of the troopers had Spencer repeaters and the guns spoke again and again.

Spur McCoy hardly believed it. In the three-hundred yards to the north end of town from the soldiers, he saw half the Cameron Raiders shot off their horses. Not more than twenty-five lived to reach the safety of the town.

The army rifles ceased fire as the Raiders came close enough to town to put the defenders there in the line of fire.

Spur let Curt Cameron and his survivors gallop into the "safety" tunnel between the first two houses before he bellowed.

"FIRE AT WILL!"

A dozen rifles spoke at once. Six men slammed off their horses, dead before they hit the ground. Now there was a steady snapping of rifle shots as the riders came in sight of one layer of gunmen after another defending their town.

Only seven of the Raiders remained on their horses as they charged through the narrow street to the first alley. They whipped down it and out of range and rode out of town as fast as their lathered mounts would take them.

"CEASE FIRE!" Spur shouted into the sudden silence.

The whole fire fight in town had lasted only twenty seconds. Slowly the men on the ground came out and kicked rifles and pistols away from the

Cameron Raiders on the ground whether they were dead or wounded.

Spur caught his horse and rode out of town toward the army camp. Troopers were checking the dead, moving the wounded into a staging area, and taking care of the small war as it should be done.

Major O'Reilly cantered up on his horse.

"We have one trooper wounded, Colonel. The rest of my men are untouched. So far we have an enemy casualty count of twenty-two dead and six wounded."

"Six or seven of them got away down the alley," Spur said. "Curt Cameron is one of the dead. He'll never lead another pillaging raid on anyone."

"Except maybe in hell," Major O'Reilly said. He nodded. "I'd say it was a good exercise. You want the wounded? We'll trade you our six wounded for the dead raiders. I'd say a large common grave out here somewhere would serve the purpose as well as any. Were any of your people casualties?"

Spur laughed, the tension broken. "I forgot to check. It's been some time since I've been in a battle." He turned and rode back into town. He suddenly felt so limp he thought he might fall off the saddle.

Aftershock. He'd seen it a hundred times in a battle, and after a battle.

In the street the Laramie defenders gathered around the wounded and the dead.

"Any of our people wounded?" Spur called.

Rutger came from the crowd.

"No sir, not a one. I checked."

"Good. Rutger, get a wagon and some help and load on the dead. The Army is going to dig the graves. One large one, the major said. Then tell Doc Asamore he's going to have about ten new patients.

Already some of the men were pulling nails out of

the boards that had been put over the store windows. Curtains were going up. Spur turned and rode back to the north. He would gladly take the wounded and get them patched up and sent on their way, but not before he grilled each one about what happened at the Shuntington ranch when Curt took it over.

That was his next job.

14

Five of the wounded from the Battle of Laramie could walk. Spur found them heavily guarded by the Sheriff's deputies at Doc Asamore's office. Spur took them on one by one.

The first two just stared at him and wouldn't say a word. He backhanded each across the face and went on to the next one on the bench. He was younger, had been crying. His left shoulder had been shattered by a round and another sliced through his thigh. He had lost a lot of blood but was not in serious condition.

"Name?" Spur barked at him.

"Billy Joe Hatcher."

"Where were you born, Billy Joe?"

"Memphis, Tennessee."

"You were in the Confederate army then. What was your rank?"

"Private, the Tennessee Fourth."

"Shut up, you asshole!" one of the other rebels shouted.

Spur ignored the soldier.

"You been with Captain Cameron since the war?"

"Yes sir."

"He's dead, you know."

The young man sniffed, tears flowed from his eyes

as he nodded.

"We know that your band has taken over ranches before, the way you did the Circle S. Can you tell me about it?"

"You do, Billy Joe and you're one dead reb," the same voice from down the bench said.

Spur spotted the man this time. He jumped in front of him, slammed a right fist into his face, smashing him back against the wall. He hung there a minute, eyes wide, then he passed out.

Spur took Billy Joe outside and sat him on a bench behind the doctor's office.

"Not sure what's in store for you, Billy Joe, but I know the sheriff is going to charge every one of you. If you tell me exactly what happened when you and Curt rode into the ranch, I'll see that you get off, and that as soon as you're able, you can jump on board the train free and clear with no charges against you and head back to Tennessee."

Billy Joe stifled his sobs and looked up. "No lie? You'd help me get clear?"

"Word of honor, Billy Joe. I'm with the United States Secret Service. I never go back on my word. Were you along with the first of the raiders when they hit the ranch?"

Billy Joe nodded.

"Tell me about it, Billy Joe. Exactly what happened."

Billy Joe wiped his eyes with his sleeve. The doctor's wife came out the back door.

"This one special?"

"Yes. He's helping me. Can you patch him up out here away from the others?"

"Of course. We're just all so thankful you helped save our town. Laramie will remember you for a long, long time, Mr. McCoy."

Spur thanked her and looked back at Billy Joe. "Tell me what happened when you first rode in to the Shuntington ranch. Was it night time?"

"Yeah. Night. After midnight. Curt said it would be easiest that way. Catch them all sleeping. No guards out, he'd checked. He'd been in town for a week making arrangements.

"He met us about a mile from the ranch and led us in, all fifty-eight of us. We had over two-hundred at one time right before the war ended. We did good then, raiding Yankee outposts and some farms and a village here and there.

"But now we was down to fifty-five. We rode in and some of the men were assigned to the bunkhouse. First they went around the bunks and picked up all the six-guns and rifles they could find. Then they woke up the cowboys and ordered them all to get dressed.

"They didn't know what was happening. One big guy refused to put his pants on so one of our guys shot him in the shoulder. After that they all did exactly what they were told.

"Curt said only thing to do with the hands was to kill them all or make them think we was going to kill them so they would never come back. We got them outside and brought around their horses. Then we roped them all together and ten of our men herded them off the ranch and rode them for five days west. By the time they had them that far most were so sick and hungry they could hardly ride. The guys pushed them into a little town to recover and warned them that if any of them showed up in Laramie or if they talked about what happened, somebody would know and would shoot them until they looked like a kitchen colander. They was scared damn good."

"Then what happened back at the ranch?" Spur asked.

"I went up to the ranch house just after we arrived. I'm good with the women folk. Curt always had me handle them until he figured out what to do. We went into the house, found the bedroom and picked up the two pistols close by the bed. Then Curt woke up the couple in the bed.

"They was surprised, mad as hell, and the man, Shuntington kept swearing and trying to fight. One of our guys, Bryce, kept knocking him down. Finally he couldn't get up any more.

"Curt took this Shuntington out to the kitchen table and tried to get him to sign the bill of sale and the grant deed, but he wouldn't. Brought out his woman and ripped her nightgown off and squeezed her tits but even when she screamed her husband wouldn't sign.

"Curt put the woman up on the table on her back and said he was going to fuck her right in front of him. That's when the guy went crazy. He grabbed a frying pan and brained Bryce with it, split open his head like a watermelon, and then he came at Curt.

"Curt had plenty of notice and he had out his Colt. He shot the guy five times and had to jump out of the way as Shuntington fell dead at his feet.

"The old woman screamed and wailed, but Curt went ahead and screwed her there on the table. Didn't even take his pants down, just opened his fly. She screamed at the top of her voice the whole damn time. Then he shot her right in her open mouth and her brains flew all over the kitchen. Then Curt laughed and shot her through each eye.

"Billy Joe," he told me. "Drag these bodies out of here and get somebody to bury them. Dig them in deep where nobody will find them."

Billy Joe looked up at Spur, his eyes pleading.

"I come right off the farm into the army. They sent me to Captain Cameron and he trained us well. We wasn't usual infantry, we went back and forth across the lines. Always had on civilian clothes. He called us his raiders.

"I never killed nobody 'cept in a straight shoot-out. Never did murder nobody like Curt and the others did."

"I understand, Billy Joe. Where did you bury the Shuntingtons?"

"In the garden. The lady had a big garden in back of the ranch house and she watered it from the river, a canal she had dug to bring water to it year round. Grew some good vegetables back there and had a peach tree and things. Half of it was all ploughed up ready for more planting.

"I had the guys dig it deep, down at least six feet. Then we covered it over and transplanted some vegetables over the spot. Both of them are in one hole. We wrapped them up in blankets first. Figured it was the Christian thing to do. I even said some words softlike as we filled in the hole."

Spur watched the young man. He wasn't over twenty-two or three. Must have been sixteen when he joined the group. What an education in butchery he must have had!

"After we get you fixed up, I'll want you to show us where the bodies are," Spur said.

"Yes sir, I sure will do that."

Spur kicked the bench, hard. Then he took Billy Joe back to the doctor who examined his wounds. Nothing was broken. He bandaged the leg and shoulder and gave Billy Joe back to Spur.

The sheriff himself rode out to the ranch with them. Billy Joe sat the horse carefully, his arm and leg hurting. Spur had little sympathy for him.

"What kind of charges on the raiders?" Spur asked.

"Talked to the district attorney. We've got attempted murder, discharging a firearm at a person, rioting, conspiracy to rob and plunder, half a dozen more. Probably drop all but the attempted murder charge and put them away in the territorial prison for ten to fifteen years."

"All except Billy Joe here?" Spur said.

"Who? Oh, the one who got away. Nothing pending on him at all. Sooner he gets on the train headed east the better. Tomorrow morning would be a good time."

Spur had brought along two men he hired in a saloon to do the digging. In the end he helped. They lifted the blanket-wrapped bodies out of the grave. All of them around the grave had kerchiefs over their noses but it didn't help much. A month old corpse is a highly decomposed piece of flesh.

The blanket-covered bodies were put in the barn and one of the men left as a guard.

Spur heard the noise again and stared at the house. They hadn't been inside.

"Somebody's in the house," Spur said. He ran for it with his six-gun out. The back door was half open. He toed it all the way out and slid inside.

A woman stood by the kitchen table watching him.

"Why you dig them up?" she asked.

"Who are you?"

"Lucia."

"Oh, yes, the topless dancer. You were the one dancing in the firelight last night. You were good."

"Thanks. Where are the men?"

"Curt is dead, along with about thirty of his outlaws. You were with them?"

"Not with them, I'm heading for St. Louis in the morning. I just met them two months ago."

"Why St. Louis?" Spur asked.

"I have some business there."

"Fair enough. You want to ride with us back to town?"

"Might. It's getting lonely here."

Spur nodded. "Get your things, we'll be leaving in half an hour."

Spur found a horse in the corral and saddled it for her. He didn't care if she wore a split skirt or not, she was riding the horse with a regular saddle.

When he came back to the house she was ready. She wore a pair of man's pants she had cut down, and a shirt that she tucked in the pants tops to show off her breasts.

She had only one small carpet bag.

"Everything I own in the whole world," she said. "I'm just a poor girl trying to make my way in life."

"By dancing and whoring," Spur said. She tried to slap him but he caught her hand. He took her carpet bag and opened it.

"Leave my things alone!" she screeched.

Spur went through everything. He found a stack of letters with a home address, a purse with over two-hundred dollars in it in greenbacks. In the back of the purse in a partially hidden slot in the leather, he saw the edge of the bank passbook. He looked at it and at first didn't believe it.

The name on the outside was Curtis Cameron, listed was a St. Louis address. In a neat small hand were entries. The last showed a balance in the savings account of $43,478.19.

"Give me that, I earned it!"

"And stole it. Curt would never give it up without a fight."

"It's mine. I'm the widow, so I'm entitled."

"Where is your marriage certificate?"

"Left it in St. Louis."

"Or that's where you'll have one forged. I think I better keep this little passbook. It will help pay for the damage to the Shuntington Circle S ranch. I can have the money impounded by the U.S. attorney in Missouri."

She flew at him, fingernails slashing, eyes furious, feet kicking.

Spur grabbed her and dumped her on the table.

"On second thought, you better find your own way back to town. The train leaves in the morning going east. You be damn sure that you're on it!"

Spur rode back to town with the others. The woman trailed them by half a mile.

He had made sure that Rutger had not heard any of the Billy Joe story, and that he had been kept busy in town so he couldn't come with them to the ranch.

The sheriff left one of the men in the barn to guard the bodies. There would be a funeral tomorrow at the ranch.

As the small group approached Laramie, Spur saw that the two companies of cavalry were still in place. Their tents were aligned as if they had been positioned by a surveyor. Half the men were taking horse drills.

As Spur rode up the company street, Major O'Reilly came to meet him.

"Sir, the troops can be ready for your inspection in five minutes if you still desire it."

"I do, sir. It is the least I can do for the service your troops performed today. I wish to commend them. How is your wounded man."

"He was not seriously hurt. His heavy cartridge belt saved his life, I'd say. The bullet was half spent by the time it penetrated the belt."

"I'd like to present that trooper with a wound medal."

"Of course sir. We have it ready."

Fifteen minutes later the eighty troopers and officers were drawn up in a formal parade formation and rode past Spur McCoy in review.

There was no band, but a bugler blew a "To the Colors" call, and the parade ended.

Spur presented the medal to the trooper who was somewhat embarrassed.

"Without your good body to accept the bullet

from the rebels, your fellow troopers would not have been permitted to fire at the raiders." Spur said. "I'm afraid even with our concentration of gunfire at the entrance to town, the raiders would have overwhelmed us and your burial detail would have had many civilians, both women and children to care for. Private Windlawn, the United States Army congratulates you!"

Spur saluted the private who smartly returned the gesture and positioned himself beside Spur and the Major as they trooped the front of the formation and then the ceremony was over.

Spur turned to the Fort Commander. "Major O'Reilly, I'll have a letter ready for your report on this action before I leave town. Again, I thank you for your help."

Back in town, it was near dark. Laramie looked almost back to normal. The boards were all down from the stores. The streets were filled with people. Some looked at the bullet holes in the buildings. A glazier was busy putting in four new windows that had been shot out.

The hardware man set up a table to accept any cartridges that the volunteers wanted to turn in.

The five walking wounded raiders were hustled into jail before the people could do them any real harm.

One more of the wounded had died. Three would be bedfast for at least two weeks, perhaps longer.

The sheriff talked to the district attorney who had filed charges of attempted murder against each of the eight men. The sheriff signed the complaints, but deleted the paperwork against Billy Joe. Spur put Billy Joe in a jail cell by himself for his own protection.

Rutger caught up with Spur as he came out of the sheriff's office.

"You found my parents?"

"We think so. You'll have to identify them tomorrow. I think it's better to have a burial on the ranch."

Rutger turned away, covered his face with both hands. He sobbed for a moment, then wiped away tears. "I figured it had to be, but knowing for sure this way is a . . . a shock. I better go and tell Priscilla."

"I'll make the arrangements for tomorrow, preacher, flowers, everything."

"Thanks."

Spur didn't feel like eating. At the hotel, he had a bathtub brought to his room with three buckets of boiling water and one of cold. For an hour he soaked the suds and the tension away from his stiff and sore body. His thigh wound was healing well. His left shoulder was still hurting.

He had two stiff drinks of whiskey and crawled into bed, but not before he pushed a chair under the door and slid the dresser in front of the window. He didn't want anything to disturb a good night's sleep.

15

The next morning Spur worked at cleaning up the Shuntington case. He rode out to the ranch with Rutger and ten quickly hired cowboys.

The preacher came with them and a simple, private ceremony took place on a slight rise under a gnarled, twisted cottonwood. Priscilla came out by buggy with Amy Young for the service, then both went back to town.

Priscilla said she wasn't quite ready to stay at the ranch where there was so much of her mother still evident. It would take some time.

Rutger dug into the business of the ranch. The outlaws had not destroyed everything. They had figured on coming back and perhaps burning it when they left, he decided.

He appointed one newly hired man as cook, and had him inventory the root cellar, the pantry and the store room. Then sent him to town with two-hundred dollars and a wagon to stock up on food and supplies.

Next he rode out on the range to get a good picture of the stock, where they were, how many were there, what they could do with a roundup and a dozen other pieces of information he needed.

Spur rode along with him to the near range and

checked the stock, then decided the ranch was in good hands.

"Be sure to consult with the lawyer to find out how you get the grant deed returned to your name, and any other legal problems that Cameron caused. Then you'll be in the clear."

Rutger shook his hand.

"Thanks, McCoy. Next time you're in this area, be sure to stop by for a drink and a steak so thick not even you could eat it all."

Back in town, Spur checked with the sheriff. Spur wrote out a statement for the court and had it notarized. The eight men would be charged with several felonies. Conviction was almost certain.

"Both Billy Joe and that woman Lucia got on the morning train headed east," Sheriff Dryer said. "I figure that we just about have the Shuntington case all wrapped."

"Not quite," Spur said. He tossed the bank saving passbook on the sheriff's desk.

"What about your costs of extra deputies and the cost of the assault on the town, medical care for the injured, board and room, and court costs. I'd suggest you ask the circuit court judge to establish a fair price for all of this, as well as an assessment from Rutger Shuntington about the losses caused to the ranch, and at least a ten-thousand dollar fee for the wrongful death for each his mother and father.

"When the final figure has been determined by the court, this account in St. Louis should be attached by the federal court and the money sent here for payment."

Sheriff Dryer laughed, a belly whopper that shook the small office. "Damn, but you think of everything. How did you get the little passbook?"

Spur told him and the Sheriff snorted. "Not exactly a legal search of a private citizen, but who cares. It's going to work out all to the good."

Spur left his final report with the sheriff, then wrote out a letter commending Major Patrick O'Reilly and his Pony Soldiers and had it delivered to the major at the fort.

His last duty was a telegram to General Wilton D. Halleck, his boss in Washington D.C. He gave a run down on the solution to the problem, and that he was evaluating his priorities. He would be in touch with his St. Louis office and Fleur Leon.

By that time it was slightly after midday and Spur stopped in the hotel dining room for a meal. He was halfway through a trio of center cut pork chops and mashed potatoes and gravy and two kinds of vegetables, when someone slid into the chair across from him.

Priscilla watched him, her face sober, her eyes red rimmed. She wore a plain dress and had not even tried to make her hair look pretty. At least she had changed from the black dress she wore at the graveside service at the ranch.

"Hello, Mr. McCoy. Do you mind if I sit here a minute. I just want to see a friendly face for a moment."

He stood and she motioned him down.

"My pleasure, Miss Shuntington. Do you wish something to eat? A cup of coffee?"

She shook her head.

He finished the pork chops and then pushed his plate away. The lady obviously had something on her mind.

"Could we walk for a spell?"

He said they could and took her out the side door and along a side street, the shortest way to the open country beyond town and the pleasant Laramie river.

Only then did she reach for his arm and hold it tightly.

"Do you mind, Spur. It really helps me."

"I'm honored."

They had crossed the tracks and soon came to the banks of the Laramie.

It's always seemed to me like the river runs the wrong way," Priscilla said. "I think of north as being up and south as down, and when water runs north . . ."

She bent, picked up a stone and threw it in the river. It was an unschooled woman's throw, herky-jerky.

Spur found a stone and made it skip across the water, bouncing six times before it ran out of forward motion and sank into the water.

"I like that," she said smiling up at him like a school girl. "Let's sit down in the grass and throw stones."

He found a place that was green and soft and helped her sit down. Her skirt made a circle around her.

"I'm basic and childlike today," she said slowly. "I've seen death, the deaths of my two best friends in the whole world. Now I have to put myself and my life back together again. I hope you can be patient and help me. I've decided that I have three days to do the job.

"Then I must go back to the ranch, take over for a while and run the house until I can find a competent housekeeper. I still want to go back to school. I know my father never believed it, but I think women should be just as well educated as men. We're just as smart, and in Wyoming we can vote and hold office. Maybe I'll be governor some day!"

She looked over at him as he threw another rock. "Only five skips, you're slipping. Can you help me reconstruct my life during the next three days, Mr. McCoy?"

"Will it be difficult for me?"

She smiled and touched his shoulder. "Not at all.

You'll take me shopping, and we'll read some books, and maybe go to church, and have a picnic and some long talks. Oh, Rutger gave me a thousand dollars and I put it in the bank, so there's no problem about money."

"I wasn't worried about money."

"Can you?"

"I hope so. I sent a telegram to Washington and St. Louis. I might get word about a new assignment any time."

"I'll risk it if you will."

"Fine. Done."

"Kiss my cheek to seal the arrangement." He did and he felt her stir.

"Tell me about your mother. Talk it out, don't try to hold anything inside. If you can talk about something like death, it's easier to deal with all the smaller problems."

She lay back in the grass and Spur felt she was totally unaware of how tempting she made herself. She was a little girl again talking about her memories of her mother. She rolled over and propped her chin on her hand as she talked. All the good times, the time she was sick, then going away to school in Denver.

Before they knew it, the shadows of the river trees swept over them and Spur stood.

"It's getting late, we should start back."

"Yes, hold my hand. I feel better already. Tonight let's have dinner in that little cafe down the street, the one run by that funny little Chinese man. Then up in my room we can play dominoes. Do you know how to play?"

He knew how to play. Dinner was pleasant. Upstairs she made him wait in his room while she changed. When he came in she wore a thin cotton blouse she said was cooler. For a moment he wondered if she were trying to seduce him, but she was little girl innocent again.

She seemed not to think about romantic things or situations. Once she bent over him to whisper a funny story and her blouse swung outward showing the sides of her breasts but she didn't notice.

Spur made no move toward her. They played four games of dominoes to five-hundred, and she won two. She stood up, looked at the wind-up clock she had on the dresser.

"Goodness, it's late, after nine-thirty. We better get to bed." She held open the door. "I'll see you for breakfast promptly at nine. Then we're going to go riding down along the river. You promised me. And I'll even show you that I can use that big .44 of yours."

She held out her cheek to be kissed and he pecked her and hurried to his room. It had been an interesting afternoon and evening. He went over most of it again and no where could he find any hidden motives or any sly purpose in her actions. She was being friendly, simple, open. Indeed, it did seem like she was trying to heal the wound of the loss of her parents with a true friend.

The next morning, Spur was up long before nine o'clock. He went to the hardware store and bought a skillet, some fishing gear, some coffee and sugar and a packet of salt. At the bakery he had them make up four big sandwiches for him and then he hurried back to the hotel in time to take Priscilla to breakfast.

Later they rode upstream, south from Laramie, past the fort and toward the Colorado territory line. She was an excellent rider. Priscilla picked out her own horse at the livery and knew how to saddle the smallish mare. She wore a divided skirt and rode astride.

After an hour's ride Spur pulled them into an open area by the stream and stopped.

"Fishing time," he said. "There should be some trout in the river. We need some for our dinner. Can you fish, too?

She could.

He had fishing line and hooks, they dug for worms and cut poles from the brush. Priscilla caught the first one, a scrappy ten-incher, and Spur got a twelve-inch trout soon after that. They caught two more, then Spur cleaned the trout and built a small cooking fire.

He cut the heads and tails off and cooked the trout flat over the fire, being careful not to overcook them. With salt and the sandwiches and water from the big canteen they had their noon time meal.

They hadn't seen a soul since they passed the fort. The food was delicious, the trout boned out easily, and they ate until they were full.

"This is so wonderful I don't want it ever to change!" She fell back in a patch of daisies and smiled at him. "Isn't this delightful, Spur McCoy?"

"Yes, relaxing, calming, refreshing. But it's not all there is to life."

"Now you are a philosopher. Spur McCoy, if you had one thing you wanted in all the world, what would it be?"

"I have it now. I have a job I enjoy, a work that helps people, that solves crimes, that puts killers behind bars or in Boot Hill. I'm satisfied with that. What would you want?"

She smiled. "First to finish school, and learn so much about just everything. Then I want to find a wonderful man and get married and have four delightful children I can raise to be senators and governors and maybe even President of the United States. I have high goals."

She sat up and moved closer to him. "There is one more thing I want and I've been worried about it. Ever since Elliot Parker forced me that day. . . ."

She looked away. Then she stared deliberately at Spur, caught his hand and pushed it inside her loose blouse.

"Spur, please, *please* show me what it's like to make love with a man you love and respect. Please, Spur, right now. It's the one last thing I need to experience so I can accept all that's happened to me in the last few days. Then I'll be able to help Rutger get the ranch moving again, and then go back to school in Denver and finish my education."

Spur felt his hand on her bare breasts. She had on nothing under the blouse. Slowly his hand curled around a breast and he felt it throbbing. Her nipple burned his palm.

Slowly she lifted up and kissed his lips. For a moment he didn't move. Then she kissed him again and her lips opened and her tongue licked his lips until they parted.

Her tongue darted inside his mouth exploring. She shivered and then her hand reached for his crotch and rubbed tenderly. His erection began and she found it and massaged it with great care.

He eased away from her lips.

"Priscilla, we can't. It's not right. I'll be going away. It's just not right."

"Spur McCoy, I'm the one asking. I know I can't seduce you, but I would if I knew how. *I need you to make love to me.* It's simple. I want you. I need to know love at its best, when it's tender and thoughtful and slow and loving!"

She watched him. He hadn't moved his hand. It rubbed her breasts gently. Her hand covered his growing erection.

"Besides, I owe you the favor. You kept me from being killed by the raiders. You saved our ranch and drove off the killers. I need to give you something. It will make me feel so much better."

Her hands slipped the buttons loose from her

blouse and she slid it off her shoulders.

Her breasts were larger than he had guessed, perfect mounds topped with wide pink areolas and blood red nipples.

"Please?" she pleaded.

"My god but you are beautiful!" he said, his voice catching.

She kissed him again, their tongues twining. Priscilla gave little moans and yelps of joy as she knew he was going to show her what true loving felt like.

When the long kiss ended, she caught his head and brought it down to her breasts.

"No one has ever kissed my breasts, Spur. Would you?"

He took a deep breath and caught the creamy white orbs, kissing each tenderly, working around them in circles that moved upward until he reached her pulsating nipples. When he kissed her second one, Priscilla moaned and then yelped. Her whole body went rigid for a moment and she clutched at him as a sharp series of spasms shook her.

Her hips pounded toward his. She rolled toward him and pumped her hips against his erection at least a dozen times before the spasms receded and she sighed and barely opened her eyes.

"Oh, god but that was marvelous! So wonderful. What is it going to be like when you push inside me?"

He kissed her and took off his shirt. She toyed with the black hair on his chest.

"Do all men have hair on their chests?"

"No. But some much more than this." Spur let her unbuckle his belt and open his pants, then he pulled them off with his short underwear and turned toward her.

"Oh my!" she said, her eyes wide. She glanced at him quickly. "He's so big. A friend at school said some are bigger than others."

Spur chuckled. "Girls talk about such things?"

"Only sometimes when we're lonely and feeling kind of wild."

She reached out, then her hand came back. "May I?"

"You better," he said smiling.

She knelt in front of him where he lay naked in the grass and touched and pulled and examined his genitals.

"I've never had a chance to look at. . . ." she ducked her head. "Hope you don't mind."

"I like it," Spur said, his hands caressing her hanging, swinging breasts.

"I like you touching me, too." A moment later she sat back, satisfied. She looked up at him. "Would you take the rest of my clothes off . . . gently?"

"If you want me to."

He removed her skirt, then a split petticoat, and when he touched her tight, form fitting drawers that buttoned to the knee and were full of tiny satin bows, she stopped him.

"Maybe that's enough for today," he said.

"Oh, no, it's just that for so long I've thought that I'd never let a man . . . you know . . . take off my clothes until I was married."

"No rush," Spur said stroking her breasts.

"Oh, that feels so marvelous." She looked at him. "Will it feel that good when you go . . . you know, when you push it inside me?"

"I've been told it's a dozen times better than anything else. That the thrusting is pure heaven."

She sighed, kissed him again, then bent and kissed his belly near his penis and put her hands on the buttons holding her drawers on.

A few moments later she pulled the drawers down and off her feet.

Her dark muff was thick and luxuriant. At once

she rolled on top of him. He kissed her again, then his hand found its way between them and caressed the triangle of dark hair.

Slowly she spread her legs and his hand found her heartland that was already wet. He touched her clit and she roared into another climax, bounding and humping at him where she lay on top of him.

Beads of perspiration collected on her forehead and she closed her eyes as the tremors shimmered and slanted through her delightful young body.

When it was over she nodded at him.

"Now, Spur McCoy, before I lose my nerve again. I want you to come inside me, right now!"

He rolled over in the grass, pushing her on the bottom. Gently he spread her legs and lifted her knees and went between them. She looked down at his stiff penis, then closed her eyes. He found her slot and slowly edged in. She yelped and he thrust harder, then he was past the membrane and sliding smoothly and well lubricated deep into her.

"Oh my god!" Priscilla whispered. "Never in the world have I felt anything so . . . so wonderful! It's magic, it's sailing over the moon! I felt nothing like this before, the first time."

Spur slid almost out and drove back in and she squealed in rapture and raced to another climax. She locked her arms around his neck and he could see the sweat on her forehead.

Ten times she climaxed as he worked her along. Then Spur could hold back no longer and he thrust forward hard half a dozen times and fired his jolts of jism into her waiting vessel.

Priscilla climaxed again as he was grunting and yelping and sounding like a steam engine. They collapsed together and held each other tightly until they could breathe normally.

She shifted and he lifted away, but she held him.

"Don't go, not yet. I want to remember this for as

long as I live."

"You will," he said. "But never tell your husband, or any other living soul. This was part of your healing, part of growing up, and it's nobody's business but ours. Promise?"

She nodded. He kissed her, then lifted out of her and sat on the grass.

They both looked at the water.

"Skinny dipping?" Spur said and they raced for the river. It was mountain snow fed from the Colorado snow pack, and they stepped in only to screech in surprise. They splashed each other a little but quickly came out of the calf deep water to lay on the grass in the sun to get warm.

Again, Priscilla talked. She told Spur about her childhood, and growing up. How good it had been on the ranch. Her parents were special people, kind and thoughtful, generous with the hands, keeping on many year round when there was a little or no work for them to do to earn their wages.

They had the smallest turnover in cowboys of any ranch in the territory.

At last they kissed once more, then dressed and put away the cooking things and got ready to ride. It was after three in the afternoon.

"Where did the time go?" Priscilla asked. She looked at Spur and they both giggled.

"Time goes fast when you're enjoying yourself, and making love with someone you love," Spur said. He did love her, perhaps just for the day, but it was real and solid even though not lasting.

They rode back to town. She said she was going to have a long hot bath and would be ready for supper at eight. Spur checked with the Sheriff, then the telegraph office. The afternoon train came through bringing in half a dozen new people, but no problems.

When he got to the telegraph office, the operator looked up and nodded.

"Tried to find you this noon, Mr. McCoy. I have two wires for you. Must be important."

Spur took the two envelopes and walked back to the hotel.

He wasn't going to open them yet. Both had to be about a new assignment. He'd get to it, eventually. First he was going to have a long, luxurious, supper with a beautiful girl. Then they would play dominoes until ten o'clock.

After that he would take a look at the telegrams. It was at times like this that Spur McCoy wondered if he had been in the field too long. Now and then he had a touch of resentment when a new assignment came in. Once in a great while, he wished he could just settle down and stay in one place for a whole six months, maybe even a year!

He could make friends, maybe even get married and have a son or two. Oh, and at least one little girl! That would restrict the kind of assignments he could take.

Spur shook his head. What in hell was he thinking about? He was a field man. He had the whole western half of the U.S. as his territory. And he had covered almost all of it from time to time.

An itch began to grow in the back of his mind. Where would he be going next? The Pacific Coast maybe. Washington State? Or way up in Montana near the Canadian border? Maybe Apache country down in New Mexico or Arizona?

Spur pushed down the itch, walked into the first bar he passed and ordered a cold bottle of beer.

He looked at the two envelopes. When the beer was drained, he tore open one of the telegrams and began to read.

"CONGRATULATIONS ON YOUR WRAP-

PING UP THE SHUNTINGTON RANCH TAKE-OVER CASE. WE HAVE A NEW PROBLEM. IT SEEMS THAT THERE IS A SERIOUS SITUATION THAT YOU NEED TO LOOK INTO AS SOON AS POSSIBLE IT'S IN. . . ."

Spur McCoy pushed the telegram back in his pocket unread. So it was a new assignment. He would read it later tonight, after he had kissed a pretty girl good night and walked back to his room.

Nothing was going to spoil his last night in Laramie. He owed the lady that much. That much and a little bit more.

Spur McCoy hurried over to the Medicine Bow Hotel. The lady had not said that he couldn't help her take her bath. There might be a good chance, if he hurried before she was through.

There was a new spring in Spur McCoy's step as he marched up the hotel stairs toward the third floor. Yes, he thought, there was an extremely good chance that he could hire on to wash a back. Who knows, maybe even a front!

Spur McCoy grinned as he knocked on Priscilla's door. Yeah, he was a field man!